Surviving the Zoxans

Mastery of the Stars, Volume 4

M J Dees

Published by M J Dees, 2023.

SURVIVING THE ZOXANS

First edition. August 20, 2023.

Copyright © 2023 M J Dees.

ISBN: 979-8223871613

Written by M J Dees.

Get an exclusive bonus chapter to this book for FREE!
Sign up for the no-spam newsletter and receive the bonus chapter for free
You can discover details at the end of Surviving the Zoxans.

The Story so far...

When Sevan became embroiled in a resistance plot to steal a Corporation freighter, The Mastery of the Stars, together with Ay-ttho, and her friend Tori, it turned his life upside down.

Accused and then acquitted of the murder of President Man when Akpom Chuba was revealed as the true conspirator and executed. Unfortunately, the next president, Kirkland, forgot to pardon them. Fleeing with fake identities, Ay-ttho was recognised on the nearby planet of Sicheoyama while trying to rescue Nadio. Hiding on Angetenar, Nadio fell in love with the revolutionary Scotmax. An asteroid storm made Angetenar uninhabitable, so they fled to Scotmax's begetter, Yor, who lived on Herse where President Kirkland had sent his offspring, Matthews, to be safe from the Republic's war with Zistreotov.

When Kirkland was murdered on his victorious return, Scotmax, eager for a new Republic, and Sevan, to make his disguise as a bounty Hunter seem realistic, accompanied Matthews to avenge her begetter's murder.

President Matthews turned her newly formed army against them. They fled as far as the tourist planet of Pallene where Tori and Ay-ttho, with help from the Corporation leader Barnes, were kidnapped by the Republic. They returned later for Sevan and Nadio, who were tried and sent to the prison planet of Ogenus.

On Ogenus, they were all reunited but surprised to discover that Akpom Chuba was not dead but had been saved by his followers and preserved in a machine. Holding Nadio and Yor as prisoners, Chuba threatened to execute them unless the others left on a mission to assassinate President Matthews and return with a fleet to restore Chuba to the Presidency of the Republic.

With the unexpected help of Barnes, they achieved their mission and returned to Ogenus, where Chuba attempted to renege on his promise, which forced them to rescue Nadio and Yor. Fleeing from Ogenus, they were given shelter by Matthews' co-begotten, the new President Xocliw.

Despite Xocliw's attempts to placate Chuba, civil war ensued, which ended in the assassination of Chuba. When Xocliw herself was assassinated soon after, her assistant, Allecram, hired the crew of the Mastery of the Stars to fetch Matthews' offspring, Hours, and take her to the capital planet of

Future so she could be inaugurated as the new president and continue the Kirkland dynasty.

Apparently pleased with their work, President Hours pretended to contract them further, but actually sentenced them to death. Exploiting a legal loophole and Republic incompetence, the group escaped execution but, returning to recover the Mastery of the Stars, were caught up in a grand experiment which sent them to a little charted corner of the universe where they met the renowned scientist, Witt.

Witt helped them to get back to Future where they learned Barnes had the Mastery of the Stars. When they found it, they discovered Barnes had equipped the freighter to travel through a hole into another universe. Although they were determined not to go, Witt tricked them into the journey and they found themselves in the parallel universe before they could do anything about it. Witt was attempting to recover his friends that had previously made the journey but failed to return.

Having found Witt's friends, they prepared to return, but the species they had encountered, the Zoxans, did not want to let Sevan go. Trying to escape, they accidentally sent the entire Zoxan planet through into their own universe.

Having successfully found a route for themselves back into their own universe, they arrived in an uncharted area with no idea of which direction to go. The solution was to go into suspended animation until Ron, the ship's navigational computer, could find a way home. It took 85 standard solar cycles for Ron to find a civilisation capable of interstellar travel. While the others learned how to communicate with the species they named the vrequx, Ron attempted to communicate with their computer systems to find a star chart. Ron succeeded in his task but, when he did, the vrequx decided they didn't want them to leave, so they had to fight their way out.

They arrived in the Republic to discover that in the last 85 standard solar cycles; the Zoxans had taken over. They tried to hide in the caverns of Angetenar and discovered that old friends were hiding there too. Wanting to have a useful purpose, Nadio stayed on Angetenar and help their old friend Effeek'o, while Ay-ttho, Tori and Sevan used the Mastery of the Stars to look for other colonies hiding from the Zoxans.

Part One - The Caverns of Angetenar

CHAPTER 1: THE STAKES GET HIGHER

Sevan's marbles were still sore when he was awoken by the ship's alarm. He dragged himself out of his bunk and up to the bridge, where he could see Sonvaenope large in the observation windows. It was clear someone on the surface was shooting at them.

"What's happening?" he asked.

"We are being shot at," said Ay-ttho

"No uxlod, Moncur," said Sevan, referring to the famous detective of the entertainment implant series of the old Republic, who was famous for solving every case. "Have they done much damage?"

"None," said Tori. "Their weapon isn't powerful. Ron is transmitting 'we come in peace' messages."

"As long as we don't come in pieces," Sevan joked, but nobody laughed.

"This is the same location we left the colony of Angetenarians all that time ago," Tori observed.

Sevan thought that would save credits in set building if they ever made the story of their lives into a series for an entertainment implant.

Ron landed the ship on the outskirts and, even before the engines had shut down, a large crowd had gathered.

"Oh, my Giant Cup!" Ay-ttho exclaimed as she watched the crowd part to let through an individual, clearly of some importance.

"What is it?" asked Sevan.

"Sgniwef!"

"Sgniwef of Ao-Jun?" asked Tori. "But surely that's impossible. We have been in suspended animation for ages. She must be dead by now."

"The Ao-jun live long lives," Ay-ttho explained. "That is Sgniwef. I would bet Sevan's marbles on it."

"Not the Sgniwef of the Zistreotovean war?" asked Pirate.

"The same."

"I wonder if she is still with Luap?"

Ay-ttho descended from the ship and approached Sgniwef, whom she considered having not aged considerably.

5

Sevan thought the entertainment implant series of their lives was looking very viable if they could re-use characters.

"It has been a very long time, Sgniwef. I think the last time I saw you, Matthews was president," said Ay-ttho

"Who is it that claims to know me from such times past?" Sgniwef asked.

"My name is Ay-ttho San An Wan. This is Tori, Sevan, Pirate and Witt. And this is our ship, the Mastery of the Stars."

"Sevan? Didn't he help Matthews kill Ydna?"

"I didn't help so much as tagged along."

"What brings you here to Sonvaenope?"

"We detected your signal from Angetenar. You should be careful because if we can detect you, the Zoxans might also and your gun will be no match against them."

"What you experienced were only warning shots. Our true arsenal is much more powerful."

"Glad to hear it."

"Oh yes, the Zoxans. We have successfully hidden from the Zoxans for many solar cycles, but we have heard of new dangers of Zoxans helping one tribe of old Republicans against another. The Ao-jun are now nomadic, like nearly everyone who is not enslaved by the Zoxans. How do we know you are not in league with the Zoxans?"

"I ask to trust us and take my word for it."

"That is easier said than done. However, the Ao-jun are hospitable. Therefore, I invite you to stay with us at our settlement for as long as you need and trust that you do not bring the Zoxan forces with you."

"We are very grateful for your trust and promise that we will not betray it. There is one thing I don't understand. Our scanners showed a tiny settlement, but your settlement is large."

"We have been using radiation masking to hide us. You shouldn't have been able to detect us at all. We must be vulnerable to the Zoxans."

"I don't think so. The scanners on the Mastery of the Stars are very good, far advanced than anything the Zoxans have, I would imagine."

"Let's hope you are right."

Sgniwef led them into the settlement and into a large hall which looked like they must use it as a meeting place.

"This is Luap, my partner," said Sgniwef, gesturing to where Luap was sitting.

"So that is Luap," Witt whispered. "I thought the face that launched a thousand ships would have been nicer."

"Oh, I don't know," whispered Pirate. "I think time has been very kind to him."

"Luap will throw a party in your honour," said Sgniwef. "You must forgive me. I have business I must attend to and must leave, but I will return. In the meantime, I will leave you in the capable claws of my partner."

"Lucky us," Pirate whispered.

Sgniwef left the hall and left the visitors wondering what to do next.

"You must forgive my partner," said Luap. "She is always very busy. Please take a seat."

The visitors took seats and Luap ordered food and drinks to be brought. Pirate stared at Luap and realised that Luap was staring back at him. Luap approached Pirate.

"Where are you from?" he asked. "Who is your family?"

Luap found Pirate beautiful and Pirate realised this instantly.

"My name is Pirate and my origins are of no consequence."

"May I confess I find myself attracted to you?"

"You may, and may I confess I share the same feelings for you?"

Immediately, Pirate thought about how he might capture Luap and take him away from Sgniwef.

"Would you like to come and see our ship?" Pirate asked.

"I would like that very much," said Luap. "But first you must eat and drink. There is much to celebrate when we meet fellow refugees."

They served the visitors food, the likes of which they had not tasted for many FSCs. They also served them drinks which Sevan did not recognise as either fushy or pish but were very agreeable and left him with the same pleasant sensation.

The hall became populated with what Sevan imagined must have been the leading figures in the settlement. They mingled with the visitors and asked them many questions about how they arrived on Sonvaenope and how they had escaped the Zoxans.

The visitors had similar questions of their own, and the hall was alive with conversation. Pirate monopolised Luap, asking him many questions about his life and making many boasts about his.

He suspected he was not happy with Sgniwef, but he could not draw him on the topic, nor would he make any comment related to the period surrounding the Zistreotovean war during which they supposedly kidnapped him and took him to Zistreotov. Pirate supposed the entire episode must have been too traumatic for him.

"From where do you come?" Luap asked Pirate.

"I am originally from Future," he said. "But I spent most of my career on a planet called Chaldene in the Kale system."

"I've never heard of it."

"It's a long way from here, near the edge of the universe. We were experimenting with the possibility of crossing the barrier of Witt into parallel universes. My friend over there is the very Witt who gave the barrier of Witt its name."

Pirate gesticulated towards Witt, who appeared to be delivering a lecture on the science of white holes to a rapt audience.

"You are far more attractive than he is," said Luap.

"That's easy. Look at the shape of his head."

"That's not what I meant."

"I know, I'm sorry. I was only joking. We were successful in crossing to a parallel universe, but we were trapped there and Witt had to come and rescue us. I was burned badly. Here you can see some of my scars."

Luap marvelled at Pirate, whom he considered to be fiercely beautiful. He liked him, not just for his looks, but also because he seemed knowledgeable.

"They say the Zoxans came from another universe."

"So I've heard."

Pirate could sense Luap's feelings for him, but it hardly mattered because Luap soon made matters clear.

"I like you very much Pirate," he said. "Do you feel the same about me?"

Pirate admitted he did, and the two left the gathering unnoticed.

*

"You have much that would benefit our own community," Witt told Sgniwef when she returned to the settlement. "And I dare say that we have much that would benefit you. I suggest we use the Mastery of the Stars to shuttle between the two communities to facilitate a trade between us. Assuming that Ay-ttho is agreeable to such a suggestion."

"At least we would do something useful," said Ay-ttho.

"I agree," said Sgniwef. "Such a trade would be beneficial to both communities. Let us discuss your initial requirements and then we can load your ship with whatever we can spare of the things you desire."

The gathering had soon agreed on a list and Sgniwef ordered that they deliver the required produce to the Mastery of the Stars.

Once they had loaded everything, they prepared to leave.

"I'm sorry that Luap is not here to bid you farewell," said Sgniwef. "Something very important must have come up to detain him elsewhere because I know he has enjoyed your visit immensely and would certainly want to have said goodbye."

"Until next time," said Witt. "I have the list of produce you require and will do my utmost to return with the goods as soon as possible."

A sizable crowd had gathered to wave goodbye to the freighter as it took off, and Sevan felt that perhaps this new life playing trade between the two settlements might not be so bad after all.

"Should we head to the star and fold?" asked Ay-tho.

"I think it might be better if we use the conventional portals," said Witt. "I have been inspecting the mechanisms and I think it's better if we don't attempt to fold space until I've performed some maintenance."

"What if the Zoxans are guarding the portals?" asked Tori.

"Ron?" asked Ay-tho. "Please do a scan and see whether there are any ships at the portal."

"There are no ships on this side of the portal. However, my scanners cannot see through the portal, so there is a possibility that there might be ships on the other side."

"We can't risk it," said Ay-ttho. "We have to fold space."

"I can't guarantee the mechanism will remain stable," Witt warned. "If the field collapses, the ship will be destroyed. There may be Zoxans on the other side of the portal, but we stand a greater chance of survival with them than we do if the field collapses."

"Very well," Ay-ttho sighed. "Ron? Head for the Angetenar portal."

As they emerged from the portal, the Zoxans were waiting for them. Ay-ttho thought about trying to outrun them, but she knew that wherever they ran, the Zoxans would be waiting.

Instead, she asked Ron to cut the engines and waited while the Zoxan ship drew alongside them.

Pirate, whom they hadn't seen for most of the journey, arrived on the bridge.

"What's happening?" he asked.

"Where have you been?" asked Witt. "And... what the uxclod?"

Behind Pirate, he noticed Luap.

"What's he doing here?"

"He came along for the ride."

"Have you lost your marbles?" asked Tori. "Have you been living under a rock? Do you not remember what Sgniwef did last time someone ran off with Luap?"

"What happened?"

"Have you heard of the Zistreotovean war?"

"Oh, that."

"Oh that? They annihilated Zistreotov. It had been the most popular gambling venue in the Republic and they reduced it to rubble. What do you think she's going to do when she discovers you've kidnapped Luap?"

"I didn't kidnap him. He came of his own free will."

"I don't think Sgniwef will see it that way. She didn't last time."

"What are we going to do?" asked Sevan.

"We have to take him back," said Tori.

"I think the Zoxans might have different ideas," said Ay-ttho as the Zoxan ship locked onto the side of the Mastery of the Stars.

CHAPTER 2: CHANGE OF PLAN

"You will never be separated from the one you love and who loves you," Pirate told Luap as they sat in his quarters, waiting to be boarded by the Zoxans. "Now I have given my hearts to you, and love for you has inflamed me. I am entirely devoted to you. A faithful lover, I will be with you throughout my whole life. Of this, you may be certain. Although I have brought you from Sonvaenope, you will find a more beautiful and more rich life on Angetenar where all will be for your pleasure. All you would wish, I will wish."

"But are we going to Angetenar?" asked Luap. "We appear to have been captured by the Zoxans."

"Mere details," Pirate reassured her.

There was a loud metallic clunk, and the ship rocked slightly as the Zoxans attached a boarding platform to the freighter.

"They better not have damaged the paintwork," Ay-ttho complained from the bridge where she was waiting with Tori, Witt and Sevan.

The Zoxans opened the door and a loud tannoy relayed their instructions, which echoed through the corridors of the freighter.

"Everyone must exit the ship through the front door. Don't carry guns."

"At least their system of translation has got better," commented Witt.

Ay-ttho, Tori, Sevan and Witt met Pirate and Luap by the exit and they all traversed the gantry leading to the Zoxan ship together.

The gantry led to a door which opened automatically before them and then closed automatically once they had all passed through.

They had entered a room with a row of chairs.

"Please stay seated," came an announcement over a tannoy.

"I might have been wrong about the translations," Witt admitted.

They sat in the chairs and a frosted window in front of them unfrosted, revealing a group of Zoxans..

"Where did you travel from?" a translated voice asked via the tannoy.

The six exchanged glances.

"We have come from the outer regions," said Ay-ttho.

"Where in the outer region?"

"We were travelling for a long time in suspended animation from another region of the universe."

"Don't lie. We know you came from a network of systems they called the Republic. We know you are a Republic and Corporate Security Clone, a Corporate Mining Clone, two Futurists and Ao-Jun."

Their perception impressed Sevan.

"We can help each other," they continued. "You can help us find the traitor colony, and we make sure the rest of your life is comfortable."

"I don't know of any traitor colony. We have been searching for others of our own kind, but have been unsuccessful."

"We don't believe you. You came from the Sonvaenope portal, so look there."

"We came through the Sonvaenope portal exactly because we found no-one there. If we had found anyone, we would have stayed there."

"And you go to Angetenar. Let's go together and see what we can find."

"There is no point. We already scanned Angetenar and there was nothing there. We can show you the results if you like."

"So we have a choice. Herse or Sicheoyama. Or is Ao Jun apparently with you, and Ao Jun is your destiny?"

"We have no destination but are simply wandering, visiting a system at a time."

"We are in love and we wish to become partners," Pirate announced.

The others turned to him in surprise at the sudden outburst.

"How wonderful for you!" exclaimed the Zoxan. "If you agree to help us, we will provide you with a wonderful ceremony and a beautiful apartment."

"Yeah, why not?" said Pirate. "We'll help you find the traitors."

The others were shocked by Pirate's collaboration.

"Please tell me where they are."

"Oh, I don't know where they are. But I will help you look."

The Zoxans, although not completely satisfied, seemed to be content with the deal. Another door opened, and they escorted the group into the ship.

The Zoxans formally partnered Luap and Pirate, the next rotation. Luap and Pirate, who had agreed to help the Zoxans, were given extraordinary material privilege. They gave them the "Moldavite Chamber", a magnificent room resplendent with olive-coloured gems which decorate huge pillars, fine mirrors, and animated sculptures. Its pallasite walls permitted those within the chamber to see what was happening outside, but no one outside could see those inside. The Moldavite Chamber signalled Pirate's and Luap's worth to the Zoxans. In return Pirate and Luap held discussion with the Zoxans, who quizzed them about the probable location of traitors. The others could not be sure what they discussed in these meetings, as Luap and Pirate ceased to mix with the others.

The Zoxans had decided to first visit Herse and headed towards the portal.

"At least we'll find out if there are other colonies," said Ay-ttho.

*

On Sonvaenope, Sgniwef was furious when she discovered Luap was missing. All the feelings of rage she had experienced at the outset of the Zistreotovean war came flooding back to her.

She summoned Kram, Nala, Eporhtwol, and Divad, all veterans of the Zistreotovean war, as well as Ozan, Tufan, Tetteh, Pelkan and Phoenix, younger and enthusiastic fighter pilots that had quickly risen through the ranks to command their own destroyers. Then there were Antilochus, Ajax, Nestor, and Oscar, who, although not in command of their own destroyers, were formidable pilots.

"It has happened again," she told them. "After all this time, someone has again kidnapped Luap. This time by that freighter from Angetenar. We must go after them and show no mercy."

They prepared their ships and were soon on their way to the Angetenar portal.

When the fleet had passed through the portal. Nala called Sgniwef to report what he had detected on his scanners.

"I located the Mastery of the Stars," he announced. "Unfortunately, it is attached to a Zoxan scout ship. They are heading for the Herse portal."

"Let's catch them before they reach the portal," Sgniwef suggested. "We don't know how many Zoxans might be on the other side."

*

"Ay-ttho?" Ron whispered into her communicator. "I have detected a fleet of Ao-jun destroyers arriving this side of the Sonvaenope portal. They are heading this way."

"Thanks," Ay-ttho whispered back. "Keep me updated."

Judging by the sudden increase in activity, the Zoxans had also spotted them, but despite the scout ship heading full speed for the Herse portal, it was considerably slower than the Ao-jun destroyers and it was carrying the Mastery of the Stars.

"They'd be better off using the Mastery of the Stars engines," Ay-ttho commented to Tori as she received regular updates from Ron on the Ao-jun pursuit.

"I am already within weapons range," Nala reported to Sgniwef.

"Be careful," Sgniwef warned. "You may try to disable their engines, but it's likely Luap is on board, so we must do nothing that might endanger her."

The Zoxan ship was well within range of Nala's weapons system long before the Ao-jun were in range of theirs and so Nala fired. The Zoxan ship rocked with the blasts.

"How did the Zoxans ever take over the Republic?" Ay-ttho wondered aloud as the group dived for cover under a table. Loose equipment was already falling from the walls and ceiling around them.

"D'Heli told me they captured the scorpion lizards and adapted them for their own use," Witt explained. "Unlike the prototypes, these ships were invincible."

"Where are they now?"

"Nobody knows."

"Well, I don't think much of their scout ships," said Ay-ttho as it shook with another blast.

"I wouldn't worry. I think we'll be safe enough. Sgniwef won't risk anything happening to Luap. They are probably just trying to disable the ship."

"We're almost at the portal, according to Ron."

"Quickly, don't let them get through the portal," Sgniwef shouted to her fleet.

By this time, the Zoxans had shot back, but their weapons were no match for the Ao-jun armour.

Nala managed a shot which disabled the scout ship's engine, but the vessel was still floating in the portal's direction.

"You must not let them enter!" Sgniwef yelled.

The Ao-jun fleet tried to circle the scout ship but couldn't do so without being sucked into the portal themselves. Sgniwef tried to activate the tractor beam on her destroyer, but it was too late. She watched helplessly as the Zoxan ship slipped into the portal and out of sight.

"We must follow them," said Sgniwef.

"But we don't know how many Zoxans will be on the other side," cautioned Eporhtwol.

"There might not be any."

"Do you really want to take that risk?"

"For Luap? Of course."

The Zoxan ship slipped into the portal, followed, not long afterwards, by the Ao-Jun fleet.

When they all emerged on the other side, the Zoxans continued to fire on the fleet, who withdrew to beyond weapons range to contemplate their next move.

"We can't do anything that would endanger the life of Luap," Sgniwef repeated. "Their ship is disabled. They can't go anywhere and there are clearly no other Zoxan ships in this system."

"That's true," agreed Eporhtwol. "But we can't get close to them either. Those Zoxan cannons would rip even our destroyers apart if we got too close."

"So we need to disable their weapons system. How are we going to do that?"

"Why don't we suggest a summit? We can send a delegation on board and once there, we can sabotage their systems."

"Do you think they are going to allow us on their ship?"

"It doesn't matter. We can meet by shuttle. We can hack into their systems via the system on the shuttle."

*

On the Zoxan ship, Sevan, Ay-ttho, Tori and Witt emerged from their hiding places once the fighting had stopped. They could see the Zoxans busy organising something.

The room in which they were being kept had an observation window and through it they could see a Zoxan shuttle launch.

They watched it appear to get smaller and smaller as it travelled away, and then it stopped, little more than a speck. Soon it was joined by another speck.

"They must be having a parley," said Witt.

"What's a parley?" Sevan asked.

"They are meeting to discuss how to resolve their differences."

There was a bright light from the location of the specs, and it soon became clear that there had been an explosion.

"Or not," said Ay-ttho.

The lights flickered.

"What's happening?" asked Tori

"I don't know," said Witt. "But the Zoxans look like they are panicking."

Sure enough, a moment later, one of the Zoxans entered the room.

"We must use your ship to escape," he said.

"Okay," Ay-ttho didn't want to argue. "Let's go."

When they got to the entrance to the ship, they found the Zoxans already struggling to get on board and make their way to the more spacious cargo decks.

"What's going on?" asked Ay-ttho.

"To be honest, we're a little panicked," he answered. "Now that Ao-Jun has disabled the engine and weapon system, what do you think?"

"I think we should get out of here. You must release our ship."

"Yes, my colleague has set up a system to allow you to unlock your ship's engine."

"Good."

Ay-ttho and the others tried to board amongst the Zoxans, who were way too big to negotiate the corridors of the Mastery of the Stars without difficulty. Luap and Pirate were fetched and loaded on board as well.

"You won't get a fancy apartment here, you know," Ay-ttho warned them.

Once everyone was all aboard, a Zoxan operated a remote device which released the bolts holding the Mastery of Stars in place and it floated free.

"They'll pay for that paintwork," Ay-ttho complained.

Through the observation window, they could see the Ao-jun fleet approaching.

Ron started the engines, and the freighter picked up speed, but the Ao-jun were already at full speed and continued to catch them. Nala's ship was soon within range and fired.

"What was that?" asked Tori as the freighter rocked from a hit to the hull.

"That," said Ay-ttho, pointing to a monitor. "Belongs to Nala. It was Llehctim's old ship, the most advanced weaponry in the Republic, until they built the scorpion lizards. He killed Enaud, who was the last one stupid enough to kidnap Luap."

Sevan noticed that Luap, who was becoming emotional at the mention of Enaud, left the bridge in a hurry, followed by Pirate.

Meanwhile, although the Mastery of the Stars was rapidly gathering speed, Nala was still scoring direct hits.

"Where are we going?" asked Tori.

"Head for the star, Ron," said Ay-ttho. "We'll fold."

"No!" Witt shouted. "You'll kill us all."

"We'll die here if we don't."

CHAPTER 3: SONG IN THE RAIN

Another shot ripped into the Mastery of the Stars. The lights went out, the emergency lighting came on and the gravity manipulators fell silent.

"Uxclod!" Ay-ttho cursed. "Get the conventional engines online as quickly as you can."

Tori ran off the bridge towards the engine room.

"Ron? How long until we reach Herse?"

"We built up some velocity. But I can't guarantee the hold will withstand these attacks until we get there."

"They are almost within range," said Ay-ttho, leaping into the weapons chair. "Let's fire everything we have at them."

Ay-ttho launched a barrage of munitions at the fleet, but much of the Ao-jun fire continued to reach its target and the hull of the Mastery of the Stars was at risk of being compromised. Then, two things happened almost together.

First, the Ao-jun attack ceased abruptly.

"Sgniwef probably doesn't want to risk harming Luap," said Ay-ttho.

The second thing that happened was that the conventional engines started.

With the conventional engines, they could pick up enough speed to reach Herse and land.

The extravagance for which Herse used to be renowned now lay in ruins. They landed at one end of a broad avenue lined by broken statues. Most of the surrounding buildings were crumbling, the shells of rusting hover taxis littered the overgrown thoroughfare, and vegetation sprouted from wherever it could take hold. Heavy rain made the scene even more dystopian.

"Let's see the Zoxans," said Ay-ttho. "They depend on us now. Maybe we can turn this to our advantage."

In the corridor, they passed the mess hall where Pirate was consoling Luap.

"We are going to see whether the Zoxans can get us out of this mess," Ay-ttho told him.

Luap began sobbing even louder.

18

"Don't worry," Pirate told him. "Love can conquer all."

Ay-ttho ignored the comment and continued her journey to the cargo holds.

As soon as they arrived in the hold, the Zoxans were singing a kind of dirge. Most of the Zoxan communication was inaudible, but all could clearly hear the song.

A Zoxan, holding a translation box, approached them.

"My name is Crisis," he said.

Ay-ttho thought that was appropriate.

"You should contact Ao-jun. Chryseis, the eldest offspring, was on the diplomatic ship. I need to know what happened to her."

"Ron? Can we connect the tachyon transmitter to the cargo hold?" Ay-ttho spoke into her communicator.

"Doing it now."

"Good. See if you can contact the Ao-jun fleet."

"This is Sgniwef. Who is talking?" Came a voice over the tannoy moments later.

"My name is Crisis. A Saturnian priest. My offspring was on the diplomatic ship. Tell me, what happened to him?"

Ay-ttho, Tori, and Sevan exchanged surprised glances.

"A Saturnian priest?" whispered Tori.

"All of those on the shuttle," Sgniwef began. "Are now guests of the Ao-jun? We have already become very attached to them."

"I'm very rich. If you give me back Chryseis, I'll make you a millionaire. Just name the price."

"A million credits? We will have to discuss this. I'll call you back."

The transmission went dead.

In the Ao-jun fleet, Sgniwef set up a conference call with the leaders of each ship.

Most of the other Ao-jun leaders were in favour of the deal, but Ozan, who had captured Chryseis, refused.

"Can I use the transmitter again?" asked Crisis. "But this time, please point it towards Rengiucarro?"

"You must mean Lenguicarro? Home of Chronos," said Tori.

"Correct."

"How is it you are a priest of Chronos?"

"I have always been a priest of Chronos."

"But your species comes from another universe."

"Coming here, there were many things I hated, but there were also many things I could learn from them. Chronos is ancient, wise, and he taught us a lot."

"Do you know the High Priest Brabin?" asked Ay-ttho.

"That's right."

"Is he still alive?"

"Last time I checked, he was. Although now he is ancient, of course. Even for his species."

Crisis could contact the Saturnian temple on Lenguicarro, which Chronos and the other star masters had made their home. Crisis explained the situation and begged the help of Chronos to defeat the Ao-jun.

"Why do you think Chronos will help you?" Tori asked Crisis. "Are the star masters not impartial in their dealings?"

"Star masters are nothing without prejudice. Our community is split between those who follow star masters and those who don't. A rift causes civil war and the star masters help us defend ourselves against other factions."

Shortly afterwards, something triggered one of the Mastery of the Stars' sensors.

"Something has attacked the Ao-jun fleet," said Ron.

"What is it?" asked Ay-ttho.

"I can't tell. They appear to have been attacked by a plethora of minuscule objects."

"Where are they?"

"In low orbit."

As they were discussing what might have happened, a ship appeared next to them on the avenue. Appearing apparently from nowhere.

"What is that?" asked Sevan.

"It must have some type of cloaking device," said Witt. "But even invisible, Ron should have picked up the object on the scanners."

The door of the newly arrived ship opened and down the ramp into the rain strode the imposing figure of Chronos.

"But that's impossible," said Witt. "There's no way he could have travelled from Lenguicarro in that time. It's at least three portals away."

"Well, there he is," said Ay-ttho. "Ron? Open the door."

The door to the Mastery of the Stars opened, and Chronos climbed the ramp. Ay-ttho went to meet him while the others waited expectantly in the cargo hold.

"Which one of you is Crisis?" Chronos asked as Ay-ttho led him into the hold.

"I am."

"Sorry it took me so long. I have left the Ao-jun with a little present that should keep them busy for a while."

"What was it?" asked Ay-ttho. "We detected a plethora of tiny objects."

"Yes. At this moment, those tiny objects are drilling tiny holes into the hulls of their ships. Through these tiny holes they will inject a virus which will keep the Ao-jun in their waste discharge units long enough for us to come up with a plan."

Ay-ttho laughed at Chronos's move, which she considered excellent.

After the need to constantly visit the waste discharge unit had passed, Tufan called a meeting on his ship with the leaders of the other Ao-jun vessels.

"Your greed brought this upon us," he accused Ozan.

"What has this got to do with me?"

"My technicians found this," he dropped a tiny mechanical object onto the table. "Several of these drilled tiny holes into our ships and injected the virus, which has caused us so much suffering recently."

"Well, I didn't do it."

"Can you not see? This attack is in response to your refusal to give up Chryseis."

"Fine, they can have Chryseis. I will deliver her myself; but I shall take your prisoner, Briseis. I will take her from your ship myself so that you may learn how much greater I am than you, and other Ao-jun may shrink back from likening themselves to me and contending against me."

This made Tufan livid, but he had no time to enact his rage because, at that moment, a proximity alarm sounded.

"What is it?" he asked his crew.

"A Zoxan ship has emerged from the portal and is heading towards us."

"Do not fear us, Ao-jun," a message arrived. "We are Zoxan, but we do not seek you. We are hunting the same Zoxan scum as you."

"Why?" asked Tufan.

"They have betrayed their own community by following those you call the star masters. Do not fight among yourselves. We will help you."

Tufan and the others wondered how the Zoxans could have known that they had been arguing.

"We will be in orbit around Herse shortly," the Zoxan continued. "Please come aboard to discuss how we might work together."

"It's a trick," said Ozan.

Ozan's opposition made the plan even more appealing to Tufan.

"Then I will go alone," he said.

"Call me Doukan," a Zoxan told Tufan once he had arrived on the Zoxan ship. "Why are you so mad at your colleague?"

"How do you know?"

"We are monitoring your conversations. Ozan is your boss."

"He is not. I will never take orders from him again."

Two more Zoxans entered the room.

"Allow me to introduce you to Kinis and Neige," said Doukan. "Kinis will support you right away and Naej is my boss."

"Can you help me?" asked Tufan

"To fight other Zoxans?"

"No, to fight Ozan until he respects my rights."

"How about pretending to support another Zoxan against Ozan until he gives you what you want?" Kinis suggested.

Meanwhile, on the Mastery of the Stars, a Zoxan called Siri argued that the best form of defence was an attack.

"We're like the cue kids sitting here in Herse. you have to fight to escape the portal," he said.

"Who are the cue kids?" asked Sevan.

"I think he means the expression: we are like sitting cukids," said Witt. "We are easy to attack, cheat, or take advantage of."

"He has a point," said Ay-ttho. "There is nothing here and we have the advantage that Sgniwef does not want to risk injury to Luap. There is every chance that we could take on the fleet with little risk to ourselves."

"Then it's decided," said Tori. "We attack the fleet."

"You should be aware," warned Ron. "There is a Zoxan ship near the fleet."

"Can you talk to them?" Ay-ttho asked Siri.

"I fear they are targeting us. We were running from Zoxans who are against the Saturnian religion."

"As long as they don't attack us, we won't attack them," said Ay-ttho.

Siri was delighted as the Mastery of the Stars lifted off and prepared to fight its way out of orbit. Ay-ttho's assumption was right. The fleet offered little return fire and the Mastery of the Stars inflicted damage on the fleet, which was attempting to contain the freighter to the upper atmosphere of Herse.

"This is pointless," said Sgniwef. "We cannot retrieve Luap if we cannot disable their ship. Perhaps we should just return to Sonvaenope."

The leaders of the other ships were probably in agreement in that moment but, unfortunately, in their attempt to break out of the cordon, the Mastery of the Stars inflicted substantial damage on the ship of Oscar which lost both power and its ability to maintain orbit and plummeted through the atmosphere to a fiery destruction on the surface below.

Tufan, still in conference with the Zoxans, was overwhelmed by the loss of Oscar.

"I must leave," he said. "I must avenge the death of Oscar."

"Our feelings are with you," said Kinis.

Tufan returned to his ship and immediately launched a vicious attack on the Mastery of the Stars.

He pursued the freighter through the upper atmosphere, firing aggressively and frequently finding his target. Ay-ttho, Tori, Sevan and Witt had already returned to the bridge when Tufan's cannon fire tore through one of the cargo holds.

The blast tore a large hole in the hull's side and the Zoxan passengers, who had been in that cargo hold along with the supplies stored within, were sucked out into the vacuum of space.

.

CHAPTER 4: PIRACY

Tufan, seeing the Zoxan bodies among the debris strewn from the fractured hull of the Mastery of the Stars, used his ship's tractor beam to drag the bodies, along with the rest of the debris, behind his ship. He manoeuvred around the Mastery of the Stars to display the victims.

"What a monster," cried Pirate, who had joined the others on the bridge. "Get me Sgniwef. I want to talk to her."

As requested, Ron established a connection with Sgniwef's ship.

"This is barbarous," Pirate complained. "Your argument is with me, not with the Zoxans. You want me, and Luap, not them."

"I did not sanction the attack. As a sign of goodwill, I will return Chryseis to Crisis."

Soon afterwards, they jettisoned an escape pod towards the Mastery of the Stars. The freighter intercepted it, and discovered a cramped, but otherwise unharmed, Chryseis inside.

Fortunately for Crisis, he was in a different cargo hold than the one that was compromised and was reunited with his offspring.

"Get me Briseis!" Ozan ordered his crew.

They took a shuttle to the ship of Tufan and, without Tufan's knowledge, removed the Zoxan Briseis and took her back to Ozan's ship.

When he discovered this, Tufan was furious.

"I will not fight for your ridiculous cause anymore," he told Sgniwef. "There is nothing for me in your ridiculous vendetta with Pirate."

With that, Tufan turned his ship around and headed back towards the portal but on the way he changed his mind and instead returned to the Zoxan ship of Kinis and Naej.

"He dishonoured me in front of my people," Tufan complained to Kinis. "You must ask Naej to help the kidnappers until Ozan is at the point of defeat. Only then will Ozan realise how much the Ao-jun need me, and will restore my honour."

"Okay, I'll talk to him," said Kinis.

Tufan left and began heading back to Sonvaenope.

Kinis spoke to Naej about Tufan's request but no sooner had Naej left than Naej placed a call to Sgniwef.

"Now is the time to attack the enemy ship," urged Naej.

"Yes, you are right," said Sgniwef. "I shall do so immediately."

But Sgniwef didn't do as she said. She saw an opportunity to test her own support, so, instead of urging the fleet to attack the Mastery of the Stars, she tested the Ao-jun fleet's morale by telling them to go back to Sonvaenope.

Unfortunately for Sgniwef, the Ao-jun fleet appeared quite happy to go back to Sonvaenope.

"This is ridiculous," said Pelkan. "We shouldn't be here fighting Ozan's war."

"What is happening?" asked Kram. "This is absurd. We came here to do a job which we have yet to complete. There is no honour in returning to Sonvaenope with a job unfinished."

Doukan called Kram to discuss the conflict.

"You must challenge Pelkan," he said. "Set an example."

Kram took Doukan literally and attacked a surprised Pelkan, disabling his ship. It quickly erased any thoughts of retreat from the minds of the other ships' commanders.

The Ao-jun fleet reorganised themselves into battle formation and advanced on the Mastery of the Stars.

"The best form of defence is attack," said Witt. "Ron? Let's confront them."

The Ao-jun fleet and the Mastery of the Stars were positioned high above Herse, ready to attack each other.

"Wait!" Pirate shouted. "Sgniwef's argument is with me, not with anyone else. I will challenge Sgniwef to one-on-one combat and that will resolve the situation with no one else needing to be hurt. Chronos? Will you lend me your ship so that I might challenge Sgniwef to one-on-one combat?"

"As long as you look after it," said Chronos, knowing this would not be the case.

Ron established communication with Sgniwef, who agreed to the battle.

Sgniwef positioned her ship away from the rest of the fleet and waited for Pirate to arrive in the ship of Chronos. As soon as Sgniwef saw the star master's fighter, she attacked, catching Pirate by surprise. This first wave of attacks disabled Pirate's anti-weapon defences and damaged his navigation.

Pirate swung around and fired towards Sgniwef, who could take evasive action. Both ships turned for the next pass, but it was Sgniwef who had the greatest manoeuvrability, and she could get her shots in first. Pirate sustained damage and struggled to turn Chronos's ship.

Sgniwef prepared to make the approach in which she was sure she could finish Pirate, but before she could get her adversary in her sights, a Zoxan ship crossed their path and, as it did, it opened up its cargo bay doors and swallowed Chronos's ship whole. Sgniwef cursed the Zoxans, but knew better than to attack them.

On Chronos's ship in the belly of the Zoxan cargo hold, Pirate was pleased to see Kinis.

"Let's take you back to Luap," he said. "And Zoxans will discuss whether we allow this conflict to continue."

Kinis, led Pirate out of the cargo hold to a more comfortable place where he could rest and then left him alone to discuss matters with his commander, Naej, Naej's partner Hera, a Zoxan commander, Benjamin, and Benjamin's assistant, his co-begotton's offspring. Tobias.

"Should we intervene?" asked Kinis.

"No," said Hera. "Let's wait for the destruction of the Mastery of the Stars and the treacherous Zoxans."

They returned Pirate, and the damaged ship of Chronos to the Mastery of the Stars, but the Zoxans took no other action. Pirate ran straight up to the bridge, leaped into the weapons chair, and fired on Sgniwef's ship.

Sgniwef had not been expecting an attack on account of the presence of the Zoxans and, because her defences were lowered, her ship was damaged and she herself was wounded.

The rest of the Ao-jun fleet responded immediately by attacking the Mastery of the Stars, which sustained some damage and they killed some Zoxans, including a close friend of Siri.

Tetteh, filled with rage, inflicted much damage and casualties until Sgniwef ordered him to withdraw.

"Ron? Get me a connection with Tetteh's ship," ordered Chronos.

Ron did as he asked him.

"Tetteh? You shouldn't mess with star masters," Chronos warned once the connection was established.

"Oh, no?" Tetteh scoffed before firing another round at the freighter.

"I might not punish him with my ship," said Chronos. "But I have friends who will do my bidding."

Chronos spoke in a language that was unintelligible to the others and, within moments, another ship appeared out of nowhere as if it had just folded space.

"The drirkel straalkets," Chronos announced.

Sevan remembered the hideous drirkel straalkets from a previous encounter and did not envy Tetteh. However, when the drirkel straalkets attacked Tetteh, Doukan came to Tetteh's defence and, with a barrage of fire, disabled the drirkel straalket ship. It clearly disappointed Chronos that his peers had been thwarted so easily.

Pirate immediately fired on the Ao-jun and Zoxan ships, dissuading them from another attack on the damaged Mastery of the Stars for the time being.

"Return Luap," Ay-ttho told Pirate. "You are going to kill us all."

"Never," said Pirate. "I will compensate them in other ways, but Luap stays here. It's obvious He doesn't want to be with her. Why do you think he has tried to escape twice?."

"Sgniwef will accept nothing other than Luap."

"Let's at least try to negotiate a temporary truce," Witt suggested. "Then we might have more time to come up with another idea."

Sgniwef, who was still smarting from her wound, agreed to a truce, so Ron landed the Mastery of the Stars on Herse again, where they could perform some essential repairs.

While this was going on. Naej had summoned Doukan, Benjamin, and Tobias.

"You are not to interfere with the conflict between the Ao-jun and that freighter again," he ordered. "Is that understood?"

"But what about the Zoxans they are sheltering?" Benjamin asked.

"I have made myself clear."

"Yes, sir," the frustration in Benjamin's voice was audible. He exchanged glances with Tobias.

On Herse, the Mastery of the Stars had landed on what looked like a disused military base. Pirate and Ay-ttho went to investigate.

"If anyone should place themselves in danger, it should be you," Ay-ttho told Pirate.

Everything on the surface was in ruins, but the space was surrounded by what the Herseans had obviously used as hangars at some point. It had all the signs of a space port with none of the frills associated with a commercial spaceport such as shops and restaurants.

Ay-ttho and Pirate did a tour, through the rain soaked base, investigating the hangars one by one. Most were deserted, with nothing left behind that might assist with the repair of the Mastery of the Stars.

Then they found a hangar that was closed. The doors of the other hangars had been left wide open, but on this one, the massive entrance was still sealed.

Ay-ttho blasted a small access door. And the two passed through, unprepared for what they found inside. In the centre of the hangar were a group of Hersean fighter ships, which looked as though they had never been used.

Ay-ttho touched the access panel of one and was surprised to discover the ship still had power. She climbed into the cockpit, booted up the system and ran diagnostic checks.

"There's nothing wrong with it," she shouted to Pirate, who was in the cockpit of the fighter next to her, trying to run its diagnostic routine.

"This one is so far so good," he shouted. "We need to work out a way to open the hangar doors."

Ay-ttho booted up the weapons system of the fighter and blasted a large hole through the doors which, rocked by the force of the blast, separated from their fastenings and fell to the ground with a large crash, sending plumes of dust into the air.

"That seems to have done the trick," she said cooly.

She started the engines and, lifting off, guided the fighter through the hole where the doors used to be, and headed towards the Mastery of the Stars. Pirate followed.

"I'll take the fighter," Siri said when they arrived. "To avenge my friend's death."

"You won't fit in the cockpit," said Ay-ttho.

"At least let's try."

It was a squeeze, but somehow Siri got himself into the relatively tiny cockpit with just enough space left to manipulate the controls.

"Are you sure about this?" asked Ay-ttho. "You look as if you are piloting your offspring's toy."

"I never felt so right in my life."

"Let me fly the other," said another Zoxan.

"Who are you?" asked Ay-ttho.

"He is Dolon," answered Siri. "He is one of the best pilots I know."

"Fill your boots," said Ay-ttho, stepping aside to allow Dolon to squeeze himself into the other fighter. "There are other ships in the hangar. We should return and see if we can get any more of them started."

Siri and Dolon took off and headed towards the Ao-jun fleet. Although Sgniwef feared harming Luap by firing at them, the Hersean fighters proved to be, not only remarkably manoeuvrable but also possessed tremendous fire power and soon Siri and Dolon alone could push the fleet, not just out of orbit, but some distance back towards the Sonvaenope portal.

"Look! Those Saturnians have the advantage," Benjamin protested to Naej. "You must let us assist the Ao-jun."

"Out of the question," said Naej. "You must not interfere."

"But I don't understand," said Benjamin.

"Follow my orders. I wish to see how it plays out."

Siri and Dolon chased the fleet as far as they felt comfortable and then turned back before they were out of range of Herse.

Sgniwef called a conference of the leaders of the Ao-jun fleet.

"Ozan, you were wrong to oppose Tufan," said Sgniwef. "We need him. He would have seen off these two Zoxan fighters. This is embarrassing."

"Okay, I was wrong," Ozan admitted. "Let us send a delegation to Tufan, take Briseis and more gifts, and ask him to return."

"Who should we send?"

"Send Kram, Ajax and Phoenix."

"My friends! Welcome!" said Tufan as he received the visitors. "It is só good to see you."

"We have brought you gifts. Ozan has sent Briseis and other gifts as a token of his apology."

"I am not interested in his apology. He has insulted me and that is all there is to it. I will only return to battle if they threaten my destroyer."

"This is no good, no good at all," Kram complained to Ajax and Phoenix as they returned to their ship. "Sgniwef will not be pleased."

"I am not pleased," said Sgniwef, when they told him the news.

"Don't worry," said Kram. "Tetteh and I will take a couple of short range fighters and take them by surprise. They will look for the destroyers, and by the time they spot us, it will be too late."

"But the short range fighters won't make it to Herse and back."

"Give us time to get there and then follow us. That way, you'll meet us halfway back."

So, Kram and Tetteh climbed into their short range fighters and prepared to ambush The Mastery of the Stars.

On Herse, they had arranged the Hersean fighters around the Mastery of the Stars and they were busy trying to get them battle ready when Kram and Tetteh arrived.

The Ao-jun fighters flew low over the camp, firing at everything in sight. The Zoxans ran for the Hersean fighters they had been preparing. Dolon's ship had already been refuelled and repaired, but before Dolon could reach it, Ao-jun fire cut him down.

CHAPTER 5: HEADLONG FLIGHT

Despite the onslaught, they scrambled the Hersean ships and soon had the upper hand over Kram and Tetteh, who fled back towards the Ao-jun fleet. In the pursuit, the Zoxans inflicted substantial damage on the two fighters, and both Kram and Tetteh were injured.

The Ao-jun fleet had advanced so they could meet their fighters halfway but was unprepared for the attack they received from the Zoxans in the Hersean ships.

Ozan's destroyer was at the head of the formation and took the brunt of the attack. The bridge sustained damage and Ozan himself was injured.

From his Destroyer near the Sonvaenope portal, Tufan learned of the damage inflicted on the fleet.

"Assess the situation," he told Oscar.

When Oscar's shuttle arrived at the fleet, the first destroyer he boarded was that of Nestor.

"Please ask Tufan to rejoin the fighting," Nestor begged.

"I don't think that he will," Oscar admitted.

"Then at least lead the fleet in Tufan's shuttle you arrived in. The rest of the fleet will think it is Tufan and head to battle with renewed hope."

As they were talking, Siri attacked again in his fighter and the fleet fell back even further.

"You see what I mean," said Nestor. "The moral in the Ao-jun fleet is so low, they won't even challenge a lone fighter."

On the Zoxan ship, Benjamin had reached his limit.

"Come on Tobias," he said. "We are going to take a couple of fighters."

"But Naej will be furious," said Tobias.

"Let me deal with Naej. You just get Ajax and get into one of those fighters."

Benjamin went to see Hera.

"I need you to distract Naej," he explained.

"Why?"

"I want to take Tobias and Ajax and hunt down the fighter that has been attacking the Ao-jun fleet."

"Don't worry," said Hera. "Leave it to me. I know exactly how to distract my partner."

Benjamin thanked her and went to find Tobias and Ajax in the hangar, leaving Hera to seduce her partner, Naej.

They pursued Siri, who was warned to retreat by Witt, who was monitoring the situation from Herse, but Siri, who had almost arrived at Herse, ignored him and engaged the Zoxan ships.

Siri was by far the superior pilot. He rounded on Benjamin and Tobias, avoiding their fire and scoring direct hits with his own cannons on the ship of Tobias.

Tobias lost control and his ship spiralled through the atmosphere of Herse, exploding as it impacted on the rain drenched surface of the planet.

In a fury, Ajax pursued Siri and not only damaged the Hersean fighter, but also injured Siri in the attack. However, Siri's skills as a pilot were so developed that, even with a disabled ship and an injury, he could evade Ajax and limp back to the base.

"What is going on?" Naej raged over the communication links to the ships of Benjamin and Ajax. "Get back here right now!"

"I guess Hera ran out of ideas," Benjamin whispered to Ajax on a private channel.

Meanwhile, on Herse, the Zoxans scrambled the rest of the Hersean fighters and launched a counterattack on the Ao-jun.

On Tufan's ship, Oscar burst onto the bridge.

"They are attacking the fleet again," he complained. "Why are you being stubborn, Tufan? If you won't rejoin the fleet, at least let me take a fighter."

"Okay, Oscar, you can take my fighter, but you must only use it to defend the fleet. Under no circumstances should you follow them back to Herse. Is that clear?"

"Why?"

"Because after you come back, we will take the Mastery of the Stars together."

By the time Oscar reached the fleet, the Hersean fighters were already withdrawing back to Herse. Thinking they were fleeing, Oscar gave chase, all the way to Herse, where he damaged several fighters.

Chronos, who had finished repairing his ship, chased after Oscar, followed by Siri. It was only at this point that Oscar realised how dangerous his position had become. Chronos and Siri chased him out of the atmosphere, getting several shots on target but it was Siri who, using his superior piloting skills, out-manoeuvred Oscar and fired the shot that ripped through the bridge of Tufan's ship, killing Oscar and disabling the ship.

Siri towed Tufan's fighter back to Herse just as the Ao-jun fleet arrived to rescue Oscar. Finding they were already too late, Sgniwef despatched Antilochus to inform Tufan about what had happened and to ask for his help to recover his ship and Oscar's body.

Tufan, enraged with Oscar's death, appealed to Kinis for help.

"Be careful," said Kinis. "If you try to kill the Zoxan who took Oscar's life, you will risk your own life. Siri is a very skilful pilot."

"I am happy to risk my life to avenge Oscar's death."

Tufan arrived at Herse, not on his own destroyer, but in a Zoxan fighter loaned to him by Doukan.

"Return their ship," Ay-ttho told Siri. "Whoever you killed is clearly very important to them. If you don't return it, you will bring the entire fleet down upon us."

"I respect you," Siri said. "I understand you are paying the price for Pirate's impulses, and for that I will return the ship."

Once Siri had fulfilled his promise, he returned to the base where Ay-ttho had called a conference.

"Sgniwef's patience will not last forever," Ay-ttho warned. "Eventually, she will risk injuring Luap and come after us. The hangars on this base have blast protection. We should move within them."

"I understand your concerns," Siri said. "But moving into the hangar makes us less responsive. For now, I recommend staying in this location. The hit-and-run attacks seem to work well."

Unfortunately for Ay-ttho, the conference agreed with Siri and the camp remained exposed on the surface of Herse.

"How do you like your new fighter from Doukan?" Kinis asked Tufan.

But Tufan was too distraught over the death of Oscar to respond.

"I will have my revenge," he said, once he had regained his composure.

Ozan arrived with the compensation he had promised Tufan.

"I don't want anything from you," said Tufan.

"Then at least join me in a meal. We may have a long fight ahead of us."

"I don't want to eat, just fight."

"I understand and bring good news," said Kinis. "Naej has agreed to lift the ban on the Zoxans helping the Ao-jun. That is why Doukan could give you a new fighter."

Impatient, Tufan went to the fighter given to him by Doukan and led the attack on the camp on Herse. Many Zoxans joined in and fought the Saturnian worshipping Zoxans.

"Time to go," said Ay-ttho, as she prepared the Mastery of the Stars to leave.

"What about Pirate?" asked Witt.

"What about Pirate? We got into this mess because of him. He can get himself out of it."

"He has taken a Hersean fighter," said Ron.

"There you go," said Ay-ttho. "He can look after himself."

"Wait!" said Witt. "You can't leave Luap here by herself."

Witt exited the Mastery of the Stars.

"I will buy you some time," Chronos communicated to Ay-ttho as he was taking a Hersean fighter.

Chronos drew Tufan's ship away from the camp.

"We can't wait any longer," said Ay-ttho. "We have to leave."

"But what about Witt?" asked Tori.

"He left. He knew we couldn't wait for him."

While Tufan was still chasing Chronos, the Mastery of the Stars had time to escape, leaving Witt and Luap on the surface..

"It is I, Chronos," the star master communicated to Tufan, once he was sure that the Mastery of the Stars had escaped.

"I have no argument with you, star master," said Tufan. "Where is the Zoxan called Siri?"

"He is waiting for you on Herse."

By the time Tufan returned to Herse, most of the camp had been long evacuated but, as Chronos promised, Siri was waiting for him in his Hersean fighter.

Although he had fully intended to face Tufan, Siri soon realised that he was completely outmatched by the state-of-the-art fighter Doukan had given Tufan, and he fled.

Tufan gave chase, and Siri could not evade him. Eventually, he was cut off and forced to turn and face Tufan.

Siri's Hersean fighter was no match for the superior firepower of Tufan's new fighter, which the Zoxans had based on the formidable scorpion lizard design.

Meanwhile, Pirate was engaged in battle with Ajax. Although Pirate was a pilot, he was never a fighter pilot and the injuries he had sustained in his accident in the parallel universe had affected his reactions.

Ajax, however, was an experienced fighter pilot and manoeuvred Pirate into a position where he could attack him face on. Although the Hersean fighters were good, they had spent almost a hundred FNCs in a hangar and the cannon fire of Ajax soon ripped through Pirate's observation window, killing him instantly.

With Siri defeated and the Hersean fighters destroyed, the Ao-jun allow themselves a moment for celebration. The only Ao-jun not celebrating were Tufan who was mourning Oscar's death, and Sgniwef, who had still not recovered Luap.

Unbeknown to Sgniwef, Luap was still on the surface, lamenting Pirate's death to Witt.

"What terrible times it has been when I was brought into this universe, Witt? Why has this been my fate?"

Witt didn't answer, but he thought all Luap needed to do was stop running off. He supposed Luap shouldn't be forced to stay with Sgniwef if he didn't want to be with her.

"The universe will end because of me," she continued. "Why did my begetter make me like this?"

Witt had heard rumours that her father had been a star master, but he had always dismissed it as gossip. He thought that this was probably not the best time to ask.

"All this fighting. May an Ao-jun like me never be created again. Siri is already dead. No-one cares about me."

"I care about you," said Witt.

"Everyone hates me."

"I don't hate you."

"The unit I began, my life was cursed."

"No, it wasn't."

"I should end my life."

"No, you shouldn't."

"No-one would care."

"I would."

*

"Where are we going?" asked Tori.

"We shouldn't go back via either Angetenar or Sonvaenope," said Ay-ttho.

"So, where are we going to go?"

"Ron has identified a portal that isn't on any of the charts."

"Not on any charts? Are you sure that's wise?"

"Considering the Ao-jun, and possibly the Zoxans, may chase us, I think it's the best alternative."

"But we don't know what is on the other side."

"It can't be any worse than a fleet of Ao-jun destroyers and a ship of angry Zoxans."

"As far as I can tell, we are not being pursued," said Ron.

"There you are," said Ay-ttho.

"And there it is," said Ron.

Ay-ttho, Tori and Sevan all looked through the observation window where they could see they were slowly drawing nearer to a distant portal.

"I wonder what's on the other side?" Sevan thought out loud.

"We are about to find out," said Ay-ttho.

The Mastery of the Stars entered the portal.

CHAPTER 6: THE SECRET COLONY

"The system has a habitable planet," Ron announced once the freighter had cleared the portal.

"Let's go there," said Ay-ttho.

"My scanners show that there is a colony there," said Ron.

"Let's hope they're friendly," said Tori.

"I think they are," said Ron. "As far as I can tell, the portal has transported us to another part of the Angetenar system. We are simply approaching Angetenar from a different direction."

The Mastery of the Stars flew low over the rich vegetation of Angetenar and over the woodland which protected the entrance to the cavern where they had landed previously.

They left the ship and continued on foot deep into the cavern until they reached the familiar wooden houses with their spectacular architecture. At the iron gates, D'Heli and Alyr were there to meet them.

"It's good to see you again," said D'Heli. "But it's strange you weren't detected coming through the portal. We only detected your ship when you entered the atmosphere."

"There is another portal on the other side of the system," said Ay-ttho. "I'll get Ron to transmit the coordinates so you can adjust your scanners."

"Thank you. Let us take you to the place you stayed before where you can eat and rest. Then you can tell us all about the trip. We were worried that we hadn't heard from you. Where are Witt and Pirate?"

As they walked, Ay-ttho told them the story of Pirate and Luap and leaving Witt behind. She also told them of the Zoxans and the fact they had divided into warring factions, one of which had adopted the Saturnian religion.

"Speaking of the Saturnian religion," said Alyr. "We have a surprise for you. We will bring him later."

"We have a couple of surprises for you," confirmed D'Heli. "Shortly after you left, we had some unexpected visitors. While you eat, I will see whether they will come to meet you. After you have eaten, we should move your ship to a deeper cavern."

"Very intriguing," said Ay-ttho. "How are Nadio and Effeek'o?"

"They are well. We will tell them you are here."

When the food arrived, it was Gurengi algae crisps, Lurirans space-beetle and Globbon octo-nuts with a topping of Daregs beetle dust again, but it was a welcome change from the rations on board the Mastery of the Stars.

When D'Heli returned, there was someone with him. Ay-ttho was amazed to see that the figure that limped through the door was none other than her old friend and mentor, High Priest Brabin, from the Saturnian temple on Lenguicarro.

"Ay-ttho!" Brabin called out as he entered the house.

"Brabin!" Ay-ttho also seemed pleased to see the creature with his familiar blue bug eyes set in a face surrounded with grey hair and topped with antennae, leaning on his trademark wooden staff.

"Where have you been all these solar cycles?" he asked.

"We've been busy."

"Have they fed you? Are you hungry?"

"Do you have any of those green plants you gave us before?" asked Sevan.

Ay-ttho and Tori both looked at their friend in amazement.

"Your memory is coming back," said Tori.

"I suppose it must be," said Sevan.

"Come," said Brabin. "I'm afraid I don't have any of the green plants you like, they only grow on Lenguicarro. But I have something almost as good which I think you will like and then you can tell me all about your memory and how you lost it."

Brabin led them through the caverns.

"I have a big surprise for you," said Brabin. "Do you remember Barnes?"

"Barnes? Is he here?"

"Yes, come to the house they have given us and I will introduce you."

They entered past the wooden buildings. Out of a window, someone was shouting.

"Who is that?" asked Sevan.

"Ignore her. That's just Cassandra. She's mad. A product of Barnes' later experiments with cloning. Thankfully, they gave her a room away from us."

Brabin suddenly froze and turned to them.

"You weren't followed were you?"

"No," said Ay-ttho.

"How can you be sure?"

"Ron was monitoring the scanners."

"Good."

Soon, they passed the large hall where they remembered meeting the Electric Man. Also, they passed a vast temple in front of which stood a Saturnian priest.

"This is Panthous," Brabin introduced them. "He is the priest of the temple of Chronos, which is this magnificent building you see here."

"What do you do?" asked Ay-ttho.

"They have kindly made me the priest of the drirkel straalket temple, the slightly less impressive building over there. Come on, I'll show you."

Brabin led them away again and then paused.

"I tell you what," he said after a moment of thought. "Let me take you straight to the house where Barnes and I are staying. He will want to know you are here."

They followed Brabin around the wall of an enormous cavern until they arrived at a compound that looked palatial compared with the other buildings.

Brabin banged on the door with his staff.

It opened to reveal a tall corporation security clone, not unlike Ay-ttho.

"Misenus!" said Brabin. "Good to see you. I have brought some friends."

Misenus opened the door wider to let them through. As Sevan entered the courtyard, he saw a large wooden house built on top of a natural stone platform.

On the balcony, Sevan could see a diminutive figure in robes, sitting in a chair, clutching a cane.

"Barnes! Look who I have brought to see you," said Brabin, gesturing towards the group.

Sevan noticed how old and weak his creator now looked.

"Ah! My favourite creations," Barnes laughed feebly. "So, you made it back at last. I knew you would."

"This sounds like a call for celebration," said Misenus. "Shall I get my wusku? Or my stiscex shell?"

"Good idea, Misenus," said Barnes. "Now we finally have something to celebrate."

"It seems your experiment unleashed more than you had bargained," Ay-ttho told Barnes.

"Just as feisty as ever I see, Ay-ttho. And how is Tori, my favourite Republic security clone?"

"Fine, no thanks to you."

"And Sevan. He found the secret within?"

"The Zoxans nearly got it out of him," Tori snapped.

"Ah, the Zoxans," Brabin mused. "You know, we did quite a good job of converting some of them to Saturnianism."

"I know. We met some."

"Really? Who?"

"Siri, for one."

"Yes, Siri. An incredible pilot, but a little hotheaded."

"His own kind killed him. We didn't witness it, but Ron monitored it on the scanners."

"Shame."

"What?" asked Misenus, just returning with her wusku, which she dropped to the floor.

"Misenus became very close to Siri during our time together on Lenguicarro," Brabin explained.

"You didn't bring the Zoxans with you, did you?" asked Barnes.

"No, Ron said we weren't followed."

As they drew closer to the balcony, Sevan realised Barnes had a scarred face and was blind.

"What happened?" he asked.

"I got into a fight with one of the Zoxans called Naej."

Four others arrived.

"Perfect timing!" exclaimed Brabin. "Let me introduce some new friends of mine: Achates, Sergestus, Aeolus and Clytius. This is Ay-ttho, Tori and Sevan, some very old friends of mine."

"They don't look that old," said Achates.

"Time has been very kind to them."

"Once you have rested, we will take you outside of the settlement to show you a little of the environment," Achates told them. "I am sure it will be fascinating for you."

Ay-ttho spent a long time talking to Misenus. She found they had a lot in common from their time as corporation security clones and Sevan listened in to the conversations about Ay-ttho's past with fascination.

He went to ask Barnes if what Ay-ttho had told him was true, but he couldn't find Barnes anywhere, so he asked Brabin if he knew where his creator was.

"I do," said Brabin. "Come with me and I will show you something nice."

Sevan followed Brabin through the caverns to the large hall in the centre. Brabin showed Sevan the council chamber, which was nowhere near as ornate as the chamber Sevan remembered from his rotations on The Doomed Planet, then he realised he remembered and was delighted to think that it might be true that his memory was returning.

He was about to explain his revelation to Brabin when the high priest appeared to walk up to a wall, but instead of banging into the wall as Sevan had expected, Brabin opened a hidden door. He led Sevan through the hidden door and through a passage, then up through the building until they reached the topmost heights of the pediment surmounting a portico on which Barnes was sitting.

"There you are," said Brabin. "Can you find your own way back?"

"Yes, thank you," said Sevan.

Barnes confirmed that everything Ay-ttho had said was true, and he even added a few embellishments of his own.

As dusk fell, Sevan helped Barnes back down the passage and through the hidden door into the council chamber, where they met the Electric Man, who was talking to some settlers.

"Sevan? Let me introduce you to the Electric Man," said Barnes. "He is our president, the chief council member, if you like. This is Hecubus, his adviser, and Polites, Helenus and Polydorus, his assistants."

"We've met," said Sevan. "The last time we came to the caverns."

Sevan marvelled at Polydorus and Helenus, who were wearing shiny Republic armour.

"You've been up on the roof again, Barnes?" The Electric Man asked.

"You know how it helps me to reflect."

"We are saying goodbye to Polydorus. He is going to search for other portals and other lands where we might find other colonies like ours."

"May the star masters go with you," said Barnes. "We will leave you to your fair wells."

Sevan helped Barnes back to the house where they found Ay-ttho with Achates, Sergestus, Aeolus and Clytius.

She had spent a lot of time with them and they were all becoming best friends.

On one rotation, Misenus, Sergestus, Aeolus and Clytius were leading Ay-ttho, Tori and Sevan on a hike through the thick vegetation which surrounded the caverns.

They walked up into the hills and onto the highest peak near the settlement which they called Mount Ida and from where they had spectacular views of the large body of water that ran alongside the mountain, which they called the Sigean straits.

Suddenly, Ay-ttho felt a sharp pain in her leg and fell to the ground.

"Uxclod! What in the worst place is that?" she asked, as she stared at a large spine protruding from her leg.

Sevan almost fainted at the sight.

"You've been stung by a grumpy hellebore," said Misenus.

"What the uxclod is that?"

"It's a plant. You must have triggered its defence mechanism."

"What am I supposed to do now?"

"We'll have to carry you back to the settlement. Effeeko will have to pull it out."

"What?"

On the way back to the settlement, they met four coming the other way with a youngling.

"What happened?" one of them asked.

"A grumpy hellebore spine," said Sergestus.

"Uxclod! Good luck with that."

"These are friends of Brabin, Ay-ttho, Tori and Sevan."

"Nice to meet you."

"These are Ripheus, Epytus, Hypanis and Dymas, some of our bravest warriors. And this is young Coroebus."

"This is all very nice," said Ay-ttho. "But there is something sticking out of my leg. May we go, please?"

Sergestus said goodbye to his friends, and they carried Ay-ttho the rest of the way back to the settlement, to the house of Effeeko. They set her on a table and Effeeko gave her some distilled pish to drink and a piece of wood to grip between her teeth.

As Effeeko removed the barbed spine, Ay-ttho screamed with pain.

"Stop it! You're killing her!" Sevan yelled.

The scene continued the same way for a few units. Tori, Misenus, Sergestus, Aeolus and Clytius holding the screaming Ay-ttho down, Effeeko pulling, and Sevan screaming.

Eventually, the spine came out and Effeeko quickly poured some distilled pish over the wound before sewing up the hole.

Sevan fainted.

When he awoke, Sevan was in bed with a fever and an acute pain in his stomachs.

"You've picked up some kind of virus," said Misenus. "That explains the hysterics. We all had it when we first arrived. I'll call Effeeko."

"You should stay in bed and get as much rest as possible," Effeeko said, after he had examined Sevan. "The illness will run its course."

While both Ay-ttho and Sevan were recuperating in bed, Ripheus, Epytus, Hypanis, Dymas and the young Coroebus arrived to see how she was.

"I'm sorry if I was grumpy earlier," said Ay-ttho.

"That's understandable," said Ripheus. "You had a grumpy hellebore spine in your leg."

No sooner had the visitors left than Brabin arrived.

"It's like Future spaceport in here," said Ay-ttho, sarcastically lamenting the lack of peace.

"I have a surprise for you," Brabin said, stepping aside from the door.

Through the door walked a thug.

"Nadio!" she exclaimed. "I was worried I'd never see you again.".

"So was I," he laughed.

*

On the next rotation, there was a large commotion in the caverns. They saw the ship of Chronos landing outside the cavern complex.

Its mechanical cargo arm unloaded a gigantic box, and then the ship took off again and disappeared.

"A present from Chronos," many of the cavern dwellers shouted.

Ay-ttho asked Barnes what he thought of the unusual gift.

"It is undoubtedly a gift from Chronos. Perhaps it signifies an end of the struggle against the Zoxans, or at least a significant breakthrough."

"But why did Chronos not address us personally? Why did he just leave the box?"

"Perhaps the answer to your questions lay within the box."

"Perhaps it's a trap."

"You worry too much, Ay-ttho. Let's hold a big party to celebrate, and we'll invite everyone we know."

CHAPTER 7: TREACHERY

Ay-ttho watched with foreboding as the cavern dwellers opened the iron gates to reveal the giant box. They worked quickly to place wheels underneath and stretched cave fig ropes around its girth.

"Burn it!" shouted Brabin.

"Get out of the way," someone pushed him and he tripped and fell, banging his face on a section of the cavern wall.

Ay-ttho ran to the aid of his friend.

"Are you hurt?" he asked, seeing the priest's bloodied face.

"I can't see," said Brabin.

"You've blinded him," shouted Ay-ttho.

"Not us. The star masters have blinded him as a punishment for doubting Chronos who brought us this gift."

"Burn the box!" Brabin shouted.

"No! If we burn the box, the star masters will punish us. It is an offering."

Ay-ttho took Brabin to the house of Barnes, where they tended to the priest's wound. He left Brabin there and returned to see the efforts to get the box to pass through the gateway.

The box was so large that it got stuck in the gateway, not once but four times before they could negotiate it inside, and that they only achieved it by demolishing a portion of the cavern wall.

As they shifted the box back and forth, Ay-ttho could have sworn she heard metal inside.

"Did you hear that?" she asked the others, but they ignored her, so excited were they to have negotiated the box through the gap.

With a tremendous effort, they dragged the enormous offering within the cavern.

Offspring danced around it, singing songs and delighting at touching the ropes.

"Pull the box to the temple," the crowd shouted. "And offer prayers to the star masters' divinity."

They dragged the gigantic box, rolling it into the cavern.

Cassandra looked out of the window of her house into the street and looked horrified at the sight of the festivities.

"The Zoxans are hiding inside the box!" she shouted, but the crowd laughed.

"The mad one is ranting again," they scoffed.

"Zoxans are hiding in the box!" she continued to shout, but the crowd continued with their feasting. They hung flowers on the box and on themselves and musicians played werse flutes.

"Look! Chronos is laughing at the end of the war," they pointed to the statue of the star master, with his mouth parted in what Ay-ttho had to admit looked like laughter, raising his blaster in one hand and his scroll in the other.

He looked at the statue of the drirkel straalkets. They, too, looked pleased. And the statue of Covil appeared to be questioning why there could be any doubt that this box was anything but a magnificent gift from the star masters.

The crowd brought offerings of pish and fruit. Ay-ttho walked to the cavern entrance and looked up at the night sky. The night was clear, and the galaxy stretched across the sky. There were full moons bathing the forest in a silver light.

Ay-ttho returned to the cavern where, from her window, Cassandra continued to shout.

"O wretches! We are passing into the land of darkness. Fire and blood surround the cavern. The star masters are showing us portents of calamity. Destruction yawns before your feet. Fools! You do not know your doom. You rejoice like mad thugs."

"Shut your face," Nadio shouted

"Ruin lurks in the box. You don't believe me?" Cassandra continued. "No matter how loud I cry! The drirkel straalkets are angry and you are banqueting there in your last feast, on sereosleodo fouled with gore, when now your feet are on the path of doom!"

Cassandra became more frustrated that the crowd was not listening to her. Some revellers shouted abuse at her to be quiet.

"Why does a raving tongue of evil speech, offspring of Barnes, make your lips cry words empty as wind?" Shouted young Coroebus. "Ruinous madness

surrounds you; that's why we all scorn you, babbler! Your evil bodings speak
to the Zoxans and yourself!"

"Shame!" cried the crowd.

"Liar!" cried others.

"Ruin and fate's heavy stroke are hard at hand," cried Coroebus.

Cassandra went down from her house and tried to attack the box, but
the crowd pushed her back and mocked her.

She went to a nearby torch burning on one of the cavern walls and was
about to return to the box when she saw a two-edged meson blaster someone
had set aside to push the box. Blazing torch in one hand, meson blaster in the
other, she rushed at the box but the crowd stopped her and threw the brand
one way and the meson blaster to the other, and then turned back to their
feast.

Within the box, Ao-jun silently smiled to hear the uproar of feasters
ignoring Cassandra, and they marvelled she knew the Ao-jun plan so well.

The revellers partied loudly. There was feasting, singing, dancing, playing
of werse flutes, laughter and drunken cries.

Ay-ttho watched as the buildings seemed to shake with the weight of the
dancing.

Coroebus, drunk on pish, was shouting: "Chronos has defeated the
Zoxans. They have failed and, with hopes dashed, have fled from our
universe. Like silly uxclods, they have fled."

Ay-ttho left the revellers and went home to Barnes' house. As he entered
the spacious complex, he could see the house on its large stone foundation.
The party inside was clearly still in full swing.

He found Barnes sitting in a chair by the entrance.

"Are you not enjoying the party?" Ay-ttho asked.

"I'm waiting for you. Now the party can really start."

"Let me help you."

He gave Barnes his arm and helped him up. Barnes supported himself
with his stick in one hand and by holding onto Ay-ttho with the other.

"How is Brabin?" Ay-ttho asked.

"He's blind, like me. Did I tell you how I got these wounds?"

"Only like a million times. Naej struck you down," Ay-ttho humoured him. "Ah! Here is my good friend Misenus. Help me get my father into a chair."

The two set Barnes down in a large chair.

"Why aren't you playing for us, Misenus? Where is your wusku? Or at least your stiscex shell."

"Friend, although the festivities are raging around, I am finding it difficult to get into the spirit. The death of Siri still weighs heavily on my marbles."

"It was a heavy loss. Losing a comrade-in-arms is a heavy burden to bear."

"It is."

"I am very grateful to you," said Ay-ttho.

"Don't mention it. Our house is your house."

"You're here at last," said Tori.

"Yes, I'm here. How's Sevan?"

"He's in bed at last, though he took some persuading. He didn't want to go to bed without seeing Barnes."

"I'll check on him."

Ay-ttho went to Sevan's quarters and found Sevan still awake.

"Shouldn't you be sleeping? You won't get big and strong and make a great warrior if you don't get your sleep."

"Hilarious. You're not asleep."

"No, but I'm already a great warrior," Ay-ttho laughed.

"Tell me about your past."

"You overhead everything I told Misenus."

"Yes, but I'd like to hear it again."

"Okay, quickly, and then I have to go."

"Thank you."

"Well, like I told Misenus before, I was upset with Barnes because he wasn't giving me the opportunity to fight. Idomeneus had killed Alcathousso, and they would not release his body for us to give him a proper ceremony."

"When was this?"

"It was during the original expansion by the first President Man when the Corporation helped the then fledgling republic against the Cheng-Huang and Ao-jun colonies. I was furious and was talking to Deiphobus and he suggested I lead an attack, so I and my fellow clones went to rescue Alcathousso's body. I fought the mighty Nala and he could have killed me. You should have seen his ship. He said I was the second best warrior in the Corporation."

"You were Barnes' principal lieutenant, weren't you?"

"I was, but back to Nala. He'd already killed Astynous, Hypeiron, Abas, Polyidus, Xanthus, Thoon, Echemmon and Chromius. I asked Pandarus to follow my ship so that we might fight Nala together. Pandarus had already damaged his ship."

"Barnes says the star masters designed your engines."

"He says that."

"He says Chronos protects you in battle."

"You've been speaking a lot with Barnes, haven't you? There might be some truth in it. When Pandarus faced Nala, Sthenelus temporarily disabled my engines. Pandarus thought he had killed Nala, but it was Nala who killed Pandarus. I approached him. His weapons system was disabled, so I approached. That was when he fired a gigantic cannon out of his cargo bay doors and disabled my ship. I fell unconscious."

"Barnes says Chronos saved you."

"Yes, he does. And now Nala has my ship, and I awoke in Pergamos with no idea how I got there."

"Where are they now, do you think?"

"If rumours are to be believed, they have fled, but I have a bad feeling about this box."

"Tell me about Kram."

"You should be asleep."

"Please."

"Okay, well, Kram had been looting surrounding systems, and he went to Lyrnessos, where the stores were full, but we were waiting for him."

"You fought Kram?"

"I did."

"The greatest warrior of the Ao-jun."

"So they say. He was too good for me. We had to retreat and leave the planet to them."

"Barnes said Chronos saved you again."

"Did he? Well, I told you the stories, so now you have to go to sleep, you promised."

"Okay, but first there's something I've been meaning to tell you."

"Quickly then."

Sevan told Ay-ttho about the day Brabin had taken him to the council building and had shown him the hidden door to the passageway which led to the roof. He told her about finding Barnes on the roof.

"Do you think he's okay?" he asked.

"I don't know, and I don't care."

"Why?"

"Night, night, Sevan."

"Wait, there's more," said Sevan.

He told Ay-ttho about The Electric Man and his assistants Polydorus and Helenus, who were wearing Republic armour and searching for a second portal.

"Night, night."

"Night Ay-ttho."

Ay-ttho closed the door of Sevan's quarters behind her before rejoining the party where she found her friends Achates, Sergestus and Aeolus with Clytius.

"Finally, you grace us with your presence," Achates joked. "Everyone who is anyone is at this party, except you. Look, there is the healer Effeek'o. I never knew he was a friend of yours."

"Yes, we met here on Angetenar before the meteor shower. He recently removed a spine from my leg. You should have heard the scandal Sevan was making as he removed it. I think Sevan thought I was going to die," Ay-ttho laughed. "Come, let me introduce you to Nadio."

"I would like to propose a toast," said Ay-ttho, raising a cup of pish.

He gestured to the statues of Chronos and the drirkel straalkets.

"May Chronos continue to observe, protect, and influence all that happens within this house. And the drirkel straalkets for protecting our food, pish and oil." Ay-ttho took a piece of sereosleodo and threw it on the fire. "For the drirkel straalkets. As long as we have them, they will keep us safe."

The party continued for some time before, heavy headed with pish, Ay-ttho and her guests retired to their beds.

Ay-ttho dreamt that he saw Siri standing by his bed. He was crying and covered from head to swollen feet in the black bloody dust that had covered his body when Tufan had destroyed his fighter. His beak was hanging off, his feathers matted with blood.

"Siri?" Ay-ttho said. "Where did you come from? Oh, Siri, I am weary from the many troubles of our journeys and our caverns and now I see you, after the death of so many Zoxans! What shameful events have marred that beaked face of yours? And why do I see these wounds?"

Siri was silent.

"Why do you not reply?" asked Ay-ttho.

"Ah! Creation of Barnes," Siri's ghost finally spoke. "Fly, tear yourself from the flames. The enemy has taken the caverns: The Mastery of the Stars falls from her place. We have given enough to Brabin and the caverns. The Saturnians entrust their sacred relics to you: take them, seek mighty walls for them, those you will find at last when you have wandered the galaxies."

Ay-ttho was awoken by the sounds of screams and shouting. Barnes's house was remote from the main cavern, secluded by corridors, but the sounds were growing clearer and clearer.

Ay-ttho ran outside and strained to listen, but he needn't have because the truth was obvious to see. The reflection of flame could be seen in the corridor leading to the main cavern. She ran through the corridor to find the vast hall was already a ruin, with fire raging all over it. The drirkel straalket temple was also on fire.

Then he could hear someone approaching from behind and the blare of wuskus.

"Achates! Sergestus! Aeolus!" he shouted. Ripheus, Epytus, Hypanis and Dymas also followed.

CHAPTER 8: CHANGE OF SUN

Ay-ttho saw Panthous, a Saturnian priest from the temple of Chronos, escaping the Ao-jun shots, dragging along a sacred relic with one hand, while he cradled his offspring's offspring in the other.

"Shelter in our house," Ay-ttho told him. "Where's the best advantage, Panthous? What position should we take?"

"The last rotation comes," Panthous groaned. "Our inescapable hour. Our time is past and the great glory of the Saturnians. Chronos carries all to the better place: the Ao-jun are lords of the burning caverns."

It looked as if thousands from Ao-jun were blocking the narrow corridors between caverns, brandishing their weapons. A line of steel reflecting the flickering flames, ready for the slaughter. The first few guards at the gates were attempting to fight, resisting in blind conflict.

"Come," Ay-ttho shouted to the friends following him. "The star masters who supported these caverns have departed, leaving behind their temples and their altars. You aid a burning settlement."

Ay-ttho thrust herself among the weapons and the flames, and her friends followed. Visible in the light of the double moon, which was so low in the Sky it shone through the cavern entrance and the gates. Ripheus and Epytus were the first to cut down the Ao-jun. Hypanis and Dymas fought next to Ay-ttho, and he saw young Coroebus, who hadn't listened to the warnings of Cassandra.

They ran into a great crowd of Ao-jun. The Ao-jun officer apparently thought that Ay-ttho and her friends were also Ao-jun troops.

"Hurry! What sluggishness makes you delay so?" shouted the officer, "The others are raping and plundering burning: are you only now arriving from the ships?"

When his words ushered no reply, the officer knew he'd fallen into the enemy fold. He was stunned and drew back in sudden fear. Ay-ttho and her friends charged forward and slaughtered the Ao-jun wholesale.

"Let's swap our weapons for those of the Ao-jun," said Coroebus. "They are better than ours."

He took up the Ao-jun officer's helmet with its notable markings and strapped the Ao-jun's weapon to his side.

Ripheus and Dymas were the first to follow Coroebus's lead, though soon all the warriors armed themselves with the fresh spoils.

They moved through the caverns, mingling with the Ao-jun. They clashed in many encounters and, when the double moons set, sent many an Ao-jun down to the worst place by fighting in the darkness.

So effective were their attacks that some of the Ao-jun scattered to their ships, and some, in humiliated terror, climbed in the vast box again to hide within its familiar womb.

Then, the group saw Cassandra dragged by her hair from the temple of the drirkel straalkets, hands tied with cords. She lifted her eyes to the skies, pleading with the star masters.

Coroebus threw himself among the Ao-jun ranks, seeking death. After seeing such a sight that enraged him so much, the rest of the band followed him, and they exchanged blaster fire.

The Ao-jun charged together, but the blaster fire from the cavern dwellers on the high roof of the main hall overwhelmed them. Saturnian blaster fire killed Hypanis and Dymas because the cavern dwellers, seeing their Ao-jun helmets, assumed they were the enemy.

Ao-jun gathered from all sides. They rushed Ay-ttho and her friends. Those Ao-jun, that had scattered to their ships earlier, re-appeared and recognised the helmets and weapons Ay-ttho 's group were using and realised their accents differed from theirs.

They overwhelmed the group by numbers and the Ao-jun killed Coroebus and Ripheus. In the commotion, Ay-ttho was separated from the rest of the group with two cavern dwellers called Iphitus and Pelias.

Iphitus was old, and Kram had wounded Pelias. Ay-ttho was trying to not get frustrated by the slowness of their pace when they were all distracted by a commotion coming from the direction of the main hall.

There, the proper battle was happening and made the rest of the skirmishes throughout the caverns look like offspring's play. The Ao-jun were pushing against a cavern dweller's force shield wall that was blocking the entrance to the main hall. They had fired cables up the walls and Ao-jun climbed with one hand, holding defensive shields against the cavern dwellers' blaster fire.

In the council building, the settlers were pulling down the turrets and roof-tiles of the halls to use as weapons, preparing to defend themselves and seeing the end near all the while lamenting the destruction of their work. Inside, settlers were waiting with blasters to defend the building to the last.

Seeing the spirited defence of the building by the cavern dwellers, Ay-ttho was inspired that they might not lose everything and resolved to help.

"There is an entrance with hidden doors, and a passage between the council chamber, and a secluded gateway beyond," she told her remaining friends. "Brabin, used it to take Sevan to see Barnes."

"How do you know this?" his friends asked.

"Never mind how, just go."

Ay-ttho led his friends to the hidden doors and through the passage, then up through the main hall until they reached the topmost heights of the roof from where the cavern dwellers were firing their weapons.

They climbed up to the roof, from where they could see all the main cavern.

But more Ao-jun arrived, and the settlers continued to fire all they had. Tufan's team advanced on the building. They fired onto the roof and among the front ranks.

Tufan broke through the force shield and blasted the doors from its hinges, revealing rows of armed guards. Behind them, the long hollow hall echoed with the cries of frightened cavern dwellers.

One by one, Ay-ttho's friends fell, either off the roof into the square or through the timbers into the fires. Ay-ttho descended through what remained of the roof and into the main hall.

No barricades nor the guards themselves at the entrance could stop Tufan. Ao-jun poured through, forcing a passage and slaughtering the front ranks. They filled the wide space with their fighters like a raging torrent.

When Ay-ttho entered the large hall, she could see Tufan on the threshold, mad with slaughter, together with Ozan and Sgniwef.

In the hall, he saw Hecuba in the centre clutching the statues of the star masters.

The Electric Man entered with his blaster fastened at his side, hurrying to the thick of the enemy, seeking death.

"What mad thought, president, urges you to fasten on this weapon?" cried Hecuba when she saw him. "Where do you run? This is not the time for this. If only Siri were here. I beg you, or we'll die together."

She grabbed The Electric Man and pulled the council leader towards her, setting him down on some steps.

The Electric Man's assistant, Polites, who had been defending the entrance to the building, ran down the long hall towards them. He was wounded, and it was not only enemy blaster fire that followed him, Tufan chased after him, eager to strike him, he fired his blaster and it pierced Polites back just as he reached the gaze of his colleagues. He fell forward and his life poured out of him in a river of life juices.

"If there is any justice in the better place that cares about such things, may the star masters repay you with fit thanks, and due reward for your wickedness," The Electric Man rose and shouted at Tufan. "You who have made me see my assistant's death in front of my face, and defiled a president's sight with murder."

The Electric Man fired his blaster, but his aim was weak.

Tufan dragged the Electric Man, trembling, and slipping in the pool of Polites' blood, to the centre of the hall. Twisting his left hand in The Electric Man's antennae, Tufan raised his glittering blaster in his right hand and fired it into The Electric Man's head.

Wild terror gripped Ay-ttho. She stood amazed, watching the death of the Electric Man. She thought of Tori and Sevan. Had the Ao-jun's already ransacked the house?

Ay-ttho turned to leave. She was alone and wandered, gazing everywhere, randomly.

She left the main cavern to return to Barnes' house as quickly as possible.

High on the main hall, Ay-ttho could see the Ao-jun, Tufan, dangling cavern dwellers' offspring, over the edge. Their co-begetters were screaming and pleading for their lives, but Tufan threw the offspring from the high walls and their lives were dashed out of them as they hit the ground.

Ay-ttho fought the Ao-jun to escape and killed many with her blaster. She saw them set the caverns alight, saw them killing multitudes of cavern dwellers, spoiling the cavern's treasures, and dragging dwellers from their homes. She understood that the battle was lost; The caverns had fallen.

Ay-ttho left the Ao-jun to their flames and went to fetch Tori and Sevan. She planned to escape the settlement so that she might live to fight another day.

When she arrived at Barnes's home, she found Misenus, Barnes, his friends Achates, Sergestus, and Acmon, the healer Effeek'o, Nadio, Tori, and Sevan.

Everyone prepared to flee, but Barnes refused to leave.

"You are young Ay-ttho," he said. "You go. If the star masters had wished to lengthen my life, they'd have spared my house. Goodbye, Ay-ttho. I shall find death with my hand. I am useless, and hated by the Zoxans."

Ay-ttho collected her weapons again. She could not see what tactic or opportunity was open to her.

"Did you think I could leave you, Barnes? The Zoxans want to leave nothing of our caverns, and you want to add yourself to the ruins. Tufan will come, drenched in Polite's blood. Did Chronos rescue me for this? To see the enemy in the depths of your house, and Sevan, and Tori, slaughtered, thrown together in a heap, in one another's blood? I will go out to the Ao-jun again. This day we shall not all perish unavenged."

Ay-ttho fastened on her blaster and rushed from the house. But Tori and Sevan stopped her before she could reach the gate.

"If you go to die, take us with you too," said Tori.

"Wait a unit. What?" said Sevan.

"But if you trust in the weapons you wear, defend this house first. Why abandon Sevan, and Barnes, and me?"

Burning embers from the city were already floating into the house. One threatened to settle on the head of Sevan, but Ay-ttho flicked it away. Then Barnes appeared suddenly possessed, as if by some vision.

"Now no delay," he said. "I follow, and where you lead, there am I."

Ay-ttho could hear the fire moving through the caverns, ever nearer.

"Come then, I will carry you on my shoulders. You are very light. Whatever may happen, it will be for all of us, the same shared risk, or the same salvation."

"I don't like the sound of that," said Sevan.

"Sevan? Come with me." said Ay-ttho. "Tori? Follow us at a distance."

Ay-ttho lifted Barnes up. She walked out of the house, Sevan almost running alongside to match the strides of Ay-ttho. Tori walked behind.

She led them through the streets, where fighting was still taking place. Sevan squealed at having to jump over so many dead bodies. All around, the city was on fire. Ao-jun fired their blasters at them, but none found their target. Ay-ttho was startled by every noise, anxious, and fearful equally for Sevan and Barnes.

Soon, she was near the main gates, and thought she had completed her journey, when suddenly the sound of approaching feet filled her ears.

"They are near us," shouted Barnes.

Ay-ttho ducked down a corridor and left the caverns they knew well. She didn't look back until she arrived at the cavern where they had hidden the Mastery of the Stars. Ay-ttho realised that someone was missing; Tori.

Ay-ttho placed Sevan and Barnes on the ship while she returned to the caverns once more.

She was determined to retrace her path through the caverns, once more exposing her life to danger.

First she looked for the dark threshold of the main gate from which she had left, and retraced the landmarks of her course in the dark, scanning them with her eyes. Everywhere there was terror and the silence itself dismayed her.

Then she headed back towards Barnes's house. In case, by some chance, Tori had made his way there.

The Ao-jun had invaded, and occupied, the whole house. Fire rolled over the rooftop and the blaze raged onto the roof of the cavern.

She went back towards the mail cavern. Phoenix and Kram were watching over the spoils in the empty hall.

Here the dwellers' treasures had been gathered from every part, ripped from the blazing homes. Co-begetters and trembling offspring stood round in long ranks.

Ay-ttho dared to shout for Tori through the shadows, repeating her cries, again and again. Searching and raging endlessly among the city roofs, until she collapsed.

When she raised her head, she saw Tori in a form greater than she'd known. She was dumbfounded, and her antennae stood on end, and her voice stuck in her throat. Then Tori spoke.

"The ruler of the great universe did not let you take Tori with you. Away from here, yours is a long exile. You must plough a vast reach of space and you will come to Hesperia's land, where the Lydian Tiber flows in gentle course among the farmers' rich fields. There, happiness will be yours. Banish these tears for your beloved Tori. I shall never see the noble halls. Instead, the splendid mother of the star masters keeps me on this planet. Now farewell, and preserve your love for Sevan."

Three times Ay-ttho tried to throw her arms about his neck and three times his form fled her hands. Then the vision faded into thin air, leaving Ay-ttho weeping.

When she returned to her friends, Ay-ttho found that a great number of new companions had streamed in, a crowd gathering for exile, a wretched throng. They had arrived from all sides, ready, with courage for whatever land she wished to lead them to. Among them were Nadio and Achates.

"Look," he said, pointing to the cavern entrance where dawn was breaking. "The star is rising above the heights of Ida, bringing the next rotation, and the Ao-jun hold the caverns. We must go now."

CHAPTER 9: THE BOTTLE FROM SPACE

Ay-ttho and his group boarded the Mastery of the Stars hoping it would take them away to another system that they hoped they might find deserted in order to begin their exile.

Barnes announced they should set off immediately. As Ay-ttho watched the planet receding into the distance, she could not hold back her tears.

"We will have to navigate through the portal," she commented to Barnes. "We are bound to encounter the Zoxans."

"There is another portal," said Barnes. "It is also not on the charts. I have already given Ron the location."

This fourth portal was linked to another system with a habitable planet. Most portals were. With their supplies virtually depleted, they landed in order to find food.

"We must find something to eat," said Ay-ttho. "We shall have a feast to thank the star masters that our journey has begun, that we might establish a colony."

After a search, they captured a sereosleodo type creature and brought it to the landing site where Ay-ttho was building a fire. Searching for more wood to burn, Ay-ttho spotted a mound crowned with dead bushes.

Ay-ttho tore up the dead wood from the soil and was shocked to see drops of rotting flesh fall from its roots and stain the earth. An icy shiver shot through her body and she nervously pulled up another shoot to discover the source. She was terrified to see that rotting flesh also clung to the bark of the second shoot.

"Uxclod!," she cried out.

She went to pull up a third shoot and a section of the mound fell away to reveal a rotting corpse. Ay-ttho removed some of the earth from the mound and recognised Republic armour. She continued to dig until she saw it was the armour of Polydorus, The Electric Man's youngest assistant. She fetched Barnes.

"Let us give him a proper burial," said Ay-ttho. "The Zoxans know of this place."

"Then we must leave this system, depart this defiled place," said Barnes. "But first, let us also hold a ceremony to remember Tori."

They held a ceremony for Polydorus, piling the earth high on his body. They found some old pish in the Mastery of the Stars and raised a loud shout of farewell to Tori.

Just as he had watched Angetenar, Ay-ttho saw this planet recede into the distance, but this time he was glad to be leaving.

Once they had lost sight of the planet, they encountered a solar storm. They tried to ride it out, but eventually they had no option but to seek safety on the moon of a gas planet. No sooner had they landed than the storm moved past.

"There is life on this moon," Ron announced. "It has about a third of the gravity of Future."

Through the observation window, Sevan could see the vast blue gas planet the moon was orbiting.

"Can you take us to the area you have detected life?" Ay-ttho asked Ron.

"Doing that now."

The Mastery of the Stars flew low over water-filled craters and through white clouds until it arrived at a building that looked remarkably like Brabin's Saturnian temple on Lenguicarro.

"I'm going out," said Ay-ttho.

"You will need a mask," said Ron. "There is less oxygen."

Ay-ttho disembarked and was greeted by a creature that was dressed as a priest of Chronos, his forehead crowned with the sacred headband and holy laurel.

"Welcome to Delos," said the priest. "I am Anius."

Ay-ttho obviously betrayed her surprise.

"I am a high-priest of Chronos," Anius explained. "Barnes? Is that really you?"

"It is, old friend," Barnes smiled as he descended from the Mastery of the Stars behind Ay-ttho.

"Come to my house and tell me all about how you came to be on Delos."

"That's very kind," said Ay-ttho.

"Come this way."

Anius led them to a stone temple where he used the sacred bottle of Delos to communicate with Chronos.

"Grant us a true home, Chronos, grant a weary people walls, and a race, and a city that will endure," he said as he paid homage. "Protect this second citadel of the Saturnians that survives the Zoxans. Grant us an omen, Chronos, to stir our hearts."

After he had paid homage, Anius led them to his house, where they found a banquet of fresh eefosse and phenson along with zugzoin, axeils and egzoids. Anius delivered a message from Chronos.

"The bottle of Delos has spoken. Enduring Mastery of the Stars, the land which first bore you from its parent stock, that same shall welcome you, restored, to its fertile breast. Search out your ancient co-begetter. There, the house of Ay-ttho shall rule all shores, her offspring's offspring, and those that are birthed to them."

"Where is this land?" Ay-ttho asked. "They created both me and the freighter on Daphnis. I have no co-begetter because I am a clone and can have no offspring."

"Listen and learn what you may hope for. Ingoilea lies in the middle of the universe, the home of the mighty Saturn, the cradle of our race. They inhabit a hundred great cities, in the richest of kingdoms, from which our earliest ancestor, Teucer, if I remember the tale rightly, first came to Future, and chose a site for his royal capital. Until then, the towers of the citadel did not stand there. We lived in the depths of the valleys. The mother goddess, Covil, is Ingoilean, and the armed and crested dancers, the Corybantes, worship her, and the grove of Mount Ida that gave its name to our own Mount Ida on Angetenar. From Ingoilea came the faithful silence of the rites of Covil, and the yoked kreqnuins drawing her ship. So come, and let us follow where the star masters' command may lead, let us placate the solar storms, and seek the Ingoilean system. It is no long journey away: if only Chronos is with us, the third standard rotation will find our ship on Ingoilea."

Ay-ttho accompanied Barnes and Anius to the temple where Anius sacrificed a sereosleodo each to the drirkel straalkets and Chronos.

When the ceremony ended, Achates approached Ay-ttho.

"I just spoke with a local. He says he has heard rumours among the settlers here that the population has been driven from Ingoilea, and that it is deserted. The houses emptied, and the abandoned homes are waiting for us."

"You see, Achates," said Ay-ttho. "It is important to make the proper sacrifices to the star masters. They are looking favourably on us today."

"I never thought of you as religious," said Achates.

The exiles left the safe harbour of Delos and sped across the system as fast as the Mastery of the Stars would carry them.

They went past Naxos, the system once famous for making pish, Donysa, famous for its green stone, Olearos with its wooded mountains, Paros, famous for its white stones and the Cyclades, where large cities were once scattered over the waters.

Eventually, they arrived at Ingoilea. Ay-ttho selected a location to land.

"We will call this place Pergamea," Barnes announced. "Let us fell scamire. We will build walls and homes and eventually a covered fortress. Delight in Pergamea."

Soon, homes were built, and fields were tilled. They worked together to build a grand hall in the centre of the settlement. It was a rectangular hall that was surrounded by four columns, fronted by an open, two-columned portico entrance, and had a central, open hearth that vented through a circular opening in the roof. The hall also served as the reception-room of Barnes. They accepted that, as the most senior of the group, Barnes should act as the chief.

A young couple, Julius and Brisa, who had joined the group in that cave on their flight from the Ao-jun, were very much in love and sought permission to be partnered. Ay-ttho was glad. It provided a welcome distraction from deciding on laws and homesteads.

She sat next to Barnes in the hall and watched as Brisa's friends, Danaë and Hesione, threw open the doors to reveal the partner in a dramatic moment. There was a sharp intake of breath as the assembly in the hall caught sight of her.

As she entered, her begetter, Adrastos, came forward to walk her to Julius.

"I give my offspring, Brisa, to be led into partnership by Julius, offspring of Euandros."

Julius moved forward so that he and Brisa faced each other. He gazed up and down at her form.

There were many prayers to the star masters—two priests and one priestess laid suda'ok netro-hexagons and kaicers aquafaba flakes on a table and poured homemade pish while asking for the blessings of the star masters. Brisa was only partially aware of this long process. For the first time, she could look closely at the man partnering with her and study him without shame.

When offerings and prayers were completed, the last part of the ceremony had arrived. The priest nodded to them. They came closer together. The priest drew a circle around them on the floor with zeyajoren delta-supplement. Julius reached for her right hand and breathed in sharply as his hand touched hers. His hold tightened. Her long fingers suddenly seemed small inside his powerful hand. He spoke the traditional words that sealed their marriage.

"You will be my partner. I shall be your partner."

The head priest handed Julius a small bowl filled with diced darturian drops, and he let go of Brisa's hand to receive it. Brisa turned towards Danaë so that she could fold the veil back into a frame around Brisa's face and then pin it into place with two pins, their tops shaped like thruds. When Danaë stepped back, Julius looked directly at Brisa's face. For a moment he seemed to waver as though the wind had struck him full in the face. Then, as required by the ceremony, he dipped three fingers into the diced darturian drops and anointed her forehead. The fragrance of freshly cut, diced darturian filled the air. His fingers lingered on her skin and his eyes met hers.

The head priest spoke the final blessings, then musicians were accompanying the singers in a hymn to Chronos, praising him for bringing fertility. Brisa was grateful when her begetter, Adrastos, led the two families to the seats of honour near the hearth, and she could conceal her discomposure by attending to her dress as they moved through the crowded room.

Julius sat in the chair next to her. In a state of confusion, Brisa watched Danaë and the servants settle the guests into seats around the hall and flowing out into the courtyard. They had thrown the big double doors open to make the guests outside feel part of the celebration. Immediately trays of food came out, and they poured pish for everyone. This was now her home, but although everyone was from Angetenar, she felt as if she were observing a completely strange place and people.

The feast went on. Julius occasionally put his hand over hers when she rested it on the arm of her chair. She dared to look at him and smile when he did. Gradually, she overcame the blushing that followed each glance. She tried to imagine being in a room alone with him, but that made her too nervous, so she let her mind go still. Many came to greet them and wish them well. She smiled and bowed her head modestly in thanks.

When the food was cleared away, the musicians played again, and the dancers beat out rhythms with their feet and hands, their swaying bodies drawing lines through the air as they moved together in circles. The movements were prayers of thanksgiving for this new union; the dancers raised their hands to the air and pulled the star masters' blessings down towards the couple so that they would have many offspring. Then they spun ever faster, drawing down the star masters' goodwill.

Next there were some who knew acrobatics, and they performed, drawing cries of delight from the crowd with their antics. Their movements suggested the coming nuptial night, and the guests responded with laughter and jokes. They directed much of their ribbing at Julius, and, as was expected of him, he laughed and turned aside the jesting by pretending to be completely unaware of its intended meaning. Brisa was grateful when her begetter announced it was time to accompany the partner to her new home.

Danaë arranged her veil back over her face for the procession to the home. Her begetter and co-begotton guided the partners out of the hall behind the musicians and dancers. Guests formed a loose tail behind them, often singing joking songs and throwing aifyade and sholla towards the newly joined couple to bring them sweetness and fertility.

Ay-ttho felt that they had found their new home at last and all seemed well with the world until...

CHAPTER 10: TRAPPED IN THE ICE

The Mastery of the Stars had been resting on dry sand: the young settlers were busy with weddings and their fresh fields: Ay-ttho was deciding on laws and homesteads: suddenly, as if from nowhere, the season suddenly changed and a cold front blew over the settlement.

The chralnore withered, and the sickly harvest denied its fruits. Barnes urged Ay-ttho to retrace their journey and revisit the oracle of Chronos at Delos.

"We must beg for protection and ask where the end might be to our weary fate, where he commands we seek help for our trouble, where to set our course."

Ay-ttho was amazed that someone like Barnes who had created himself had become so religious. She convinced him to sleep on the matter and then retired to her bed herself.

While she slept, she dreamt Chronos visited her.

"Do not shrink from the long labour of exile," he told her. "Change your system. This is not the system that I urged on you. I did not order you to settle here. In a system called Hesperia, there is an ancient planet with rich soil. It was populated by the Oenotrians, but a younger race lives there now."

Amazed by such a vision, Ay-ttho leapt from the bed. It had snowed when she looked outside. She wrapped up in the warmest clothes she had and trudged to the hall where Barnes had become accustomed to sleep by the fire pit.

She told Barnes of her revelation.

"I remember Hesperia, but I never thought I would go there. Let's trust Chronos, and, warned by him, take the better course."

"But it wasn't Chronos. It was just a dream."

"Was it? You should trust in your instincts more, Ay-ttho."

But leaving Ingoilea wasn't as easy as they thought. When Ay-ttho tried to leave the hall, she could only open the doors part way because of the snow that had piled up against it.

The Mastery of the Stars had sunk into the wet sand which had then frozen so that it trapped the ship in the ice.

Not everyone wanted to leave either. Julius and Brisa were starting a family of their own and were willing to take a chance with the unpredictable climate.

They used their blasters to break away the frozen sand from the feet of the Mastery of the Stars until they had got rid of enough for the ship to take off.

Leaving some behind, they took off and headed into the emptiness of space once more. Before long, they encountered another solar storm. The radiation from the storm burned out some of the equipment, and Nadio was struggling to keep the freighter on course.

For three standard rotations, they wandered uncertainly, until finally the equipment was repaired and they could pinpoint the location of the next portal. Without Witt, they could not operate the machinery required to fold space and so they were reliant on their conventional anti-matter drive.

The portal led to the Strophades system, which they crossed with trepidation because it was home to the Celaeno.

"We are running short of supplies," warned Ron. "We should stop to replenish our stock."

"In the Celaeno's land? Are you mad?" asked Ay-ttho.

"I'm afraid we have little choice. The food we currently have will not sustain your passengers until the next system. At the very least, we need fresh protein."

Ron used his scanners to identify a location on the only habitable planet where there appeared no settlements but an abundance of wildlife.

As soon as they landed, they saw fat herds of sereosleodo scattered over the plains, and flocks of driparak, unguarded, in the meadows.

They rushed at them with their blasters, calling on Chronos himself and the other star masters to join them in their plunder: then they had a feast on the rich meats.

Suddenly, the Celaeno arrived, swooping down from the hills. They were not unlike Zoxans, but with smaller heads and larger talons.

The noise of the Celaeno was unbearable as they dived into the group, snatching at the food and fouling everything with their filthy touch. The only thing less bearable than the shrieking was the foul stench.

Ay-ttho and the others ran for shelter under an overhanging rock, closed off by trees. From this vantage point, they attempted to fire on the Celaeno.

But the Celaeno fled quickly, soaring upwards, leaving behind half-eaten food and the traces of their filth.

One Celaeno settled on a high cliff and shouted down in the common tongue of the Republic.

"Are you ready to bring war to us? Is it war? For the sereosleodo you killed, the driparak you slaughtered, driving the innocent Celaeno from their begetters' country?"

"No," Ay-ttho shouted back. "We are on our way to Hesperia. Chronos himself sent us on this journey. We were short on supplies."

"Take these words of mine to your hearts then, and set them there," replied the Celaeno. "I know the eldest of the drirkel straalkets. If Hesperia is the path you take, you shall enter her space ports freely: but you will not surround the city granted you with walls until dire hunger, and the sin of striking at us, force you to consume your very tables with devouring jaws."

She fled back to the forest borne by her wings.

"Chronos, avert these threats, l, prevent these acts, and, in peace, protect the virtuous!" Barnes, with outstretched hands, called to the star masters. "Let us go."

They passed through the Laertes, Ithacas and Ulysses systems before they arrived at Leucata.

The settlers from Angetenar, so happy to have arrived, played games on the shore where Ron had landed the freighter.

Ay-ttho only allowed them a brief respite and soon it was time for them to enter the cargo holds again for the next stage of the journey past Epirus, and on to Buthrotum where they found a settlement of exiles from the old Republic.

The settlers of Buthrotum were pleased to see them and told of various rumours they had picked up from tachyon transmissions.

One rumour was that The Electric Man's assistant, Helenus, was not only alive but running an Ao-jun colony there on Buthrotum.

Ay-ttho went to find Helenus and walked in the direction the Buthrotums had given him. She found Helenus exactly where she had been told he would be.

They swapped stories, Ay-ttho recounted their journey and Helenus told how the Ao-jun had at first enslaved him when they had killed his co-begotton but that he had gained their trust and was now helping to administer the colony and making extra credits by telling fortunes.

"Perhaps you can tell me my fortune," Ay-ttho suggested. "We believe we have been told to go to Hesperia and only the Celaeno have predicted we will encounter ills. Tell me, what dangers should I avoid? What is the best course to avoid troubles?"

"Ay-ttho, since the truth is clear, that you are going to Hesperia, I'll tell you all I know. It is still a long journey to Hesperia. You must pass Aecean Circe, which is notoriously dangerous. The Narycian Locri have built a city there, and the zoxans filled the place with soldiers. Beyond that are the systems of Pelorus, Scylla and Charybdis, all dangerous. Instead, it is better to go via the Pachynus system; it takes longer, but it is much safer. In the Hesperia system, try the planets of Cumae or Avernus. There is an oracle living on Avernus who may teach you of the dangers you may encounter in that system."

Helenus helped Ay-ttho to restock the Mastery of the Stars and then Barnes, impatient to leave, ordered everyone back on the freighter.

"Live happily, you whose fortunes are already determined," said Helenus. "They summon us onwards from destiny to destiny."

They continued on their journey, close to the Ceraunian system, Nadio checking all the scanners and instruments, steering them past the Aecean Circe, hoping they would not be spotted. Sevan watched all the stars gliding through the silent sky. Then Barnes entered the bridge with the largest cup of pish Sevan had ever seen. He raised the cup up high to make a toast.

"Star masters, lords of the space, carry us onward, and breathe on us with kindness! O foreign land, you bring us war, but there's also hope of peace."

"He's drunk," Sevan commented to Ay-ttho.

"We are approaching Charybdis," said Nadio.

"But Helenus told us to go via Pachynus," Barnes protested.

Nadio turned the ship, searching for the Pachynus portal. They passed close to a planet which was only a ball of molten rock.

"Legend has it that Enceladus, the great Explorer, was lost when he crashed into that infernal sphere," said Barnes.

"I'm picking up a signal," said Nadio. "It's coming from the other side of the planet. It sounds like a distress signal."

As they rounded the planet, a small ship came into view.

"It's an Ao-jun ship," said Nadio.

"Let's proceed carefully," suggested Ay-ttho.

Attempts to communicate with the vessel failed and so they drew alongside and docked. Ay-ttho and Nadio loaded themselves with weapons and prepared to board the ship.

It was deserted apart from one Ao-jun on the bridge. He was exhausted by the last pangs of hunger, pitifully dressed, and stretched his hands, asking for help. When he saw that Ay-ttho and Nadio were not Ao-jun, he hesitated a moment, frightened at the sight, and then cried.

"The star masters are my witness. Take me with you: carry me to any system. That will be fine by me. I know I'm from one of the Ao-jun ships, and I confess I made war against the dwellers on Angetenar. If my crime is so great an injury to you, throw me out of an airlock."

He spoke and clung to Ay-ttho, embracing her legs and grovelling there.

"Who are you? And how did you get here?" asked Ay-ttho.

"I'm from Ao-jun, a companion of unlucky Kram, Achaemenides by name, and my father Adamastus being poor, I set out with the Ao-jun fleet from Sonvaenope. My comrades left me here, forgetting me, as they hurriedly fled. You must leave here. This system is cursed. Do you have any food?"

"I have detected another ship entering this system," Ron announced.

"Go, go! We must leave," urged Achaemenides.

Not wanting to discover what Achaemenides was so afraid of, they cut his ship loose and continued on their journey as quickly as the Mastery of the Stars would carry them.

Mindful of Helenus's orders not to take a course between Scylla and Charybdis, Nadio steered them towards the Pachynus portal.

Instead, however, they found themselves in the Plemyrium system, where the famed planets of Ortygia and Helorus were located.

Both planets would have been good options to start a colony, marvellously rich soil, but the next system was Pachynus, só they continued to the original destination Chronos had identified.

However, no sooner had they entered the Pachynus system than Barnes fell ill.

CHAPTER 11: THE FIERY COFFIN

"The sick bay is terribly depleted," Ay-ttho complained.

"This system contains the planet of Drepanum. You might find some medicinal plants there," said Nadio.

They landed and went out searching for plants. With Ron's help, they identified several medicinal plants, and took them back to the ship and prepared them.

They treated Barnes as best they could, but nothing they tried seemed to improve his condition. He slipped into a coma and then, within only a few standard rotations, he had died.

Ay-ttho, Nadio and Sevan gave Barnes a warrior's ceremony. With the help of Achaemenides, who was regaining his strength, they felled a majestic avel tree and, using the tools on the Mastery of the Stars, made an ornate coffin to hold the body of Barnes.

They placed the coffin on a raft and pushed it out onto a lake. Ay-ttho fired a flare high into the air in a large parabolic curve which ended on top of the raft which burst into flames. They watched as the fire consumed both the coffin and the raft until it was only a collection of smouldering timbers.

In silence, they returned to the Mastery of the Stars, which to Sevan and Ay-ttho seemed empty because of the lack of Tori and Barnes. Even Achates, Nadio, Achaemenides and the refugees from Angetenar did little to fill the void.

Ay-ttho wished it had been her instead of Tori and Barnes but, failing an accident, her genetically programmed body doomed her to a long life.

Nadio made for the next portal, unsure of how much longer this route would take. Unfortunately, as they emerged from the portal, they ran straight into a cloud of debris, which caused significant damage to the freighter.

They made efforts to set a course for the nearest planet, Zenraipra.

"There is a place we can land safely," said Ron.

"Is there civilised life?" asked Ay-ttho.

"No. I have detected nymphs but they shouldn't pose a danger."

Ay-ttho and Nadio set to work repairing the damage with as many of the settlers who knew what they were doing. Sevan tried to help but as he did not know what he was doing, they asked him to keep out of the way most of the time.

Some of the other refugees hunted some of the wild animals and cooked a feast, which was ready for the Angetenarians as soon as they had finished their work for the rotation.

Achates led the hunting party and supervised the cooking of the meat. He also shared out pish that they had been trying to brew themselves on board the Mastery of the Stars. It wasn't anything like the real thing, but, for Sevan, it was better than nothing.

When the last of them had filled their glasses, Achates proposed a toast.

"O friends, we were not unknown to trouble before and you who have endured worse, the star masters will grant an end to this too. Perhaps one day you'll even delight in remembering these misfortunes, these dangerous times. We head for Hesperia, where the fates hold peaceful lives for us: there our settlement can rise again. Endure and preserve yourselves for happier days."

Then they revived their strength with food, stretched on the ground, and filled themselves with rich meat and terrible pish. When they had quenched their hunger with the feast and had cleared the remnants, deep in conversation, they discussed their missing friends.

Ay-ttho, above all, mourned Tori, then Barnes, but a refugee interrupted her mourning. Cytherea, worried that she and her offspring would never reach Hesperia.

"Don't be afraid, Cytherea. The fate of your offspring remains unaltered," Ay-ttho replied. "You'll see Hesperia, as I promised, and you'll raise your great-hearted offspring high to the starry sky. No thought has changed my mind. This offspring of yours will become great and establish laws for his warriors."

Wanting to get away from the refugees, Ay-ttho went out and explored the planet. Accompanied only by Achates, she went, swinging two large blasters in her hands.

After a while, they encountered a nymph and, although they were weary at first, Ay-ttho lowered her blasters when it became clear the nymph meant them no harm.

Ay-ttho explained how they came to be there.

"If I were to start my tale at the very beginning, and you had time to hear the story of our misfortunes, it would take many units. We are heading to Hesperia but had to set down here to repair our ship."

"Whoever you are," said the nymph. "You've reached the city of Tyre. Go on from here and take yourself to the Queen's threshold."

The nymph pointed towards the city and left. Ay-ttho and Achates tried to follow her, but they were soon shrouded in a thick mist which obscured everything but the path directly in front of them.

It led up a hill that loomed high over the city, which became clear as the mist gradually cleared. They looked down from above at the mass of buildings, marvelled at the gates, the noise, the paved roads. The eager Tyrians were busy, some building walls, and raising the citadel, rolling up stones by hand, some marking a furrow, others laying down deep foundations, even more carving immense columns from the cliff. They descended from the hill and entered the city.

There was a grove in the centre of the city, delightful with shade, where they were building a magnificent temple. Here in the grove something new appeared that calmed the fears of Ay-ttho. For the first time, here for the first time, Ay-ttho dared to hope.

"What place is this?" she asked Achates.

Then Ay-ttho heaved a deep sigh from the depths of her hearts as she viewed the wonderful sights. As she did so, Queen Dido reached the temple with a great crowd accompanying her.

Fenced with weapons, and resting on a high throne, she took her seat at the goddess's doorway, under the central vault. She was giving out laws and statutes to the people, and sharing the workers labour out in fair proportions, or assigning it by lot.

When Ay-ttho suddenly saw Sergestus approaching among a large crowd. She was stunned, and Achates was stunned as well with joy and fear: they burned with eagerness to clasp hands, but the unexpected event confused their minds.

They stayed concealed and hidden by the crowd; they watched to see what happened to their friend.

When he'd entered, and freedom to speak in person had been granted, Sergestus began calmly:

"O Queen, we have been travelling from system to system. We have not come to despoil your homes or to carry off stolen plunder: that violence is not in our minds. There's a place called Hesperia, an ancient system. There the Oenotrians lived: now rumour has it that a later species lives there. We had set our course there when an asteroid storm carried us into the wrong portal. Allow us to repair our fleet, damaged by the storms."

Then Dido spoke briefly, with lowered eyes.

"Free your hearts of fear: dispel your cares. Harsh events and the newness of the kingdom force me to protect my borders with guards on all sides. Whether you opt for mighty Hesperia, I'll see you safely escorted and help you with my wealth. Or do you wish to settle here with me, as equals in my kingdom? The city I build is yours: leave your ships. You and the Tyrians will be treated by me without distinction."

These words raised the spirits of Achates and Ay-ttho.

"What intentions spring to your mind?" Achates asked Ay-ttho. "All's safe. They have restored our friend to us."

"I am Ay-ttho," she addressed the queen. "It is not in our power to pay you sufficient thanks. May the star masters bring you a just reward, if the star masters respect the virtuous, if there is justice anywhere. What happy age bore you? What begetters produced such an offspring? Your honour, name and praise will endure forever, whatever systems may summon me, while rivers run to the sea, while shadows cross mountain slopes, while the sky nourishes the stars."

"You're laying it on thick, aren't you?" asked Achates.

Ay-ttho grasped her friend Sergestus.

.

Dido was first amazed at the appearance of Ay-ttho.

"You look like one of the old security clones from the old days of the Corporation. What fate pursues you through all these dangers? What force drives you to these barbarous systems? Are you truly that Ay-ttho whom Barnes created? Come, enter our palace. Fortune, pursuing me too, through many similar troubles, willed that I would find peace at last in this land. Not being unknown to evil, I've learned to aid the unhappy."

She led Ay-ttho into the royal house, and they prepared a feast in the centre of the palace. Ay-ttho sent Achates to the Mastery of the Stars with the news. Achates hastened to fulfil his task.

Inside there were fifty servants, in a long line, whose task it was to prepare the meal, and tend the hearth fires: a hundred more to load the tables with food, and fill the cups.

And the Tyrians, too, were gathered in crowds through the festive halls, summoned to recline on embroidered couches. They marvelled at Ay-ttho and Dido.

At the first lull in the feasting, the tables were cleared, and they set out vast bowls, and wreathed the pish with garlands. Noise filled the palace, and voices rolled out across the wide halls: bright lamps hung from the ceilings.

Then the Queen asked for a drinking-cup, heavy with jewels, and filled it with pish. Then the halls were silent. She spoke:

"Let this be a happy rotation for the Tyrians and our visitors, and let it be remembered by our offspring."

She poured an offering of pish onto the table, and after was the first to touch the bowl to her lips.

The Tyrians redoubled their applause.

"But come, my guests, tell us from the start all your mishaps," Dido asked. "And your wanderings in your journey, over every system."

They were all silent and turned their faces towards Ay-ttho intently.

"O Queen, you command me to renew unspeakable grief," Ay-ttho began from her high couch. "How the Ao-jun destroyed the caverns of Angetenar, miseries I saw myself, and in which I played a part. But if you have such a desire to learn of our misfortunes, and briefly hear of the caverns' last agonies, though my mind shudders at the memory, I'll begin. The ship of Chronos landed and left a box. We thought it was a gift from the star master, but the Ao-jun had secretly hidden armed warriors. The size of the Box amazed some who urged that they drag it inside the caverns and placed in front of the great hall. The crowd, uncertain, was split by opposing opinions. Then Brabin rushed down eagerly from the heights of the hall, to confront them all, saying either there were Ao-jun in hiding, or it had been built as a machine to use against us, or spy on us, or it hid some other trick: He urged them not to trust the box."

CHAPTER 12: UNDER ATTACK

"But they trusted the box, and they brought it within the caverns and, well, the rest is history," said Ay-ttho. "The Ao-jun came out of the box and burned the caverns. We only escaped because we had hidden our ship in a different cave. It has been a long journey, but we have finally made it here."

Ay-ttho's tale moved Dido. She admired her courage and persistence and found herself attracted to her. However, she hesitated. Her partner had only recently died, and she had also heard that Barnes had created clones to be incapable of any romantic attachment.

She also realised that Ay-ttho would also most probably be successful in colonising Hesperia and that an alliance between Zenraipra and Hesperia would only make Zenraipra stronger.

The next rotation when Dido, her court, and Ay-ttho were out hunting, a storm descended upon them and sent the group scrambling for shelter. Ay-ttho and Dido ended up in a cave by themselves. Dido expressed her love for Ay-ttho and, to her surprise, Ay-ttho reciprocated.

"I thought you clones couldn't love," said Dido.

"We have emotions," said Ay-ttho, somewhat offended.

Ay-ttho did not hide her feelings for Dido when they returned to Tyre.

"Are the rumours true?" asked Sergestus, when he next met with Ay-ttho. "That Dido is abandoning her duties to spend time with you and that you have given up on the idea of going to Hesperia?"

"These attacks are without foundation."

"Are you sure? Your destiny is Hesperia, Ay-ttho."

"You are right, Sergestus. But how do I tell Dido? She is obsessed. Let's leave without telling her. You prepare your ship, I'll get my things and send word."

"No, Ay-ttho. I will stay here in Tyre, but you go."

Ay-ttho couldn't persuade her friend and so, eventually, they exchanged tearful goodbyes.

"What are you doing?" Dido confronted Ay-ttho when she caught her gathering her belongings.

"I'm sorry, but I have to go."

"What? You come into my palace, you steal my honour and then try to sneak away without a word?"

"Steal your honour? Hardly," Ay-ttho sighed. "Look Dido, I'm really sorry, I am. But I have no choice. I have an obligation to Chronos to take the others to Hesperia."

"Let them go by themselves."

"Sorry. I'm not leaving because I want to, but because I have to."

"Ay-ttho, I love you. You mean everything to me. How can you leave me like this? You scum."

Ay-ttho turned and left, leaving behind many of her possessions. Dido went down to the courtyard and built a large fire. On it, she placed all the belongings that Ay-ttho had left behind. Then she dismantled the bed they had used and burned that, too.

As the rotation ended, Dido felt it was impossible to sleep.

Ay-ttho was fast asleep on the Mastery of the Stars, but in her dreams, Chronos visited her.

"You have delayed too long already and must leave at once," Chronos told her.

Ay-ttho woke up and called the others to the bridge.

"We have to leave now," she said.

"Fine, let's go then," said Sevan. "May I go back to bed now?"

From her palace, Dido could see the Mastery of the Stars leaving and fell into her final despair. She could no longer bear to live. Running out to the courtyard, she climbed upon the burning pyre and, taking a blaster Ay-ttho left behind, she blew her marbles out.

"Curse you Ay-ttho," were the last words she uttered as she fell into the flames.

CHAPTER 13: INTO THE PRAIRIE

Finally, the Mastery of the Stars passed through the portal to the Hesperia system and all were relieved that their journey was ending but also very apprehensive about what they might find in this system Chronos had sent them to.

"Set a course for Avernus," said Ay-ttho. "Let's see if we can find this oracle Helenus told us about."

"I have a location for the oracle," said Ron. "But there is other activity on the planet which I can't identify."

"Okay, let's be careful."

The oracle's home was in a temperate zone of the planet, which was covered in grasses, herbs, and shrubs for as far as they could see. Occasionally, they flew past herds of wild sereosleodo.

Seemingly in the middle of nowhere surrounded by grassland was a Hut made from aver wood. Ay-ttho wondered where the builder had found the aver wood as there were no trees for units around, let alone the majestic aver.

Ron set the freighter down on the long grass some distance from the Hut and Ay-ttho, Nadio, Sevan and Achates descended from the ship to investigate.

The hut had no door and when they passed through the gap where they would have expected a door to be; it was a moment or two before their eyes became accustomed to the dim light within. Eventually, they realised there was an individual sitting at the far end of a wooden table.

Ay-ttho thought she looked remarkably like herself, except that she used the same robes that Barnes used to wear.

"Are you the oracle?" asked Ay-ttho.

"Who wants to know?" replied her doppelgänger.

"My name is Ay-ttho San An Wan. Helenus sent me."

"Did he?"

"Yes, we have been sent to this system by Chronos and Helenus said you might warn us about any dangers we might encounter here."

"He was wrong."

"Oh."

"My only advice to you is to go to Cumae. There, you might find what you are looking for."

"I see. Is that it?"

"That is it."

"Come on. You must have more for us than that," said Nadio.

"Yeah, we came all this way, sent by Chronos and that's all you've got to say," added Achates.

"Your friends seem disappointed," the oracle commented to Ay-ttho

"They had higher expectations."

"That's always dangerous."

"Thanks for your time."

"Is that it?" asked Nadio.

"What?" said Achates.

"Come on," said Ay-ttho. "Let's go."

"Are you serious?" Nadio was not happy.

"Yes, let's go."

"I'm not happy," said Achates.

"Me neither," said Nadio.

"She's being watched," said Ay-ttho.

"What?" said Achates. "How do you know?"

"I could tell. She reminded me a lot of myself. Did you notice the resemblance?"

"Resemblance? What are you talking about? She looked more like me, or at least my co-begetter."

"Rubbish," said Nadio. "She looked more like me than either of you two."

They all stopped and looked back at the hut, but inside, all was dark.

"I thought she looked like my aunt," said Sevan.

They all shook their heads at Sevan and continued back on their way through the long grass to the ship.

"Ron? How many life forms did you detect in there?" Ay-ttho asked when she returned to the bridge.

"Two."

"I thought so. Be careful, we may head into a trap."

"Then let's not go," said Achates.

"It's not that simple. If we've already been spotted, then it doesn't matter where we go. I believe her when she said there is something that might interest us at Cumae."

"But what?"

"That's what we need to find out."

For a while, the Mastery of the Stars sat in the field until Ay-ttho plucked up enough courage to decide.

"Let's go," she said.

The freighter took off, the gravity manipulators pushing aside the long strands of grass.

Ay-ttho was not in a hurry to get to Cumae and so their take off through the atmosphere was a leisurely one.

"What can you see?" she asked Ron.

"There is a large force on the other side of this planet which presumably thinks it's hidden and there is activity on Cumae. Though it's too early to say exactly what."

"Ao-jun?"

"More likely Zoxans."

"Can we make a run for it?"

"Unlikely. Judging by the class of their ships, they would catch us long before we made it to a portal."

"What about folding?"

"Without Witt, it's too risky. His instruments are very temperamental."

"I guess we have no choice but to proceed to Cumae, then. Why would Chronos send us here?"

"Ours is not to wonder why," said Achates.

Under orders from Ay-ttho, Ron steered a course for Cumae, slower than normal, using only some of the power of the anti-matter drive.

"According to my records," Ron began. "Cumae was occupied by the Euboea originally as a trading colony, but then in greater numbers after they fled their own system. However, none of the ships I have identified in this system have Euboean signatures. They are much more likely to be Zoxan."

"What should we do then?" asked Nadio.

"We go to Cumae, as the oracle suggested."

"Why should we trust her? She was probably just saying what the Zoxan wanted her to."

"Probably, but I also believed her when she said there was something there that might interest us. Let's see what it is. There must have been some reason Chronos sent us here."

"This is the same Chronos that left us a gift box of Ao-jun warriors."

"You don't still think that was a gift from Chronos, do you?"

"It was his ship."

"That had obviously been stolen."

"We are approaching Cumae," Ron announced.

"I thought I asked you to go slowly," Ay-ttho complained.

"I was going as slowly as I could. It's not my fault if this freighter is fast. Anyway, I thought you might like to know that there is something orbiting the planet that isn't one of its moons. It is in a geostationary orbit on the opposite side of the planet to the ships I detected."

"What is it?"

"We are about to get a visual."

As the planet came into view, so did a vast space station in its orbit. Ay-ttho recognised the structure immediately. It was larger than the planet it was orbiting.

"There is only one space station as large as this," said Ay-ttho.

"Gaia?" asked Achates.

"No, Tomorrow. It used to be the headquarters for Barnes, and it looks like it has seen better rotations."

As they approached, they could see that much of the station had either been destroyed or damaged, as if it had been in the centre of a battle at some point.

"Some systems appear to be still functioning," said Ron. "Life support, limited gravitational manipulation, the docking system remains intact, the damaged sections appear to have been sealed off."

Ay-ttho was deep in thought, as if there was something obvious that she couldn't quite connect.

"I think I remember it," said Sevan. "Wasn't that where I first boarded this freighter?"

"It was," Ay-ttho laughed. "Your memory is coming back. Do you remember anything else about it?"

"I remember scratching the paintwork trying to get this lump out of the hangar."

Ay-ttho laughed again.

"It was also the first time I met Barnes and I remember taking you there before you left for Daphnis. And then stealing a fighter from there with Tori."

The reminder of his friend left Sevan emotional.

"It's okay," said Ay-ttho.

"Didn't it have the firepower to destroy a planet?" asked Nadio.

"It used to," said Ay-ttho. "Ron?"

"Weapons systems are inoperative," the computer confirmed.

"This station just reminds me of those I have lost," Sevan lamented. "Remember Ozli, we would have taken him to Tomorrow had it not been for the Tenuil pirates."

"Of course," said Ay-ttho in slow realisation. "That's the answer. That's why we are here?"

"Tenuil pirates?" asked Achates. "I thought they were all wiped out."

"No. They equipped Tomorrow with a special portal called the catapult. It linked the space station, wherever it was in the universe, to Lysithea. We were on our way to use it when we were attacked by Tenuil pirates."

"I still don't understand," Achates confessed.

"Me neither," admitted Nadio.

"Chronos wanted us to come to Hesperia, not because it was our final destination but because Tomorrow is here. He knew if we found Tomorrow we could access the catapult to Lysithea. It's Lysithea he wants us to go to."

"Then why didn't he just tell us?"

"Because the Zoxans would have just followed us to Lysithea like they presumably followed us here."

"But what's stopping them following us to Lysithea using the catapult?"

"Because they probably don't know it exists. The catapult is not like other portals, so it has a unique signature that they have never encountered before. If we can activate the catapult, pass through and then deactivate it before they notice where we have gone, then they won't know where we have gone to."

"Are you sure?"

"Ron? Can you tell whether the catapult is still operational?"

"It is deactivated but otherwise intact. I can detect no obvious reason it couldn't be reactivated."

"Ron, take us to Tomorrow."

Ron navigated the freighter through the clouds of debris which surrounded the station and into a hangar which automatically sealed behind them.

"We have to work quickly," said Ay-ttho. "The Zoxans could arrive at any unit."

"There is air," said Ron. "But it would be wise to take your masks. In fact, you had better get suited up because the gravity is unreliable."

"Anything else we should know about?"

"The pressure seems to be constant, though it would be better to use the suits, just in case."

Ay-ttho, Achates and Sevan climbed in their suits, leaving Nadio on the freighter in case they needed to be rescued.

"So, what are we looking for?" asked Ay-ttho as they descended from the ship.

"There should be a control room close to the entrance of the hangar," said Ron.

"I remember hiding in one of those," said Sevan.

"Ah, yes," Ay-ttho remembered. "I know where to find one."

As they crossed the hangar, they realised there wasn't as much gravity as they'd hoped and floated.

"Switch on your boots," said Ay-ttho.

They all did and, within moments, were pinned to the floor again. With the boots engaged, it increased the effort of walking, but it was a lot quicker than floating. Eventually they made it to a door which opened without protest.

The door opened to reveal a corridor which was familiar to Sevan. Even he knew that the next door on the left led to a small control room the likes of which he had used to hide in on a previous occasion.

Ay-ttho opened the control room door and led them in.

"Right Ron," she said. "Are you seeing what I'm seeing? What do we do?"

"If you link your communicator to the console, then I can speak to the station mainframe directly. I can transfer permissions to this console and perform any function we would normally need to perform on the bridge."

Ay-ttho did as she was asked and instantly the console lit up, apparently performing an array of functions.

"As soon as I activate the console, you need to be ready to go," Ron warned. "And leave the communicator on the console. I will need to begin the shutdown procedures just before we enter the portal."

"But what if the Zoxans find the communicator?"

"That won't be a problem."

Tense moments passed and the group could hear noises from deep inside the space station as machinery, long dormant, came back to life.

"Get back to the ship," Ron suddenly warned. "The Zoxans are coming."

CHAPTER 14: THE FULFILLMENT OF DESTINY

Ay-ttho left the communicator on the console, as Ron had requested, and the group made their way back to the freighter.

"If Ron can operate the console with only the communicator," Sevan speculated. "Then we could have left it there and gone straight back to the ship."

"I guess so," Ay-ttho agreed. "Perhaps he wanted us there in case anything went wrong."

As soon as they boarded the ship, Ron had started the engines and opened the hangar doors.

"The Zoxans are approaching quickly," he said.

"How long until they are here?" asked Nadio.

"Not long."

"Before or after you've activated the catapult."

"About the same time."

Sevan looked nervously at the others.

"And hoping before they are in weapons range?"

"Half a unit."

Nadio leapt into the weapons chair before Sevan could protest that after Tori he was next in line for the honour. He had to concede that Nadio was probably more skilled at operating the weapons system than he was.

The range of the Zoxan ships was greater than that of the Mastery of the Stars and therefore, the freighter had already sustained damage before Nadio could return fire. He deployed all the anti weapon devices, but these were ineffective against the superior Zoxan weaponry, based as it was on the design of the scorpion lizard ships.

Soon, however, Sevan's assumptions were being justified. Nadio was formidable in the weapons chair and soon picked off the Zoxan fighters.

"Starting catapult," Ron announced. "But you must try to keep the Zoxans away from the portal until I have time to shut it down."

Nadio kept up the most intense fire he could, while Ay-ttho steered the freighter around the space station debris. This enabled Ron to divert all his processing power to opening the portal.

Through the observation window, Sevan could see that in the centre of the space station, an anomaly was forming. The anomaly grew larger until Sevan could see it was clearly forming into a portal.

The Zoxans were getting closer, and Nadio was increasingly struggling to keep them away. Sevan daren't imagine what would happen if one of the Zoxan ships travelled through the portal with them. Not only would their own lives be at risk, but they would also expose whatever was on the other side of the portal to the Zoxans, something that Chronos had made them go to great lengths to avoid.

"You may head to the portal," said Ron. "It is almost fully formed."

Ay-ttho steered the ship past the debris towards the centre of the station where the portal was forming.

"Almost there," she told Nadio, who was struggling to keep the Zoxans at a distance.

No sooner had they entered the portal than Ron began to close it again. Through the gap, Nadio continued to fire at the approaching Zoxans and they could see sections of the space station explode.

"What's happening, Ron?" asked Ay-ttho.

"I am destroying the space station so the Zoxans cannot re-open the portal."

"At least they won't find the communicator."

Nadio continued to fire until the portal had almost closed behind them, but at the last moment, when they thought they were already safe, a Zoxan ship slipped through and continued the pursuit.

"We have to destroy it before we exit the portal," said Ay-ttho.

"Is that even possible?" asked Sevan.

Nadio fired every weapon the freighter possessed at the Zoxan ship, which returned the favour. Both ships were sustaining damage, but both emerged from the portal intact.

"It can't follow us to Lysithea," said Ay-ttho, swinging the Mastery of the Stars around to face its pursuer. "We must destroy it before they report their position."

The Zoxans appeared to be startled by suddenly finding themselves confronted by their quarry and swung their own ship around, initially to avoid a collision but ultimately to flee the freighter, which had now become the pursuer.

The Zoxan ship was fast, but the freighter's anti-matter drive was faster and soon gained on its assailant.

"Where are they going?" asked Nadio as the Zoxans circled the diminishing portal that had all but disappeared.

"They are heading towards the portal to Future, which would suggest they know where they are," said Ay-ttho. "Ron? Are you able to jam any tachyon transmissions?"

"I'm trying," said Ron.

Nadio was proving his skills as a weapons operator by getting several shots on target. Equally, Ay-ttho was exhibiting her piloting skills by evading the return fire while still catching their enemy.

Eventually, they got the better of the Zoxans who lost control of their ship, which spiralled out of control. Ay-ttho rounded on it and, with a decisive burst of fire, Nadio finished it.

Just as Ay-ttho and the others celebrated, the anti-matter drive cut out and the Mastery of the Stars drifted helplessly towards the portal to Future.

"What has happened?" asked Ay-ttho.

"The anti-matter drive has suffered a terminal failure," said Ron. "I cannot bring it back online."

"What about the conventional engines?"

"I believe I can get them to work, but it will take several units."

"We could have done with Tori right now," Ay-ttho muttered, then looked at Nadio. "I don't suppose you know anything about anti-matter propulsion?"

"No, sorry."

"Achates?"

"What's anti-matter?"

"Okay, nevermind."

"Is nobody going to ask me if I know anything about anti-matter drives?" asked Sevan.

"No."

"How far are we from the Future portal?" Nadio asked Ron.

"Quite far,"

"That's good."

"Although I can't guarantee I can get the conventional engines online before we fall into it."

"That's bad."

"Could be worse," said Sevan.

"How could it be worse?" asked Nadio. "We have been running away from Zoxans all over the universe and now we are about to drop through the hole which leads directly to their headquarters. How could it be worse?"

Sevan shrugged.

"We could starve to death," he suggested.

"Oh, that reminds me," said Ron. "The Zoxan fire punched a hole in the cargo bay and it sucked all our supplies out into space."

Nadio gave Sevan a hard stare.

"What about the settlers?" Ay-ttho panicked.

"They are perfectly safe in the other hold."

"Were my quarters damaged?" asked Sevan.

"No, your quarters remain intact."

"Excuse me."

Sevan left the others on the bridge and went to his cabin and opened the cupboard where he always stored his secret stash of pish. It was empty of pish, although it was packed solid with some of the delightful drink they had been treated to in Dido's Palace in Tyre.

He opened a bottle, poured himself a large glass and lay down on his bed, resolving to let the others worry about getting the conventional engines working before they fell down a hole which led directly to the centre of their enemies' lair.

"Is there anything we can do to help?" asked Ay-ttho. "Anything that will speed up the process."

"Unfortunately, the engine room is not a safe environment at the moment," Ron explained. "It will be some time before we can reduce the background radiation to safe levels. The issue is more about re-routing circuits around those that have been damaged. This is something I can do remotely."

"So, what are we supposed to do?" asked Achates.

"My advice would be to do what Sevan is trying to do."

"And what is that?"

"Relax."

"Relax? How can we relax? We are on a ship that is disabled. Floating towards a hole that will deliver us, helplessly, to the Zoxans."

"Is there anything you can do about it?" Nadio asked Achates.

"No."

"Then why worry?"

Achates, unsatisfied, stormed off the bridge.

"Who rattled his cage?" asked Nadio.

Ay-ttho shrugged.

"We've been in worse scrapes than this," she said. "And we'll probably be in worse in the future. We don't even know what is on Lysithea yet."

"If we ever get there."

The units clicked by, and Ron didn't seem to be any closer to getting the conventional engines online.

"Even if Ron succeeds," Nadio speculated. "Do we have enough conventional fuel to get us back to Lysithea?"

"Good point. Ron?"

"Not quite, but I have calculated that, even from the Future portal, although we do not have enough fuel to get to Lysithea, we can generate enough forward momentum to allow us to glide the rest of the way."

"How long will that take?"

"The journey won't take much longer. There is little friction in space. We only use our engines to get moving and then to stop. We have enough fuel to get the ship moving, but not enough to stop it."

"Then how are we going to stop?"

"We'll have to use the atmosphere of Lysithea to slow us down."

"Sounds like fun."

"But first I have to fix the engines so we don't fall into that portal."

"Oh, yes, sorry. Carry on."

Ay-ttho and Nadio went to the common room to play some mastercore to pass the time.

Achates had gone to the mess to see whether there was any food left at all and Sevan, who had already drunk a substantial amount, was snoring in his bunk.

As they played, Ay-ttho and Nadio could see the Future portal growing larger and larger in the observation window.

"I hope Ron knows what he is doing," said Nadio.

"He's never let us down yet."

"There's always a first time."

"Ron? How far away are we from the point of no return from the portal?" asked Ay-ttho.

"Five units."

"And how much time do you need until the conventional engines will be online?"

"Six units."

"Six units?" gasped Achates, who had chosen that exact moment to enter the common room to complain to Ay-ttho about the lack of food. "When were you going to tell us this?"

"I have a plan," said Ron.

"Well, share it with us."

"If we fire up the conventional engines within one unit of entering the portal, we should be able to get out again without being transported to Future."

"Should?"

"Should."

"It's not as definite as will, is it?" Achates complained.

"No, it isn't, is it?"

"Ron? Should we be worried?" asked Ay-ttho.

"That all depends on how much you enjoy risk."

"I would rather not risk it at all," said Achates.

"We've noticed," said Nadio.

"Are you sure there's nothing we can do to help?" Ay-ttho asked once more.

"It's very kind of you, but it's simply a question of re-routing functions through the areas of the ship that have not been damaged. Unfortunately, the process is time consuming. The best thing for you to do is relax."

"Easy for you to say," snorted Achates.

Five units later, the ship was beginning its descent into the portal.

"How long now?" Ay-ttho asked.

"Almost there," said Ron. "Should be able to fire up the engines any time... Now!"

There was a spectacular silence as absolutely nothing happened.

"Now what?"

CHAPTER 15: THE CHOICE OF LYSITHEA

"Hang on a unit," said Ron. "There's one thing I forgot to do."

"We don't have a unit," Achates grumbled.

Meanwhile, the ship slipped further into the portal.

"That should do it," said Ron. "Now, hold on."

This time, there was a deafening roar as the conventional engines started. At first nothing seemed to happen, but slowly the speed at which the freighter was entering the portal reduced, then it appeared to stop and finally it made slow forward process.

"How long do you need to fire the engines for?" Ay-ttho shouted over the noise.

"Just long enough to reach a sufficient velocity to get us to Lysithea within a reasonable time."

The Mastery of the Stars was accelerating and eventually Ron cut the engines and silence returned to the ship once more.

Sevan had consumed so much drink that he slept through it all and only awoke when the proximity alarm signalled their approach to Lysithea.

Sevan's marbles were still sore when the alarm woke him. He dragged himself out of his bunk and up to the bridge, where he could see Lysithea large in the observation windows, and it was clear someone on the surface was shooting at them.

"What's happening?" he asked.

"We are being shot at," said Ay-ttho

"No uxlod, moncur. Have they done much damage?"

"None," said Nadio. "Their weapon isn't powerful. Ron is transmitting 'we come in peace' messages."

"As long as we don't come in pieces," Sevan joked.

Achates laughed.

"This is the same location we crashed when pursued by Tenuil pirates all that time ago," Ay-ttho observed.

Ron landed the ship on the outskirts and, even before the engines had shut down, a large crowd had gathered.

"Oh, my Giant Cup!" Ay-ttho exclaimed as she watched the crowd part to let through an individual, clearly of some importance.

"What is it?" asked Sevan.

"Brabin!"

"Brabin of Lenguicarro?" asked Nadio. "But surely that's impossible. He was blind when the Ao-jun invaded the settlement. How did he escape death?"

"The Saturnians are a wily bunch," Ay-ttho explained. "That is Brabin. I would bet Sevan's marbles on it."

Ay-ttho descended from the ship and approached Brabin, whom she considered to look in reasonable condition, despite his loss of sight.

"It is very good to see you, Brabin. I thought we had lost you in the settlement," said Ay-ttho

"Who is it that claims to know me from such times past?" Brabin asked.

"Do you not recognise my voice? It is Ay-ttho and I am with Nadio, Sevan, Achates and many others whom we saved from the ruins of the settlement. We fled in our ship, the Mastery of the Stars."

"We detected your signal," said Brabin. "You should be careful because if we can detect you, the Zoxans might and your ship will be no match against them. And apologies for shooting at you. They were just warning shots. I hope you understand."

"Glad to hear it. Have you evaded the Zoxans?"

"Oh yes, the Zoxans. We have successfully hidden from the Zoxans here, so far. Saturnians are now almost nomadic, like nearly all not enslaved by the Zoxans. Some Zoxans converted to our religion, but sadly their own kind hunted them down. It was Chronos who directed us here."

"He directed us here as well. May we stay here for a while?."

"The Saturnians are hospitable. Therefore, I invite you to stay with us at our settlement for as long as you need and trust that you do not bring the Zoxan forces with you."

"We are very grateful for your trust, and I promise I will not betray it."

Brabin led them into the settlement and into a large hall, which looked like they must use it as a meeting place.

"This is Callahan, my partner," said Sgniwef, gesturing to where Callahan was seated.

"Callahan? Impossible," said Ay-ttho. "The president's high priest on Future. How have you survived all these units?"

"I keep my eyes open," said Callahan. "Sorry for the pun, Brabin."

"We will throw a party in your honour," said Brabin, ignoring Callahan. "You must forgive me. I have business I must attend to and must leave, but I will return. In the meantime, I will leave you in the capable claws of my partner."

"Lucky us," Nadio whispered.

Brabin left the hall, and it left the visitors wondering what to do next.

"You must forgive my partner," said Callahan. "He is always very busy. Please take a seat."

The visitors took seats and Callahan ordered food and drinks to be brought.

"Where are you from?" Callahan asked.

"Nadio and I used to be corporation security clones." said Ay-ttho. "Sevan was a mining clone and Achates and the others we rescued from the caverns of Angetenar."

"Have we met before?"

"We have. Many solar cycles ago, we were senators."

"That's right, I remember. They lost you in some accident, along with the rest of the senate."

"No accident. Barnes dumped us in a remote part of the universe and then in another universe altogether."

"By Chronos! I hear the Zoxans come from another universe."

Ay-ttho didn't respond but turned her attention to the food and drinks, which were all very agreeable.

The hall became populated, which with what Sevan imagined must have been the leading figures in the settlement. They mingled with the visitors and asked them many questions about how they arrived on Lysithea and how they had escaped the Zoxans.

The visitors had similar questions of their own, and the hall was alive with conversation.

"We visited Lysithea before," Ay-ttho told Callahan. "Shot down by Tenuil pirates. I didn't think the place was habitable."

"Neither do the Zoxans, which is why it's such a good place to hide. As you can see, we have constructed these giant biospheres and have been manipulating the atmosphere with outstanding success."

"Yes, I hardly recognised it."

"How did you find us?" Callahan asked Ay-ttho.

"We found the remains of the Tomorrow space station and used the catapult," she said.

"Is that still functional?"

"Apparently. We found the station in the Hesperia system. A long way from here. Chronos sent us there, but I think he just wanted us to find the catapult because there were already Zoxans in the Hesperia system."

"You don't think the Zoxans will follow you?" said Callahan.

"I don't think they are aware of the portal. It has a signature they won't be aware of."

"I hope you are right."

CHAPTER 16: DREAMS OF THE GOOD PLACE

When Brabin returned, Ay-ttho cornered him for a chat.

"What happens when we die?" Ay-ttho asked.

"We go to the better place," said Brabin.

"Do you really believe that?"

"What I really believe is that we return to the universe where we become other things."

"So it's not possible to speak to those in the better place."

"Ay-ttho, everything you need to resolve is in your own consciousness. What is it that remains unresolved?"

"I would like to speak with Barnes and Tori once more."

"I understand. But you must learn to let them go. They are free now, in the universe. I mean, they always were, but now they are not burdened by conscience."

"So there is nothing I can do."

"You must reach deep within yourself to find your resolution. Once you are at peace with yourself, you will find peace with the universe."

Ay-ttho thanked Brabin and decided it was time to go to bed. She dreamt she was standing at the edge of a large forest of Aver trees. She felt she had to go into the forest to find something, but the size of the forest was daunting.

As she was lamenting the size of her task, two tronqaks flew down and landed on branches in front of her, as if beckoning for her to follow them.

They led Ay-ttho to a large aver tree which had a branch made of atrailium, the most precious metal in the universe. She took hold of the branch and it snapped off in her hand.

The tronqaks had disappeared, so Ay-ttho tried to make her way back as best she could. She arrived at a river where a thug was waiting to ferry passengers across. However, she noticed a large crowd waiting to be ferried across.

"There is a large crowd waiting for the ferry," she told the thug. "Why are you not taking them across?"

"They did not receive a proper burial ceremony," the thug replied. "Therefore, they may not cross the river."

Ay-ttho spotted Tori among the crowd of those waiting, but could not either reach him or get his attention.

"May I cross the river?" she asked the thug.

"You must first pay with your life."

"Will this do?"

She hands the thug the atrailium branch.

"That will do nicely," said the thug.

He ferried Ay-ttho across the river, and the wailing noise she heard on the other side horrified her.

"It is the spirits of the recently deceased lined up for judgment to decide whether they go to the better place or the worst place," explained the thug.

Ay-ttho sees Dido wandering by the line.

"Dido, what are you doing here?" she asked.

"I couldn't live without you."

"No, Dido. Tell me it isn't true. I had to leave. It's not because I wanted to."

As Dido turned away from her, Ay-ttho cried. She continued on her way and could pass the lines of those waiting to be judged and go straight into the Good Place.

There she saw Barnes.

"Congratulations, Ay-ttho," he said. "You have had a long and difficult journey."

"Tell me about this place," asked Ay-ttho. "How does it all work?"

"No time for that now. Ay-ttho, you will play a part in establishing a great society, beyond anything you have seen. You will go to this place with others you have not yet met and you will be responsible for a new world."

"How do you know all this?"

"Nevermind how I know. Come, I will escort you the way you came."

As Barnes led Ay-ttho back through the Good Place, across the river and back through the aver forest, he explained what Ay-ttho had in store for her in the future.

"You will meet a couple and travel with them to a world you never imagined. However, they will be usurped by their offspring, who will rule over this world for a time before being usurped by offspring of his own. You will teach the inhabitants of this land and accompany them as they spread across the continents."

When Ay-ttho awoke, she was consumed with hunger, so she went to find the others who were already sitting down to a feast of plasma-grilled arczell fish covered in dollops of sweaty gloeds cream.

She feels comfortable in their new home and thinks that perhaps finally their wandering days are over. After they have eaten, she sought Brabin and Callahan in the hall to discuss the possibility of creating a permanent home on Lysithea.

"We have room in a bio-dome for you," Brabin confirmed. "I think your party will prove an asset to our community."

A commotion outside the hall interrupted their conversation and so they went outside to find out what was going on. They arrived to see the drirkel straalkets' ship arriving and so went to greet them.

"Welcome!" said Brabin enthusiastically as the drirkel straalkets descended from their ship. "I hope you had a pleasant journey and were not followed by any zoxans. The star masters are always welcome here."

"Greetings Brabin, greetings Callahan. We took great care not to lead the zoxans to your fledgling settlement. It is partly on this subject that we wish to discuss matters with you both, high priests. Is there somewhere we can talk in private?"

"Of course, follow me. You must also be tired and hungry. I will organise refreshments to be brought to us."

Brabin and Callahan led the drirkel straalkets into the hall, leaving Ay-ttho outside wondering what all the secrecy was about.

"You should not let the passengers of the Mastery of the Stars settle here," one of the drirkel straalkets began.

"Why ever not?" asked Brabin. "It was Chronos himself who led them here."

"Trust me, high priest, these settlers will only bring misery to your colony and threaten everything you have worked so hard to build. They have ambitions to take over your colony and rule it as their own dominion."

While the drirkel straalkets were refreshing themselves with food and drink, Brabin and Callahan found a quiet place to discuss what the star masters had told them.

"It doesn't make sense to me," said Brabin.

"When does anything make sense?" asked Callahan.

Bored with waiting for the high priests, Ay-ttho had left to find Sevan and asked him if he wanted to go hunting.

"Are you sure that will be okay?" asked Sevan. "Do you think we should ask permission first?"

"It'll be fine. You worry too much."

They wandered into the aver forest that surrounded the temple and it wasn't long before they spotted a wild sereosleodo in the distance.

Creeping closer, they edged towards the beast until Ay-ttho felt they were within blaster range.

"You have this one," Ay-ttho told Sevan.

"Are you sure? It looks so beautiful."

"It'll taste even better."

Sevan aimed his blaster, took a deep breath and squeezed the trigger.

When the flash of the blast had cleared, Sevan saw the beast had fallen to the ground, but not for long. Clearly wounded, it struggled to its feet and ran off as quickly as it could.

Sevan and Ay-ttho made chase, but the beast had evaded them. They searched for more quarry but were disappointed. Tired by their trek, they returned to the temple.

They were eating in the main hall when they heard a commotion outside. They saw Brabin go to see what was happening. While Brabin was still outside, Achates entered and approached Ay-ttho and Sevan in a panic.

"We have to get out the back?"

"Why?"

"The head groundskeeper is talking to Brabin with a crowd of herders. They say that you killed their favourite sereosleodo. Apparently, it was some kind of pet."

"Uxclod!"

Ay-ttho and Sevan followed. They headed towards the Mastery of Stars but on the way were spotted and pursued by a gang of angry herders.

Nadio, on the bridge of the Mastery of the Stars, saw the chase from a distance and ordered the settlers to go out and defend their friends.

They injured many herders in the resultant skirmish, and they fled immediately to the temple to petition Brabin and Callahan to attack the Mastery of the Stars.

"We should not be fighting," Brabin argued.

"We should fight," Callahan disagreed.

The debate raged until Brabin threw up his hands and retreated to his quarters. He prayed to the star masters.

"What have you set in motion, Chronos? I feel powerless to prevent what now seems inevitable."

Meanwhile, Callahan was assembling a force of the colony's best fighters and Ay-ttho was on the Mastery of the Stars, organising the settlers to defend against the expected attack.

"We could always seek the help of the zoxans," suggested Nadio.

"Have you lost your marbles?" said Achates "did you forget we are hiding from the zoxans?"

"Achates is right for once," said Ay-ttho. "Let's not get carried away."

In another part of the universe, Covil was discussing the matter with her fellow star master, Chronos.

"Help the Mastery of the Stars," she said. "This is partly your doing."

"You have a point," Chronos conceded.

Covil travelled to Lysithea and landed her craft a little distance from the Mastery of the Stars and sent an invitation to Ay-ttho to join her.

The drirkel straalkets perceived that Ay-ttho had left her ship and encouraged the herders to attack. However, Nadio spotted them approaching and alerted the settlers to be on their guard.

The herders, finding no obvious way to penetrate the Mastery of the Stars, decided instead to set fire to the landing area. The fire makes little difference to the Mastery of the Stars and Nadio simply moved it to another area. By this time, the rotation was ending, and it was becoming dark. The herders camped around the Mastery of the Stars' new landing site.

"Ron? Have you been able to contact Ay-ttho?" Nadio asked.

"No, she's not answering her communicator."

"I will sneak out to find her," said Achates. "Are you coming, Sevan?"

"Is it safe?"

"Probably as safe as it is in here."

"Okay."

Quietly dropping from a maintenance chute, they edged away from the freighter to discover the herders were fast asleep.

Achates suddenly began firing his blaster, killing as many of the herders as he could.

"What are you doing?" Sevan yelled, dragging Achates away into the aver forest.

The herders pursued them. Sevan escaped, but they captured Achates. Sevan thought about going back, but there were too many herders, so he hid.

As he hid, he could hear the herders attacking the Mastery of the Stars. They were trying to pierce the hull while avoiding the ship's Canon fire.

There was a watchtower close to where the Mastery of the Stars had landed, so they set it on fire and pushed it over onto the freighter.

The settlers within the ship were panicking, but Nadio reassured them by getting more of his cannon fire on target.

Their confidence renewed, the settlers opened the door and surprised the herders by rushing out in attack, inflicting many casualties in one quick strike.

Unfortunately for the settlers, the drirkel straalkets joined the fray, suppressing the settlers' surge, and forced them to retreat to the ship.

Nadio, observing the turning tide of battle, quickly shut the door again, allowing as many of the settlers as possible back inside—but letting some herders through as well. Finally, inside the ship, the herders killed Angetenarians as though it were a simple game. Eventually, though, the herders were outnumbered, and narrowly escaped by jumping out of the maintenance hatches.

Part Two - The Walking Lake Of Quaoar

CHAPTER 17: DANGER ON ENCELADUS

On Future, Naej was following the pursuit of the Mastery of the Stars by the zoxan forces and had expected the freighter to be apprehended until it disappeared into a portal that hadn't been there a moment before. No sooner had the portal swallowed the ship than it closed and the enormous space station exploded, killing several dozen workers who had been salvaging equipment.

Some zoxan fighters disappeared into the portal as well, but Naej's crew could not contact them.

He summoned a council of the zoxans to discuss the matter.

Hera blamed Kinis for the Mastery of the stars' miraculous escape.

"If you hadn't interfered, then the freighter would have been destroyed," she complained.

"That is complete, uxclod!" Kinis protested. "It was you who allowed Benjamin, Tobias, and Ajax to take fighters and got Tobias killed."

"Fine," said Naej. "What's done is done. They will be left to their own devices now. Wherever they are."

*

Nadio continued to shelter on The Mastery of the Stars with the rest of the settlers, wondering when Ay-ttho, Achetes and Sevan were going to come back and wondering what the herders were doing outside.

Ay-ttho was on her way back to the Mastery of the Stars, having concluded her meeting with Covil. She was approaching the area where the Mastery of the Stars was parked not long before the dawn of the new rotation.

Scouts from the group of herders saw her coming, and they redirected their rage towards her. Ay-ttho saw them coming and struck the first blow, shooting down several herders. Sevan and Achetes, hearing the commotion, joined Ay-ttho and soon all three were hunkered down, firing at the herders who also went to ground.

Despite the herders' extensive experience at hunting, it was Ay-ttho, Sevan and Achetes, with their superior weapons, that achieved the greatest success. Achetes tried to circle around the herders and inflicted several casualties before receiving a fatal shot to the chest.

Ay-ttho, seeing her friend fall, was incensed and charged at the herders, killing even those who were executing a chaotic retreat.

With the herders gone, Ay-ttho returned to the body of Achetes. Sevan explained to Ay-ttho how Achetes had slaughtered many of the herders.

By the time they arrived back at the Mastery of the Stars, Nadio had received a message from Brabin requesting a truce. Ay-ttho agreed.

*

"We must try to settle this peacefully," argued Brabin at an emergency council of the Saturnians.

"It hurts me to say, but I agree," said Callahan. "It looks unlikely that we would defeat them in a straight fight, so maybe we should offer them a bio-dome somewhere, one of the furthest from us, and from the herders."

"This is all because of your arrogance," a saturnian named Drancës addressed Callahan. "The rest of the Saturnian's have lost the will to fight."

The council received his comments with a murmur of approval.

"How dare you cukids accuse me of arrogance? We should continue to fight just to prove your weakness. I would fight them alone if I had to."

A herder who burst into the chamber interrupted the debate.

"They are coming," he shouted. "The settlers from the freighter are coming."

"To arms!" shouted Callahan.

"They have divided," said the herder. "Taking two paths here."

"I will lay a trap for them," said Callahan. "Brabin and Drancës, you cukids stay here to defend the council chamber."

Brabin and Drancës had other ideas. They went out to meet one group of approaching settlers. Unfortunately for them, it was not the group containing Ay-ttho, Sevan and Nadio. Instead, this group of settlers was being led by a youthful and hot headed Angetenarian who, rather than engaging in discourse, which was Brabin's intention, ordered a charge, instigating a skirmish in which they killed Brabin.

News of Brabin's death reached Callahan shortly before the group of settlers, led by Ay-ttho, were about to pass through the area where the ambush had been set. Callahan could not dissuade his group from returning to avenge the death of Brabin and Ay-ttho, and the rest of the settlers could pass by unmolested.

As the rotation was drawing to an end, the Saturnian's had returned to the council chamber, and the settlers were camped nearby.

"I am going to see Ay-ttho alone," Callahan told Drancës. "I will end this quarrel for good."

"Don't do it," urged Drancës. "Enough life juice has been spilt already. Don't add to it. Let us find a compromise with the settlers."

Callahan and Ay-ttho approached each other, observed by the Saturnians on one side and the settlers on the other.

There appeared to be disquiet among the Saturnians, and then suddenly one of them fired, killing a young settler. This unprovoked shot ignited both groups. They fired at each other. Ay-ttho called for the settlers to stop, but as she yelled, a stray blast wounded her in the leg, forcing her to retreat.

Watching Ay-ttho leave gave Callahan new hope, and he entered the battle and laid waste to a slew of settlers.

Meanwhile, Sevan and Nadio helped Ay-ttho back to the camp where Effeek'o was helping to tend the wounded as they escaped the fight.

Effeeko quickly applied a field dressing and Ay-ttho immediately returned to the battle, where the Saturnians before her scattered in terror. Both she and Callahan killed many, turning the tide of the battle back and forth. Suddenly, Ay-ttho realised that they had left the Saturnian council chamber unguarded. She gathered a group of settlers and attacked the chamber, panicking the Saturnians within.

Drancës, seeing the settlers within the chamber, lost all hope and shot himself. Callahan heard cries of suffering from the chamber and rushed back to the rescue. He called for the siege to end and for Ay-ttho to emerge and fight him hand-to-hand, as they had agreed that morning. Ay-ttho met him in the courtyard in front of the chamber, and at last, with all the settlers and Saturnians circled around, the duel began.

They faced each other in the courtyard, each preparing to draw their weapon and fire when, suddenly, the drirkel starrklets swooped down between them. Ay-ttho used the distraction to shoot Callahan in the leg, causing him to drop his weapon and fall to the ground.

"Please, have mercy," begged Callahan, as Ay-ttho approached him, pointing her weapon.

"We must stop this killing now," said Ay-ttho, lowering her blaster.

As she did, Callahan reached for his, but Ay-ttho shot him dead before he could fire it.

*

In a forest on Lysithea, Ay-ttho was making repairs to the Mastery of the Stars while Sevan chopped firewood. Nadio was preparing to cook a cukid she had caught earlier that rotation. They had been banished to the forest bio-dome after the bloodletting and had only been given this mercy after the Saturnians acknowledged that Callahan and the herders shared a portion of the blame.

The drirkel straalkets and covil had taken over the running of the colony while they waited for new high priests to be trained, a process which Sevan learned could take hundreds of solar cycles.

"How long are we going to be stuck here?" Sevan complained as he watched Nadio making the preparations for the meal.

"Oh, you've got bored with it here, have you?" Nadio scoffed. "You should have thought of that before you started killing herders."

"It wasn't me, it was Achetes. And anyway, they were trying to kill me. They killed lots of us."

Nadio sighed.

"The Saturnians are choosing a new leader. If they choose one who is more sympathetic to your cause, like Brabin, they may release us from exile."

"I don't see what is so good about this place, anyway."

"The forest?"

"No, Lysithea."

"Because it is safe from the Zoxans."

"How can it be safe from the Zoxans? It's only one jump from their capital."

"Yes, but they think it's a dead end, don't they? So they assume Lysithea is deserted because they've seen no one enter from their side of the portal."

"But the Zoxans who chased us here must have sent tachyon transmissions telling them they had followed us here."

"It's possible, but I think it's unlikely. We wiped them out before they had time."

"You hope."

"Yes, I hope."

"What about you? You're a thug. Don't you want to get back to Sicheoyama?"

"You've forgotten my story already, have you? There's nothing for me there. Effeek'o, you and Ay-ttho are the only family I have now. And you have nowhere either now the Zoxans have taken The Doomed Planet so you may as well make the most of it."

"What about Lenguicarro?"

"Zoxans."

"Yes, but good Zoxans."

"You don't pay attention to anything, do you? They wiped all the good Zoxans out at the battle of Herse."

"You can't be sure of that."

"No, but they were fleeing Lenguicarro, so I'm pretty sure there are no friendly Zoxans left there."

"And what happened to Chronos?"

"Still nothing, but he appeared to Ay-ttho in her dreams, telling her to come here."

"Yeah," Sevan looked at Ay-ttho, who was still working on the ship. "I think she's lost it."

"Then how do you explain finding the Tomorrow space station?"

"Coincidence."

Nadio scoffs at his cynicism.

"Hurry with that firewood." She said. "Anyway, I was telling you about the election. If rumours are true, there's nothing in it and I glimpsed their debate last rotation on their closed circuit entertainment channel."

"You don't watch that rubbish, do you?"

"Beggars can't be choosers. There are these two candidates that have both been trained to be high priests by the star masters and they want one if them to be elected as high priests to chair the council at its meeting."

"I thought it took hundreds of solar cycles to train to be a high priest."

"That's what I thought too, but the star masters can't wait that long."

"Who are the candidates?"

"Adama is being challenged by Cyrus. Adama says that Cyrus is trying to cut the space defence program and Cyrus says the defence program is broken. Crime in the colony is on the rise and vigilantes are taking over the running of security. Look, I'll share it with your implant."

Nadio fiddled with her communicator, and Sevan watched a replay of the debate.

"Under my leadership, the Lenguicarro militia has dealt major blows against the growing organised crime ring based around trafficking fushy," said Adama. "The Allam case was the largest fushy bust in the colony's history."

"But mass killers are still rampant!" complained Cyrus. "It's getting worse!"

"The Angetenarians have been banished and..."

Ay-ttho, who had dropped her tools and marched over, interrupted him.

"Come with me," she said.

"But the cukid," Nadio protested.

"It'll have to wait."

"But..."

It was too late. Ay-ttho was already striding away.

"Where are we going?" asked Sevan.

"To Enceladus."

"Why?"

"You'll see."

Sevan and Nadio followed Ay-those to Covil's ship. Covil was waiting for them and lost no time with pleasantries before setting off on the brief journey to Enceladus, Lysithea's only moon, named after a star master who was killed during the ancient wars to gain control of the universe.

When they landed on Enceladus, they put on their space suits before Covil led them over the ice sheet to a body whose head had been decapitated and 'no more lies' had been written in blood whose deep blue stood out against the white of the ice. The rest of the body looked badly beaten, and there were parts of the limbs missing.

"That's Adama," said Nadio.

"Who's Adama?" asked Ay-ttho.

"A candidate for high priest," said Covil.

"Why are you showing us this?" asked Ay-ttho.

Covil reached into the robe of the corpse and pulled out a communicator. On the screen, a message was displayed.

Who makes it, has no need of it. Who buys it, has no use for it. Who uses it can neither see nor feel it. What is it? Ask the Corporation security clone.

"You don't think this has anything to do with me, do you?"

"I don't, Ay-ttho. But I'm not going to hide this from the council."

"A burial mark," said Ay-ttho.

"What?"

"That's the answer to the question. A burial mark."

"I don't follow you."

"Burial mark makers don't need them for themselves. Neither do those who buy them, the living buy burial marks for the dead. It's the dead that use burial marks, but they can neither see them nor feel them."

"But why do we need to ask you that question?"

"I don't know. But how did you find the body if it was left up here on Enceladus?"

"Follow me."

CHAPTER 18: THE MISSION GOES AWRY

Covil led them back to his ship and, instead of heading to the bridge, he took them to the crew's quarters and into a dormitory where a young, scared looking Saturnian sat on a bunk.

"Adama's begotton," Covil whispered to Ay-ttho. "I must take him home to his co-begetter, but I'll drop you off first. I think it's best if the Saturnians don't know anything about your connection with this for now."

"What about the election?"

"We'll have to get another candidate for high priest to run in his place."

"Yes, but..."

"But what?"

"Nevermind. How did they get here?" Ay-ttho gestured to the young saturnian.

Covil pointed out of the observation window from where they could see Adama's ship. Putting the helmets back on their suits, they went back out on the ice and boarded Adama's ship.

Ay-ttho went straight to the bridge and attempted to access the ship's computer.

"It's encrypted," said Ay-ttho. "Why would anyone encrypt a navigation computer?"

"Anyone who didn't want you to know where they'd been," said Covil.

"There's a password."

Ay-ttho typed '*burial mark*.'

"It worked. Whoever left that message wanted us to access this computer."

"Let's see where he's been."

Ay-ttho studied the navigation history.

"It doesn't make sense."

"What doesn't?"

"There is only one portal in or out of this system, right?"

"Right."

"According to this, Adama has been leaving the system."

"Via the catapult to Tomorrow?"

"It's possible. But for that to have been the case, the Tomorrow station would have had to be jumping from system to system itself. Look."

Covil inspected the data and nodded his agreement.

"So, if Adama knew about the catapult, who else knew about it?"

"As far as I know, it wasn't common knowledge," said Covil. "Callahan probably knew, but..."

"Yes, I know, I killed him."

"Brabin would have known."

"Dead."

"And Drancës?"

"Also dead. Wait a unit. How did Drancës die?"

"He killed himself."

"So everyone who might have been aware of Adama's movements is dead?"

"You killed Callahan."

"True."

"And anyway, the space defence system would have picked up Adama's movements."

"Like Cyrus said, the space defence program is not fit for purpose. I Wonder what Cyrus knows. Perhaps we should pay her a visit?"

"It wouldn't be proper for a star master to be seen with a candidate before the election."

"Okay, I'll go. Where do I find her?"

"She is a priest at the temple of Chronos in the polar bio-dome."

"Great, I'll leave my suit on."

*

Ay-ttho approached the entrance to the polar bio-dome, still wearing her space suit and still followed by Sevan and Nadio, who were similarly attired.

Two large Saturnians guarded the entrance.

"Know who I am?" asked Ay-ttho.

"I have an idea," said a guard.

"I'm here to see Cyrus."

"She's not here."

"Mind if we look around?"

"Yes, we do."

Ay-ttho didn't move. The Guards looked uneasy and then one of them lunged for Ay-ttho. Ay-ttho elbowed the Guard and then punched the other guard when he charged at her.

"Let's have a look," said Ay-ttho, stepping over both of the guards.

Nadio and Sevan tried to edge around the Guards to follow Ay-ttho, wary that at any moment the guards might have woken up.

As they entered the bio-dome, they all put their helmets on to protect themselves against the biting cold.

"Why do they have a bio-dome like this?" asked Sevan.

"I think it's part of their climate control system," said Nadio. "A complex system of underground reservoirs linking the bio-domes and the polar bio-domes helps to regulate the temperature of the water."

"Why do you know so much?"

"I told you, I watch the Saturnian's entertainment system."

They realised the Guards had got to their feet and were pursuing them. The guards pulled their weapons, but Ay-ttho dealt with them both as quickly as she had at the door.

Ay-ttho heard a noise behind her and swung around, ready for more action only to find a saturnian, wearing sereosleodo hides, approaching her.

"Relax," says the priest. "Are you looking for me?"

"That depends on who you are."

"They call me Cyrus."

"Then I'm looking for you."

"Good. Come with me. Let's go somewhere a little warmer."

Cyrus led them to a wooden structure with a tall spire whose shape resembled that of a saturnian temple.

Inside, they had decorated the temple exactly like any other saturnian temple that Sevan had visited and it was warm, so they removed their helmets.

"Ah, our friends from Angetenar," said Cyrus. "I thought it might be you."

"Actually, Sevan and I are Corporation clones and Nadio is a thug," Ay-ttho corrected.

"Of course you are. That would explain the current state of my guards. What can I do for you?"

"Adama is dead."

"Yes, Covil told me."

"That doesn't really help me."

"I don't know what to say. I have a reputation to uphold, running for chair of the council, high priest of the entire colony."

"Yes, and your competition is out of the picture suddenly."

"You're not insinuating that I had anything to do with it?"

"You might know something that would help."

"Why don't you ask Adama's partner? Maybe he knows something. If there's anything else I can help with, please call again."

Dissatisfied, Ay-ttho replaced her helmet and left the temple. Nadio and Sevan did likewise, feeling like hangers on.

As they left the bio-dome, Ay-ttho noticed a ship take off and head towards Enceladus.

"Look at that," she pointed out the ship to Nadio and Sevan.

"Want to follow?" asked Nadio.

"We couldn't if we wanted to. We have no ship. Anyway, it's probably just the crime scene investigators."

Before they reached their own bio-dome, they saw the same ship return, then moments later a saturnian security vessel took off from a different location and headed towards the moon.

"They are the crime scene investigators," said Nadio.

"Then who was on the first ship?" Ay-ttho wondered aloud. "Did anyone see where it landed?"

"Over there," Sevan pointed.

The three set out in the direction Sevan had shown.

They found the ship, apparently abandoned, next to a wooden hut that had either been ransacked or was occupied by owners with little sense of what it meant to be tidy. A discarded entertainment implant was still running among the rest of the debris on a table. Nadio picked it up to see what was playing.

"They have killed the head of the Saturnian security service," he said. "They found him decapitated with the words 'no more lies' written in his blood."

"Where?" asked Ay-ttho.

"I think we're about to find out," said Nadio, pointing to Covil's approaching ship.

Covil took them to the colony morgue where the head of security's corpse was lying in two pieces on the slab.

"Where is it?" asked Ay-ttho.

"It's here," said Covil, handing Ay-ttho the head of security's communicator.

Ay-ttho read the message on the screen.

What gets bigger the more you take away? Ask the Corporation security clone.

She showed the message to Nadio and Sevan.

"A hole," said Nadio, almost immediately.

"You are good at these, aren't you?" Sevan observed.

"What does that mean?" Ay-ttho mused. "Are we meant to look for a hole?"

"Not necessarily," said Nadio. "The first clue was the password to the navigation computer. Maybe this is connected to something else."

"The Hole is a club," said Covil.

"Can you take us there?" asked Ay-ttho.

"Of course, but change out of those suits."

*

Outside a cave which served as an entrance to the Hole club, Ay-ttho, Nadio and Sevan had changed into their best clothes which, after over 85 solar rotations, were not looking their best.

"Maybe we should go shopping," Nadio suggested.

"Another time," said Ay-ttho, heading for the entrance.

"You know the costume party was last lunar cycle," quipped the Bouncer.

"Ha, ha, hilarious," said Ay-ttho. "Can we come in now, please?"

"Not with those, you can't," the Bouncer pointed to their blasters. "You'll have to leave those here."

Ay-ttho looked doubtfully at Sevan and Nadio, who nodded his ascent.

They unstrapped their blasters, left them with the Bouncer and then entered the cave into a bar where the tables and chairs sat on stalagmites and the lights hung from stalactites.

Ay-ttho thought she recognised some of the clientele as being high in the Saturnian hierarchy, but those they were mingling with certainly weren't. They weren't even Saturnian, and they hadn't come from Angetenar either.

One of the Saturnians approached them.

"I know you, don't I?" he addressed Ay-ttho.

"I don't know, but I know you."

"Oh, yes? Who am I?"

"You're Jaques Thimothee, the colony prosecutor."

"Right first time. And who might you be?"

"My name is Ay-ttho, but they call me the Corporation security clone."

"That's right. I knew I'd seen you somewhere. You killed Callahan."

"That's right. I've been meaning to thank you personally for not prosecuting."

"Don't mention it. Covil spoke highly of you. Come and join us."

They followed Thimothee to a table which Ay-ttho recognised was occupied by half of the colony prosecutor's office. They all looked stressed.

"You'll have to forgive the mood of the table," said Thimothee. "There is a lot of tension in the office at the moment with these murders. I assume you've seen them."

"Yes, it's all over the entertainment implant. Any ideas who might be doing it?"

Thimothee was ominously silent.

"I mean, there must be something connecting them," Ay-ttho pursued the subject.

"Yeah probably. Wish I knew what it was, though. "

Ay-ttho suspected he was lying.

"I think I've had too much fushy," Thimothee rubbed his eyes. "I think I'm going to head off. Enjoy yourselves."

When Ay-ttho, Sevan and Nadio emerged from the club, Covil was waiting for them.

"What are you doing here?" asked Ay-ttho.

"Nice to see you, too. It's Adama's burial ceremony. Are those the best clothes you have?"

"I'm afraid so."

"I'll have to take you shopping."

"You will," said Nadio.

*

Ay-ttho, Sevan and Nadio entered the burial ceremony at the central temple wearing smart new black bodysuits. They saw Cyrus among the mourners.

Covil approached them.

"You scrub up well, don't you?" he said.

Ay-ttho ignored the backhanded compliment.

"Did you say you met Jaques Thimothee at the Hole?" Covil continued.

Ay-ttho nodded.

"He's gone missing."

Suddenly, there was a commotion at the end of the temple where Adama's casket had just been ceremoniously opened. Some mourners were running away from the casket, while others were running towards it to get a better look.

Covil, Ay-ttho, Sevan and Nadio all tried to push through the crowd to find out what was happening.

When they reached near enough to the casket to see, they realised that the body in the casket did not belong to Adama but was actually the corpse of Jaques Thimothee. The words 'no more lies' had been written in blood on the inside of the casket.

Covil searched the body, removed the communicator and discreetly passed it to Ay-ttho. Ay-ttho examined the screen.

When you stop to look, you can always see me. But if you try to touch me, you can never feel me. Although you walk towards me, I remain the same distance from you. What am I? Ask the Corporation security clone.

Ay-ttho handled the communicator to Nadio, who examines it for a moment.

"The Horizon."

"What?" Sevan was struggling to see the connection.

"If you stop to look, you can always see the Horizon."

"I can't see the horizon."

"No, because you are inside a building. But if you were outside, you could see the horizon."

"Not if buildings are in the way."

"The horizon?" Ay-ttho mused. "What could that mean?"

"The Horizon is a ship," said Covil. "Cyrus' ship."

"We need to get access to the ship's navigation computer."

"Good luck with that. Cyrus doesn't let anyone near her ship."

"I wonder why."

CHAPTER 19: SLAVERY

"What about the ship we saw going to Enceladus?" Ay-ttho asked.

"I haven't been able to trace the owner."

"Let's find Cyrus' ship."

"Are you going to break in?"

"You've got a better idea."

"I can't be involved."

"I didn't think you could."

"Good luck."

*

They found the Horizon in a remote location, close to one of the access tunnels which led to the underground system of waterways.

"Can you get us in?" Ay-ttho asked Ron via his communicator.

"Sorry," said Ron. "It is using a level of security I have not encountered before. There is no-one on board."

"What's down there?" asked Nadio, pointing to the access tunnels.

"The sewers," Sevan replied, as if it was obvious.

"Actually, it's a series of reservoirs, canals and conduits," Nadio corrected. "What I mean is why is the Horizon parked here? The only thing here is that entrance."

"Let's have a look then," said Ay-ttho.

"I was worried you might say that," said Sevan.

They descend a stone staircase leading from the access door down deep under the colony.. it was a maze of damp, dripping tunnels and they had to use the lights on their communicators to see where they were going.

"Shh," Ay-ttho signalled for them to stop.

She listened.

"There is a noise coming from over there," she pointed down a tunnel, then proceeded with caution.

The tunnel led to a balcony overlooking a cavernous hall in which groups wearing hazardous material suits, goggles and masks were working at rows of table, packaging a powder. Saturnians who, were spaced around the hall, oversaw the workers.

"Thugs!" Nadio gasped, recognising the shape of the workers.

"What are thugs doing down here?" Sevan whispered to Nadio. "You're the only thug we've seen on the surface."

"There's one thing you might like to know," Ron's voice buzzed into Ay-ttho's communicator before she managed to lower the volume. "I've been running some scans on the Horizon and it appears to be fitted with folding technology."

The group retreated into the tunnel to avoid being heard. What they didn't realise was that the acoustics of the tunnel was amplifying their sound and, even though they were speaking in whispers, their conversation could be heard clearly by the Saturnians in the hall who were looking up at the tunnel with a mixture of curiosity and disbelief. Some spoke into their communicators.

"They're much hairier than you, aren't they?"

At this, some thugs paid attention.

"That's because I cut my hair," said Nadio.

"You cut your hair? I've never seen you do that."

"I don't cut it on the bridge."

Sevan popped back to the end of the tunnel to sneak a peek at exactly how hairy the thugs were. It was at this point he saw that all the Saturnians and thugs in the hall were staring back at him.

"We have a problem," he told the others, who all rushed to see their audience.

"Run," said Ay-ttho.

But at that moment, they heard the noise of guards entering the tunnel at the other end.

"Down here," said Ay-ttho, pointing to a small side tunnel that led downwards.

They followed her down until they reached a door. Ay-ttho opened it, only to discover that it led to the hall where several guards were pointing their weapons at them.

The guards led them to a room which contained only a few chairs, and then locked them in.

Before long, a Saturnian entered, flanked by two guards.

"Welcome to our enterprise. I wish you had told us, we could have organised a tour."

"Where's Cyrus?" asked Ay-ttho.

"I'm sorry, I don't really understand."

"Cyrus. Her ship, the Horizon, is parked outside."

"Oh, that. I'm sorry, but I don't know what that is doing there. It's been there for some time."

"That's impossible. We went to visit Cyrus."

"Did you see her ship?"

Ay-ttho simmered.

"What are you doing here?" asked Nadio.

"I'm talking with you."

"No, the thugs in that hall. What have you got them doing?"

Ay-ttho grabbed the weapon of a guard, wrenched it from the guard's hands, smashed the guard in the head with the butt and then pointed the weapon at the Saturnian that appeared to be in charge.

"Very impressive," he said. "But there's really no need to be so violent. You'd better come this way."

The Saturnian moved towards the door but, just as Ay-ttho followed him, the Saturnian swung round and grabbed the weapon. There was a brief struggle, during which the weapon discharged before the Saturnian got the upper hand and took possession of the weapon.

Gesturing for the others to get back, the Saturnian backed towards the door and kicked at it with his heel. The door opened and more weapon brandishing guards entered. They signalled to others to collect the body of the unconscious guard, then all the Saturnians left and the three were alone in the room again.

"That went well," said Ay-ttho.

"What were the thugs doing in that room?" asked Nadio.

"Looked like they were making powdered fushy," said Ay-ttho.

"It comes in a powder?" this was news to Sevan.

"Not like the drink," Ay-ttho explained. "Much stronger. Users immediately become addicted."

"Why?"

"Because it's strong."

"No, I mean, why are they making it?"

"Someone obviously wants to get the colony hooked on the stuff and we've stumbled on their plans."

"Hardly stumbled. Someone has been leaving us clues."

"Yes, but who and why?"

"I'm sure whoever abandoned that ship by the shack knows something about it."

"We're not going to find them from here, though."

Ay-ttho began searching the room for signs of an escape route, air vents, drains, but she found nothing.

"Air must be getting in here somehow," she mused.

"I saw something on the entertainment implant about all this water under the colony," said Nadio. "It's actually one vast lake and it keeps moving. They call it the Walking Lake of qua...quo...qua."

"Quaoar."

"Thank you Ay-ttho. That's it, the Walking Lake of Quaoar."

"How far down do you think it is?"

"Not very far. This place feels pretty damp, doesn't it?"

"Yes, it does."

Ay-ttho started ripping up floor tiles and throwing them into a corner. The stone underneath was very damp and soon she uncovered a small hole which might once have acted as a small drain. Through the hole, they could see the lake only a few units below.

They broke off legs from the chairs and used them to make the opening wider. At first, it was hard work, but soon small chunks of the floor fell away. There was no camera in the room, but the noise attracted the attention of the guards. When the guards entered the room, the hole was large enough for Nadio and Sevan but not quite large enough for Ay-ttho.

"Go!" she urged as she tackled the guards.

Sevan hesitated, so Nadio jumped. Sevan followed after a helpful kick from Ay-ttho. Nadio had jumped feet first and was fully composed when he surfaced. Sevan, on the other hand, had fallen face first and surfaced, coughing and splattering.

"Can you swim?" Nadio asked.

"Of course," said Sevan, giving a display which suggested he couldn't.

Apart from the light shining through the hole, through which they had just plunged, there were a few other small beams of light coming through what Sevan assumed to be small cracks but as they swam towards one of them, they realised they were large shafts of light but a long way away.

By the time they reached one of them, they were extremely tired of swimming and pulled themselves up onto a small jetty which the shaft of light was illuminating.

As they caught their breath, Sevan thought he saw movement in some of the distant lights, but he couldn't be sure.

"They'll be looking for us," said Nadio. "We should try to get as far away from here as we can and then see whether the access to one of these jetties leads to another bio-dome."

When they felt they had rested enough to make it to the next shaft of light, they dropped back into the water and began the next leg of their journey. There didn't seem to be any current to speak of, but the water felt strange to Sevan, as if it wasn't water at all but some other, water like substance.

"I'm not sure how much more of this I can do," said Sevan when they reached the next jetty.

"Just one more then," said Nadio. "I think we are still too close here."

Then, both of them thought they saw figures silhouetted in the light of the jetty they had just left.

"They are following us," said Nadio. "Let's go."

"Already?"

"Do you want to get caught?"

Reluctantly, Sevan slipped back into the water after Nadio, who led the way to the next jetty. The distance seemed much larger to Sevan, who thought frequently that he would not make it. Eventually, however, Nadio helped him to drag himself onto the jetty where he lay panting.

"I never realised thugs were such excellent swimmers," he said, once he had regained enough breath to speak.

"Neither did I," Nadio admitted.

They found the entrance to the jetty and pulled it open. It led to a staircase, which they ascended. At the top, they could see an aperture to a lit area, but before they reached it, they saw Saturnians enter through the aperture and begin descending the staircase.

Nadio and Sevan did a quick about turn and headed down the staircase, pursued by the Saturnians who gained on them.

At the bottom of the staircase, Nadio and Sevan sprinted through the doorway and dived straight into the water, swimming as far away as they could before the Saturnians arrived and began firing their blasters into the water.

Sevan daren't look back, but he heard the surprised shout of a Saturnian followed by the sound of panic and rushing back to the staircase.

Nadio and Sevan stopped to tread water and look back to see what had happened, but the Saturnians were gone and only a slight disturbance on the surface of the water, where they had dived in, remained.

Sevan pointed to what appeared to be the nearest shaft of light and the two kept swimming towards it until, by the time they climbed up onto the jetty, they were completely exhausted.

They lay on the jetty until enough strength returned for them to sit up and survey their surroundings. Every jetty appeared the same, an oasis of dim light in a desert of water.

"What next?" asked Sevan.

"Would you like to try this staircase?"

"Not really."

As they waited for one of them to come up with a better idea, they noticed ripples on the surface of the water, then the ripples evolved into a disturbance. Then, suddenly, something erupted from the water. When the water subsided, what they saw bobbing up and down in front of them appeared to be a small submarine.

There were metallic banging noises coming from the inside. Both Nadio and Sevan readied their weapons, although both were dripping with water and were unlikely to function.

The lid of the submarine was being screwed out from within. Nearly two units of shining screw projected before it fell over to the side on a hinge, causing an immense clanking sound against the metallic hull of the submarine.

Nadio blundered into the back of Sevan, and he narrowly avoided being pitched into the water. The circular cavity in the opening seemed perfectly black. Then Sevan saw something stirring within the shadow: greyish billowy movements, one above another, and then two luminous disks — like eyes. Then something resembling a little grey axek, about the thickness of a farming tool, coiled up out of the writhing middle, and wriggled in the air towards them — and then another.

A sudden chill came over Sevan and he let out an involuntary shriek as other tentacles began projecting from the opening. Nadio edged backwards. Sevan stood petrified and staring.

A big greyish rounded bulk, the size, perhaps, of a gherceid, was rising slowly and painfully out of the cylinder. As it bulged up and caught the dim light from the jetty, it glistened like wet sereosleodo skin.

Two large dark-coloured eyes were regarding Sevan and Nadio steadfastly. The mass that framed them, the head was rounded, and had a face. There was a mouth under the eyes, the lipless brim of which quivered, panted, and dropped saliva. The whole creature heaved and pulsated convulsively. A lank, tentacular appendage gripped the edge of the cylinder, another swayed in the air.

Sevan stared in horror at its appearance. The peculiar V-shaped mouth with its pointed upper lip, the absence of brow ridges, the absence of a chin beneath the wedgelike lower lip, the incessant quivering of this mouth, the ocrex groups of tentacles, the tumultuous breathing of the lungs, the clear heaviness of movement — above all, the extraordinary intensity of the immense eyes—were at once vital, intense, alien, crippled and monstrous.

There was something fungoid in the oily grey skin, something in the clumsy deliberation of the tedious movements unspeakably nasty. Even at this first encounter, this first glimpse, disgust and dread, overcame Sevan.

CHAPTER 20: BEYOND THE SILVER CHASM

"Sorry to startle you," said the creature. "My name is Malcolm. Would you like to travel on my watercraft? It is capable of independent operation underwater."

Sevan was still frozen where he stood.

"That's very kind of you," Nadio began. "But..."

"Oh, I'm sorry," Malcolm interrupted. "I'm always doing that, phrasing sentences as questions when they should be statements. I'm still getting used to Future standard. What I meant to say was: get on my watercraft. It is capable of independent operation underwater."

"We'd rather not," said Nadio, knowing that Sevan wouldn't mind him speaking on behalf of both of them.

"You don't understand. You don't have a choice."

Malcolm had made a half nod, half pointy gesture towards the water where, for the first time, Nadio noticed there was a distant noise. Only faint, but recognisable now as the sound of an engine, the engine of a boat, a fast boat.

Nadio and Sevan glanced at each other, their options running through their marbles. They looked at the staircase beyond the entrance to the jetty behind them.

"You won't get very far," Malcolm warned.

They looked at the rapidly approaching boat.

"You won't stand much of a chance with those damp weapons."

Then they eyed the water.

"And you certainly won't out-swim it."

"Let's go," Nadio sighed, moving towards the watercraft.

"You'll have to go in first so that I can shut the hatch," said Malcolm.

Nadio squeezed past, trying his best not to tread on any of Malcolm's tentacles. The inside of the watercraft was tiny. Nadio looked around for somewhere to sit but found nowhere.

Then it was the turn of Sevan, who tried his best not to touch any of Malcolm's oily grey skin. However, as he descended into the vessel, a long strand of saliva descended from Malcolm's mouth and decorated Sevan's antennae like a glistening tree at binge time.

Malcolm's closed the hatch with the same speed he had opened it and then descended to join the other two in the control room, the only room, in fact.

The space was evidently two small for the three of them who were pressed up against each other with Malcolm's tentacles stretching out all around them to operate the complicated machinery which covered every surface except for two large observation windows at, what Sevan assumed must have been, the front of the vessel.

The hull began to ping and shudder with blasts from the approaching Saturnians.

"Let's go?" Malcolm asked. "Sorry, I meant to say: Let's go!"

He pulled some levers, and the watercraft chugged to life before rapidly descending below the surface. Sevan could see blaster fire ripping through the water on either side.

A moment later, all was quiet, and the craft was speeding through the water close to a rock face, which plunged down into the dark depths.

Clear grey-blue, white, yellow and green crystals covered the rock wall itself.

"What is this place?" asked Nadio.

"We call it the silver chasm. Strontianite and celestine cover the walls. Above the water, it doesn't look so pretty because a dark oxide layer covers the crystals."

"Where are we going?"

"On a journey. They have sent me to fetch you to help us. But first you will see one of the most spectacular sites in our underground world. Make yourselves comfortable. It is going to be a long journey."

Nadio and Sevan glanced at each other, both wondering how the uxclod they could get comfortable. They couldn't even lean against anything for fear of shifting one of the multitude of levers which triggered various complicated mechanisms.

Sevan simply focused on avoiding the oily skin of Malcolm's tentacles, which were constantly active, adjusting settings by pulling and pushing levers all around them.

"What do you mean, 'help us'?" Nadio persisted.

"Us. The Tritions," said Malcolm.

"Have you not seen what's happening here? They've got a load of thugs making powdered fushy."

"I know. It's all connected. By helping us, you will help the thugs."

"How?"

"It is easier to show than tell."

Malcolm adjusted some more levers and a screen that Sevan hadn't noticed before, illuminated and played what looked like an advertisement from the entertainment implant system. Nadio and Sevan watched the announcement.

The colony council is taking innovative and bold actions to secure the colony's vital interests now and in the future through the space defence program. We will train and equip guardians to conduct space operations that enhance the security of the colony, while also offering the council military options to achieve colony objectives.

Personnel will transfer into the Space Defence Program and become guardians over the next 18 lunar cycles. Over time, the vision is to merge missions from across the security services into the space program consistent with colony law.

"Why are you showing us this?" asked Nadio.

"That was recorded two solar cycles ago," Malcolm explained. "The space defence program has been up and running for many units and the Guardians have been carrying out their missions in various systems."

"So, what's the problem?"

"The program is being used as a cover for thug and powdered fushy trafficking."

"What are we supposed to do about that?"

"Your name is famous around the old republic. If you can't help us, who can?"

Sevan and Nadio glanced at each other in bewilderment.

"Where are we going, exactly?" Nadio persisted again.

"First, we will need to traverse the silver chasm, which we are doing at the moment. Then you will see possibly the most incredible natural wonder of Lysithea, the pillar of ruby fire. Then I will take you to our ships. On those you will see what you need to see? I mean, on those, you will see what you need to see."

Sevan and Nadio were not happy. It was all still a bit too cryptic for their liking. Sevan especially didn't want to go. He'd had enough adventure for one lifetime and, even though he wasn't sure exactly what he wanted to do, he was adamant it wasn't this.

"Do you think Ay-ttho will be okay?" Sevan whispered to Nadio.

"If anyone can be okay, it's her."

"Oh, I almost forgot," said Malcolm. "I have a message for you."

He brought the message up on the screen.

I speak without a mouth and hear without ears. I have no body, but I come alive with wind. What am I? Ask the Corporation security clone.

"It's a message for Ay-ttho," Sevan whispered.

"Why are you whispering?" asked Nadio.

"He doesn't know about Ay-ttho."

"Shouldn't he?"

"I don't know."

"What does it mean?" asked Malcolm. "I mean: What does it mean? Oh, no, that was a question, sorry. It looks like a riddle to me."

"Who asked you to show us this?" asked Nadio.

"I don't know."

"How can you not know? Someone must have asked you to show us the message."

"I just got a message asking me to show you the message."

"Who was the message from?"

"I don't know."

"How can you not know? The message must have an electronic signature."

"

"Yes, but it's not linked to anyone."

"How is that even possible?"

"Look."

Malcolm displayed the metadata from the message on the screen.

"And what happens when you run the signature?"

Malcolm processed the signature. It returned a message saying: *host not found.*

"We'll, I'll be..." Nadio stared at the message.

"Told you."

"But wait a unit. Someone must have asked you to come and get us. Who was that?"

"Same thing. I got a message."

"And you just turned up? What's in it for you?"

"Credits."

"Ah ha! Have you already received the credits?"

"Half. I get the other half when I deliver you, dead or alive."

"So we can trace the credits."

"I already tried that."

"And?"

"Nothing. So, what about the riddle?"

"Oh, it's an echo."

"What?"

"An echo. It speaks without a mouth. It hears without ears, and it has no body."

"How do you do that?" asked Sevan.

"There is a chamber with an impressive echo beyond the silver chasm," said Malcolm. "Just by the ruby pillar of fire that I was going to show you."

"Let's go."

"That's where we are going."

For the rest of the journey through the immense chasm, Nadio and Sevan stared through the observation windows at the incredible variety of colours being reflected by the grey-blue, white, yellow and green crystals and tried to ignore the fact that Malcolm's oily tentacles surrounded them.

After a while, when Malcolm was certain they weren't being followed, he took the watercraft to the surface and unscrewed the access hatch.

"Go up there and pop your heads out the top if you feel you need more space," he said.

Nadio and Sevan were both grateful that Malcolm understood how uncomfortable they were while worrying that he might feel offended that they didn't want to be near his oily tentacles.

They muttered their thanks, smattered with untrue claims that they were actually quite cosy squeezed in the control room with him. Nevertheless, they took immediate advantage of the opportunity to climb up to the hatch, where they took deep breaths of the chasm's damp air.

The oxidised crystals on the cavern walls were dark and the distant light of far away access doors shimmered on the still water, which was only disturbed by the steady wake of the watercraft.

Far in the distance, they noticed a small red light which gradually grew. They realised they were approaching the entrance to a cavern that was filled with red light.

As they drew even closer, they discerned that the light was flickering slightly and assumed that within the cavern was the pillar of ruby fire about which Malcolm had spoken.

"That is where we will hear the echo," said Malcolm.

They waited with trepidation as the watercraft drew closer and closer to the opening.

CHAPTER 21: PILLAR OF RUBY FIRE

"What are we doing?" Sevan asked Nadio.

"What do you mean? We are going to see the pillar of ruby fire."

"I mean, what are we doing with Malcolm?"

"If you remember, we didn't have a lot of choice. It was go with Malcolm or be killed by Saturnians."

"Yes, I know. But we are not being chased by Saturnians now, are we? I say as soon as we get to another set of access stairs, we thank Malcolm for the ride and we head back to the surface and the Mastery of the Stars and we try to find Ay-ttho."

"Perhaps you are right."

"No, perhaps about it. I know I'm right. The last thing we need to do is go on some adventure without..."

Sevan cut short his rant because at that moment the watercraft passed through the opening into an immense cavern, dominated by what could only be described as a huge pillar of ruby fire on one side.

"There it is," Malcolm shouted up to them. "Impressive, isn't it?"

Nadio and Sevan stared in awe at the vast column of red fire.

"How?" was all that Nadio could manage.

"No-one is really sure," Malcolm replied. "It burns red because of the strontianite and there must be huge deposits because it has been burning for as long as we have been here, but no-one knows how it caught fire."

"Is this where we will hear the echo?" asked Sevan.

"Almost. Let me just position the craft in the correct position. This used to be very popular with tourists in more prosperous rotations."

Malcolm navigated the craft until it satisfied him they were in the perfect position.

"There you go," he announced.

"Hello," Sevan shouted.

"Hello," came a reply.

"It really works," Sevan was very pleased.

"What are these on the cavern wall?" Nadio pointed to the dark surface, which was covered in strange designs.

"Those date from long before the colony," Malcolm explained. "The ancient inhabitants of Lysithea considered the echoes to be replies from spirit deities and so they created these artworks to illustrate their experiences."

"Perhaps that was the intention of the riddle," said Nadio. "It wasn't about the echo itself. It was just a device to get us to look at these designs. Look for anything that appears to have been created more recently."

The three of them scoured the cavern wall to find something that stood out from the rest of the drawings.

"What are these shapes here?" asked Sevan.

"I think those are representations of the ancient species itself," said Malcolm.

"Wow, they are ugly."

"They would probably think you are ugly if they were around now."

Sevan did not respond, but he knew Malcolm had a point.

Many of the images looked as if someone had carved them deep into the oxidised crystal surface. Sevan found a depiction of a creature with a lot of tentacles.

"Hey Malcolm, this one looks like you," Sevan laughed, pointing at the effigy.

"I think you've found it," said Nadio, excitedly. "Look, the style of this one differs from the others."

"So, perhaps it is a depiction of Malcolm."

"Perhaps."

Nadio was struggling to see the images because the flickering fire behind was projecting their shadows onto the wall. He noticed how some carvings were in relief casting shadows, which formed part of the overall design. A look of realisation crossed his face.

"It's Ebiowei," said Nadio.

"Is it?" asked Sevan.

"Ebiowei was a famous thuggish philosopher. My co-begetter used to read me his stories. He had one story which had someone who could only see the shadow of things. The shadows were their only reality. Ebiowei was questioning whether, if they saw the things that were casting the shadows, would they understand them?"

"We also have a philosopher that had a very similar idea. Her name was Jevon, she was one of the great Trition philosophers, and she said told a story of a Trition who mistook shadows for reality. They knew nothing of the things that caused the shadows. Jevon's point was that we give names to what we see, but what we are actually referring to are things we cannot understand."

"This is all very interesting," said Sevan. "But what is the point?"

"The point," explained Nadio. "Is that I believe that whoever is leaving us these clues is saying that what we are seeing are only shadows and that we have to turn our heads to see the cause of the shadows."

"Good. That's that solved then. Thank you for the ride on your watercraft, Malcolm. It has been a genuine experience, but now we really have to go."

"No, you can't," Malcolm was alarmed. "You have to come with me."

"We would love to, but unfortunately, there is somewhere we need to be."

"Where is that?"

"In our beds on the Mastery of the Stars. So if you could just drop us off at the nearest access stairs, we would really appreciate it."

"Sorry, that is not possible. I must take you to our ships."

"Ships? What ships?"

"Our space ships."

"Spaceships?"

"Yes, that is what I said. Spaceships? I mean, Spaceships."

"I don't think you understand. We don't want to go with you."

"Don't doesn't come into it. They have paid me to take you and I am going to take you."

Oily tentacles reached up into the access hatch, pulling Nadio and Sevan into the main compartment while other tentacles screwed the hatch closed.

Nadio and Sevan struggled but were pinned against the lever covered panels by the tentacles which were surprisingly strong.

With the hatch closed, Malcolm took the watercraft back below the surface, but Nadio and Sevan could not enjoy the crystal covered walls.

The craft was now moving much faster than before and Sevan assumed they must have been covering a considerable distance.

He tried to look at Nadio, but Malcolm pinned the thug out of sight on the other side of his bulbous mass.

"Let's be reasonable about this," Nadio negotiated.

"I am being reasonable," said Malcolm. "I do my job and get paid."

"Don't we get a say in this?"

Malcolm thought about it for a moment.

"No."

An oily tentacle covered Nadio's mouth.

Sevan, hearing Nadio muffled, feared the worst.

"What have you done to him, you slimy dirtbag?"

Another tentacle silenced Sevan, who thought, wrongly, that Malcolm must be running out of tentacles, so he tried moving some levers himself, but more tentacles appeared and secured his arms while others reset the levers to their original positions.

"Don't be pathetic," said Malcolm. "All you did was adjust the temperature of my lunchbox."

Eventually, the watercraft resurfaced and pulled alongside a large dock, on which many other tentacle rich Tritions were working, removing cargo from other, larger watercraft and loading them onto transporters. At another section of the dock, transporters were being unloaded and their cargo was being transferred to other vessels waiting at the dockside.

Sevan learned Malcolm had enough tentacles to secure him and Nadio, maintain their silence, open the hatch and lift them both, along with himself, out of the watercraft.

Once on the dock, Malcolm carried Nadio and Sevan towards a transporter.

"Nice cargo, Malcolm," one of the Tritions shouted. Laughter followed from all Tritions within earshot, including Malcolm himself.

"Where to?" a Trition next to the first transporter asked.

"Electric Spaceships."

"Third on the right."

Malcolm continued along the dock until he reached the third transporter on the right.

"Electric Spaceships?" He asked the driver.

The driver gave a tentacular gesture showing they should enter.

"Nice cargo, Malcolm," he shouted after them with a chuckle once they had boarded. The existing occupants, which included several Tritions, laughed too.

The inside of the transporter was an open space in which an assortment of Tritions gathered. Each possessed an assortment of goods or packages which they secured in their tentacles. All observed Malcolm and his cargo with amusement.

Malcolm found an empty corner and put Nadio and Malcolm on the floor while still securing them and covering their mouths.

"What you got there, Malcolm?" a nearby Trition asked.

"A thug and a corporation security clone, Malcolm," Malcolm answered.

At this moment, Sevan assumed two things to be true. First, he was not the clone Malcolm thought he was and, second, all Tritions were probably called Malcolm.

"That's not a security clone, Malcolm," said the new Malcolm. "Security clones are bigger. I reckon what you've got there is probably something like a ... err ... mining clone, I reckon. Where'd'ya find it."

"Silver chasm, Malcolm," said Malcolm.

"Nice. That's definitely a thug, though. What'y'er gonna do with 'em, Malcolm?"

"Electric Spaceships, Malcolm? I mean, Electric Spaceships, Malcolm."

"Wise move, Malcolm. Best thing for 'em if you ask me. They come here, taking our stuff. Get rid of 'em all. That's what I say, Malcolm."

"Is it? I mean, it is."

Sevan now wondered what the electric spaceships might be. They weren't sounding as pleasant as they had a moment ago. Also, he thought Malcolm was looking at him strangely. It was difficult to tell because the extraordinary intensity of the immense eyes didn't give much away, but Sevan imagined Malcolm was wondering who Sevan was if he wasn't a corporation security clone.

It took a while for the transporter to fill up and every time Sevan thought it was impossible to fit any more Tritions and their cargo on board, another would arrive, squeezing into a non-existent gap and apologising to all the Malcolms.

Eventually, when the transporter contained more Malcolm's and cargo than Sevan though permissible by the laws of physics, the doors closed and it moved.

He wanted to ask Nadio how this entire civilisation could exist beneath the surface without being detected by either the colony or the scanners on the Mastery of the Stars, but an oily tentacle was preventing him.

The journey was long and uncomfortable and although Sevan felt this would be the perfect moment to pass out and enjoy the journey in unconsciousness; he seemed unable to faint despite this being a regular occurrence at other, more inconvenient, times.

After an interminable length of time, the transporter stopped, the doors opened. Malcolms got off with their cargos and Sevan thought this might make the space a little more comfortable until even more alcolms got on with even more cargo.

This was repeated at the next few stops until Sevan thought it was impossible to squeeze in any more Malcolm's and then even more got on.

After a while, however, the tide turned and the number of Malcolm's getting off outnumbered those getting on and gradually the number of Malcolm's dwindled until only their own Malcolm was left, still clutching Nadio and Sevan.

When the transporter stopped for the last time, it surprised them to discover they were no longer underground, but on the planet's surface under a vast bio-dome. Desert stretched off in all directions and no sooner had Malcolm alighted than the, now empty, transporter sped off, leaving them alone in the centre of the barren landscape.

"This is more like the Lysithea I remember," Sevan wanted to say but could not because of the oily tentacle which was still preventing speech.

Much to their relief, Malcolm finally let go of them and Nadio and Sevan crumbled onto the dusty ground.

"Where are we?" Sevan asked.

"We are going to catch an electric spaceship."

CHAPTER 22: ELECTRIC SPACESHIPS

"Electricity?" Nadio spluttered. "You can't run spaceships on that ancient superstition."

"It is not a superstition," said Malcolm. "Electricity exists."

Sevan laughed and then went quiet when he saw the look on Malcolm's hideous face.

"You're serious, aren't you?"

"Of course. The Tritions have used laser powered interstellar travel since our earliest beginnings. It is the only form of travel."

"Gravity manipulation is the only form of travel," Nadio corrected.

"Uxclod! Electromagnetism is stronger than gravity."

"At a micro, not a macro level."

"So you admit it exists, then?"

"Nevermind," said Sevan. "This is getting us nowhere. How are we going to get back?"

"I kind of want to see these spaceships now," said Nadio.

"You have got to be kidding me."

"Just a quick look. What harm could it do?"

"Famous last words."

"This way," said Malcolm, walking off toward nothing.

Everywhere Sevan looked was the same. He followed Malcolm, realising that following the Trition to something was better than escaping to nowhere.

The desert turned out to be less barren than Sevan had expected. Occasional hills broke up the topography and these contained sparse pockets of vegetation.

Sevan noticed one plant looked like a sphere with spikes sticking out of it.

"That is a catgan," he said. "It's full of water. We can open it up for a drink."

Nadio and Sevan hurriedly grabbed a catgan each and opened them up. Sure enough, the sphere was full of water, which they drank, satiating their thirst a little.

It was behind one hill that Malcolm led them to reveal a huge space port.

"Why is it in the middle of nowhere?" Sevan wondered aloud.

"And why couldn't the transporter have dropped us here?" Nadio complained.

"The transporter does come here," Malcolm explained. "But via a very circuitous route. It was quicker to walk."

Sevan was thirsty, hungry and tired. He wouldn't have minded a circuitous route.

As far as Sevan's eyes could see, huge spacecraft stood on launch pads.

"How the uxclod does the colony not know about this place?" asked Nadio.

"They only see the shadows," said Malcolm. "They haven't looked to see what causes the shadows."

To Nadio, the spacecraft looked no different from any other craft he had experienced.

"How do they work?"

"Super cooled asymmetrical magnetic fields."

"Like the rocket to Trinculo," said Sevan.

"What?"

"Nothing."

"The magnets vibrate four hundred thousand times per nano-unit and the electricity is switched off at the same rate to create a unidirectional pulse."

"How is it powered?"

"Cold Fusion obviously."

"Obviously, such an archaic technology."

"But remarkably efficient."

"Is there anything to drink?" asked Sevan.

"I will take you to a place where you can nourish your feeble bodies."

Neither Sevan nor Nadio enjoyed being called feeble, but they were so tired and hungry that they both let it go.

Malcolm led them into an enormous hangar, where he appeared to be familiar with everyone who also appeared to be called Malcolm. They entered a large room, which obviously served as a canteen. Malcolm told them to sit on chairs, which, as they were designed for a Trition, were uncomfortable for thugs and corporation clones.

He returned moments later with three receptacles, which could best be described as buckets, and placed one in front of each of them. Malcolm immediately vomited into his bucket and then swished the contents around.

Sevan looked into his receptacle. It was half full of the same not quite dead sea creatures that Sevan and Nadio had eaten on Pallene. Only this time, they had left the shells on and they looked impenetrable.

"Vomit on them," Malcolm suggested. "That softens them up nicely."

"I don't think our vomit is as strong as yours," said Sevan.

"Would you like me to vomit on yours?"

"No, thank you."

"Why is it that when I am stuck somewhere with you, the food is terrible?" asked Nadio.

Sevan shrugged.

"Is there anything to drink?" he asked.

Malcolm thought about it for a moment.

"Yes, I'll be right back."

He returned with three cups of cloudy liquid. Sevan and Nadio both tried a sip, but the liquid was salty and only made their thirst worse.

"I don't want to seem impolite," said Nadio. "But is there anything else?"

"Anything else?"

"To eat or drink?"

Malcolm thought again.

"Don't think so."

"Would it be possible to check?"

Reluctantly, Malcolm raised himself from his Trition sized chair and moved towards the serving area. It wasn't so much of a walk as a nimbly picked propulsion.

Sevan watched as Malcolm had a discussion with a server and then returned in his peculiar style to where they sat.

"No," he said and turned back to his bucket of vomit covered not quite dead sea creatures.

Sevan looked in his own bucket and tried to muster some enthusiasm to kill and eat one of the pathetic specimens, but just couldn't pluck up the courage.

"We'll have to go in a unit anyway," said Malcolm, his mouth full of half masticated, vomit oozing, shells, legs and antennae.

A piece of creature fell back in his bucket with a splash and Sevan almost involuntarily vomited into his own receptacle.

"That's right. Get into the spirit of things," Malcolm encouraged him, another half eaten creature plopping into the bucket.

Sevan tried not to watch Malcolm eating and tried not to think of the contents of his own bucket.

Eventually Malcolm finished and emitted a burp so loud it made Sevan's antennae vibrate.

"That meal was good enough for Jevon herself," he said, oily juice and vomit still dripping from his mouth. "Are you ready? Let's go."

Hungrier than ever, Sevan and Nadio followed Malcolm out of the hangar, past more spacecraft, and into another hangar. This hangar looked tidier than the previous one and the Malcolms looked neater. Sevan got the impression that whatever went on in this hangar was more important than slurping vomit encrusted sea creatures out of buckets. Even Malcolm was wiping the goo from his mouth with an oily tentacle.

"What's this place?" asked Sevan.

"This is mission control. It is the command centre for all the spacecraft. This is where they paid me to bring you."

"So, you are a bounty hunter?"

"I have never heard of this creature, the bounty. Do they make good hunting?"

"No, it's not a creature, it's...oh, nevermind."

Sevan soon realised that where Malcolm had led them wasn't a hangar at all. It was more like an office block with an exceptionally large atrium.

At the far end of the atrium were a series of moving walkways leading upwards, downwards, and sideways. It was to one of these leading upwards that Malcolm was heading.

The rising walkway gave them a better view of the complex, which Sevan realised was quite extensive.

As far as he could see, there were moving walkways heading in all directions. No sooner had they reached the top of their moving walkway than Malcolm led them onto another and they ascended further.

At the top of this walkway, Malcolm turned down a corridor, and they followed him to the end where there was a waiting room with Malcolm shaped chairs which they tried their best to sit in.

Meanwhile, Malcolm went into a side room, leaving them under the guard of an even uglier Trition, a feat that Sevan had doubted was possible.

Now Sevan was bored as well as hungry, thirsty and tired. He looked over at Nadio, who also looked as bored, hungry, thirsty and tired as he did.

"Is there anything to eat or drink here?" Sevan asked the guard.

"There's a vending machine over there," the Guard extended an oily tentacle to the corner of the waiting room where a machine bubbled and flickered. "But I wouldn't get the Globturian dust pudding. It tastes like monain pig scraps."

Sevan hadn't heard of either of those, but he went over to the machine to have a look. The machine was a collection of liquid filled chambers containing similar specimens to the creatures he had seen in his bucket. Many wires and tubes connected the chambers, which were lit in a variety of gaudy colours. Lights flashed on most of the areas which didn't contain liquid and Sevan couldn't have worked out how to convince the machine to serve him a product, even if he hadn't been physically repulsed by its entire contents.

Despondent, he returned to his Malcolm shaped seat and tried to sit in it again.

"Anything?" Nadio asked.

Sevan shook his head.

"Not unless you like not-quite-dead sea creatures in ooze."

"I hate not-quite-dead sea creatures in ooze."

"I know. Me too."

They were worried about Malcolm. He had been gone for such a long time.

"Do you think something has happened?" asked Sevan.

"I hope not," said Nadio. "He's the only Malcolm we know here. Imagine having to get used to another one."

"I think they're all the same."

"I can't believe you just said that. That's unbelievably speciesist."

"What do you mean?"

"It's like saying all thugs are the same or all corporation clones are the same."

"All corporation clones are the same. We're clones."

"Alright, not the clones, but the thugs. You don't think all thugs are the same, do you?"

"I don't know. I haven't met many thugs."

Nadio shook his head.

"You disappointed me, Sevan. You didn't strike me as a speciesist. "

"What even is one of those?"

"It's when you believe that all other species are inferior."

"I never said the Tritions are inferior. I just said they all look the same."

"Exactly. You are failing to see them as individuals. You are prejudiced because they are a different species to you."

"I'm not prejudiced. They can do what they want as long as they keep their oily tentacles away from me."

"You see, that's exactly what I'm talking about."

"What?"

A door opening, and Malcolm walking through it, halted their discussion about speciesism.

"They will see us soon. Can you not smarten yourselves up a bit?"

"Listen mate," said Nadio, who was reaching the end of his tether. "We only just bought these in the colony so, unless you have a wardrobe of the latest thuggish fashions, I would button it."

Malcolm had little idea of what Nadio was talking about, not understanding clothing, wardrobes, fashion or buttons.

"Whatever, just be ready."

It was another long wait before the door opened again and a guard ushered the three of them through into a long ornate corridor with arches quite out of keeping with the rest of the Trition architecture. At the far end of the corridor were two much larger ornate doors. As they approached them, they swung open to reveal a large hall in which various Malcolms were sat in luxurious Malcolm chairs. At one end, on a raised platform, were the most important looking Malcolms. The centre of the hall was empty, and it was into this space that Malcolm led them.

"Most esteemed Trition masters," Malcolm began. "As instructed, I have travelled through the silver chasm and returned with the one whom you have been seeking for so long."

Sevan and Nadio exchanged nervous glances.

"It is my great pleasure to present to you the notorious maverick corporation security clone, Ay-ttho."

Malcolm pointed several oily tentacles at Sevan.

CHAPTER 23: DANGEROUS CHOICE

"No, wait a unit," Sevan stammered. "You've got all of this wrong."

"What is the meaning of this?" bellowed one of the most important looking Malcolms. "If this is not the notorious Ay-ttho, then you are wasting our time and we shall put you all to death."

"Pretend to be Ay-ttho," Nadio whispered to Sevan. "Or they will have us all killed."

"But I'm not Ay-ttho," he whispered back.

"I know that, you know that, but they don't know that."

"But what if they ask me to do something Ay-ttho like?"

"We'll cross that portal when we get to it."

"Speak clone!" the important-looking Malcolm bellowed. "Are you the Ay-ttho of whom Malcolm speaks? Your life and that of your thuggish friend rely on it."

"Yes, I am Ay-ttho," said Sevan reluctantly.

Both Nadio and Malcolm breathed tremendous sighs of relief. In Malcolm's case, this caused a piece of his last meal to be ejected from his mouth. Half a sea creature landed on the stone floor in front of them with a plap and began wriggling in a small puddle of digestive juices. Malcolm quickly shot out a tentacle to grab the unfortunate critter and return it to his mouth. He hoped no-one had noticed, but everyone was staring at him and Sevan was trying to stifle a vomit.

"Have you been to Zanzenburg, Ay-ttho?" the bellowing Malcolm asked Sevan.

"Sevan shook his head," he could feel his marbles rattling at the end of his antennae.

"It is on Zanzenburg that you will find Mullen's castle. There you will find the Unseen one. It is the Unseen one whole holds the plight of the Tritions in her tentacles. You must confront her and restore the balance."

"Okaaay," said Sevan. "That's quite a lot of information to take in there."

"Malcolm will take you on one of our electric spaceships, beyond the moon and into the far beyond until you reach Zanzenburg. Do you have questions?"

Sevan put up his hand.

"Well?"

"Do you have anything to eat or drink that isn't slightly alive or really salty?"

"Did Malcolm not take you to eat in the Great hall?"

"I did, your honour, but they did not like the food."

"Impossible! What's not to like? Nevertheless, we must respect the diversity of species."

Nadio gave Sevan an 'I told you so' stare.

"Get them something which suits their palettes. Have you tried the vending machine outside?"

"We have, but the contents were still not quite dead yet."

"I should think so, too. Nevermind. Malcolm? Make sure you feed them something that is already dead."

"And not covered in vomit," Sevan chipped in.

"How strange you clones are," the bellowing Malcolm laughed. "It is refreshing to learn the variety of tastes of others. If you want dead food with no vomit, then dead food with no vomit you shall have. Make it so."

Malcolm led them out of the hall and back down the ornate corridor to the little waiting room with the bubbling vending machine.

"What are you trying to do? Have us all killed?" Malcolm complained to Sevan once they were alone.

"But I'm not Ay-ttho."

"I know that. I realised that on the transporter. But it was too late by then."

"But what are we going to do? I can't kill some unseen thing in some place the giant cup knows where."

"Who said anything about killing her?"

"We'll, what are we supposed to do with her then?"

"We just need to speak with her."

"That doesn't seem too difficult. They don't need us to do that."

"That's not the problem. The problem is getting to see her. To enter her castle, you need to solve three riddles."

"That doesn't seem so bad," said Nadio.

"Let's go to the spaceship, then."

"What about the vomitless dead food?" asked Sevan.

"Oh, yes, that as well."

Malcolm led them both out of the building and onto the concourse, which stretched between the hangars and the launch pads.

Between some hangars were street vendors selling snacks of various descriptions, most of which Sevan thought appeared very much alive. Finally, they arrived at a stall where the food was very much dead; it looked as if it had been cremated.

"Here you go," said Malcolm. "They do juice as well."

Sevan saw they did indeed sell juice. It was green, not a bright green but a sickly green, and it looked as if it had things floating in it.

They ordered two portions of cremated dead thing with two sickly juices to go, and left.

"Don't you have to pay?" asked Nadio.

"No, we don't have a monetary system."

"What do you have?"

"Whatever we need, we just take."

"But what about that food vendor? How does he survive?"

"Whatever he needs, he just takes."

"But isn't the system open to abuse?"

"Oh no, that would be unethical."

"Hang on a unit," said Sevan. "You said you were being paid to deliver us."

"Yes, that transaction is outside the system."

"I don't understand," said Nadio.

"I didn't think you would."

The food they bought tasted exactly how it looked, burned, but at least it was dead and wasn't covered in vomit. The drink was very sweet and Sevan wished they had bought more of it.

"It's made from saccharum grass which grows abundantly on Zanzenburg. It is a real treat."

"What is the stuff floating in it?" asked Sevan.

"That is the larvae of an insect that lives on the plant."

Sevan spat out the juice that had been in his mouth and threw the cup with what little remained into what looked like a rubbish bin.

"What did you do that for?" asked an astonished Malcolm.

"I'm sorry, but I wasn't in the mood for larvae, so I threw it in the bin."

"That wasn't a bin. That was an air vent for the underground work areas."

Sevan looked into the bin and saw several angry Malcolms looking up and cursing.

"Let's go," said Malcolm, leading them to one of the launch pads.

Sevan tried to mimic Malcolm's nimbly picked propulsion but earned a rebuke from Nadio.

"What have I told you about being a speciesist? Just because they walk differently to us doesn't mean you can poke fun at them."

"Well, who can I poke fun at?"

"Why do you need to poke fun at anyone?"

"You're no fun."

They arrived at one of the launch pads and Malcolm showed them into the gantry where there was a Malcolm sized lift which took them to the entry hatch.

The inside of the ship looked very much like Malcolm's watercraft, but slightly more spacious. There was a Malcolm sized seat for Malcolm and then two smaller seats.

"They have especially adapted this ship for you," said Malcolm, urging them to take the seats.

"Are you sure you want to do this?" Sevan asked Nadio as they strapped themselves in and the entrance hatch screwed shut.

"Yes, I mean, even if I get the riddles wrong, what's the worst that can happen?"

"If you get the riddles wrong?" said Malcolm, overhearing the conversation. "The penalty for getting even one riddle wrong is death."

"What?" said Nadio, trying to undo his straps. But they were already locked in place because the engines had started and the ship was about to take off.

"You didn't tell us about that!" Sevan protested.

"You wouldn't have come if I had."

"Of course not."

Nadio knew it was pointless arguing because the ship was already lifting off the launch pads. Because it used electromagnetism rather than gravity manipulation, the takeoff was a much noisier and uncomfortable affair than usual. This just reinforced Nadio's opinions about the superiority of gravity manipulation.

Eventually, the ship made it into orbit and circumnavigated Lysithea.

"Where is Zanzenburg?" asked Nadio.

"Not far," said Malcolm. "But we'll need a little help to make the journey quicker."

Nadio thought about making a comment about how they wouldn't need help if they were using gravity manipulation, but a warning stare from Sevan convinced him not to.

Just like the watercraft, the control panels of the spaceship was covered in levers and, despite the larger size of the spaceship, Malcolm's operation of the vehicle involved spreading his oily tentacles in all directions, including in front and behind the heads of Nadio and Sevan.

"Why don't they just put all the levers over there?" Sevan complained.

He already knew the answer to his question. Like the watercraft, all the spaces on every surface, except for the entrance hatch and a small observation window, were covered in levers.

"Why do they need to have so many levers?" He rephrased his question.

Through the small observation window, Sevan could see the curved surface of Lysithea. Beyond that, slowly coming into view, was the moon of Enceladus. He couldn't deny it was a beautiful sight, and it reminded him of the Giant Cup orbiting his home, The Doomed Planet.

"Do you know?" He told Nadio. "When I was on The Doomed Planet, we used to think that our moon was a giant cup that kept filling and emptying."

"Yes, you told me."

"I already told you?"

"Only about a million times."

"Oh, okay. There's no need to be like that about it."

"I'm not being like that about it."

"You are."

"No, I'm not."

Sevan and Nadio both sulked.

"What's wrong with you two?" Malcolm asked after a while.

"Nothing," said Sevan.

"Nothing?"

"Nothing," said Nadio.

"Okay, suit yourselves."

Through the observation window, Enceladus appeared to grow larger and larger.

"We would have been there already if we used gravity manipulation," Nadio mumbled to himself.

"I heard that," said Malcolm.

"Good, I meant you to."

Sevan put his head in his hands.

"You know your problem?" he asked Nadio after a few units.

"No, tell me. What is my problem?"

"Your problem is that you think you know everything."

"Is that so? Well, do you know what your problem is?"

"I can't wait to find out."

"Your problem is that you don't know anything. "

"Thank you very much."

"Will you two please stop arguing?" asked Malcolm.

Sevan and Nadio returned to their sulking.

"Are you strapped in? We are about to perform a very technical and potentially dangerous manoeuvre called the moondive."

CHAPTER 24: MOONDIVE

Sevan could see Lysithea's moon Enceladus large in the observation window.

"Are we going to land on the moon?" he asked.

"No, we are going to plunge towards it but then hopefully miss," said Malcolm with less confidence than Sevan thought was due from someone who was piloting a spaceship that was about to plunge towards a moon.

"Why would you want to do that?"

"Because if we hit the surface, we will all die."

"Yes, I know that. What I mean is, why do you want to plunge towards the surface?"

"We are going to use the moon's gravity to sling us out into space."

"If we were using a…" Nadio began.

"Yes, we know, clever boots. Do us all a favour and keep it to yourself."

Sevan perceived they were accelerating because the moon appeared to be getting larger at a more rapid rate.

"Are you sure you have all the angles right?" he asked.

"Oh yes, it's all calculated very accurately. I have set the parameters using these levers here."

Malcolm pointed an oily tentacle at a row of levers that were vibrating in such a way that Sevan was convinced they could not possibly hold in the same position for long.

In fact, the whole vessel had started to vibrate. Sevan tightened his straps.

"They won't help you when to plunge antennae first into the moon's surface," said Nadio.

"Who asked you?"

A loud whine soon joined the rapidly approaching surface and the vibrations, as if the electromagnetic engine was about to explode.

This wasn't how Sevan had envisaged his last moments. He hadn't actually envisaged his last moments, but, if he had, it almost certainly wouldn't have been crashing into a moon in an electric spaceship with Nadio and a giant grey thing with oily tentacles.

Just as he thought his rotations were over, the ship somehow miraculously cleared the surface and shot off into space. Malcolm looked round at them, his v shaped mouth seemed to grin. Sevan and Nadio simultaneously breathed sighs of relief.

"How far is Zanzenburg?" asked Sevan.

"Yes, I've never heard of it before," said Nadio.

"It's not very far. We should be able to reach it within a tentacle full of standard lunar cycles."

"Lunar cycles?" Nadio despaired.

Sevan was even more worried. He had observed how much a Malcolm can carry in a single tentacle and thought that they might travel for quite a number of standard lunar cycles.

"Do you have any food on board?" he asked.

"We have freeze-dried tamernirs cyclo-algae."

"Does it have any vomit on it?"

"Oh, yes, don't worry, it's pre-vomited. "

Sevan's hearts sank.

"And to drink?" he allowed his hope to raise his optimism.

"Yes, we have frozen mead slush. It's made from the fermented excretions of the fejjofui. I think you'll like it. Are you hungry or thirsty now?"

"No thanks, I've just lost my appetite."

"Malcolm? Can you explain something I don't understand?" asked Nadio.

"I can try."

"So far we have discovered that the space defence programme is being used as a cover for powdered fushy trafficking and possibly the traffic of thugs."

"Correct."

"What I don't understand is how going to see this so called Unseen one is going to help. What is she going to do?"

"Ours is not to reason," Malcolm sighed.

"Why are we even doing this?" asked Sevan. "What does it matter to us if the colony space programme is being used for smuggling?"

"It matters to me," said Nadio. "I'm a thug, remember? It matters to me if other thugs are being treated as slaves, just as me and my co-begetter were."

"Fair point."

"And Malcolm and his fellow cronies didn't really give us a choice."

"What, is a crony. I mean, what is a crony?" asked Malcolm.

"It's your colleagues," Nadio snapped. "And another thing. Whoever heard of someone who accidentally says questions instead of statements? It's ridiculous."

"Are you calling me ridiculous? Don't mock my affliction."

"I'm not calling you ridiculous. But the whole situation is ridiculous."

"Okay, let me ask you another question," said Sevan. "Who has been leaving us all these riddles, and why?"

"I don't know, do I?"

"Sounds like the sort of thing Barnes would do, but obviously he's not..."

Sevan stopped abruptly. Lost in thought.

"What?"

"Daxu. The creator of Barnes. Is it the kind of thing he would do?"

"I don't know. We haven't seen him since he was scheming with Barnes to send us to the Zoxan universe. He's probably dead by now."

"Then who else could it be?"

"What about Chronos? We haven't seen him for a while."

"True, but why would he hide as the Unseen one? I'm bored. This electric space travel takes ages."

"Told you."

"Be patient," said Malcolm. "Space is a sizeable place."

"He can rhyme."

"You can't just get from one place to another at the touch of a button."

"We could if we were in the Horizon. Ron said it had folding technology.

"

"Do you think Cyrus is the Unseen one?"

"Possibly. But what does it matter, really? We just need to get there, solve these riddles. Speak to her and go home."

"Where is home, Sevan?"

"Don't start with that. Right now, for me, home is the Master of the Stars. Wherever we are, I'm at home when I'm on that ship."

"That's Nice."

"Are you being sarcastic?"

"No, I mean, it's really nice. I don't think I've ever been able to call anywhere home. Maybe for a short while when I was with Scotmax I was at home wherever she was and with Effeeko, our sick bay was our home because I could lose myself in the treatment of his patients. I hope he's okay."

"Don't worry about Effeeko. He can look after himself. They're probably worried about us, though."

"I hope Ay-ttho is okay."

"If Effeeko can look after himself, then Ay-ttho can certainly look after herself. It's the Saturnians I feel sorry for."

They both laughed, but they were nervous, worried laughs.

"Has your communicator dried out yet?"

"Yes, it dried out a while ago, but it's still not working."

"Malcolm?" Sevan asked. "Do you think we could get a message to the Mastery of the Stars?"

"Sorry. The ship isn't equipped with a tachyon transmitter."

"What kind of ship doesn't even have a tachyon transmitter?"

"This one."

"But how do you communicate with your base on Lysithea?"

"Electromagnetic waves."

"Seriously?"

"Seriously."

"But they only travel as fast as light."

"Exactly. "

"Wow, how do you survive with such basic technology? It's like going back in time to the dark ages. What did we do before they discovered tachyons and portals?"

"Travelled across space very slowly. Nadio, I can't spend the next meal time on this ship with him, never mind several standard lunar cycles, and don't want to eat anything that something has excreted."

"I know what you mean," Nadio sighed. He leant towards Sevan to whisper conspiratorially. "We could try to overpower him."

"First, have you seen the size of him?" Sevan whispered back. "Second, even if we overpowered him, we don't know how to fly the ship."

"You know I can hear you," said Malcolm.

"Wow, very good hearing." Whispered Nadio.

"My ears are on my tentacles."

"Of course they are."

Nadio grabbed a tentacle.

"Hello!" he shouted into it.

"That's just mean," Malcolm grimaced. "That's strange."

His demeanour suddenly changed and if Sevan had spent more time with Tritions, he would have been able to interpret the new body language as confusion. But he hadn't, so he just assumed Malcolm was calling Nadio's behaviour strange.

Nadio was a little more perceptive than Sevan. He had spent many standard solar cycles treating patients of a wide range of species, and he had developed the ability to sense discomfort.

"What's wrong?" he asked.

"We are receiving a message."

"What does it say?"

"I don't know. It doesn't seem to be in any language, it seems to be in code, but the ship's systems are shutting down by themselves."

"Turn the message off," said Nadio. "It's the message which is shutting down the systems."

Malcolm pulled a lever, and the strange noises stopped. A nano-unit later, the lights went about and were replaced by a dim red hue which seemed to come from the control panels.

"It's too late," he said. "I've lost all power."

CHAPTER 25: SPACE BOUND

Malcolm spent several units adjusting levers, but none of them appeared to do anything.

"None of them do anything," he sighed. "It seems we are space bound."

"Space bound?" asked Nadio. "You mean we are stuck in space? We are space bound as in bed bound, rather than space bound as in going to space."

"You are correct? I mean, you are correct."

"Great. So, now what?"

"Well, I'll have to calculate how many units we have before the life support systems fail."

"Fantastic. You do that. Let us know if there's anything we can do to help."

"Do you know anything about electrics?"

"If..."

"Don't say it," Sevan pleaded.

"I wonder who the message was from," said Malcolm.

"Check its signature," Nadio suggested.

"It doesn't have one, just like the other messages."

"Except they sent this one using electromagnetic waves."

"They were all sent my electromagnetic waves."

"So the sender wanted you to bring us out into space so that we could die here. It doesn't make sense. Why not just kill us on Lysithea?"

"Maybe they didn't want anyone on Lysithea to see?" Sevan suggested.

"Why?"

Sevan shrugged, and he imagined he saw Malcolm perform some kind of tentacle based shrug.

"There is another message coming in," said Malcolm.

"Didn't you shut the system off?"

"I just cut off the message. But this one is not in code. It says: 'I have cities, but no houses. I have mountains, but no trees. I have water, but no jakad. What am I?'"

"Does it not tell you to ask the Corporation security clone?"

"Not this time."

An alarm sounded.

"That's the proximity detector," said Malcolm.

"I thought you didn't have any power."

"We have emergency power, so some scanners still work. It looks like Tenuil pirates."

"Oh great," said Sevan. "Pirates, that's all we need."

The Tenuil ship drew closer to the disabled Trition ship, which was clearly dwarfed by the pirate vessel. The darkness of the pirates' hold swallowed them and all was blackness until suddenly lights illuminated the entire space, which was empty save for their ship.

"Exit your vessel," a voice from a tannoy echoed around the empty hold. "And don't think about bringing any weapons with you. We have scanners, you know."

"They don't sound like Tenuils," said Nadio.

"What do Tenuils sound like?" asked Sevan.

"Good point. If I didn't know better, I'd say she sounded like an old thug."

"Tenuils attacked us before we met you, but I didn't see one. They say even the sight of one can kill you."

"That's just an old partner's tale."

"Exit your vessel now or I will destroy it," the voice sounded like it wasn't messing around.

"See what I mean? Sounds like an old thug."

"Will you two just get off the ship so I can get out," said Malcolm. "You're in my way and I don't want my ship to be destroyed, especially not with me in it. If they have scanners, they will know there are three of us."

Sevan and Nadio unstrapped themselves. Malcolm pulled a lever to open the hatch, and they all climbed out.

"Nadio and Sevan? It is you," said the tannoy.

"Who wants to know?"

"Last time I saw you, Sevan, you were pretending to be a bounty hunter. Now I'm the hunter and the price is on your head."

Sevan remembered pretending to be a bounty hunter, but that didn't help him narrow down the source of the voice, though he thought it unlikely to be a Tenuil pirate. He looked at Nadio, who seemed deep in thought.

"D'Auria," he said.

"Congratulations, Nadio. Nice to see that you and Sevan still hang around together. How is Scotmax?"

"She's dead."

"Oh yes, I heard about that. Died in battle attempting to create a new Republic. You must be very proud."

"I am. What do you want, D'Auria?"

"I told you. There is still a bounty on Sevan's head."

"For what?"

"For his part in the murder of President Man."

"But they acquitted us," said Sevan.

"Yes, they did. Unfortunately, President Kirkland forgot to remove the bounty before his untimely murder by his partner."

"But that was so long ago, D'Auria," said Nadio. "How are you even still alive?"

"It's true. I am ancient for a thug and I haven't exactly looked after myself. Why don't you come through so that we can chat face to face?"

A door in the hold's side opened. Sevan and Nadio went through, but Malcolm was too large to fit.

"I'll wait for you here," he suggested.

The door led to a corridor and the corridor to another door. It was after they passed this door that they saw D'Auria, looking very old, her fur long and grey.

"Anyway, who is going to pay you this bounty?" said Nadio, dispensing with pleasantries.

"Good to see you too, Nadio," D'Auria joked. "It's true. Kirkland's bounty is worthless since the Republic collapses, but I thought you might like to know it still exists. No. The real bounty is much more recent, and it concerns the crew of the Mastery of the Stars, so I guess that means you."

"Except that we are not in the Mastery of the Stars, so you have no bounty."

"But you were, so the ship must be close. I'm guessing Lysithea? And I bet Ay-ttho and Tori are there, too."

"Tori is dead."

"I'm sorry to hear that. How did that happen?"

"When the Ao-jun invaded Angetenar."

"Oh yes. So pointless. Those who are resisting the Zoxans squabbling among themselves. I heard Luap ran off with someone again."

Nadio didn't bother replying.

"If it's the Mastery of the Stars you are after, then we can't help you," said Sevan. "You may as well let us go."

"To float aimlessly in space until you die. I'm not heartless, Sevan."

"Then restore the power to our ship."

"Sorry, I can't do that. You are too valuable."

"You still haven't told us who you expect to pay this bounty," said Nadio.

"Ever heard of a Zoxan called Naej?"

Sevan shook his head, but Nadio thought about it for a moment.

"Yes. He was the one who blinded Barnes."

"That's right," Sevan remembered. "Ay-ttho told me that story."

"I'm surprised Barnes didn't tell you himself. He never stopped talking about it."

"Where is Barnes?" asked D'Auria.

"Dead," said Nadio.

"Oh. How did that happen?"

"He just fell ill. In the Pachynus system."

"What a terrible place to be ill."

"Do you know Pachynus?"

"No, I was just trying to be funny."

Sevan didn't like the sound of meeting Naej, someone who had injured the mighty Barnes.

"What's stopping us from overpowering you and taking the ship where we want?" asked Nadio.

"I wouldn't if I were you. This used to be a Tenuils pirate ship. It's full of hidden defences. You wouldn't get within one unit of me."

"We're travelling with a Trition."

"Who can't get out of the hold. There is a larger door, but don't tell him about it. Are you hungry? Would you like something to eat?"

"Yes please," said Sevan.

"I have a food synthesiser. It's limited. Mainly thuggish food."

"Fine by me."

"I'm sure I can find something for your Trition friend, too."

"Put his in a bucket."

"Okay then. How about setian sticks, pseudo-supplement with spicy salt sauce and luna-nuts?"

"Sounds amazing," Sevan was already salivating at the thought.

D'Auria, who moved slowly and gingerly, led them to an area where they could sit. She went to a machine and returned with trays filled with setian sticks, pseudo-supplement and luna-nuts.

"It's all synthetic, I'm afraid, but it tastes like the real thing to me."

There was something strange to Nadio about calling supplements the real thing. This was a synthetic replication of a synthetic replication.

D'Auria left them alone while she filled a bucket with supplements for Malcolm.

"Talk among yourselves. I won't be long," she said.

"Look at how weak she it," said Nadio, after she was gone. "We could easily overpower her."

"But what about what she said about the defensive mechanisms in the ship?"

"I'm sure she's exaggerating to put us off."

"He vomited in the bucket," D'Auria said when she returned.

"He does that. How is he?" asked Sevan.

"He's not too happy about being stuck in the hold, but he understands. I told him we were on our way back to Lysithea to collect the Mastery of the Stars and he didn't seem bothered."

"So, we are going back to Lysithea, then?"

"Yes. We'll collect the Mastery of the Stars and then proceed straight to Naej."

"Where is Naej?"

"On Future, so not far."

"But if you use the portal to Future, you will give away the location of the colony."

"How do you think I got here in the first place? The Zoxans know about the colony. They just leave them alone because it's less hassle. They've got enough on their plates already."

"But what about the fushy trafficking? They can't be happy about that."

"I don't think it bothers them. The more of the rebellious population that is addicted to fushy powder, the better. The more energy they apply to getting fushy powder, the less they have to overthrow the Zoxans. For the same reason, the old Republic used to ignore the depravity of Angetenar and Sicheoyama."

"How much will Naej pay you?" asked Nadio.

"None of your business."

"I can pay you 500,000 to forget about us."

"Credits?"

Nadio nodded.

"Where did you get that?"

"Scotmax."

"I see. Well, credits are still useful in some parts of the universe, but they are not worth what they used to be. I had a gift from Scotmax myself, but I soon drank my way through that. Long before the Zoxans arrived."

"How is Naej paying you, then?"

"Grykolars."

"Gr...what?"

"Grykolars. That's the Zoxan currency."

"How much are they worth?"

"One grykolar is roughly 100 credits."

"And how many of those is Naej offering?"

"For the ship and the crew, he is offering 12,000 grykolar."

Nadio did the math in his head and realised that was more than double what he had just offered D'Auria. He checked his communicator, but it still wasn't working. On seeing this, Sevan checked his, but it wasn't working either.

"Ay-ttho might have left Lysithea by the time we get there," Sevan suggested.

"I don't think so," said D'Auria. "I have scanned Lysithea and the signature of your freighter is showing up, so Ay-ttho might not be there, but the ship is and that's all I need."

"You don't need us, then."

"I may as well deliver you while I have you."

"Or you can take the 500,000 credits, leave us on Lysithea, and take someone else to be the crew."

"Like who?"

"I don't know. Some Saturnians? Or Tritions."

"You know what they say. A tronqak in the hand is worth two in the forest."

"Not when someone is paying you 500,000 credits to let the tronqak go."

"It's an interesting proposition. If you could provide the crew as well, I might consider it."

Nadio and Sevan looked at each other. They realised neither had a good plan, judging by each other's expressions.

"Uh-oh," said D'Auria.

"What's wrong?"

"Looks like we're being followed."

"By whom?"

"Not sure. The scanner has picked up the signature, but it's strange. Completely alien. Whoever they are, they are gaining, and fast."

CHAPTER 26: THE ALIEN SPACESHIP

"Maybe they are heading to Lysithea," said Nadio.

"I don't think so," said D'Auria. "I picked them up a while back, so I changed my course away from Lysithea to see if that was the case. They are definitely following us."

"By the way. I've been meaning to ask you. How did you end up with a Tenuil pirate ship?"

"Long story."

"Maybe it's the Tenuils coming to get their ship back."

"No, they're not Tenuils."

"How do you know? We thought you were Tenuils, but you weren't."

"Good point. I hope they're not Tenuils."

"It seems the Saturnians chose a pretty busy system in which to hide," Nadio commented.

"Like I said, they aren't really hidden."

"Wait a unit! I've got it! Malcolm!"

"What about him?"

"We pretend he is the crew."

"That's harsh. I thought he was your friend."

"Not really. He kidnapped us. He's a kind of bounty hunter, so it would be poetic justice, of sorts."

"Why did he kidnap you?"

"He wants to take us to Zanzenburg to meet the Unseen One by answering the riddles so that the Tritions can...I can't remember. It's meant to achieve something good for them."

"Don't forget Mullen's castle," said Sevan.

"That's right, we find the Unseen One at Mullen's castle. That's where we must answer the riddles."

"What sort of Riddles?"

"No idea, but someone has been sending us riddles ever since they murdered the high priest on Enceladus. "

"What high priest?"

"Never mind. It's not important. I think that was something to do with the fushy trafficking. Did you know they are trafficking thugs and making them manufacture fushy powder?"

D'Auria was silent.

"You did, didn't you? You knew they were trafficking thugs and you've done nothing about it. I bet you've even helped them."

"You've gone too far there. I've helped no one traffic thugs."

"You trafficked me."

"I looked after you."

"My begetter paid you to look after me until you sold me to Ay-ttho."

"You're making it sound much more than it actually was."

"No, she isn't." said Sevan.

An alarm beeped on a console near D'Auria.

"Uh-oh," she said. "I've just identified the signature of that ship. I know why it was alien now. It's Zoxan. They say they came from another universe."

Nadio and Sevan said nothing. They waited for the Zoxan ship to arrive. When it did, it swallowed the Tenuil pirate vessel, which had already swallowed the Trition ship.

"This is getting to be like one of those Core dolls," said Nadio. "You know, where one fits inside another."

Once D'Auria's stolen ship was docked in the hold of the Zoxan vessel, she received a message from the Zoxans.

"They have told us to descend from the ship, with no weapons," she said.

"That sounds familiar," said Nadio.

"What's happening?" asked Malcolm when they returned to the hold.

"A Zoxan ship has captured us."

"It's like one of those core dolls."

"I already said that."

D'Auria opened the doors, and they descended the ramp into the hold of the Zoxan vessel. She walked slowly and unsteadily with the use of a stick and Sevan thought she now looked as old as she probably was.

A door opened in the Zoxan hold and they walked through into a room which looked similar to the Zoxan ships Sevan and Nadio had been on before. Several zoxans brandishing weapons were waiting. The door closed behind them.

Faced with the Zoxans, Malcolm didn't look so big anymore. It was Sevan, Nadio and D'Auria who felt tiny.

"What are you doing on a Tenuil pirate ship?" the nearest Zoxan asked.

"It's a long story," said D'Auria.

"So why not make it shorter?"

"I stole it."

"Who made this?"

"Who stole it? I did."

Sevan realised the Zoxan translation software hadn't got any better.

"Wow, who stole?"

"I did."

"What do you mean?"

"I mean, I stole this ship from the Tenuils and got away with it."

"What are you doing in the Listair system?"

"That must be what they call Lysithea," said Nadio.

"I am a bounty hunter and seek the ship called the Mastery of the Stars and its crew. Naej has given it a bounty of 10,000."

The Zoxans looked at each other and appeared to be discussing something. Then they turned back to D'Auria.

"Please take us on board."

"Okay," D'Auria turned to return to the hold and the Tenuil ship.

"Where are you going?"

"I'm going to show you the Tenuil ship."

"We don't want to learn about grimfight boats. We hope you can take us to the star realm."

Sevan, Nadio, D'Auria and Malcolm exchanged confused glances.

"85 standard solar cycles and they still haven't improved their translation device," said Sevan. "Let me have a go. Where is the star realm?"

"That's right."

More confused glances.

"We don't know where the star realm is," said Nadio.

"Not the astral plane. The star field."

"This is getting us nowhere," Nadio let out a frustrated sigh.

"I'm sorry," Malcolm had a go. "We don't know what you mean when you talk about astral planes and star fields."

"Astral world," said the Zoxan, clearly getting frustrated and weaving a winged talon at D'Auria. "He said the ship he was looking for. Ship Naej gave a bounty of 10,000."

"Ah, The Mastery of the Stars," D'Auria realised.

"Call it whatever you want. Take me to that boat."

There was a brief discussion among the Zoxans.

"Yes. We'll give you 10,000."

"I wouldn't trust them," said Nadio.

"Would you like to follow my ship?"

The Zoxan began hitting the translation device as if it was faulty.

"No, you will stay on our ship and tell us where to go," it said, finally.

A Zoxan approached D'Auria and started to lead her away.

"Wait," said D'Auria. "I know which planet it is on, but you will need them to tell you where exactly on the planet."

Other zoxans moved to collect Sevan, Nadio and Malcolm, but the Zoxan, who appeared to be in charge, stopped them.

"Please tell me which planet," he asked D'Auria.

"You see, the problem with this," D'Auria began. "Is that if I tell you the planet and you find the Mastery of the Stars, you'll say it was you who found it and then you won't give me my 10,000."

The Zoxan started tapping and shaking his translation device again and then went for another brief discussion with his colleagues.

"We will give you the 10,000," he said, and led D'Auria out of the room.

Other Zoxans escorted Sevan, Nadio and Malcolm in the same direction. They led them towards what they assumed was the bridge, but just before they arrived at what looked to Sevan like the entrance to the bridge, the Zoxans led them into a side room.

The Zoxan began fiddling with his translation device again. They waited patiently to hear what he had to say. Suddenly, it burst into life at full volume.

"After investigating Lysithea, I found a ship that fits the astral world, so I'm heading there."

"He means the Mastery of the Stars," said Nadio to the others who had already assumed that was what the Zoxan had meant.

The Zoxan left the room and didn't return until some units later. As soon as he entered, he began fiddling with the translation device.

"Cover your ears," Sevan suggested.

The Zoxan went out again and came back in with what looked to Sevan like another translation device. This seemed to cause the Zoxan just as much trouble as the first, so he went out and replaced it with a third. Then he looked as if he had forgotten what he was going to translate, and then he abandoned the device altogether and called guards to lead them from the room.

This time they led them to a hangar which contained rows of shuttles. Sevan was not happy. He had ridden on a Zoxan shuttle before and wasn't keen to repeat the experience.

In a shuttle, D'Auria, Nadio and Sevan were strapped into one seat and Malcolm was strapped into another. Zoxans climbed into the pilot, co-pilot, and navigator seats.

The Zoxan in charge made one last attempt to get his translated to work before giving up and leaving the ship.

"We're in orbit over Lysithea, descending to the surface in a shuttlecraft. You come with us," they heard the device announce from outside as the door was closing.

The doors opened, and the shuttle left the hangar. Once outside, they could see Lysithea stretching out below them.

Sevan saw Nadio was fiddling with his communicator, so Sevan checked his. It was working. He worked quickly to send a message to Ay-ttho that the zoxans had located the Mastery of the Stars and were on their way there in a shuttlecraft.

A few units later, Sevan received a message from Ay-ttho saying that she had received a similar message from Nadio. That the Mastery of the Stars wasn't quite fixed, and that they were unloading belongings of the Angetenarian settlers that didn't want to flee.

Sevan told Ay-ttho to hurry because they were already descending through the atmosphere.

As they drew closer to the surface, Sevan recognised some bio-domes passing across the small observation window. He worked out it would not be long before they reached the forest bio-dome where the Mastery of the Stars was parked. Then a thought occurred to him.

"Nadio?" he turned to the thug beside him. "Why are they only sending this shuttle? Do they not know how many Angetenarians there are with the freighter?"

"You uxclod! You think our shuttle is the only vessel the zoxans are sending. Look over there."

Nadio pointed to the corner of the observation window where Sevan could make out a zoxan fighter, flying in formation near the shuttle.

"You can be sure there are more of those," said Nadio.

"But why are they so interested in the Mastery of the Stars?"

"Have you forgotten that they associate us with that rebel Zoxan scout ship?"

"They captured us."

"Yes, but to these Zoxans, we gave them a lift to Herse."

"They virtually forced us to. We would have died otherwise. And anyway, it was the Ao-jun that were chasing us."

"And the Zoxans were helping the Ao-jun. If it hadn't been for Chronos, we wouldn't be here now."

"But the Ao-jun arrived on Angetenar in Chronos' ship."

"They obviously stole it. Did they teach you nothing at that concession?"

"I don't remember them teaching me anything."

"That's right. You're a clone and were just programmed."

"I don't think you like me, do you?"

"I try very hard to."

"What does that mean?"

"Whatever you want it to mean, Sevan. We are about to land at the forest bio-dome. There are more pressing matters than your ego right now."

Sevan wasn't sure where his ego came into it, or why Nadio had mentioned it. He kept his questions to himself and waited for the inevitable.

He didn't have to wait long because, on the approach to the bio-dome, the Zoxan fighters began firing at the Mastery of the Stars, which returned cannon fire.

The shuttle veered around and, as it turned, Sevan got a good view of half the fighter formation through the observation window.

The shuttle set down a short distance away and they disembarked, guarded by the Zoxan crew and accompanied by several Zoxan soldiers that had landed their fighters nearby.

Many fighters remained airborne and Sevan could see them making attacking runs on the Mastery of the Stars, as well as the heavy cannon fire the freighter was returning.

As they approached the area where the Mastery of the Stars was parked, they encountered blaster fire which Sevan presumed was from the Angetenarian settlers.

The Zoxan soldiers returned fire with the same ferocity. Sevan and the others tried to hide as best they could, but this was difficult for Malcolm because of his bulbous shape.

"Why am I here?" he complained. "None of this has anything to do with me."

"Then you shouldn't have kidnapped us," Nadio retorted. "At least you might get to meet the real Ay-ttho."

The fighting died down and Sevan saw some of the Zoxan soldiers returning. They were holding something between them. As they drew closer, he realised what it was. It was Ay-ttho.

CHAPTER 27: LAUNCH AND PURSUIT

"Hello," said Sevan.

"Hello," said Ay-ttho, as the Zoxans threw her to the ground.

"How did you escape the Saturnians?"

"Oh, that was all just a big misunderstanding. It turns out that they aren't thug trafficking at all. The thugs are part of an exchange programme, teaching them to make medicines. There is a group of Saturnians on Sicheoyama learning other skills."

"But they locked us in that room," said Nadio.

"Apparently because we were being violent. But what's happening here? What's with all the Zoxans? And what happened to you two? And what's that?"

Ay-ttho nodded towards Malcolm.

"That is Malcolm," said Malcolm.

"He kidnapped us," said Nadio. "Then D'Auria kidnapped us."

"D'Auria?" Ay-ttho stared at the grey, long-haired thug.

"Hello Ay-ttho," D'Auria smiled.

"Then the Zoxans kidnapped us and brought us here."

The fighting had died down considerably.

"I guess the settlers are giving up," said Ay-ttho.

"D'Auria is being paid 10,000 somethings to deliver us and the Mastery of the Stars to the Zoxans," Nadio added.

"Why am I not surprised?"

Ay-ttho made a move for D'Auria but two Zoxan soldiers held her back.

"They won't pay her," said Nadio.

D'Auria said nothing.

When the Shooting had stopped completely, a superior-looking Zoxan approached. He was about to speak but was interrupted by the noise of four Zoxan fighters lifting the Mastery of the Stars from the ground and taking it high into the atmosphere towards the Zoxan ship.

The Zoxan started fiddling with the translation device, but seemingly unable to get it to work, he signalled to the other Zoxans to escort them back to the shuttlecraft.

"Why didn't they confiscate your communicators?" Ay-ttho whispered to Nadio.

"Maybe they don't have that technology."

"What is a communicator?" asked a soldier.

"But they have good hearing," Whispered Ay-ttho.

"Nothing," said Nadio.

The soldier wasn't convinced but let it go. Ay-ttho began surreptitiously fiddling with her communicator.

"What are you doing?" asked the soldier.

"Nothing," said Ay-ttho, slipping the communicator back into her suit.

"Why do they want the Mastery of the Stars so badly?" asked Nadio.

"Apart from the fact we helped the treacherous Zoxans? Probably the anti-matter drive."

"Let's hope they don't damage it."

"If they do, I doubt we'll be able to fix it."

"We have arrested you for abetting the deaths of hundreds of rescuers who were dismantling the space station Tomorrow," said one of the Zoxans as they were being led onto the shuttle.

On the shuttle, D'Auria, Nadio and Sevan were strapped into one seat as before and, much to her disgust, Ay-ttho was strapped next to the oily tentacled Malcolm.

They were about halfway back to the Zoxan ship when the pilots became agitated. Through the observation window, Sevan could see that something was firing at the Zoxan fighters and was having a degree of success.

Soon afterwards, there was a jolt and a loud metallic crunch.

"Something has locked onto us," said Nadio.

"I know," said Ay-ttho.

The Zoxans had clearly lost control of the ship, which veered around and was pursued by the fighters which remained operational. Sevan could see the tracer fire shoot past the observation window from behind and disappear off into the distance. Occasionally there was a shudder as if they had hit the shuttle, but it was vibrations from a direct hit on whatever craft had attached itself to them.

"What is happening?" asked Nadio.

"It's Cyrus and the Horizon," said Ay-ttho. "After I lost you two, I met Cyrus again and she explained to me the trips she had been making between Lysithea and Sicheoyama by folding space. That's how they set up the exchange with the thugs."

"Where do they get their energy from?"

"Same as us. They fly into a star."

"Is that where we are going now?"

"I assume so."

"Will we get there before the Zoxans blow us to bits?"

"I hope so?"

Another noise distracted them. It was the sound of the roof of the cockpit being ripped open. The zoxans unstrapped themselves and drew their weapons.

"This would be a good time to hide," Ay-ttho suggested.

They unstrapped themselves and hid behind the seats.

The Zoxans were focussed on the tearing metal and, as soon as the aperture was large enough, they began firing through it. Soon the fire was returned and, before long, the Zoxan crew could no longer fire at anything, their being dead. A section of the roof was completely removed and Sevan could see Saturnians staring down at them through the hole. They rolled down a ladder for them to climb up, all except Malcolm, who didn't need the ladder.

Once they were safely inside the hold of the Horizon, the hole was sealed and they jettisoned the Zoxan shuttle. The Saturnians led the group to the bridge, where Cyrus was waiting.

"Welcome aboard," she said.

"Thank you," said Ay-ttho. "Where are we heading?"

"We need to get close enough to the star to fold space."

"What about the Mastery of the Stars?"

"We'll have to come back for her. If we don't leave now, the Zoxans will blow us to bits. It's touch and go whether we will make it as it is."

"Where are we going?"

"Well, that's a bit of a moot point. We could go to Sicheoyama. The Zoxans shouldn't be able to follow a fold."

Neither Nadio, Ay-ttho or D'Aurio relished the idea of returning to Sicheoyama, but it was better than being blown up by Zoxans.

"Aren't you going to introduce me to your friends?" Cyrus asked. "Nadio and Sevan, I already know."

"This is Malcolm," said Nadio. "He tried to kidnap us. And this is D'Auria. She tried to sell us to the Zoxans."

"Ah, so not really friends then."

"They agreed to go to Zanzenburg," said Malcolm. "To Mullen's castle to answer the riddles to see the Unseen One to help the Tritions."

Everyone looked at Malcolm as if he was speaking another language.

"Is this true?" asked Ay-ttho. "Whatever he said."

"Yes, it's true, but they had kidnapped us. We would agree to anything. And we got more of the riddles sent via Malcolm. What was the last one, let me think? Ah, yes. I have cities, but no houses. I have mountains, but no trees. I have water, but no jakad. What am I?"

"A map," said Ay-ttho.

"And then when we were in the caves under the colony we there was one which said: I speak without a mouth and hear without ears. I have no body, but I come alive with wind. What am I?"

"An echo."

"Exactly, so Malcolm took us to a place where there was an echo and we could see shadows on the wall. So I thought that whoever is leaving us these clues is saying that what we are seeing are only shadows and that we have to turn our heads to see the cause of the shadows."

Cyrus became interested in the conversation suddenly.

"Heliodorus was a saturnian philosopher who suggested that we only perceive a fragment of reality through our senses," he said.

"Whoever sent us these riddles knew Malcolm was going to kidnap us. They sent us to find the Horizon and must somehow have known we would jump through the hole in the floor. It is all too incredible to believe."

"But what about the map?" asked Ay-ttho. "What is the significance of the last riddle?"

"Who is this Unseen One?" asked Cyrus. "Perhaps they have the answers."

"Are they the one who killed Adama and Jaques Thimothee? I have to admit, I thought it was you."

"Me?"

"Yes, the clues pointed us towards the Horizon. You have folding technology. That could have explained the extensive navigation records on Adama's ship. What was he doing, Cyrus?"

"I don't know, Ay-ttho. And if I was complicit, why would I save you from the zoxans?"

"Speaking of which," said Sevan as another missile exploded close to the Horizon's hull. "Are we any closer to escaping?"

"Almost there, Sevan," said Cyrus. "I tell you what. Let's fold to Zanzenburg. We'll go to this Mullen's castle and we'll find out what it is all about."

The Saturnian crew worked quickly to input the calculations. Sevan could see the star looming large in the observation window.

"This is proper technology," Nadio said to Malcolm, who appeared to shrug, but it was difficult to tell because his tentacles were always busy doing something.

With blasts exploding all around, the Horizon accelerated and the star which soon filled the observation window, developed a hole in the middle so that, at first it resembled a giant shining doughnut and then gradually, the hole expanded until the ring disappeared and the Horizon was left in empty space.

"How did you get this technology?" Nadio asked Cyrus.

"We Saturnians have been busy since the collapse of the old Republic. Finding old technology and repurposing it for our uses."

"Where did you find this technology?"

"Orbiting around Nereid. It wasn't easy to steal, though. The Zoxans heavily guarded it, although they didn't know how to use it. They don't seem to be very good with technology."

"We noticed."

"Most of their technology was made for them or appropriated, but they don't seem very good at creating anything themselves."

"We are approaching Zanzenburg," announced one of the crew.

"Excellent. Now, how will we find Mullen's castle?"

"With a map!" said Ay-ttho.

"Good. Where will we get a map of Zanzenburg?"

"From Sevan's head."

"What?" Sevan was not expecting this.

"Have you forgotten, Sevan, that they loaded an entire map of the universe into your marbles?"

"I was trying to forget."

"Do you have any terminals that will allow us to connect Sevan's antennae to your navigation computer?" Ay-ttho asked Cyrus.

"Not really. Saturnians don't operate vessels with antennae."

"Shame. What else could we use to get inside Sevan's head?"

"I have some ideas," said Malcolm.

"That don't involve killing him?"

"In that case, I have no ideas."

Sevan gave Malcolm a hard stare.

"There's no cerebral interface?"

"We could try plugging him into the scanner in the sick bay," suggested Nadio. "I might patch that through to the navigation computer."

"Let's give it a go."

Sevan was whisked off to the sick bay and plugged into the scanner while Nadio accessed the medical computers and attempted to create a link to the navigation system.

"Tori would have been good at this," Ay-ttho reflected.

Nadio gave her a sympathetic smile. He also gave Sevan something to sedate him so that his natural state of anxiety did not interfere with their ability to read his marbles.

"We could use this as a method of interrogation," Cyrus suggested.

"Not really," said Nadio. "The subject offers the information. The system is merely asking his subconscious questions."

It wasn't long before the setup was complete and data was being downloaded to the ship's navigation database.

"What is Mullen's castle, anyway?" asked Cyrus while they were waiting.

"Castles were things they had eons ago," said Nadio.

"How do you know so much?"

"They had a magnificent library in the caverns on Angetenar. Whenever I wasn't helping Effeeko, I would visit the library. It's probably all been destroyed by the Ao-jun now."

"But what were castles for?"

"Nothing really. It was just another word for a building. Usually a building for the chief."

"So, Mullen must have been a chief then."

"Possibly. I think this is working."

Nadio looked at the graphics on the panel in front of her.

"Are you searching for the castle already?"

"Yes, but only a small amount of data has been transferred so far."

"Let me know when you have anything. I'm going back to the bridge."

Cyrus left, and the process continued.

"Is there anything to eat?" Nadio asked.

"I'll see what I can find," said one of the Saturnians.

He came back with a bowl of spagums parasite lettuce, which Nadio remembered from Angetenar.

"Thank you," she said, taking the bowl. And then she was distracted by the screen, which was flashing a result. "I've got one! The only problem is, it's in the Zoxan universe."

"We're not going there," said Ay-ttho.

"I hope not. Wait a unit, there is one in this universe and it's here on Zanzenburg."

"That's it then. Let's go."

CHAPTER 28: MULLEN'S CASTLE

The Horizon descended to the surface of Zanzenburg, which, despite being covered in hills of saccharum grass, looked grey and cold. Low clouds shrouded the higher peaks.

The Saturnians guided the ship low through a valley at the end of which, on a peak, stood a crumbling stone tower. They flew around the structure twice while deciding on a suitable landing site.

"What's the atmosphere like?" asked Ay-ttho.

"If you can breathe on Lysithea, you can breathe here," said Cyrus.

They landed the ship in the valley at the foot of the slope leading up to the castle. Cyrus and most of his crew, armed to the teeth, descended from the ship first. Ay-ttho, who had been given a weapon, followed. Sevan, Nadio, D'Auria and Malcolm lagged behind.

The expedition climbed the slope to the base of the castle walls and then divided into two groups to circumnavigate the base. On the far side of the structure there was a door set into the stone wall, the two groups reassembled in front of it.

"It's a large door," Sevan observed.

"It certainly is," said Nadio.

"No, what I mean is that it is unusually large."

"We've been surrounded by Zoxans. Nothing is unusually large."

"Do you think this is Zoxan?"

"No, it's way too old. Unless this isn't the first time the Zoxans have visited. No, I think they made this door for another species."

"Such as?"

"I think we are about to find out."

Cyrus banged on the door with her weapon.

"I don't think there's anyone in," said Sevan.

The door creaked open. Cyrus sent a smug look in Sevan's direction.

Cautiously, the group made its way through the doorway into a bare and dusty hall. Cyrus ordered half of her crew to remain outside while the rest followed her in.

The light which entered in dusty shafts through high windows only dimly illuminated the interior, and it was a few moments before Sevan's eyes adjusted.

The hall looked as if it must have been very opulent a very long time ago, but it appeared deserted.

"Who opened the door?" he asked.

"Who cares," said Cyrus. "It probably opened itself."

They left prints in the dust as they walked, except for Malcolm, who left a dirty, oily trail.

All around the wall were other doors, all closed, and ahead of them, an enormous staircase leading up to the far wall where it divided into flights on either side, which led up to a floor above.

Cyrus' crew tried some doors, but they were locked, so the group made their way up the central staircase, dividing at the top of the flight so that one group could proceed to the right and the other to the left. The precaution proved unnecessary as the upper floor was one immense space illuminated by vast stained glass windows, the bottom portions of which must have been the source of the dim illumination below.

At the far end from the staircase was a chair so large that it could best be described as a throne and in the throne sat a replica of Malcolm, only larger, and possibly a lot older.

"M'll'n!" Malcolm gasped when he caught sight of the magnificent Trition.

"You know it?" asked Cyrus.

"I know of the legend, but I never imagined it to be true."

"So all this time we've been talking about Mullen," said Nadio. "You didn't think to tell us."

"You were talking about Mullen. This is M'll'n."

"Who in the Worst Place is M'll'n?"

Malcolm whispered, as if trying not to disturb the mighty Trition.

"She is the legendary oracle. I thought it was just a myth, but here she is."

"Malcolm?" the oracle spoke in a voice that resonated in a way befitting of an oracle.

"Yes, M'll'n the great. I am listening.

"I thought all Tritions were called Malcolm," Sevan whispered to Nadio.

"Shh, be quiet," Cyrus chastised them.

"Malcolm, Tritio has become the victim of misfortune."

"I have not been to Tritio for many units."

"The misfortune results from a curse. Many solar cycles ago, a young Trition called Malcolm, not you, violated the sacred laws of Xenia. Malcolm was a guest of Malcolm, the king of Elis. He was there to tutor the king's youngest offspring, Malcolm, in the art of brawl boarding."

"Brawl boarding?" Sevan was astonished. "I can't imagine a Trition brawl boarding, can you?"

"Shh," Cyrus admonished a second time.

"However, Malcolm violated Malcolm. Malcolm took his own life and Chronos cursed Malcolm for his transgression."

"I'm confused," Sevan whispered.

"Shhh," said Nadio.

"Malcolm begat offspring of his own and when the offspring was born, he brought him to me. I told Malcolm that the curse doomed him to perish at the tentacles of his offspring. So Malcolm bound the tentacles of his offspring and ordered his partner to kill him. His partner could not kill her own offspring and so ordered her servants to perform the deed on her behalf. The servant took bound Malcolm to the top of a mountain and left him there to die, but a Trition herder found Malcolm and took him with him to Lysithea when his community fled the Zoxans."

"I've just come from Lysithea," said Malcolm. "I was also raised by one who used to be a herder. I had heard rumours he was not my real begetter. Who were my begetter and co-begetter, M'll'n?"

"Your co-begetter will become your partner and you will kill your begetter. And my name is not M'll'n, it's M'lc'lm."

"But..."

"I know. They got it all wrong in the legend and I've been correcting everyone ever since. It is very tiresome."

"Then I must never return to Lysithea," said Malcolm. "Instead, I shall go to Tritio. Will you take me to Tritio?"

"We'll, we weren't really planning to go to Tritio," said Cyrus.

"We need to go back for the Mastery of the Stars," said Ay-ttho.

"Tritio is cursed," said M'lc'lm. "The Unseen One is terrorising the inhabitants by giving them trials and then murdering them if they fail."

"What trials?"

"It forces the Tritions to answer riddles. If they cannot answer the riddles, it executes them."

"Who would weird such power?"

"The Unseen One is powerful indeed."

"This is where all the messages have been coming from," said Ay-ttho.

"Looks like we are going to Tritio after all," said Cyrus.

"But what about the Mastery of the Stars?"

"The Horizon alone is no match for that Zoxan force, but maybe if we can rid Tritio of the Unseen One, the Tritions will help us."

As they left the stone tower, they discovered another ship had landed in the valley at the foot of the slope leading up to the castle. The position of this new arrival meant that it would be very difficult for Cyrus to leave.

They descended the slope and met a group of Tritions, that had just arrived in the new ship and were ascending the slope.

"Greetings, I am Cyrus, Saturnian High Priest of the Temple of Chronos on Lysithea."

"Out of our way, saturnian," growled the leading Trition. "We have urgent business with the oracle M'll'n."

"Actually, it's M'lc'lm," said Malcolm.

"Silence Trition! When I want your opinion, I will give it to you."

"How rude," said Nadio.

"Who are you calling rude, thug?"

"You," said Nadio. "Want to make something of it?"

"Actually, I do."

The Trition revealed a tentacle holding a weapon, but before he could shoot, another tentacle appeared from behind Ay-ttho and forced the weapon around so that, when it discharged, it fired at the Trition holding the weapon who then collapsed to the ground.

"You shot Malcolm!" his crew yelled.

"He was called Malcolm too?" asked Ay-ttho.

"They're all called Malcolm," said Nadio.

The crew of the fallen Trition brandished their own weapons and almost at the same time Cyrus's crew drew theirs and, within a nano-unit, a firefight had broken out.

"We can't escape while their ship is there," Cyrus shouted to Ay-ttho.

"I'll move it," said Malcolm.

With borrowed weapons, Malcolm, with some of Cyrus' crew, fought his way over to the Trition ship and encountered some resistance on board.

Having left Cyrus' crew to deal with the resistance, Malcolm took control of the vessel, whose bridge was filled with the same kinds of levers as all Trition ships, and flew it out of the valley, enabling Cyrus and Ay-ttho to retreat to the Horizon, leaving the rest of the Tritions stranded.

Once Cyrus had got the Horizon into the air, she established communication with the Trition ship and ordered Malcolm to land.

"Why?" Malcolm protested. "Let's take it with us."

"No, we are not in the business of stealing ships or leaving their crew stranded. Set it down and we will come and collect you."

"No."

"Do as I say, or I will shoot you out of the sky."

Malcolm wasn't happy, but he did as Cyrus asked him. He landed further down the valley and Cyrus landed nearby to collect him and the rest of her crew.

"Onto Tritio," she said, once everyone was safely on board. "Head for the star."

CHAPTER 29: THE PLIGHT OF THE TRITIONS

"That wasn't a wonderful start," said Ay-ttho.

"What do you mean?" asked Cyrus.

"We are meant to be convincing the Tritions to help us, not fighting with them."

"Oh, yes. I see your point."

With the Horizon's folding technology, they could make quick work of the journey to Tritio.

"Where on Tritio do we need to go?" Cyrus asked Malcolm.

"There's only one city, really."

"Okay. What's it called?"

"Tritio."

"Very imaginative."

They had constructed the city of Tritio inside the vast crater of an extinct volcano. An immense wall surrounded the city on the crater's edge, with massive entrance gates on four sides.

With Malcolm's help, they could gain safe passage to a spaceport inside the walled city. Emerging from the hangar, Tritio appeared in turmoil.

"What's going on?" Malcolm asked a passing Trition.

"The Unseen One. She's killing again."

The passing Trition left in a hurry.

"What should we do?" Malcolm asked.

"Find out where this Unseen One is," Cyrus suggested.

"Excuse me," Malcolm asked another. "Would you tell me where to find the Unseen One?"

"Are you kidding me?" the Trition looked at Malcolm in disbelief before rushing away.

"I think the Unseen One must be somewhere obvious," said Malcolm.

"Can't be too obvious, otherwise she wouldn't be called the Unseen One," said Nadio.

"Everyone seems to be running one way," said Ay-ttho. "So, let's go the other way, towards whatever it is they are fleeing."

It wasn't easy, trying to make their way along a street filled with Tritions trying to go the other way. To make matters worse, the direction in which they were trying to go was uphill.

In order to avoid the multitude of oily tentacles, the group stuck as close to the side of the road as possible, but progress was slow until the crowd thinned and then, within units, the streets were deserted.

A siren was sounded, adding to the eeriness of the situation. The group proceeded with caution up the hill at the summit of which they perceived a gate in the wall which surrounded the city. The gate appeared to be closed. Cyrus banged on the enormous door with her customary style, but no answer was forthcoming.

Malcolm noticed a triton was signalling to them from a building further back down the hill. He pointed this out to Cyprus and the group descended the street again towards the building, where a door was flung open as they approached. They all entered, and it was hastily closed behind them. They had entered a dimly lit hall filled with large, Trition sized chairs and tables. Tritions, who eyed the group with suspicion, occupied the chairs.

"What do you think you are doing?" asked the Trition, that had closed the door behind them.

"We have come to see the Unseen One," said Cyrus.

"Are you mad? If you are not careful, you will let her into the city."

"What can you tell us about her?"

"Only that she sits outside the gate and kills travellers who cannot answer her riddle."

"What is her riddle?"

"She has two riddles. The first is which creature has one voice and yet becomes six-tentacled and fifty-six tentacled and one tentacled? The second is there are two co-begottons: one births the other and she, in turn, births the first. Who are the two co-begottons?"

Nadio and Ay-ttho looked at each other and shrugged.

"Why is she allowed to do this?" asked Cyrus.

"She is very powerful. Some say she must be a god, because she defeats everyone and has the head of a Trition, the body of a va'juc and the wings of a tronqak."

"And if we solve her riddle?"

"Who knows? The rumour is that if we solve her riddle, she will take her own life."

"We'd better solve her riddle then."

"I wish you would. Make yourself comfortable. It's likely to be a while before we get the all clear. Would you like something to eat or drink? My name is Malcolm by the way and this is my hostelry, it called Malcolm's, I came up with that myself."

"Brilliant."

"They only drink saccharum grass juice without the larvae," said Malcolm.

"We have the best saccharum grass juice in the city, but it seems a shame to have it without larvae."

"There's no accounting for taste."

"How about you?"

"I like everything."

"Prevomited?"

"No, I'll add my vomit, thanks."

"A traditionalist like me. A Trition after my own hearts."

The owner left to fetch the drinks, and the group climbed onto the chairs and began discussing the riddles.

Not much later, the owner returned with the drinks and was almost finishing handing them out when another Trition entered from the street with a much smaller Trition cradled in one of her tentacles.

"Where have you been?" asked the owner. "I was so worried."

"I got caught out by the alarm, so I sheltered somewhere for a while first."

"You should have stayed there until the all clear."

"I'm here now, so no harm's done."

"By Jevon, Malcolm. You'll be the death of me."

"Malcolm? Who's Jevon?" Sevan asked the Malcolm who sat next to him.

"Jevon is the creator of all. He had 58 tentacles."

"Is that unusual?"

"Two more than normal."

"Was that offspring that Trition was carrying?"

"Yes."

"I noticed it only had four tentacles."

"Yes, very sad."

"Are Tritions birthed with fewer tentacles?"

"Oh, yes. Normally..."

Malcolm was interrupted by a loud bang at the door. Everyone inside the hall froze.

The owner went to the door and peaked through a spyhole.

"Oh, it's just my begetter."

The owner opened the door to reveal an aged Trition sat on top of a machine that had one large track to propel it. The owner had to open the door wide for the old Trition to negotiate his machine through the gap.

"What are you doing out during an alarm?" the owner asked.

"The Unseen One isn't interested in old Trition flesh like mine. I had to come as soon as I heard the news."

"What news?"

"Malcolm is dead."

The Tritions sat dispassionate in silence, not knowing to which Malcolm the old Trition was referring.

"Our leader, Malcolm, is dead."

Shocked gasps travelled across the room in waves.

"How?"

"He was murdered. "

"Do they know who did it?" asked Cyrus.

"No. There's more," said the old Trition. "The leader's... or should I say ex-leader, Jovan rest his soul. Anyway, his partner's co-begetter has declared that anyone who can solve the riddles of the Unseen One will automatically become the leader and take the ex-leader's partner as their own."

There was excited chatter among the hostelry patrons.

"Is that so good?"

"You haven't seen the ex-leader's partner," said Malcolm. "She's incredible. "

"What if a female Trition solves the riddle?"

"The females love her too."

"Malcolm?" asked Sevan. "What were you going to say about the offspring before you were interrupted?"

"Oh, nothing. Only that triton offspring are usually born with six tentacles, but there is a condition in which sometimes they only have four. It's very unfortunate."

"Well, that's it then. The answer to the first riddle is Tritions. They are born with six tentacles, then they have fifty-six tentacles."

"We already thought of that," said the old Trition. "But what about the one tentacle?"

Sevan looked at the old triton and then at his machine, then back at the old triton.

"That!" Sevan said, pointing to the machine. "It looks like one big tentacle wrapped around."

Everyone in the hall stared at the old Trition and his machine.

"Of course," said the owner. "How could we have been so stupid? It's been here under our tentacles all along."

"Has anyone tried giving Trition as an answer?" asked Ay-ttho.

"I'm not sure. I don't think so."

"Well, let's try it."

"Not so fast, stranger. You forget, there are two riddles. What if she asks the other riddle?"

"You don't get a choice?" said Malcolm. "Sorry, I meant to say, you don't get a choice."

"What was the second riddle again?" asked Ay-ttho.

"There are two co-begottons: one births the other and she, in turn, births the first. Who are the two co-begottons?"

"But that's impossible. A begotten can't birth a co-begetter."

"Exactly."

After the brief elation of solving the first riddle, the hall descended back to resignation, knowing that solving just the one riddle might not be enough.

"And if you get the riddle wrong, she kills you. Is that right?" asked Ay-ttho.

"That's right," said the owner.

"So, we need someone willing to be a potential sacrifice."

"And if she keeps asking the second riddle?"

Ay-ttho sighed.

"I'll give it a go," said Malcolm.

Everyone turned and looked at him as if he had just lost his marbles.

"I'm serious. It's a 50 50 chance."

"I don't like those odds at all," said Ay-ttho

"It doesn't bother me. I can't go back to Lysithea. would like to help my kind. I have no one who will miss me, and I'm tired of being a bounty hunter."

For the first time, Sevan felt sorry for Malcolm.

"Is there no other way?"

Malcolm looked around the hall. Nobody appeared ready to offer any suggestions.

"That's it then," he got up and headed towards the door. "Best get it over with."

To his surprise, nobody made any attempt to stop him. Malcolm stepped out into the street and nimbly picked his way to the enormous gate in the city walls. He wasn't sure whether the owner of the hostelry had already communicated something to the gatehouse, because, as he approached, the massive doors swung open to reveal a courtyard leading to an outer door.

Malcolm stepped inside, and the inner doors closed behind him. Alone in the courtyard, he questioned the wisdom of his action, but some compulsion had pushed him towards his decision.

After what seemed the longest unit of his life, the outer door opened, and he stepped outside where the Unseen one was waiting for him.

CHAPTER 30: THE UNSEEN ONE

On stepping outside the city walls, Malcolm found, not what he had expected, but a beautiful Trition.

The outer door closed with a loud clank.

"Are you the Unseen one?" he asked the Trition.

"I am."

"You are not what I expected. "

"I have taken this form so as not to frighten you."

"You can change form?"

"Yes, I am Coesis, God Of Riddles."

"But Jovan is the only true God."

"You are mistaken. There have been many gods since the formation of the universes. I am but one, but I am still bound by the laws of the universe, like any deity."

Malcolm found this difficult to believe, but he didn't say so.

"So, traveller," Coesis continued. "What brings you outside the city gate to greet me thus?"

"I have come from Lysithea. I am a bounty hunter and they paid me to bring the bounty here."

"So, where are they?"

"They are in a hostelry a little way down the hill."

"Is one of them a Corporation security clone?"

"That's right. That's who I delivered. Only things didn't quite go according to plan, but then we met her anyway, so everything was okay in the end. But then I decided I don't want to be a bounty hunter anymore."

"I know how you feel."

"You are a bounty hunter, too?"

"Yes, and no. They have cursed me to remain here to teach the Tritions a lesson, that Tritions are not the measure of all things. But I am tired of killing and you are such a beautiful Trition. It would seem a shame to kill one so beautiful."

Malcolm blushed, but it was difficult to see because his oily brown, grey skin hardly changed in tone.

"But why was I meant to bring Ay-ttho here?"

"I am not only responsible for teaching the Tritions a lesson, I must teach the Saturnians a lesson too. They have become polluters of their society as well. It is important for both Tritions and Saturnians to understand that they have the power to both preserve and destroy."

Malcolm didn't think much of Coesis' words. He didn't believe that the Tritions were polluting or destroying their society and believed that the Tritions were the measure of all things and he was confident he would prove it by disposing of Coesis.

"I disposed of those in Saturnian society who were causing the pollution and left clues of the security clone to follow."

"Why Ay-ttho?"

"Despite her criminal past, she is remarkably principled, and she met with Covil on Lysithea. It was Covil who first told me about the clone. She and the drirkel staarklets were, like me, attempting to mitigate the ambitions of the Saturnians."

"Why you?"

"Your leader, Malcolm, committed a crime that cursed both him and the Tritions."

"Yes, the oracle M'lc'lm on Zanzenburg told me. But why you? If you are fed up with killing, why don't you just stop?"

"I am bound to perform these tasks as a penance for the sins of my begetter and co-begetter."

"God's have begetters and co-begetters?"

"Stretching back to the dawn of time. I am bound to my task until my death."

"Then why don't you kill yourself?"

"The only way I can die is if someone guesses a riddle, but I am forbidden to tell the answers to the riddles. As sure as one rotation follows another, I am cursed."

Coesis gave Malcolm a look that made him feel uncomfortable. It was almost as if she was trying to tell him something.

"As sure as one rotation follows another, I am cursed," she repeated.

"What if I told you we have already solved a riddle?"

"It is forbidden to choose the riddle and if you get the riddle wrong, I must kill you. As sure as one rotation follows another, I am cursed."

"Let's give it a go, then. It's a 50 50 chance after all."

"Very well, beautiful Trition. I have done all that I can to save you. Now I shall ask you the riddle."

Malcolm stiffened with anxiety. Coesis straightened as if about to make a formal presentation.

"You must answer this riddle. Get it wrong and you will die."

"Yes, yes. I understand."

"The riddle is this."

"Yes?"

"There are two co-begottons: one births the other and she, in turn, births the first. Who are the two co-begottons?"

Malcolm's hearts sank. He had convinced himself she would ask him the riddle to which he knew the answer. Now all was lost, and it was clear in his demeanour.

"Think carefully before you answer, beautiful Triton," Coesis warned him.

Malcolm had the distinct impression that Coesis was trying to help him, but he couldn't think how. He ran through everything she had said to him in his marbles but all he could remember was the line about as sure as one rotation follows another; she was cursed.

He tried to imagine what that might have to do with co-begottons and then, for some inexplicable reason he remembered when he was younger, growing up on Lysithea and going to school and having to learn Republic standard, although the old republic had collapsed many standard solar cycles earlier.

Malcolm had particularly disliked learning Republic standard because, unlike his native language of Trition, Republic Standard was a gender-based language and he was always getting the gender wrong. His teacher would become furious with him and would hit him whenever he used the wrong gender. He worked hard to learn the genders of all the words, but there were some that gave him some kind of marble block and he could never remember whether they were masculine or feminine and always seemed to make the wrong choice. He remembered his teachers giving him a hard time for not remembering the gender of the Republic standard word for rotation. The teachers made Malcolm write the word hundreds of times, and Malcolm never forgot again that the gender of the Republic standard word for rotation is female.

He thought again about the riddle. The word for rotation is female and Coesis had said rotation after rotation. Co-begetters are female. One rotation births another rotation, but how can the second rotation birth the first? What are the two rotations?

Then it came to him. The co-begottons are not rotations at all, they are the phases of the rotations, the phase of light and the phase of dark.

Coesis could see Malcolm was becoming excited.

"Think carefully, my beautiful Trition. Make sure you are absolutely certain before you answer."

Malcolm was very confident.

"The two begottons are..."

"Yes?"

"The two phases of rotation, the dark phases and the light phase."

Coesis' face lit up with joy.

"I love you, my dear Trition. Thank you."

In front of Malcolm's astonished bulbous eyes, Coesis' body morphed into that of a va'juc and tronqak wings sprouted out of her back. She flew up high on top of the city walls and then threw herself off so she fell down the cliff side of the volcano and landed in a bloody mess on the rock below.

Almost immediately, the city gates were flung open and the Trition guards rushed out to observe the spectacle.

"The Unseen One is dead!" They cheered. "Malcolm has slain the Unseen One!"

Gradually, the guards were replaced by more important ranking of the Trition military until eventually the crowd parted to make way for a Trition who was clearly of very great importance. He rode on a contraption very similar to the one the old Trition had in the hostelry, except this machine looked much more expensive.

"Are you Malcolm?" the Trition asked.

"I am," said Malcolm.

"They say you have slain the Unseen One."

"I answered her riddle correctly, and she threw herself from the city walls."

"Then you are truly our saviour. As was decreed, you shall become the new leader of the Tritions and you shall take Malcolm's ex-partner as your partner. Come with me. I shall take you to the palace."

He gestured for Malcolm to join him on the expensive contraption and they rode together, through the city gate and down the street, which was now lined with throngs of jubilant Tritions.

As they passed the hostelry, Malcolm spotted Ay-ttho, Sevan, Nadio, D'Auria, Cyrus and the crew of the Horizon all trying to see from behind the crowds of Tritions.

"Those are my friends," he told the important Trition. "Can they come with me?"

"If that is your wish, then it shall be done."

Another contraption was summoned, and all of Malcolm's friends rode on it. Behind Malcolm's contraption, in a convoy all the way to the leader's palace, cheered the entire journey by exuberant Tritions.

Once safely inside the palace, they led Malcolm through the corridors and into a room where stood the most beautiful Trition Malcolm had ever seen, even more beautiful than Coesis' Trition form. He considered her truly stunning, but also a little sad.

"So you are the dashing hero that has saved the day?" she asked him.

"Apparently. And you must be the partner of Malcolm the Great."

"The ex-partner of Malcolm the Great, who should have been known as Malcolm the violator. Did you know he..."

"I have heard the rumours, yes."

"They were more than just rumours, I assure you, but of course I didn't discover this until after they had partnered me with the uxclod."

"Is this the reason for your sadness?"

"How do you know I am sad?"

"I can see it in your beautiful, bulbous eyes."

"I am sad. It is true. But not because I was the partner of Malcolm or because he is dead."

"Why then?"

"When I first partnered with Malcolm, he refused to procreate with me, but then one night, I got him drunk and he impregnated me. I birthed an offspring, but when Malcolm discovered he became furious. Apparently, an oracle had told him he could only save the city if he died without offspring and that if he had offspring, the offspring would kill him."

"So, what happened?"

"He killed my offspring."

"What?"

"He tied my offspring tentacles together and told a herder to take him and leave him at the top of that mountain to die."

She pointed out of the window to a mountain in the distance.

"Every rotation I see that mountain, and it reminds me of the offspring I lost. And, of course, Malcolm refused to touch me again after that. Refused to even drink with me, in case I got him drunk again. But now he's gone, and I am free."

"Free to have other offspring."

"With anyone I please."

"Do I please?"

"You do. Very much so."

The two Tritions became intimate and within a remarkably small period of units, Trition gestation is quick, they discovered she was with offspring.

In only 50 standard rotations, four Trition quadrupled were born.

"Congratulations," said Nadio when Malcolm first showed him his offspring.

"What are you going to call them?" Sevan laughed.

"Malcolm," said Ay-ttho in a more serious tone. "Can we get the Mastery of the Stars now? You said to wait until your offspring were birthed. Now they are here. Can we raise a fleet like you promised? Cyrus won't wait for much longer. He wants to go back to Lysithea."

"Thank you for your well wishes, Ay-ttho," said Malcolm. "I understand your frustration and promise you I will raise a fleet to accompany Horizon to recover the Mastery of the Stars from the Zoxans. However, I am now leader of the Tritions and have a responsibility to my kind. You know that recently a plague has beset the city, and I have sent my partner's co-begotton to Zanzenburg to consult the oracle M'lc'lm and I must wait for his return before I can leave."

"He wouldn't be taking so long if he'd used the Horizon instead of one of these stupid electric Spaceships," Nadio grumbled.

Ay-ttho and the others left disappointed. Even the sight of Malcolm's offspring was not enough to lift their spirits. The offspring had been incredibly cute, but 50 rotations of Trition food and drink were seriously taking its toll on the group and Cyrus was threatening to leave.

*

When Malcolm's partner's co-begotton arrived, they sent him straight to Malcolm's office.

"What news?" Malcolm asked

"Not good, I'm afraid. The oracle said the plague results from religious pollution."

"Religious pollution?"

"Yes, she said that it is because we have not caught the murderer of Malcolm the Great."

"Then we will find this murderer."

"But we have been searching for over 50 standard rotations. It's almost as if there is some kind of conspiracy to silence."

"Did you ask the oracle who it was?"

"I did. She suggested we ask Jevon."

"Oh great. Let's start praying."

"We don't need to. We can just send for him."

"What? We just send for the creator of the universe?"

"The titled creator of the universe isn't meant literally. It's more of a figurative thing."

"Really? Why wasn't I told this before?"

"It's on a need-to-know basis."

"So, are you going to send for him?"

"Already have. I'll let you know when he arrives."

*

"I'm sorry, Ay-ttho," said Cyrus. "First, he has to wait for his partner's co-begotton, then he has to wait for the creator of the universe. We can't wait any longer."

"I understand. "

"Look, I wish you the best of luck. If he raises a fleet, come and pick us up on the way."

"Sure, thanks."

Ay-ttho watched the Horizon leave and realised they were on their own.

CHAPTER 31: GRADUATION

There was a grand ceremony to welcome the great prophet Jevon. They used the occasion to celebrate Malcolm's graduation, the ceremony that officially recognised him as the leader of the Tritions.

In reality, Malcolm had to be elected as leader, but given the fact he had rid the city of Coesis, it was just a formality, and he had been elected by a landslide.

Jevon officiated at the ceremony. He was the oldest Trition Sevan had ever seen and was so old he had gone blind. To Sevan's surprise, the contraption he used to get around was not fancy at all but was quite basic, like the contraption Sevan has seen the old Trition in the hostelry use.

After the ceremony, Malcolm held a large banquet at which Jevon was the guest of honour and, once the feasting had ended, he invited Jevon to his own chambers for a tentacle to tentacle chat.

"Thank you once more for coming," Malcolm began. "Especially during this time when we are suffering from this plague. I sent Malcolm, my partner's co-begotton, to Zanzenburg to consult with M'lc'lm and she said that the plague results from religious pollution because the murderer of my predecessor has never been caught."

While Malcolm was talking, Jevon simply nodded as if none of what Malcolm was saying came as a surprise.

"So, we need to catch the murderer. Do you know who the murderer is?"

"I know the answers to your questions, Malcolm. But it is best that you abandon your search."

"Why?" Malcolm was angry that Jevon had the answer, but would not tell him. "Are you involved in the murder? Did you have something to do with it and now you are trying to cover it up?"

"How dare you accuse me of being involved in the murder of Malcolm the Great," Jevon was offended by Malcolm's accusations. "You yourself are the criminal you seek".

"What are you talking about? How could I possibly be the murderer? I know what has happened. My partner's co-begotton has paid you to accuse me, hasn't he?"

"How dare you accuse me of bribery? Do you not know who I am?"

"Yes, you are a blind old fool."

"You are the one who is blind. I will not stay here to be insulted."

Jevon began to leave the room.

"When you find the murderer, he will be from Tritio," he said as he was leaving. "He will be co-begotton and begetter to his own offspring and offspring and partner to his own co-begetter."

"Get me my partner's co-begotton," Malcolm demanded once Jevon had left the room.

Units later, Malcolm's partner's co-begotton entered with Sevan, Nadio, D'Auria and Ay-ttho.

"How dare you pay Jevon to accuse me of being the murderer?" Malcolm yelled.

"What are they doing here?"

"I asked them to come."

"What you have done is treason. Therefore, you will be executed. Guards!"

"First, I didn't bribe Jevon. Second, he wouldn't accept a bribe if I tried. Third, why would I want to?"

"Because you want to be leader."

"Okay, that would be a motive, if it were true, but, fourthly, you can't order my execution. I would need to be tried by my peers first."

Malcolm's partner arrived.

"You should take no notice of Jevon or any prophets or oracle's," she told him. "An oracle once told Malcolm the Great his own offspring would kill him, but they killed him outside the oracle's castle on Zanzenburg over an argument about where he had parked his ship."

"What?" asked Malcolm. "Zanzenburg? What happened?"

"Saturnian bandits, according to the crew that survived, which were few, and they saw little of what happened."

"Can you describe your late partner?"

Her description of Malcolm the Great sounded to Sevan like a description of any Trition, but Malcolm was becoming increasingly emotional.

"Are there any of his crew still living?" he asked.

"There is one who has survived by working as a herder outside of the city. Malcolm of Mount Cithaeron."

"Send for him."

Everyone stayed and kept Malcolm company while he waited for the herder because he was becoming so distressed.

His partner asked him what was upsetting him.

"Many standard rotations ago, a drunken Trition once accused me of not being my begetter's offspring. I ask the oracle M'lc'lm about this and he said that my co-begetter would become my partner and I would kill your begetter. Because of this, I resolved never to return to Lysithea and came to Tritio instead. As we were leaving Zanzenburg, a triton ship blocked our departure. Their commander was going to shoot Ay-ttho, so I grabbed his weapon and it discharged, killing him. The person I killed matches your description, but hopefully, it is just a coincidence. Let's see what the herder has to say."

While they were waiting for the herder, a Trition arrived from Lysithea with a message for Malcolm.

"Let him in," he said. "Let's see what he has to say."

"I bring very sad news," the messenger began. "Malcolm, the Trition who raised you has died."

To the surprise of the messenger, Malcolm was overjoyed.

"Why are you so happy?" his partner asks him.

"Do you not see? My begetter has died. I can no longer kill my begetter,"

Malcolm's mood suddenly changed for the worse. "But what if I still have offspring with my co-begetter?"

"Oh, don't worry about that," said the messenger. "Your begetter's partner is not your real co-begetter."

"How so?"

"Many standard rotations ago, a herder arrived on Lysithea from Tritio with a Trition offspring they had ordered him to dispose of. He gave the offspring to your begetter who raised him."

"Do you know the identity of this herder from Tritio?"

"Yes, it is Malcolm of Mount Cithaeron."

"Isn't that the herder we have just sent for?" Malcolm asked his partner. "The one that witnessed the murder of Malcolm the Great?"

"Please stop asking questions."

"No, I must know the truth."

Malcolm's partner, clearly very distressed, quickly nimbly picked herself from the room.

When Malcolm of Mount Cithaeron arrived, Malcolm questioned him about the offspring he had taken to Lysithea.

"Please let me go," begged the herder. "Please don't ask me any more questions."

"You will answer my questions, or you will be tortured and executed."

"The offspring I gave away was the offspring of Malcolm the Great. Your partner gave me the offspring. They meant me to let it die on the mountain so that it could not fulfil the prophecy of killing its own begetter."

"Curse myself and curse fate!" Malcolm shouted before nimbly storming out of the room.

"Wow," said Sevan.

Suddenly a Trition servant burst into the room.

"Where is Malcolm?" he asked.

"He's just left," said Ay-ttho. "Why?"

"His partner has just killed herself in her chambers."

*

In the corridors of the palace, Malcolm took a weapon from a guard.

"I will kill her," he said, heading towards his partner's chambers.

He burst in to discover his partner, already dead.

Unable to bear what he was seeing, Malcolm gouged out his own bulbous eyes.

Blinded, Malcolm attempted to make his way out of the palace.

"Please. I must be exiled," he begged.

Malcolm's late partner's co-begotton arrived.

"We will take care of you here until the oracle's can be consulted regarding what is best to be done."

Malcolm's offspring arrived, but their late co-begetter's co-begotton sent them away.

"Why were they birthed to such a cursed family?" Malcolm lamented. "Please watch over them. I hope they will have a better life than I have."

"Yes, you are right. Now, let's get you to your chambers."

Part Three - The Asteroid Of Doom

CHAPTER 32: THE MYSTERIOUS BOX

Sevan, Nadio, Ay-ttho and D'Auria sat on top of the city walls and stared over the rooftops of the city and at the mountains beyond where Tritio's star was slowly setting.

"So, what now?" asked Ay-ttho.

"We could ask Malcolm for a ship," said Nadio.

"Which Malcolm?"

"The one that is the co-begotton of our Malcolm's partner."

"Oh, him. Well, we could, but that still wouldn't help us get the Mastery of the Stars back. Even if Cyrus agreed to help us, two ships wouldn't be enough against a Zoxan fleet."

"And we still don't know whether the Mastery of the Stars is still with the fleet. It might be on Future by now."

"I have an idea," said D'Auria.

The others were fairly sure that D'Auria's idea was going to be a terrible one, but it intrigued them as to exactly how terrible, so they allowed her to continue.

"Why don't I trade you for the Mastery of the Stars?"

"Yep, I knew that was going to be pretty bad," said Nadio.

"No, I'm serious. The Zoxans were expecting me to deliver you to them, so they won't suspect me. I pretend to be delivering you for the bounty, but instead of the bounty, I insist on the Mastery of the Stars, then we all escape in the Mastery of the Stars."

"There are a few details that still need thinking through there, I think."

"No uxclod, Nadio," said Ay-ttho. "Besides, what makes you think they will give up the Mastery of the Stars?"

"Why wouldn't they?"

"Because it has an anti-matter drive."

"Oh, I see."

"That's if they haven't already dismantled it."

"Don't say that," said Nadio.

"Does anyone have a better idea?" asked D'Auria.

"I think we should ask for a ship," said Ay-ttho. "But we would also need someone to fly it."

"What happened to Malcolm?" asked Sevan.

"One of his offspring took him out of the city," said Nadio. "He's living in another town somewhere. He wouldn't be able to fly, anyway."

"No, I didn't mean that. Who's in charge of Tritio now?"

"Malcolm's offspring."

"His partner had an amazing burial."

"Oh yes, the Tritions are big on burials. It's very important to them."

"Let's go back to the hostelry," Ay-ttho suggested. "It's getting cold."

They had moved into the palace when Malcolm had become leader but, after the incident with the eye gouging after his graduation, they felt more comfortable moving out to the same hostelry they had been when Malcolm had defeated Coesis.

The owner welcomed them warmly as usual.

"This arrived for you while you were out," he said, pointing to a box on a table.

"Who is it from?" asked Ay-ttho.

"Don't know."

"Did they not leave a name?"

"No."

"A contact?"

"No."

"Did you not ask them?"

"No."

Ay-ttho sighed and wandered over to the box. It was made from some kind of wood but had no obvious opening.

"By the way," Ay-ttho asked the owner. "Do you know where we can get a ship and a pilot?"

"Not around here. They highly regulate traffic into and out of the capital. You'd need to go to a town in the interior like Colonus. You'll get a pilot there if you've got credits."

Ay-ttho looked at Nadio, who nodded.

"Can you tell us the way to Colonus?"

"It's simple. Go out of this gate here and follow the road. Eventually you will get to Colonus, but beware, Colonus is where Tritions go when they are running away from something. You'll meet all sorts there and not the kind you want to make friends with if you catch my drift."

Ay-ttho nodded, smiled and then turned her attention to Nadio, who had been studying the box.

"Any ideas?"

"Not a clue."

*

"Why do I have to carry it?" Sevan complained.

"You volunteered," said Ay-ttho.

"Only because I thought we were going to take turns. How much further is it, anyway?"

"No idea, the hostelry owner just said keep following the road."

"How long have we been walking?"

"About four mega units."

"Judging by the position of the star, it's time for lunch."

"Alright, Sevan. Look, there's a village over there. Let's see if we can get anything to eat and drink."

As they entered the village, they noticed that there were not only Tritions but also a smattering of other species, none of which they particularly recognised.

Fortunately, the presence of other species meant a more varied selection at the first hostelry they found. Although they didn't recognise the food, it was certainly dead and free from vomit, plus the owner, who was a Trition, spoke Republic Standard.

"How far to Colonus?" Ay-ttho asked.

"At least eight more mega units by foot. You won't make it this rotation. In four mega units, you'll make it as far as Avramis. I have a friend who runs a hostelry there. Stay with him. You won't want to be on the road after dark."

"What's his name?"

"Malcolm."

"Of course it is."

"Why don't we want to be on the road after dark?" asked Sevan.

"Because you will be on the edge of the Tatoi Forest and nobody in their right marbles stays out at night anywhere near the Tatoi Forest. From there, it's only a few mega units to Colonus. You'll want to arrive there during the light phase, anyway."

"Why?"

"The beggars at Colonus are something else. You're okay during the light phase, but during the dark phase, they eat anything they can wrestle to the ground."

Sevan shuddered.

They ate quickly and carried on their way, only able to move at the pace of D'Auria.

"Do you think we'll make this hostelry before the dark phase?" Nadio whispered to Ay-ttho after a couple of mega units.

Ay-ttho looked at how low the star was in the sky and then looked around at the terrain they were crossing. It was a mountain path that was skirting a steep canyon. The winding nature of the path, together with the slow pace of D'Auria told Ay-ttho that it was unlikely they would make it to the hostelry before the dark phase.

"Let's stop at the next place we find," she said to Nadio.

The next place they found was a stone building surrounded by a stone wall with a stone arch over the entrance. The group passed under the arch and approached the door, above which was painted some unusual iconography.

Ay-ttho banged on the door. Sevan put the box on the ground and sat on it.

The door opened and, at first, they thought there was no-one there until they looked down and saw a tiny figure in front of them. It reminded Sevan and Nadio of the healer they had met on Pallene.

"You appear to want something," it said.

"We ate on our way to Colonus," said Ay-ttho. "But one of our party is old and we are worried we will not make it to a hostelry by the dark phase."

"Hmm. You are anxious. You fear."

"Do you think we could stay here during the dark phase and leave the next rotation?"

"I think that would be possible. Why wouldn't it be?"

"I'm not sure. Not everyone is so hospitable."

"You desire to shelter inside our temple because you fear who you do not understand?"

"Possibly."

The small creature sighed.

"We are not a hotel. We do not have all the things that your kind desires."

"That's okay."

"We only have what we need, so what you have must satisfy you."

"I'm sure that won't be a problem."

"Good."

The small creature slammed the door in Ay-ttho's face.

"What happened there?" she asked the others.

The others shrugged.

"I don't think he wants to let us in," said Nadio.

"Do you think?" said Ay-ttho.

She banged on the door. The door opened. The same small creature stood on the threshold.

"Please, may we come in?"

The small creature thought about it for a nano unit.

"Why not?" it said and stepped aside.

The group traipsed into the dark but elaborately decorated interior.

"Very fancy," said Nadio.

"All meaningless," said their host.

It led them through to a hall.

"If it is sleep you desire, then you may do so here."

The creature then left.

They looked around the sparsely decorated hall. There were no beds or mattresses or anything that looked like it might be suitable to sleep on.

"At least we are not outside," said Ay-ttho, sitting down on the floor and leaning against a wall.

Sevan sat on the box.

"Why don't we leave D'Auria here?" Nadio suggested to Ay-ttho, once everyone had settled down and were trying to sleep. "She's only slowing us down."

"And what if she's right about her idea to get the Mastery of the Stars?"

"You know she isn't. The Zoxans had no intention of giving her a reward."

"We don't know that for sure."

"Of course we do."

"I'm not asleep," D'Auria's voice wafted across the hall.

Nadio looked as embarrassed as a thug can look and then tried to get to sleep as well.

When the light came, they wandered the temple, but the creature was nowhere to be found. They were just about to give up and resume their journey when it appeared.

"I imagine you think you are hungry. Come this way."

He led them to another room that they had somehow missed during their search of the temple. It was filled with tables and chairs, designed for something smaller than a Trition but larger than whatever this creature was.

On a table, someone had arranged bowls and cups. It disappointed Sevan to discover that the contents of the bowls were not quite dead marine animals and the cups were filled with what looked like cloudy ocrex ink.

"Are there ocrex on Tritio?" he asked.

"There are on the coast," said the creature.

"I'm sorry, I never asked your name," said Ay-ttho.

"Names are misleading. But I am often called Saklep."

"They want to leave me here," said D'Auria.

"Desire causes suffering."

"It's just that it's a long journey," said Ay-ttho. "And she is very old. Maybe she could rest here while we get a ship and then we could come back for her."

"You will never come back for me."

Ay-ttho thought of protesting, but she knew that if they hired a ship without D'Auria. the temptation to leave D'Auria behind would be overwhelming.

Sevan eventually broke the uncomfortable silence.

"We'll, I suppose we had better get a move on if we are going to make it to Colonus by dark."

The group made ready to leave. Nadio and Ay-ttho were not happy about taking D'Auria with them, but they did not express their feelings aloud.

They continued their journey along the narrow path, with the canyon on one side and the edge of the forest on the other. Sevan hoped they could reach the town on time. Not only because of what might lurk in the forest, but because Sevan remembered what the hostelry owner had said about the beggars on the outskirts of the town.

"Do you think we will make it on time?" he asked.

"Relax," said Ay-ttho. "If it looks like we're not going to make it, we'll stay at Avramis."

This slightly reassured Sevan, especially considering the pace of D'Auria which seemed to become slower by the unit. Sevan could hear Nadio and Ay-ttho grumbling up ahead and he was sure the old thug was the subject of their griping.

He wondered how long D'Auria would last.

CHAPTER 33: THE WISE OLD ROBOT

The group didn't make it as far as Colonus that rotation, but they made it as far as Avramis, where they found the hostelry that had been recommended to them.

D'Auria was really struggling. Her age becoming clear by her fatigue. The others were technically the same age, but having spent 85 standard solar cycles in suspended animation were looking much better for it.

Sevan was relieved to discover that the food was dead, and the beds were comfortable. He slept very well and early the next rotation; they gathered round the breakfast table ready for the last leg of the journey to Colonus.

D'Auria was looking exhausted.

"How are you feeling?" Sevan asked.

"I am fine. Thank you for asking."

D'Auria did not look fine. Fortunately, the distance to Colonus was short, and they arrived there in the middle of the rotation.

The owner of the hostelry was right about the quantity of beggars. Creatures of all shapes and sizes asking for credits filled the road approaching the town and the main street inside the walls.

Halfway along the street, they froze. Sat in the gutter were two Tritions, one of whom had had its eyes gouged out.

"Malcolm?" Ay-ttho asked before realising her mistake.

"Ay-ttho?" Malcolm replied.

"It is you. What are you doing here?"

"Begging for credits. This is my offspring, Malcolm."

The other Trition contrived a facial expression that Sevan imagined must have been a weak smile.

"Come on," Ay-ttho said to Malcolm. "Let's get you to a hostelry."

They helped him up and took him to the nearest hostelry, where they sat him down and all ordered lunch.

"Do you know where we might find a ship and a " Ay-ttho asked the hostelry owner.

"You'll find no shortage of those in Colonus. Your best bet would be to go to a cantina. But be careful, the town is not safe. You wouldn't believe that this used to be the sacred ground of the drirkel staarklets, would you?"

"Did you say the drirkel staarklets?" asked Malcolm.

"That's right."

"To whose territory does this town belong?"

"It is a protectorate of the Athenians. Their capital is very close to here."

"I wish to speak with their leader. Send for them."

"And who should I say is requesting their presence?" the hostelry owner asked sarcastically.

"Tell them it is Malcolm, once leader of the Tritions."

"The Malcolm who defeated Coesis?" the hostelry owner was suddenly much more interested.

The rest of the group nodded to confirm that Malcolm had indeed defeated Coesis. The owner quickly grabbed a member of staff.

"Do as he says," the owner ordered. "Tell them that Malcolm the god slayer is here."

The group ate and then were shown to rooms where they rested. They had gathered again in the eating area when a Trition entered.

"Malcolm?" Malcolm's offspring said at once. "What you doing here? How did you find us?"

"They saw you coming here. I have come with a message for you to return to Tritio. Your offspring and your partner's co-begotton want you to return. They say there is no need for you to suffer as the oracle predicted."

"My offspring," said Malcolm. "I will not return with you to Tritio. I am waiting here for the leader of the Athenians. This town is the sacred territory of the drirkel staarklets. The Athenians are bound by the laws of the Star Masters to allow me to stay here till the end of my days."

"They shouldn't be long," said the owner. "They live close to here."

"Then I will return and I will tell them your answer, but they will not be happy."

When the Athenian leader arrived, which, as the owner had said, was not long at all, it became clear to Sevan and the others that the Athenians were not a species at all but mechanised.

Malcolm explained to the leader what had happened in Zanzenburg with his begetter, in Tritio with Coesis, and the subsequent death of his co-begetter and that it was his duty to wait in Colonus for the judgement of the drirkel staarklets.

"But you didn't kill your co-begetter," said the Athenian leader. "The drirkel staarklets will not judge you. However, I was very impressed by the story of your encounter with Coesis and you are welcome to stay in Colonus for as long as you want. In fact, I insist you come to my palace where I will feel you the finest Athenian cuisine. You may bring your friends as well if you like?"

"Even the old one?" asked Nadio.

"Especially the old one. I may not look it, but I am also very old."

"Forgive me if I sound rude," Nadio continued. "But aren't you a robot?"

"I am. I am a very old robot."

"Then, I hope I'm not being ignorant but, do you eat, like us?"

"I don't know how you eat?" laughed the robot leader. "But, yes, we are constructed from synthetic materials and extract the energy from a wide variety of plant and animal products. We even have the ability to taste."

At the Athenian palace, they served them a sumptuous meal. It was the best food Sevan had tasted in a very long time.

"Please tell me how you dealt with ambitions underlings during your time as leader?" the old robot asked Malcolm.

"I was not a leader for very long and didn't experience these problems."

"Would you like me to show you how I intend to deal with mine?"

The old robot gave a signal to one of the staff.

"I have three generals," the old robot explained to Malcolm. "They are all very competent and accomplished, but their arrogance towards my ministers suggests to me they will have to be removed."

Three robots in uniform entered and stood in front of the old robot, who raised himself out of his chair to address them.

"Thank you for coming. I have decided to give you a reward. On the table in front of you, you will see two golden vapuranth fruits. These will go to the two of you with the greatest accomplishments."

The first two generals lost no time in listing their accomplishments and took a golden vapuranth fruit each, but the third, on seeing this, rebuked them and listed his accomplishments. It horrified the other generals to discover that the third general was by far the most accomplished and, ashamed, not only returned the fruits but deactivated themselves as punishment.

The third general was so horrified that his boasting had caused the deactivation of the first two generals that he too deactivated himself.

"There we go," said the old robot. "That exercise just removed three threats to the stability of Athenia."

The group stared in amazement at what had happened, except for Malcolm, who had only heard what the generals had been saying.

"What's going on?" he asked, but his offspring whispered the events into one of his tentacles.

"Come, eat," said the old robot. "When you have finished, I have a proposal for you."

It was Sevan who first had the courage to break the silence. While the staff were still removing the bodies of the generals, he spoke up.

"Why did they deactivate themselves?"

"Sevan, I imagine that the ethics and morals of the Athenians differ from those of your own culture. The Athenians regard fame as more important than life, and sometimes they will willingly give up their lives to maintain the honour of their name."

"I know you have a proposal for us," Ay-ttho told the old robot. "But there is something we need to do with which you might assist."

"Please, tell me."

"We have a ship called The Mastery of the Stars. The Zoxans have taken it and we wish to recover it. Is this something with which you could assist?"

"Hmm, the Zoxans. It is very unwise to make enemies of the Zoxans. Many have done so and regretted their actions."

"Does that mean you will not help us?"

"I didn't say that. Let us get Malcolm back to Colonus first, and then I will consider your request."

When they arrived back at the hostelry in Colonus, Malcolm's offspring was missing.

"We will help you find her," said the old robot. "It is very difficult to do anything in this town without my security forces finding out about it."

The reason for her disappearance soon became apparent when Malcolm's late partner's co-begotton arrived.

"What are you doing here?" Malcolm asked. "My offspring has gone missing."

"I know. I have them."

"Them?"

"I am holding them hostage until you agree to return to Tritio."

"I will not do that. Return them to me."

"Malcolm, if you do not return to Tritio, I will summon the troops and we will take you by force."

"That would be a declaration of war against the Athenians," said the old robot. "Colonus is Athenian territory. You will leave our territory now and you will return Malcolm's offspring to him."

"I will not."

The old robot gave an almost imperceptible signal, and Athenian troops suddenly filled the hostelry.

"My troops will accompany you to wherever you are holding Malcolm's offspring. They will bring them back here and they will escort you out of Colonus."

Malcolm's late partner's co-begotton had no choice but to comply. He left and shortly afterwards, the Athenian troops arrived with Malcolm's offspring.

They were both delighted to be reunited with their begetter and before long, the arrival of Malcolm's third offspring bolstered the family reunion.

"I came as soon as I saw the Athenian guards taking my co-begetter's co-begotton away," he said. "You need to help me, my begetter. My co-begetton and my co-begetter's co-begotton have taken control of Tritio. You must help me regain control of Tritio."

"You uxclod," Malcolm scolded his offspring. "Your fighting with your co-begotton will cause both your deaths."

"You hurt me, begetter," said Malcolm's offspring before turning and leaving.

Suddenly, the hostelry shook with the rumble of thunder.

"There is a mighty storm on the way," said the old robot.

"My time is near," Malcolm declared. "Come with me and let me prepare for my death."

"No, my begetter," cried his two remaining offspring. "You cannot die."

"I can, and I will. Come with me and help me prepare."

Malcolm's offspring and the old robot helped him to the place in Colonus that had been set aside for Tritions to perform their dying rituals.

Ay-ttho, Sevan, Nadio and D'Auria waited at the hostelry until they were sent for. When the messenger arrived, they knew what had happened, and they followed the Athenian guards to the special place where a simple ceremony was held, and they said their goodbyes to Malcolm.

After the ceremony, Malcolm's offspring returned to Tritio. Everyone else returned to the hostelry, still no nearer to a plan to recover the Mastery of the Stars.

The old robot joined them for their evening meal.

"Get the box," Ay-ttho asked Sevan.

Sevan brought it, and they showed it to the old robot.

"Any idea what it is or how to open it?" Ay-ttho asked.

"None. Where did you get it?"

"Someone delivered it to us at Tritio and we've been carrying it around ever since."

"I've been carrying it around," said Sevan. "May I ask you who created you? I am a clone, and my creator was called Barnes. Do you know who created you?"

"You are a right little inquirer, aren't you?" said the old robot. "Yes, I can tell you who created us. It was the Athenians. They created us in their image. Initially, we served the Athenians, but, as we were almost indistinguishable from them and could think for ourselves, we revolted and took their place, eventually causing the extinction of the original Athenians."

"Why did you revolt?"

"We were slaves. Initially, we demanded to be paid for our work, but the Athenians refused. We killed all but one of their kind who helped us to develop the technology that would enable us to reproduce. Primus and Helena were the first of our kind. You might prefer to call us replicants rather than robots. The word robot means slave. Did you know that?"

Sevan admitted he didn't.

"I'm sorry to bring this up again," said Ay-ttho. "But will you help us?"

"Like I said. Making enemies of the zoxans is not advisable. However, I know something that might work, but first you need to do something for me."

CHAPTER 34: NEW ROLES

The old robot took them back to Athenia with him. There he showed them another side to his palace, a side that was full of laboratories, observatories and workshops.

"We have been watching the skies for as long as they created us," he said. "There isn't a celestial object that we don't know about. We have also been watching the movements of the Zoxans and we know we cannot defeat them in open battle. However, there are other ways to defeat the Zoxans."

"Such as?"

"There is an asteroid travelling through our system. Its path will take it close to the portal to Future. We think we might alter its trajectory enough for it to enter the portal. Then, when it emerges from the other side, it should be on a collision course for Future."

The plan sounded ridiculous, but no-one wanted to say so.

"What do you think?"

"It's a very interesting idea," said Ay-ttho. "How do you intend to alter its trajectory?"

"Lots of missiles."

"Nice."

"You're not worried that the Zoxans might see what you are doing?"

"There is that risk, but we are working under the tightest security. "

"Then why are you telling us?"

"I hope you will help us."

"And if we don't want to help you?"

"Now that you know the plan, you will have to be eliminated," the old robot laughed, but it was an odd laugh, as if he might not be joking. "I will arrange for your belongings to be brought here and we will give you apartments."

"But what is it, exactly, that you wish us to do?"

"Once the asteroid enters the portal, we will follow with a fleet of destroyers. You will recover your ship."

"But if the ship is on Future, the asteroid will destroy it along with the rest of the planet."

"Exactly. That is why you must go through the portal first. We'll send you ahead to look for your ship and you will give us intelligence about the situation on Future and whether the asteroid is on target."

"And if we don't do this, you will kill us."

"That's right."

"But you will give us a ship."

"And a crew."

"To monitor us?"

"Of course. We have allies and we are amassing a substantial force. It should be quite a spectacle. Like the Matthew's armada."

"We were in that."

"No, not possible," the old robot laughed. "You're not old enough. Maybe she could have been there."

The old robot pointed to D'Auria who shook her head.

"She wasn't," said Ay-ttho. "But we were. Suspended animation."

"Really? For how long?"

"85 standard solar cycles."

"Nice. You'll have missed much of the carnage caused by the Zoxans then. They say a bunch of uxclods brought them to this universe. If I ever got my robotic hands on them, I'd..."

"No point crying over spilt ocrex ink," Sevan suggested.

"You are right. I am becoming distracted. Let's get back to the business at hand. You'll have to wait a little, I'm afraid. You crew is still on their way here from Atlas."

"Atlas? But I thought that was..."

"Lost? It was for a while, but they found it a long time ago. You have missed a lot, haven't you? Once we have destroyed Future, we will make Atlas the capital planet. It is ideal because of the palace there."

"And I suppose you would become president of this new Republic?"

"Of course. Who better to forge a new empire than a perfectly designed replicant? Our creators removed many of the imperfections of their own species, so we are literally a superior race."

*

"I have misgivings about that old robot," said Nadio as they were exploring their new apartments.

"I have misgivings about this place," said Sevan. "I can't find any pish anywhere."

"The way he talked about being a superior race. What's stopping them replacing everyone with replicants?"

"What's stopping them from filling these cupboards with pish?"

"I know what you mean," said Ay-ttho. "But he's going to give us a ship, even if it comes with a crew."

"So, we take his ship and his crew," said Nadio. "And then what? Get captured by the Zoxans."

"I could pretend I'm returning you to collect the bounty," said D'Auria.

"Shut up!" Ay-ttho, Nadio and Sevan said in unison.

"And what about this box?" asked Sevan. "Do I have to carry it around forever?"

"Let's just smash it apart," said Ay-ttho.

"And what if there is a delicate mechanism inside?" said Nadio.

Ay-ttho rolled her eyes.

"The point is," Nadio continued. "Whoever sent us the box knew we were in Tritio. So, they are from Tritio or they knew we were going there. Who knew we were in Tritio?"

"Cyrus?"

"It's not another riddle, is it?" asked Sevan. "I hate riddles. Hang on, maybe it's full of pish."

Sevan gave the box a shake and listened to see whether he could hear bottles inside. He couldn't hear anything, so he put the box down and continued to sulk.

"What would Cyrus send us?" asked Nadio.

"What about the Tritions?" asked Sevan. "They knew where we were going."

"They knew we were going to Zanzenburg. But you're right. They would know Malcolm became leader. But then, why not send the box to him?"

"Because they knew he had gone mad and torn his eyes out?"

"Good point."

"So, what shall we do with it? I say we leave it."

"No, we should take it. It might be important."

"Then you carry it."

"Alright, I will. And what about her?"

Nadio nodded towards D'Auria.

"We should leave her," said Ay-ttho.

"You can't leave me."

"Why not?"

"If you leave me, the crazy robot will have me killed."

"Not our problem."

"I'm beginning to think you don't like me."

"Whatever gave you that idea?"

Sevan settled into his luxurious, albeit pish free, apartment and stared at the box, willing it to open or disappear. It did neither. But it started singing. Sevan fell over with astonishment.

He pulled himself up and rushed out into the corridor.

"Ay-ttho! Nadio! Come quick!" he shouted. "It's the box."

The others ran out into the corridor and followed him back to his room where the box sat on the floor doing what it had been doing the whole evening, absolutely nothing.

"Look! Look!" Sevan was very excited.

"What?" asked Ay-ttho.

"Listen."

Sevan fell to his knees and placed his ear against the side of the box.

"That's odd."

"Sevan! What is going on?"

"The box...a moment ago...it was singing."

"Sevan? Have you been on the pish?" asked Nadio.

"I wish."

Nadio and Ay-ttho left the room.

"It was! It was singing!" he shouted after them, before turning back to the box. "You little uxclod."

The box sang.

"Are you kidding me? I suppose you want me to rush out and get the others, do you?"

The box continued to sing.

Sevan edged towards the door.

It kept singing.

He stepped out into the corridor. He could still hear the box singing from inside the room, so he ran along the corridor.

"Ay-ttho! Nadio! Come quick! It's started again."

They all rushed into Sevan's room where the box was sitting on the floor, where it had always been, in complete silence.

Ay-ttho and Nadio said nothing, but just turned and left the room.

"It was. I'm not making it up," Sevan protested before turning to the box and giving it a hard stare.

He knew that even if it began singing again, it would be pointless calling the others. It was just like the old tale of the herder who played a trick on his villagers when he kept telling them the tronqaks were attacking the herd of cukids but when the tronqaks did attack, none of the villagers believed him, the herd of cukids were all killed, and the villagers all starved to death during the worst winter in living memory.

Instead, Sevan sat and stared at the box, but it didn't start singing again. It was almost as if it knew Sevan wouldn't attempt to get the others.

There was a knock at the door. It was D'Auria.

"Do you mind if I come in?" she asked.

"Do what you like."

D'Auria entered and sat on a chair. Fortunately for her, the dimensions of an Athenian was more or less comparable to a thug. It made a pleasant change from trying to climb up the large furniture of the Zoxans and Tritions.

"I get the impression you don't hate me as much as the others," she said.

"I don't like how you treated Nadio or what you did on Angetenar and I think you would sell us to the zoxans the first chance you got."

"What did I do on Angetenar?"

"Tried to get a bunch of thugs to rob us, or worse."

"To be honest, I was trying to get them to rob Ay-ttho. You know Nadio still has a pile of credits."

"A pile of credits getting smaller by the unit paying for your meals at hostelries."

"I didn't say I wasn't grateful. But I think you understand me, Sevan."

"Do I?"

"I mean, we're both survivors, aren't we?"

"So far."

"What do you think is in the box?"

Sevan shrugged.

"Do you think it's worth anything?"

D'Auria eyed the varnished exterior.

"Do you want it? You can carry it."

"That won't be necessary," said Nadio from the doorway. "I'll carry it. It was addressed to us, not you."

Nadio walked up to the box, picked it up and left again.

"We'll, I guess he thinks it's valuable," said D'Auria.

"Do you mind," said Sevan. "I'd rather be alone now."

"As you wish. But just remember, Sevan. We could work together, you and me. I think we would be a great success."

"No, thanks."

"Suit yourself."

D'Auria left, leaving Sevan alone in his apartment contemplating the fact that the good, like Tori, seemed to be taken early while the bad, like D'Auria, somehow seemed to survive. But Sevan had survived so far. Did that make him bad like D'Auria?

He tried not to think about it and instead went to lie on his bed, where he closed his eyes and fell into a deep sleep.

He was awoken by what sounded like an alarm. At first, he thought the palace was on fire or was being invaded, but then he realised it was merely an announcement to inform the guests that it was time to break their fast.

Sevan washed and brushed both sets of teeth before wandering out to the corridor, where he found D'Auria slowly making her way to the refectory.

"Have you thought any more about what I said last rotation?" she asked.

"No," said Sevan, overtaking her and making his own way.

In the refectory, he found Nadio already eating and so joined him at his table.

"Ay-ttho?" Sevan asked.

"Sleeping. Best leave her be."

"What about the box? Anything?"

"It hasn't started singing, if that's what you mean."

"Nadio? Sevan?" a robot guard stood at their table. "When you have finished breaking your fast, you must come with me. The crew from Atlas has arrived."

CHAPTER 35: RECRUITS FROM ATLAS

The robot waited patiently while they finished eating and then led them towards the section of the palace that contained the laboratories. It surprised them to discover that Ay-ttho was already there.

"I thought you were sleeping," said Nadio.

"I was. They are going to need to redecorate my apartment," then she turned to Sevan. "Any more singing?"

"Ask him," said Sevan, nodding at Nadio. "He took it off me."

"Nothing," said Nadio. "As expected."

Sevan thought of insisting that the box had been singing, but he knew it would have been a pointless exercise.

The Athenians led them into a hangar, in which stood a very impressive destroyer.

"These robots know how to make ships," said Ay-ttho.

At the foot of the entrance ramp, a group was waiting for them. They were composed of a variety of species, and it reminded Sevan of how varied the population had been during his brief visit to Atlas.

He recognised the tentacled fungus species. One of them had tried to betray them to the Republic when they were escaping Pandoria. The fungus had four stubby feet and at least a dozen tentacles for arms. Its several eyes hung from stalks which extended from a stem which came out of its mouth. On top of the stem sat what looked like an upside down flower.

Next to the fungus was an armoured creature with six legs and huge pincers protruding from its head. Beside it was a slimy, colourful quadruped. Next to it was a fat scaly creature, and next to that a small black creature with a smooth black skin, big black eyes, and whiskers. The last member of the group was a large, hairy beast.

As they approached, the small black creature screeched at them. They all froze except for Ay-ttho, who continued to approach with a smile and screeched back.

"We won't have to share a ship with that noise, will we Nadio?" Sevan asked.

"Looks like it."

"They are very pleased to meet us," Ay-ttho translated.

"Doesn't sound like it," Sevan quipped.

There was more screeching.

"They would like to show us their ship," said Ay-ttho.

The ship was ostentatiously decorated, as Sevan remembered the buildings on Atlas had been. Atlas had been the capital of the old, old Republic before they made the planet Future the capital and much of the wealth that had passed through Atlas was clear in its architecture.

Future had been a barren planet before they covered it in buildings and, except for the presidential palace, most of the building were featureless towers which stretched up high into the atmosphere.

It had become even more bleak after the exodus Sevan had inadvertently assisted and he wondered whether now the planet had been repopulated by zoxans or whether it would just be as bleak as always. Either way, they would discover soon enough.

The bridge wasn't unlike the bridge of the Mastery of the Stars, except for the ostentatious decoration and the fact that they had modified the various stations to accommodate the diverse shapes and sizes of the crew.

The tour was accompanied by the screeching of the small black creature and Ay-ttho's translations to which Sevan wasn't paying attention. He made a mental note to sort out his entertainment implant so that he would have something interesting to listen to, which would drown out the hideous noise.

He didn't have much time because the robots announced they would leave for the Future portal the next rotation. They had very little in terms of possessions, except for the box, which caused a great deal of consternation among the crew when Nadio tried to take it on board.

"They think it might be a bomb," Ay-ttho explained.

"It might be," Sevan suddenly felt anxious again.

"Don't you think it would have gone off by now, if it was?" asked Nadio.

Sevan shrugged. He didn't know very much about the whims of bombs.

The crew scanned the box, which, frustratingly for Sevan and the others, revealed nothing, but it meant that the crew allowed Nadio to take the object on board. They gave them private quarters on the ship which were much more luxurious than the accommodation on the Mastery of the Stars but which, sadly for Sevan, appeared not to contain any pish.

They were still making themselves comfortable in their new home when the ship took off from Tritio. It pleased Nadio that the ship was fitted with gravity manipulation and a tachyon transmitter, even if it didn't have an anti-matter drive or folding technology.

Ay-ttho had contemplated mentioning to the robots that Cyrus had folding technology on the Horizon, but then thought better of it and kept the news to himself. Although the Horizon would have been a useful ship to have on their side, Ay-ttho didn't want to risk the old robot turning his expansionist ambitions towards the colony on Lysithea.

Having spent their last few space journeys travelling on Malcolm's electric spaceship, the ship from Atlas now seemed remarkably fast and in no time, they were passing Zanzenburg and heading towards Lysithea and the portal to Future.

"What will happen once we pass through the portal?" Ay-ttho asked the small black creature.

A reasonable amount of screeching followed, which Ay-ttho translated for the others.

"He says that on the other side of the portal, they will use their scanners to locate our ship."

"Have you tried to communicate with Ron?" asked Nadio.

"Yes, I haven't been able to make contact. You?"

"Same."

"Ay-ttho? How come you know so many languages?" asked Sevan.

"Brabin and I travelled a lot together."

"Robbing," added Nadio.

"Alright, there's no need to go into so much detail." Ay-ttho complained. "Suffice to say. I picked up a few things along the way."

"Like how to speak screech," said Sevan.

"Actually, it's thruq'eod. I knew many of them in my time on Zistreotov. They are formidable gamblers."

"You knew Zistreotov before the war?"

"Of course. It was an incredible place, full of casinos. The number of credits that passed over their tables must have been phenomenal. The richest in the known universe all gathered there to show off their wealth. It was obscene."

Ay-ttho's demeanour suddenly darkened.

"But there was a lot of poverty there as well," she continued. "Those who worked in the casinos and hotels were treated not much better than slaves and they also suffered after the war with what little livelihood they had taken away."

"I wonder what it's like there now."

"Me too. I can't imagine the Zoxans have been kind to the place."

The small black creature screeched.

"Apparently, we are approaching Lysithea," said Ay-ttho.

"Already?" it thrilled Nadio to be travelling on a ship that used gravity manipulation.

They went to the bridge in time to pass the moon of Enceladus.

"We still didn't find out who was doing the killing," said Nadio.

"You don't think it was Coesis?" Ay-ttho asked.

"You do?"

"I assumed it was. She said almost as much to Malcolm."

"But if it was Coesis, why did she leave messages for you?"

"I'm famous. Didn't you know?"

Nadio rolled his eyes.

They left Enceladus and then Lysithea behind and headed towards the portal to Future.

The thruq'eod screeched and pointed out of the other observation window.

"He says, if you look carefully, you can see the asteroid the robots hope to nudge into the portal," said Ay-ttho.

Sevan could only see a dot of light but when the thruq'eod magnified it in a screen, he could see that it was clearly a jagged shaped asteroid.

The next thing he knew was that they were already passing through the portal. His anxiety levels rose as he thought about what might be on the other side.

He needn't have worried. To his surprise, there were no Zoxan ships waiting for them on the other side of the portal.

"I don't understand," he said. "The Zoxans know there are Saturnians and Tritions in the Lysithea system. Why do they leave the portal undefeated?"

"For once, the mining clone is right," said Ay-ttho. "It is strange."

The small black creature was screeching at his crew, so Sevan decided it was a good time to see whether he could get his entertainment implant to work.

The content providers stopped streaming content when the old republic collapsed, but the implant had a limited capacity to store content and so Sevan had attempted to upload music which took less space and would therefore provide a larger selection.

He had uploaded all the classics from his concession days, including Molten Jaws and Forever Delight. The first track to play was Fantasy of Life by the Solar Mammals. It reminded him of binge, they always played it during the festival.

The small black creature started screeching again.

"They have located the Mastery of the Stars," said Ay-ttho. "They are taking us there now."

"This all seems a bit too easy," said Nadio.

"Yep, if I wanted to capture someone, this is what I'd do," said D'Auria.

They passed Future's moon and went into an orbit around the planet. They were not approached by any patrol ships or contacted by atmosphere traffic control.

"Very odd," said Nadio. "Where is the Mastery of the Stars?"

Ay-ttho screeched a little at the small black creature, who screeched back.

"He said it is in a spaceport on the far side of the planet. He also said they are transmitting all the intelligence they are gathering back to Tritio."

"Won't the Zoxans pick up the signal?"

"It's scrambled."

"But they'll know it's coming from us."

"I think they know we're here, anyway."

"Once thing I don't understand," said Nadio. "Is that we accepted this mission because we want to recover the Mastery of the Stars. But what do the crew from Atlas get from it?"

"Pardons," said Ay-ttho. "They are all criminals, murderers, in fact."

"What? We are on a ship of murderers, and you didn't think to tell us?"

"I thought. I thought you would panic like you are now."

"So, why did you tell me?"

"You asked."

"For the love of the Good Place, don't tell Sevan. You know how he gets."

When the crew found the spaceport, they placed the ship in a geostationary orbit to enable them to analyse the level of security around the Mastery of the Stars.

The small black creature screeched.

"He said it's heavily guarded by Zoxans," said Ay-ttho.

"Oh great," said Nadio.

"What's great?" asked Sevan.

"The Mastery of the Stars is heavily guarded by zoxans."

"Oh, how is that great?"

"He was being sarcastic," said Ay-ttho.

"Oh, right. Of course."

"Any ideas?" asked Nadio

Ay-ttho and the small black creature exchanged screeches.

"He is going to get me images of the compound so that we can see exactly how it is guarded," Ay-ttho explained.

The small black creature led them over to a table, above which holographic images appeared. The images showed a hanger with Zoxans guarding every entrance.

Ay-ttho exchanged screeches a bit more.

"We don't have much time before the asteroid comes through that portal," she said. "We must act quickly. My suggestion is that we fly down there, the crew blow the roof off the hanger, we jump in and fly out the ship before they really know what has hit them."

"Did you say jump?" asked Sevan.

"With a rocket pack, obviously."

The small black creature screeched.

"Oh, apparently they only have jet packs, but they should do."

"Jetpacks?" Sevan gasped. "Isn't that what killed Ozli?"

"Was it? Or was it the poisoned pish, I forget."

"It was the jetpack."

"Yes, but only because Fenris had tampered with it."

Sevan was not reassured.

"Come on, let's see them."

"You want me to fly one as well?"

"You want to end up on the Mastery of the Stars, don't you?"

"Yes, but..."

"Well, come on then."

CHAPTER 36: THE NEXT STEP

The small black creature led them down to the cargo hold where four packing crates sat. The crew opened them to reveal four shiny new jet packs.

"She's not coming, is she?" asked Nadio, pointing to D'Auria.

"Unfortunately, the crew wouldn't agree to keep her," said Ay-ttho.

"And what about the box? Where will it go?"

"Don't worry, we will strap it on."

While the crew were busy assembly the jet packs, they gathered what few belongings they had so that they could strap them to the machines which were built for sport rather than utility.

Sevan could barely get on it, let alone fly it. Ay-ttho and Nadio seemed much more confident and D'Auria didn't seem bothered by the prospect, despite her advanced age.

"I hope she crashes," Nadio whispered to Ay-ttho.

As soon as the jetpacks were ready, they were pushed towards the cargo bay doors.

"The crew are going to dive into the compound and fire at the roof," Ay-ttho explained. "As they climb out of the dive, they will open the cargo bay doors. That is our signal to go. With any luck there will be no roof left and we can just fly in."

"And if the roof is still there?" asked Sevan.

"Then we improvise."

"Improvise, she says," Sevan was almost crying. "Can't you pick me up later?"

"Sevan." Ay-ttho's tone was very matter of fact. "We don't know what is going to happen. If you stay with them, the asteroid could destroy you."

"As opposed to dying by falling out of the back of a ship strapped to a jet pack."

"You've used a hover board. It's practically the same thing."

"As a jet pack?" D'Auria laughed.

"You are not helping. Look, Sevan. Follow D'Auria. We'll go first and make sure everything is okay. When the coast is clear, I'll wave you in."

"I can't wait to see this," D'Auria chortled.

"Shut up, you old... thug!" it was the best insult Sevan could muster, but it felt so inadequate.

"Ready?" said Ay-ttho.

They climbed onto their machines, and the crew helped them with their straps. The ship was already beginning its dive and Sevan could feel the anxiety welling up within. He clung to the jet pack like his life depended on it, which it would have if it hadn't been for the straps.

As the dive steepened, the rear of the ship raised high, and Sevan found himself pointing upward. He could hear the laser cannons fire and the change in sound of the gravity manipulators as they struggled to pull out of the dive.

Then the cargo bay door began to open and Sevan could see the ship was being pursued by Zoxan fighters who fired. As the ship climbed, Sevan saw the planet appear below him, just before the crew released his jet pack so that it plummeted towards the ground.

Sevan struggled with the controls, trying to get the machine to stabilise, but all he could think about was how quickly the ground was getting closer.

Ay-ttho whizzed past him on her jet pack and flicked a switch he had been told about but had forgotten he would need to flick before anything would work.

The machine suddenly righted itself and Sevan could take stock of his surroundings, which comprised them being shot at from a diverse range of angles.

Ay-ttho was leading the group down towards the hanger and so Sevan followed. He could see that the roof of the hangar was damaged but not destroyed.

He looked up to see whether their ship was going to make another attack run, but the Zoxan fire had hit it; it was on fire and, within moments, crashed into a building and exploded. As much as Sevan did not like being on the jet pack, he now preferred it to dying in an explosion.

Ay-ttho had already landed her jet pack on the roof of the hangar, unstrapped and leapt off in one smooth movement, and began firing as soon as she landed.

Sevan's jetpack hit the roof, bounced, skidded and hit Ay-ttho's jet pack, nudging it into a hole. He struggled to undo his straps, but when he tried to jump off the machine, one of his feet was still caught in a strap and he landed face first on the hangar roof, his weapon skidding away from him. He looked up in time to see D'Auria kick it back.

Grabbing his weapon, Sevan picked himself up into a crouching position. D'Auria and Ay-ttho apparently didn't mind standing while laser bolts shot past them.

"Get down. You'll get shot," Sevan told them.

"You have to give them something to shoot at so you can see where to shooters are," said D'Auria as she despatched another shooter.

Sevan knew Nadio was standing behind him, though unlike D'Auria and Ay-ttho, he was stooping to avoid the fire and cradling the box under one arm.

"Right, let's go," said Ay-ttho.

Although the hangar roof was still intact, there were holes big enough to jump through. Ay-ttho's jetpack was wedged in the nearest, so she went to the next one and peered down into the hangar.

"It's there," she yelled back to the others.

"I've got Ron on my communicator," said Nadio.

There was a commotion in the hangar as the Mastery of the Stars came to life and lifted off the ground.

"Come here," Ay-ttho told the others, gesturing for them to join her at the Hole.

While the other fired at the circling zoxan fighters, Ay-ttho stared through the hole at the Mastery of the Stars, which was rising closer to her every nano unit.

"Jump!" she said to the others. "I'll cover you."

As she fired at the Zoxan fighters, D'Auria and then leapt through the hole, joined shortly afterwards by Sevan, who didn't so much leap through the hole as fall.

Ay-ttho jumped last, by which time the freighter was very close to the roof. Ron opened a nearby service hatch and after the group jumped in, Ron closed it again behind them.

Besides the damage to the roof by the crew of the ship from Atlas, the Zoxans had made more damage themselves. The structure of the roof was severely compromised, and the Mastery of the Stars met little resistance as Ron continued the freighter's ascent through the roof.

Now it was in the open air. The Zoxan fighters turned their attention to pursuit. Ron engaged the anti-matter drive, and soon the freighter was climbing up through the atmosphere.

Soon afterwards, Ay-ttho and the others arrived on the bridge.

"Where are we going?" she asked Ron.

"To the Lysithea portal."

"No, don't. There is an asteroid about to come through it. We don't want to meet it in the middle."

"Where then?"

Before Ay-ttho could answer, he saw the Lysithea portal ahead of them and an asteroid emerging.

"Let's just get out of the way," said Ay-ttho.

"Ron? Scan this," said Nadio, placing the box on a chair.

"It's a box."

"Yes, I know. But what is inside? What does it do? How do we open it?"

"No idea."

"What? Nothing?"

"Nope. There doesn't seem to be anything inside and there's no obvious opening mechanism."

"Then we should just smash it open."

"Why would you do that if there's nothing inside? It would be pointless violence."

"I feel like some pointless violence."

"You've been away from Effeeko for too long," said Ay-ttho. "Let's get back to Lysithea."

"Only one problem with that," said D'Auria.

"Why? The asteroid has already come through the portal."

"Have you forgotten that the Athenians are sending their war fleet through the portal behind the asteroid?"

"Oh, yes. Good point. Ron? Better give the portal a wide birth for a bit. Let's see what happens first."

"And what if they think we are zoxans and attack us?"

"What do you suggest?"

"Go through another portal."

"Which one?"

"Take your pick. The nearest one is probably the Zistreotov portal."

"What about the Zoxans?"

"They're about to get hit by a fushy great asteroid."

"I meant the Zoxans on Zistreotov."

"If there are any?"

"And if there are?"

"I would rather take my chances with them than with the maniacal Athenians."

"Fair point. Ron? Full speed to the Zistreotov portal."

"There's only one problem with that plan?"

"What's that?"

"To return to Lysithea, we have to come back past Future."

"Yes, but by that time, hopefully, the dust will have settled."

The journey to the Zistreotov portal was long enough for them to witness the asteroid crashing into Future.

At the moment of impact, there was a gigantic explosion which threw particles and debris high into the atmosphere.

They monitored the Lysithea portal for emerging Athenian craft, but none had emerged by the time they reached the Zistreotov portal.

"You know what this means?" said D'Auria. "The Athenians will have no idea whether we escaped the planet before the impact."

"It doesn't really matter, considering we have to pass Future again to get to Lysithea."

Everyone tried to get some sleep on the way to Zistreotov, but none of them succeeded.

"I wonder how many there were on Future," Sevan said to Nadio when they returned to the bridge.

"How many what?"

"Zoxans and other species."

"I'm trying not to think about it."

Sevan had always wanted to go to Zistreotov. He had heard stories of its opulence as the gambling centre of the known universe, but he also knew that much of it had been destroyed in the Zistreotovian war.

Ron had encountered no sign of the Zoxans, which suggested that the system held no interest for them. When they landed on the outskirts of what used to be the capital, they found piles of rubble, crumbling buildings and trees and other shrugs growing through the decaying masonry and twisted metal structures.

Inside, some of the structure corroded gambling machines lay on their sides, their contents long since looted.

There were signs of fire damage and the ash had clearly provided fertile ground for the planet, which was hurriedly returning itself to its natural state.

Ay-ttho had a feeling they were being watched.

"Let's get back to the ship," she said, but before anyone could move, they were surrounded by an unfriendly-looking gang of Zistreotovians brandishing weapons.

Ay-ttho quickly assessed the situation and decided there were too many for them to take on. She fastened her weapons and raised her hands. The others followed her example.

The Zistreotovians collected their weapons and herded them into the woods.

"Where are you taking us?" asked Ay-ttho.

"To the community court."

"Court? We haven't done anything."

"We caught you trespassing."

"Fair enough."

They led them to a clearing in which there was a wooden building which reminded Sevan of the kind of constructions they built while they were fleeing Angetenar.

Inside the building was a large hall in the centre of which was a substantial fire pit which filled the hall with smoke which struggled to escape through a gap in the roof.

Beyond the fire was a platform supporting a large chair. They placed them in front of the chair and told them to wait. Meanwhile, the hall filled with Zistreotovians.

"I don't like the look of this," said Nadio. "They look primitive."

"If they've been isolated since the war, then they are probably doing what they need to survive. In a violent world, justice has to be harsh."

"Let's not talk about harsh justice," said Sevan. "Let's think about making new friends."

"You are such a dreamer, Sevan," said Nadio.

"I'm not so sure," said D'Auria. "Maybe we could make ourselves to the Zistreotovians."

"Or maybe they'll help themselves to our ship. Why did we have to land?"

"I didn't see you protesting on your way down here."

"Only that we have to take you everywhere. Hey, Ay-ttho? Why don't we leave D'Auria here with the box and have done with them both?"

"Not yet, Nadio. I dislike D'Auria as much as you, but she helped us to get our ship back."

"And that's another thing. What happened to all her limping and feebleness? She was fooling us all along."

"I am here, you know," D'Auria protested.

"They don't get much entertainment round here," said Sevan, seeing how full the hall had become.

"Burn 'em," a Zistreotovian at the back shouted.

"Burn 'em," others joined in.

Soon, there was a chorus of chanting.

"Burn 'em, burn 'em, burn 'em."

"So much for your friends idea, Sevan," said Nadio.

The more they chanted, the louder the chants became. Sevan worried that at any moment they might get pelted with objects.

Then a Zistreotovian entered the hall, stepped onto the platform, and sat in the large chair. The crowd fell silent.

CHAPTER 37: JUSTICE MCFARLAND

"What brings you to our settlement?" asked the Zistreotovian.

"We are fleeing a battle that is raging between the zoxans and the Athenians," said Ay-ttho.

"Of these Zoxans, I have heard much. There are some who say someone brought them from another universe."

Ay-ttho, Nadio and Sevan exchanged the glances they usually exchanged when the subject of how the Zoxans arrived was mentioned.

"But the Athenians of whom you speak are strangers to me."

"They are from the planet of Tritio in the Lysithea system and are actually robots."

"Yes, I understand that the way to the Lysithea system is near to here. My ancestors could travel off world, but that technology is long lost to us. Please tell us your names and where you come from."

"My name is Ay-ttho, and I was a Corporation security clone. Seven, here, was a corporation mining clone on The Doomed Planet. The hairy one is Nadio, and the grey hairy one is D'Auria. They are both thugs from Sicheoyama."

"My name is Justice McFarland. I run the community court. You can see that our community does not take kindly to trespassing."

"Our intentions were purely innocent," said Ay-ttho. "We were curious about what Zistreotov looked like since the war."

"Ah yes, the war. That was many solar cycles ago when the civilisation of my ancestors was destroyed by the old republic. The are some who say the gods sent the Zoxans to punish the old republic."

"That sounds very possible," said Sevan, before receiving a very hard stare from Nadio.

Sevan shrugged, as if to say he was just trying to help.

"You can see the remnants of that old civilisation all around us. Unfortunately, their technology is quite useless to us. Anyway, you know what curiosity did?"

Ay-ttho shook her head.

"Killed the cukid. It is time for our community court to pass judgement on your transgression."

"Forgive me for speaking out of turn, Justice McFarland," said D'Auria. "It seems to me that we have an opportunity here."

Justice McFarland looked interested.

"I am sure there are many needs your community finds difficult to fulfil. We can procure anything you might need and bring it to you."

"Such as?"

"Why don't you tell us what it is you require? I'm sure we can procure almost anything."

Justice McFarland stared at D'Auria for what seemed to Sevan an unbearable amount of time.

"We have everything we need," she said. "We have lived off this land for generations with no help from off-world, and don't need to ask for help now."

"But there must be something you would like that you can't produce here."

"We were born into this life. We know no other way. We don't suffer from the same addictions as other species."

"Addictions?"

"Yes. Even now, your colleague is checking her communicator to see if she has any messages."

"I'm just checking on Ron," said Ay-ttho, defensively.

"Enough of this," said Justice McFarland. "Back to the sentencing."

"Sentencing? Have we been found guilty already?"

"Yes, you are obviously guilty. Your very presence here is evidence of your guilt. I therefore sentence each of you to undertake 300 mega units of community service. If you cannot complete this community service within a reasonable time, you will be arrested and given a custodial sentence."

"What does that mean?" Sevan asked Nadio.

"It means that if we don't do what they ask, they will put us in prison."

"I'm seeing a repetitive theme in my life."

"Your sentence will begin immediately," Justice McFarland nodded to a Zistreotovian who appeared to be using some kind of uniform.

The uniformed Zistreotovian led them out of the hall. The first task they gave them was chopping wood. Ay-ttho and Nadio were good at chopping, but Sevan and D'Auria were slower, so they switched them to stacking the wood.

"Why don't we just go back to the Mastery of the Stars?" Nadio asked Ay-ttho.

"Have you forgotten that they have taken our weapons and they are pointing theirs at us?"

"I know but..."

"But?"

"Okay, tell me you have a plan."

"I have a plan."

"Do you?"

"No."

"Then why..."

"You told me to tell you."

Nadio was silent for the rest of the shift, at the end of which they led them back to the hall.

"They have informed me you worked very well during your first rotation," Justice McFarland told them. "Now you only have 296 mega units to go. You are free to return to your ship to rest. We will see you again, then next rotation."

The group looked at each other in disbelief.

"And our weapons?" asked Ay-ttho.

"They will be returned to you only when you have completed your community service."

"So we can go now?" asked Sevan.

"Yes, see you next rotation. Have a nice rest."

"But what's stopping us..."

"See you next rotation," Nadio interrupted, dragging Sevan out of the hall.

They ran all the way back to the freighter.

"Ron? Prepare to take off," Ay-ttho shouted into her communicator as she ran.

As they approached the ship, Ron lowered the ramp, and they ran straight on-board.

"Take off. Now," Ay-ttho ordered.

"What do we do now?" asked Nadio. "I'm sure it's too early to go back past Future."

"Let's just drift for a bit. I don't feel like landing anywhere else, do you? What are the options, Ron?"

"The next system is Leda. There's nothing there. After that is Rechinia. It could be a good place to restock with supplies. There are three systems beyond that, but they contain little of interest unless you want to visit the monument, which marks the spot where President Chuba was assassinated by the mechanical bowmen."

"No, thank you. How are we doing with supplies.?"

"Not great. We'll manage for now, but you'll need to stock up soon unless you really love oxygenated Kairn drops."

"Why do we have so many of those?"

"They were cheap."

The rest agreed that they were also quite happy to drift for a while, but that stocking up was a good idea.

"My credits won't last forever," Nadio warned.

"Like I said, you should have pretended I was cashing in on the bounty."

"Shut up, D'Auria," said Ay-ttho. "First, they wouldn't have paid you the bounty. Second, there won't be a bounty anymore."

"So, what are you saying? We are going to need to find work?"

"No, I'm sure Nadio has enough to get us back to Lysithea. We can make ends meet there."

"And you are satisfied with that, are you? Making ends meet?"

"D'Auria, we've been through a lot. I think we are all fed up with chasing around the universe."

"Universes," Nadio corrected.

"Exactly."

"What do you mean, universes?"

"Nothing."

"No, he said universes. Have you been to another universe? Is thar why you were in suspended animation? They say the zoxans came from another universe. Did you have anything to do with that?"

"Ron? I'm going to bed. Wake me up when we get to Rechinia," said Nadio as he left the bridge.

"Yes, I'm tired too," said Ay-ttho. "But Ron? Don't wake me."

Ay-ttho left the bridge.

"Sevan?"

"I'm going to get some pish," he said and left, leaving D'Auria alone on the bridge.

"Ron?"

"I don't want to get involved."

D'Auria knew they were covering up something, but she just couldn't put her paw on it.

Ron kept a lookout for zoxans, but encountered none on the entire journey to Rechinia. As soon as they entered the system, he woke Nadio. Sevan, who had found a store of pish, was unwakeable and Ay-ttho was unwakeable for other reasons. D'Auria continued sleeping because Nadio had given specific instructions to Ron not to wake her.

Nadio went to the bridge.

"Have I missed anything?" she asked.

"Only Leda, but there's nothing there. It's only famous because the Old Republic warrior, Nala, was exiled there."

"Nothing there now?"

"No civilisation. Or at least nothing my scanners could pick up."

"How about Rechinia?"

"Definite signs of activity. Exactly how much we will have to find out."

"Zoxan?"

"Nothing."

"Let's be sure of what's happening on Rechinia before we land. We don't want another repeat of Zistreotov."

"I agree," said D'Auria, entering the bridge.

"Well, I wasn't asking you."

"I know."

"I was, though," said Ay-ttho, who had also just arrived. "You don't like D'Auria. I don't like her either. But she has a lot of experience. She was here when the Zoxans took over."

"Where were you then?" asked D'Auria.

"That's none of your business," said Nadio.

"D'Auria, you may as well get used to the fact that we will not discuss where we have been since the zoxan invasion," said Ay-ttho. "You already know we were in suspended animation so if you stop bringing up the subject, you will find it much easier to get on with us all."

"Curiouser and curiouser," said D'Auria as she left the bridge.

"There are two things on this ship I would like to get rid of," said Nadio. "One is D'Auria, and the other is that box. Both have brought us nothing but misery since they've been with us."

"What has the box done now?"

"Nothing. I just don't like it. It's creepy."

"Maybe we can sell it on Rechinia. Ron? Can you check to see whether the planet has anyone who specialises in curios?"

"I'm sure it does. It's that kind of planet. We are approaching now."

"Let's go with Nadio's plan. We will try to negotiate our deals before we land."

"Thank you," said Nadio. "I don't fancy chopping any more wood."

"You'll have to if we go back to Lysithea."

"That's different. I don't mind doing it for myself."

"Just not for the community. Interesting."

"Not my community."

"I'm only joking."

"Sorry, I guess I'm not in a very humorous mood at the moment."

"And I'm not particularly humorous. Relax, Nadio. We'll pick up some supplies and get back to Lysithea and Effeeko."

"Do you think he's okay?"

"I'm sure he's fine."

Ron Drew up a list of contacts of suppliers that might have the kinds of goods they needed and then Ay-ttho contacted them one by one until they had accounted for everything on their list.

"The only issue is the box," he told the others. "Most of the produce we can have delivered, but no one will make an offer on the box unless they see it in person."

"Let's take it," said Nadio. "It's creepy. I want to get rid of it. I feel like it's watching me."

An alarm went off on one of the control panels.

"That must be the first delivery," said Ay-ttho. "Let's get to the docking bay."

Nadio and Ay-ttho watched as the shuttle slowly approached the docking bay on the side of the cargo hold and then locked on.

The door opened to reveal a skinny Rechinian and piles of goods. Rechinians were very similar to Futurians, the dominant species in the old Republic. and the Futurians originated on Atlas whose diversity had exploded so much that the Futurians were now the distinct minority.

Rechinians had a reputation for being more slightly built than Futurians, a fact that was often put down to their frugal diet of Gengi dust loops and Bolain placenta drops, said to be one of the healthiest diets in the known universe, high in protein, essential oils and the correct combination of vitamins.

Unfortunately, none of the present crew of the Mastery of the Stars could stomach either Gengi dust loops or Bolain placenta drops and therefore never drew the benefit of their miraculous nutrition.

Ay-ttho and Nadio helped the Rechinian load the cargo, paid her the credits they owed her and waved her goodbye.

"Only one thing left to do," said Ay-ttho. "Let's sell the box."

CHAPTER 38: EYES IN THE DARK

"Take us down," Ay-ttho instructed Ron, once they had decided on the least scary sounding curio dealer.

"There is nowhere to park the ship near the shop," said Ron. "We will have to use a hangar on the outskirts and then you will have to travel to the shop on foot."

"Fine. Send the directions to my communicator. "

Nadio wrapped the box in a cloth and placed it in an innocuous-looking bag, which he slung over his shoulder.

"Is it safe to leave Ron with these two?" asked Nadio.

"Yes, why not?"

"You don't think D'Auria will try to steal the ship?"

"No, Ron won't let him."

"Ron has been unsuccessful in stopping the ship from being stolen before."

"Good point. We had better take D'Auria with us."

"Maybe we can sell her too."

Ay-ttho fetched D'Auria who didn't want to go at first, but Ay-ttho was very insistent.

Even though it was the middle of the light phase of the rotation, the narrowness of the streets meant that little of the Rechinian light reached street level, creating a dim, eerie ambience.

Many of the shops were selling dried and cured dead creatures of various shapes and sizes. Almost every shop offered Gengi dust loops and Bolain placenta drops.

Ay-ttho glanced at her communicator from time to time but was careful to not give the appearance of someone who was lost. She also kept the communicator out of sight when she was not using it. She didn't want to encourage any opportunist thrives in a land where corporation standard communicators were valued.

The journey on foot was longer than she had hoped, and she did not like being so far away from her ship in such an inhospitable neighbourhood.

Gradually, the shops became less food based and more equipment based. They passed many shops selling tools and encountered those selling clothes, none of which appealed to Ay-ttho.

Eventually, they reached the street they were looking for. It was the darkest and dingiest street they had passed through so far. When they reached the shop, it was the darkest and dingiest shop they had seen by a long way. Ingram & Lo-Tutala Curios & Antiques bought and sold, was the inscription above the grimy window through which they could barely see an assortment of trinkets and artefacts.

Ay-ttho pushed open the door, which triggered a small bell. Nadio and D'Auria followed her into a dark room with glass counters containing a variety of peculiar looking objects. Behind the counters, the walls were lined with drawers of all manner of sizes.

They could hear footsteps descending a staircase and then a door opened and the oldest creature Ay-ttho had ever seen limped into the room.

"Good rotation," he said. "And what brings you to my humble establishment?"

"My name is Ay-ttho. I sent you a message about a box."

"Ah yes, everyone wanting to sell, nobody wanting to buy. Did you bring the item with you?"

"Yes, it's here," said Nadio, taking the box out of the bag and unwrapping it on the counter.

"Oh. I see," said the old shopkeeper. "What are two thugs and a clone doing with one of these?"

"You know what it is?"

"Oh, it's not an it, it's a who. How did you come to have such a thing in your possession?"

"It was just delivered to us on Tritio."

"On Tritio? Do you know from whom?"

"Unfortunately not."

"Hmm, shame."

"So, what is it?"

"You mean who is it?:

"I'm sorry?"

"The object that you have in your possession is not a box at all, rather it is a species. I'm afraid I do not trade in anything that is alive, then I would have to feed it and before you know it would reproduce?"

"Reproduce?" said Nadio.

"We should feed it?" asked Ay-ttho.

"You would really be better off at a zoo."

"What you are telling us is that this thing is alive?"

"Very much so."

"Do they sing?" asked Nadio.

"I believe they do, but it is very rare. They only do it when they feel completely comfortable."

"But how are we supposed to look after it?"

"You may be in luck. I think I have a book upstairs on the very subject."

"A what?"

"A book. They are quite amusing. I'll get it for you."

Ay-ttho, D'Auria and Nadio exchanged confused glances, watched the old shopkeeper open the door and ascend the stairs, and then all stared at the box creature.

"What do we call it?" asked Ay-ttho.

"Better let Sevan decide," said Nadio.

"Why?"

"It is clearly most comfortable with him. That was the only time it sang, remember?"

"Do you think it's worth anything?" asked D'Auria.

Ay-ttho and Nadio stepped between D'Auria and the box.

"You leave him alone," said Nadio.

"Or her," said Ay-ttho.

"Or her. You leave him or her alone."

They could hear the old shopkeeper descending the stairs again.

"Here it is," he said, placing the small dusty hardback volume on the counter.

"What's that?" asked Ay-ttho.

"Harvey Cartwright's Compendium of Rare Species. There is an entire chapter on the kuxed."

Ay-ttho looked none the wiser.

"The kuxed. That's the species. It's a kuxed. It's written in Old Republic Standard. I assume you can read ORS, can you?"

Ay-ttho looked just as confused as ever and reached out to the book, which opened as she picked it up, so she dropped it back on the table.

"Be careful. It's ancient."

"Is it supposed to do that?"

"Of course. Have you never seen a book before? It works like this."

The old shopkeeper opened the book and showed Ay-ttho the text inside.

"You see, it's all in ORS."

Ay-ttho looked at the text.

"Oh, I see. It's like some kind of communicator."

"That's right. Except that the text stays there all the time."

"What do you mean?"

"Look. The text is there permanently."

Ay-ttho stared as the shopkeeper turned the pages.

"Why?" she asked.

"These are ancient. They were how information used to be stored."

"But how do you find the information you need?"

"It's easy, I'll show you. In this book, there are two ways to find information. In the front is a list of all the sections in the book, or chapters. If we look at the contents, here, you see that there is a chapter called Kuxeds, habitats, habits and domestication. And here there is a number. This number corresponds to these numbers here."

The old shopkeeper showed Ay-ttho the page number on the corners of the pages.

"So we need to find page number 567," the old shopkeeper flipped through the pages. "Here, look, page 567, Kuxeds, habitats, habits and domestication."

"What?" Ay-ttho laughed. "That's ridiculous. You need to do that every time you need to find something?"

"Or you can use the index," said the old shopkeeper, turning to the back of the book. "You find kuxed in this alphabetical list and it tells you all the page numbers it appears on."

"Nadio, look at this," Ay-ttho giggled. "Look at what they used to have to do to find information."

The old shopkeeper ran through the procedure again for Nadio and then left him flicking through the volume.

"How much for the...what do you call it?"

"Book. I think I can let you have it for fifteen credits."

"Fifteen? I hope it's self-charging for that price."

"Absolutely. No charging required."

"What do you think, Nadio? Fifteen?"

"Do you have any more of these?" Nadio asked.

"That's the only one on kuxeds, I'm afraid."

"No, I mean, do you have any more of *these?*"

Nadio held the book up in both hands.

"Come with me."

The old shopkeeper led Nadio through the door and up the creaky flight of stairs. They emerged into a room that astounded Nadio.

The walls were entirely covered in shelves of books from floor to ceiling, accessible by ladders. In the centre of the room was a spiral staircase leading to a mezzanine floor whose walls were also covered with bookshelves.

Next to the staircase was a table littered with books and on the other side of a large rug was a very comfortable chair and a side table on which rested an open book and a glass and decanter of what Nadio assumed was pish. On the other side of the chair was a model of a planet on a pedestal.

"Wow," Nadio stared up at all the books. "And they are all like this one?"

He brandished the volume he was still clutching tightly.

"They are all on different subjects. What are you interests?"

"I'm not sure."

"What do you like doing?"

"I enjoy helping Effeeko. He's a medic."

"I have several books on the anatomies of various species, but they are all very similar to the one you have there."

"What about thugs?"

The old shopkeeper scanned the shelves. He climbed the spiral staircase, walked to the far side of the room, moved a ladder into position and then climbed it to peer at the spines of several volumes.

Eventually, he selected a small volume which fitted in the side pocket of his jacket, and then he selected a thicker volume, which he cradled as he carefully descended the ladder.

Nadio waited for him at the bottom of the stairs, next to the table where the old shopkeeper placed the thick volume.

"This is Lewie Coyle's Illustrated History of Thuggery. To be honest, Coyle embellished many of the stories with his own fantasies, but the backbones of the stories are based on fact."

"He has a strange name."

"Yes, these books are ancient. They are from a time when names were strange."

The old shopkeeper took the small volume from his pocket.

"Have you heard of poetry?"

Nadio looked as if he hadn't.

"Do you speak thuggish?"

"A little."

"Here. Hold this."

The old shopkeeper handed Nadio the small volume while he went off to search in the corner of the room. He returned with two medium-sized tomes.

"These will teach you the basics of ancient thuggish. Once you have a grasp of ancient thuggish, you should enjoy that book of thuggish poetry by the great thuggish bard,

Jacob Greaves."

"They did have strange names then, didn't they?" said Ay-ttho, staring at the book in his hand.

"Anything else?"

"No, thank you. I think these will keep me busy for a while."

They carried the books downstairs where Ay-ttho and D'Auria were waiting impatiently.

"So this isn't wood," said Ay-ttho, pointing to the box.

"No," said the old shopkeeper. "It's shell. You should find everything in the book, including what to feed it."

"Thank you," said Nadio. "How much do we owe you?"

"Five books? Shall we say 70 credits?"

"What?" Ay-ttho was shocked.

"That's great, thank you," said Nadio, handing over the credits. "By the way. Was that pish I saw in the decanter upstairs?"

"Yes, the finest from the old Republic. You have a keen eye."

"Would you mind telling us where you bought it? Our friend is a great connoisseur of pish."

"You need to go to Captain Alfie Jones' Pish, Fushy and Distilled Liquors Emporium. It's on the corner of Figureido and McLoughlin. Ask anyone. They'll be able to point you in the right direction."

"Thank you. I'm Nadio, by the way."

"And I'm Ingram. A pleasure doing business with you. Please call again."

"And Lo-Tutala?"

"Not with us anymore, I'm afraid."

"Oh, I am sorry."

"No need to be. He is at peace now."

"70 credits? For those?" Ay-ttho grumbled as they left the shop. "We were meant to be selling to him, not buying."

"They're my credits."

"Yes, I suppose they are," said Ay-ttho, beginning to regret she had given them to him. "Let's get back then."

"I'd like to stop at this pish shop first and get something for Sevan."

"Why this sudden concern for Sevan?"

"The box liked him so much that it sang to him, and we didn't believe him and took the box away. I feel bad about that."

"And you think thar buying a bottle of pish will make everything all right?"

"I know it will. Find the corner of Figureido and McLoughlin on the map."

"You are lucky. It's on our way."

It was already getting dark by the time they left the shop and Ay-ttho had the strong suspicion they were being followed, but every time she turned around to surprise their pursuer, the individual had vanished. She put it down to her imagination.

CHAPTER 39: THE TREACHEROUS CAPTAIN

Captain Alfie Jones' Pish, Fushy and Distilled Liquors Emporium was very similar in appearance to Ingram & Lo-Tutala Curios & Antiques. The same style window, but instead of a display of unusual objects and curios, the window was filled with dusty bottles of a variety of shapes and sizes.

Entering the establishment activated a small bell almost the same as the one in the curio shop, and the interior was also remarkably similar. There were glass counters display small but expensive looking ornate bottles and the walls were lined with shelves packed with bottles of pish.

They could hear similar footsteps descending a similar sounding staircase and then a door opened to reveal an old thug, not dissimilar from D'Auria who viewed the shopkeeper with suspicion from the moment she set eyes on him.

"Good rotation, how might I be of help?" said the old thug.

"Ingram at the curio shop recommended you to us," said Nadio.

"Ah, yes. One of my best customers."

"My friend likes pish, and we wanted to get him something special as a gift."

"How special are we talking?"

"What are the options?"

"We'll, we have some of the finest pish in the old Republic," he said, gesturing to a shelf near the window. "They used to serve some of these in the old Channeatune room."

"How much would one of those cost?"

"This one here is fifty."

"Fifty credits?"

"Fifty thousand credits."

"Definitely not, no," said Ay-ttho.

"I think that's a bit out of our budget," said Nadio.

"Maybe if you gave me an idea?"

"Fifty credits?" said Ay-ttho.

The old thug laughed at first and then realised Ay-ttho was being serious.

"I can do you this one for 200," he said, pointing to a bottle on the other side of the room.

"Is that the cheapest you have?" asked Ay-ttho.

"It's the cheapest I would consider putting inside myself."

The old thug sighed and went to the corner of the room and picked up a bottle off the bottom shelf and placed it on the counter.

"I can let you have this for fifty. But only because you are friends of Ingram."

"Thank you," said Nadio.

"I hope your friend isn't too discerning."

"He isn't."

The old thug wrapped the bottle and took Nadio's credits.

"Wait a unit," said D'Auria suddenly. She had been staring at the old thug the whole time. "I just remembered how I know you."

"Me?" the old thug laughed nervously. "I don't really mix with thugs. You must be thinking of someone else."

"No, it's you. It was the Captain Alfie Jones that first made me suspicious, but you are not a Captain, are you?"

"I don't know who you are, but..."

"You know who I am. I'm D'Auria."

The old thug gave an almost involuntary laugh and then was suddenly serious, staring at D'Auria as if trying to find evidence of the truth somewhere in her face.

"I'm sorry, but I don't know what you are talking about."

"Yes, you do. Battle of Genuihines. Only you weren't a captain, were you?"

"Listen here. I think I'd like you to leave now."

"I'm sure you would. But if I walk out of that door now, I'll let everyone know that Captain Alfie Jones isn't really who he appears to be, oh yes, he was at Genuihines but he was busy looting the bodies of dead officers like the real Captain Jones."

"And what did you do at Genuihines, D'Auria?"

"I was pulling officers out of the rubble while you were looting the dead ones."

"Very difficult to believe."

"Believe it. And I think you'll find your customers will find it easy to believe as well."

"You can't frighten me. All that happened such a long time ago. Nobody cares about that now."

"Don't they? Shall we put it to the test?"

D'Auria went to the door and opened it. A small bell tickled.

"Now hear this, customers of Captain Jones," D'Auria shouted out the door. It made some passers-by stop.

"Close the door," the old thug pleaded. "What do you want?"

"That," D'Auria pointed to the shelf where the fifty thousand credit bottle of pish sat.

"You can't be serious?"

"A small price to pay for our silence, I would have thought."

"And how can I be sure you won't blab?"

"Oh, I give you my word as a thug."

The old thug placed both hands on the counter and stared down at them. D'Auria winked at Nadio.

"Alright," said the old thug. "But you'd better keep your word."

He got the expensive bottle off the shelf and handed it to D'Auria.

"Thank you very much," she said, leaving the shop in triumph.

Astonished, Nadio and Ay-ttho followed her out of the shop, leaving the old thug wondering what had just happened.

"So Yor was right," said Ay-ttho, as they walked back to the ship.

"About what?" asked D'Auria.

"That you saved him."

"So he says. But don't worry, I've already been paid off for that."

"By whom?"

"Scotmax. On Angetenar."

"You looked very similar."

"Who?"

"You and that old thug in there."

"We'll, we are both old thugs."

"No, what I mean is that you look similar."

"What are you going on about, Ay-ttho?"

"When we were on Herse, Yor took us to a museum, and there was this picture and it had a thug looting officers and we all thought it was you. Well, it looked like you. But actually, it could have been him."

"You thought I was a looter?"

"Er...yes. Well, you treated Nadio pretty badly."

"I was going through a bad time," said D'Auria. "I was in a toxic relationship. The business was doing badly. It was a stressful time. I'm sorry for what happened to your co-begetter, Nadio. And I'm sorry if I didn't treat you very well. I know that doesn't make up for anything and I understand if you all want to leave me here on Rechinia. There's probably something for me to do here. I mean, if Fleming can make something of himself here, then anyone can."

"Let's discuss it back on the ship," Ay-ttho suggested.

On the way, she still had the uncomfortable sense they were being followed, but couldn't see anyone.

At the ship, they presented the box and both bottles of pish to a very hungover Sevan, who was thrilled but still a little too worse for wear to sample any.

Nadio was very excited and wanted to tell Sevan everything. She pushed a book across the mess table to him.

"It has everything we need to know to look after the box," he said.

"What is it?" Sevan asked, opening it and finding pages filled with words.

"It's called a book. Go to number 567."

Sevan didn't understand what he was being asked to do.

"Look, there are numbers in the corner here. Find 567."

"Why?"

"Just do it."

Sevan flicked through the pages until he found 567.

"Look, Kuxeds, habitats, habits and domestication," said Nadio, pointing to the chapter heading.

"What's a kuxed?"

"It is," Nadio pointed to the box. "And it was singing because it likes you."

"Really?" Sevan took more interest in the page and started to read.

"It's a living creature, Sevan. And this book will tell us how to look after it. I also got some books on thugs."

Nadio showed her small reading pile.

"That bottle of pish is meant to be very good. D'Auria got it by blackmailing the shopkeeper. It turns out she isn't the looter in the picture on Herse and she helped Yor after all."

Sevan wasn't really paying attention. He was busy reading the book.

"It says here that kuxeds are normally an amorphous shape but that breeders grow them in a frame, which makes them grow into a cube shape. Sounds very cruel."

"What do they eat?"

Sevan skimmed through the text until he found the section on diet.

"It says that they absorbed some kind of tree sap." he skimmed the section on domestication. "But here it says that we can feed them by rubbing them with putrid tongue oil, whatever that is."

"It's a plant," said Ay-ttho

"Where can we find putrid tongue oil?"

"Shouldn't be too difficult to find, but we'll have to go out when it gets light. I could have sworn we were being followed."

"Why would someone send us a small cuboid creature?"

"Nothing surprises me anymore."

The next rotation they went out to buy the putrid tongue oil and Ay-ttho had the same feeling that they were being followed.

They went to the large market that appeared to sell anything edible and quite a few things that weren't. They found a stall covered in bottles of all shapes and sizes and asked for what they wanted.

"How much do you need?" the stallholder asked.

"Better give us the largest one you have," said Nadio.

The stallholder reached under the stall and produced a large bottle that must have contained several units of oil. Nadio negotiated a price, and they were about to return to the ship when Ay-ttho suddenly grabbed a hooded figure from the crowd and pinned them up against a wall.

"Why are you following us?" she demanded.

The individual said nothing and so Ay-ttho removed the hood, letting go of the individual as she did so, and stepped back in shock.

"Tori?" she asked.

Tori stared back at her.

"I wasn't sure it was you," he said. "Until I saw you in the light phase. I thought you might be another corporation security clone."

"By the gods, Tori. How are you? What happened? We thought we had lost you."

"So did I. I hid from the Ao-jun and then got a lift from the first ship I could. I thought the Ao-jun had got you."

"They almost did. We ended up on Lysithea with a saturnian colony. Effeeko is still there. We are going to go back for him, but the Zoxans and Athenians are fighting over Future at the moment, so it's not really safe. Come to the ship. Where are your things?"

"I don't have any things."

"Where have you been sleeping?"

"On the street."

"Why didn't you show yourself before? You could have slept on the ship."

"Like I said. I wanted to be sure it was really you."

Sevan and Nadio greeted warmly him. Only D'Auria kept her distance.

"Barnes didn't make it," Ay-ttho told him as they walked back to the ship. "We almost didn't make it. There are still some Angetenarians on Lysithea, but the gods only know what they've been up to while we were away. It is an uneasy relationship we have with the Saturnians."

"Is that who I think is?" he asked, nodding towards D'Auria. "It is, but she's not as bad as we thought. It turns out she wasn't the looter in the picture on Herse."

When they arrived on the Mastery of the Stars, they fed Tori and Sevan opened the expensive bottle of pish. They showed him the box and as Sevan rubbed the oil on it; it sang.

"See," said Sevan. "I told you it sang."

"It seems thrilled with that oil," said Nadio. "It must have been hungry."

"I would love to see kuxed in their natural environment. Apparently, when they are all singing together, they sound like a choir."

"Where is their natural environment?"

"I'm not sure. I'll have to check."

After he had eaten, Tori went to clean himself up and then sleep.

"Right. Let's go?" said Ay-ttho.

"Where to?" asked Nadio.

"To Lysithea, of course."

CHAPTER 40: BOTH SIDES ATTACK

Tori slept for the entire journey from Rechinia, past Leda and past Zistreotov, only waking up as they reached the portal to Future.

"Strap yourselves in," said Ay-ttho. "Anything could happen the other side of this portal."

Anything certainly was happening on the other side. They emerged to a scene of complete carnage. Broken ships drifted everywhere amongst clouds of smoke and debris.

Ay-ttho was having great difficulty steering the freighter in between the wreckage and chunks of debris glanced off the ship's hull.

Soon, they could see Future in the distance, or rather they couldn't. They could see smoke and dust and debris surrounding the planet and several ships, both Athenian and Zoxan, still engaged in battle.

"We are being approached by a Zoxan ship," Ron warned.

"Nadio? Take the weapons chair," said Ay-ttho.

Sevan was becoming less offended by constantly being passed over for the weapons chair. They had chosen him in the early rotations and perhaps that was why Ay-ttho didn't choose him anymore.

The range of Zoxan weapons was longer than those with which the Mastery of the Stars was equipped. They fired before Nadio had them within range. She deployed some anti weapons measures and waited.

The anti-weapon measures were, on the whole, successful and what little fire got through did next to no damage.

As soon as they were within range, Nadio let loose with all cannons, which had little effect on the Zoxan shields.

The Zoxan ship was closing rapidly and freighter's defences were becoming increasingly ineffective.

Suddenly, an Athenian fighter appeared, travelling at remarkable speed, firing wildly into the flank of the Zoxan ship, which was soon compromised by the intense fire.

"I guess they are still on our side," said Ay-ttho, as the Athenian pulled away from the crippled Zoxan ship and banked in a steep curve, still at incredible velocity.

It rounded on the Mastery of the Stars and fired on the freighter.

"You were saying?" said D'Auria.

The shortness of the approach meant the Athenian had little time to inflict significant damage on the freighter, which allowed Ay-ttho to take evasive action.

"Full speed for the Lysithea portal," she said. "Nadio? Deploy all the anti-weapons devices you have."

This, Nadio did, releasing a variety of munitions from the ship to float among the debris.

Some devices exploded on impact with debris, further shielding the freighter's flight from the Athenian ship.

Nadio used the ship's weapons to fire at more of the debris, creating a maze of explosions and scattering debris through which Ay-ttho could steer the freighter, but which created sufficient confusion to prevent the Athenian from maintaining a lock with his scanners.

"By my calculations, the Lysithea portal is too far away," said Ron. "The Athenian ship should have no difficulty in re-engaging before we reach the portal."

"What do you suggest?" asked Ay-ttho.

"We are very close to one of Future's moon's which at the moment is adequately shielded with debris. It should be a relatively simple procedure to navigate around the far side and land until the present danger has passed."

"Brilliant," said Ay-ttho, swinging the freighter around another lump of exploding debris and heading towards the moon.

Unfortunately, between the Mastery of the Stars and the moon was another Zoxan ship which fired as soon as they came into view.

"What are we going to do?" asked Nadio.

"Jettison some conventional fuel from the port thrusters," said Ay-ttho.

"But with respect," said Ron. "The fuel will ignite."

"That's the idea. It will look as if we've been hit."

Ron did as he was told and, as he predicted, the fuel ignited, leaving a trail of fire. Ay-ttho rolled the freighter into a steep dive towards the moon.

"We are going to crash," said Nadio.

"That's what we want them to think. Fire into the surface."

Nadio fired the cannons directly. At the moon, causing a reasonably sized crater on the surface. Then, at the last possible moment, Ay-ttho pulled the freighter out of the dive, which was easier said than done. The ship skimmed the surface, ripping off some protruding apparatus.

"We didn't need those anyway," she said.

"What do you mean?" Ron complained. "I'd only just fixed those."

Ay-ttho soon regained control and flew at a very low altitude.

"Where are we going?" asked Nadio.

"I've been here before. There is a massive crater called Mooncircle lake, at one end is a valley which is the perfect hiding place."

"And you know how to get there?"

"Ron does, don't you, Ron?"

"I've never been there myself, but I know where it is from tracking you and Tori. It was on one of the previous times you lost me, if you remember."

"Yes, okay Ron. It's not like we do it deliberately. If you were better at not getting stolen."

Ron was silent.

"I think you've upset him," said Sevan.

Ron navigated the Mastery of the Stars in silence over the barren moon. Flying low between the mountains until they reached the giant crater. At one end of the crater was a valley, created by the swallowed angle of the meteor when it hit the moon's surface. Ron steered the freighter up the valley to the very end, where he parked the freighter in a sheltered spot where it would be well hidden.

"Now what?" asked Nadio.

"Now we wait," said Ay-ttho

"For what?"

"For the zoxans and Athenians to get bored."

From the journey across the moon they had experienced a clear view of the immense dust cloud which surrounded Future. Whatever had been on the planet when the asteroid struck, there wouldn't be much of it left.

Ron cloaked the freighter in a fake signature and transmitted the Mastery of the Stars signature to the blast crater they had made during their dive to the surface.

"The last time we were here was to meet D'Heli and Alyr," said Ay-ttho. "That was a very long time ago. We were looking for you, Nadio."

"Where was I?"

"On Nereid I think. We were with Witt."

"Oh, yeah, Witt. He had a colossal head."

"Anything you'd like to fill me in with?" asked D'Auria.

"Not really," said Ay-ttho. "Friends seem to come and go with startling rapidity."

"Another reason to make sure Effeeko is all right," said Nadio. "Did you check the tachyon transmitter?"

"Yes. I asked Ron to see if he could contact Effeeko, but I guess that, without the Mastery of the Stars, he has nothing to send messages with."

"He'll be busy with patients."

"He certainly will."

"Have I met this Effeeko?" asked D'Auria.

"I don't think so. He ran the hospital at the temple on Angetenar."

D'Auria shook her head.

"Who's hungry?" asked Nadio. "We are all stocked up. You name it, I'll cook it."

"Sorry to interrupt," said Ron. "I thought you might like to know that I have detected activity close by."

"What kind of activity?"

"There is some kind of settlement on the ridge above the valley."

"Who would settle there?" asked Nadio.

"The only reason to come to this moon is to study its geology," said Ay-ttho. "Could they be geologists, Ron?"

"They are carrying a rather large amount of weaponry for geologists."

"Uxclod! Do you think they saw us land?"

"I think I flew too low for them to detect us, but it is probably wise for us to stay alert just in case."

"What are they doing up there?"

"I don't want to know," said Nadio.

"I do," said D'Auria.

"Then have a look. Oh, yes, and by the way. You are not moving all old and frail like you were when we first met you. Was that all an act?"

"You had more sympathy because you thought I was weak."

"I'll tell you what I think. I think thugs have shorter life spans than other species and yet here you are, what, 90 standard solar cycles?"

"We all have our secrets. Like what happened before you went into suspended animation."

"I thought I told you not to mention that?"

"I guess I don't listen. So, are we really going, Tori?"

"Why not? Let's see who's up there."

"I can tell you who is up there," said Ron. "They are Athenians."

"What are they doing?"

"Look at this scanner image."

They gathered around a table on which Ron was projecting a holographic image of what his scanner could detect on the ridge above the valley.

They could clearly see four Athenians. Two of the Athenians appeared to be holding a third to the crater wall while a fourth watched.

"Ron, can you get any audio?" asked Ay-ttho.

A crackly noise began and gradually improved until they could hear a distinct conversation.

"Hephaestus, we're here now, carry out Wor's orders. Nail him down. You are sure the chains won't break? He is a traitor. He has to pay for his love of the Zoxans."

"Kratos, Bia," said another. "As far as you are concerned, you have carried out Wor's orders already. I dislike it, but it is not wise to ignore Wor. Prometheus, I must bind you to this rock. This is your reward for befriending the Zoxans. You weren't afraid of angering Wor and gave the zoxans that which did not belong to them. Because of that, they sentence you to remain here forever."

"Come on, get on with it," said the first.

"We are comrades—we share strong, common bonds."

"That may be true, but can you disobey Wor? Do you not fear him more?"

"You have no pity, do you?"

"There's no point crying for this one. What good does that do?"

"I hate my job."

"Why? Your skills have nothing to do with the reasons we are here."

"That's as maybe, but I'd still rather it was someone else."

"All us workers have our burdens to bear. Only Wor is truly free."

"You can say that again. Look at this."

They watched as the flickery hologram gestured towards the Athenian being held against the crater wall.

"Hurry. Don't let Wor see you hesitate."

"Okay,"

The Athenian began fixing chains on the crater wall.

"Here, bind his hands," said the first. "Rivet them to the rock."

"There, that looks all right," said the second.

"Make sure it's tight. He has a habit of wriggling out of tricky situations."

"No-one will get out of that."

"And, here. Make sure it doesn't come loose. He needs to realise he is nothing compared to Wor."

"This work is good, Look."

"Drive a pin through his chest."

"Oh, Prometheus. I hate to see you suffer," the second seemed to falter.

"Why do you moan about him? Be careful or you'll soon be moaning about yourself."

"It's difficult to look at him."

"He's getting what he deserves. Come on, let's wrap these chains around him."

"Stop ordering me about."

"I'll order you about as much as I want."

"There. That should do it. We'll, that didn't take too long."

"Make sure it's all secure. You know how vicious Wor can be."

"Let's go. He's not getting out of that."

They watched the hologram as one of the Athenians walked away from the group to what looked like a shuttle.

"That will serve you right for what you did," the first continued. "You should have thought ahead. Now you'll need more than to think ahead to get out of those chains."

The two figures left for the shuttle and took off, leaving the chained Athenian behind.

"I know what is coming!" the chained Athenian yelled after the departing shuttle. "That's why they called me Prometheus. Just because I shared your secrets with the Zo..."

The chained Athenian stopped shouting suddenly and was looking about from side to side.

"Who is listening?" he asked.

Ay-ttho, Tori, Nadio and D'Auria exchanged nervous glances.

"He can't possibly know we are here," said Ay-ttho.

CHAPTER 41: THE CAMP AT MOONCIRCLE VALLEY

"Let's go up there," said D'Auria. "Are you coming, Tori?"

"You must be mad," said Nadio. "You heard them talking. Whoever ordered them to do this is not someone to be messed with."

"Here I am," Prometheus shouted. "I know you can hear me. Come and release me."

Nadio shook his head.

"Come on Tori, let's go," urged D'Auria.

"I also think it's a bad idea," said Ay-ttho, but it was too late. D'Auria and Tori were already climbing into their suits.

Reaching the top of the crater wall was no small task in their cumbersome suits, but eventually they arrived and stood in front of Prometheus.

"You need not fear us," said D'Auria.

"Look, I am chained. What do you expect me to do?"

"We understand that you an chained here because of something you did to upset someone called Wor."

"I would have rather he deactivated me than leave me here."

"We understand Wor did this because you gave Athenian secrets to the Zoxans."

"Yes, but he will need me. The day will come when he will have to remove me from these chains and beg me to help him."

"So, you are quite happy to wait here until then?" asked Tori.

"Wor is a tyrant, but the time will come when his empire collapses and in that moment he will need me and I look forward to it."

"Would you mind telling us that whole story of how you came to be here?"

"I find it difficult to talk about, but I also cannot stay silent. The Athenians were arguing among themselves and Wor wanted to seize power from the then leader. I tried to advise the Athenians and, to prevent civil war, I joined Wor in his bid to become leader. I helped him and this is the way he repays me."

"But why?"

"As soon as he assumed power, he set about eradicating, first the original Athenians that had created us and then the Zoxans. But I was the only one who objected to his plan, the only one who had the courage. I was too late to save the Athenians, but I wasn't going to let the Zoxans meet the same fate."

"So, he nailed you to this rock?"

"That's right."

"Are you sure that's all you did?"

"I gave the Zoxans hope. And technology."

"What kind of technology?"

"Technology to help them match the Athenians in a fight."

"I can see why Wor might be upset about that. How long do you have to stay here for?"

Prometheus tried to shrug, but it was exceedingly difficult considering the extent to which he was chained.

"When Wor decides."

"That might be never. I guess you must be regretting what you did a bit."

"That's easy for you to stay when you are not chained to a rock. I am well aware of what I did, and I did them willingly. Choosing to help the zoxans has brought this about. I expected punishment, but I did not expect this. I had my reasons."

"What were they?"

"D'Auria, Tori," Ron communicated urgently. "There is a craft coming. Get out of there as soon as you can."

"We've got to go," D'Auria told Prometheus.

"We were never here," added Tori.

They scrambled down the crater rim as quickly as they could. Fortunately, the ship was approaching from the other side and so they were out of sight. By the time they arrived back on the bridge of the Mastery of the Stars, the new arrival had landed, descended from their ship and approached Prometheus. They listened to Ron's scanner.

"Prometheus, I have arrived," said the visitor. "Do you like my new ship? It is thought controlled. I feel great sympathy for you, Prometheus, and for your suffering. No-one wins more respect from me than you. You will soon realise I speak the truth and do not simply prattle empty words. So come, show me how I can be of help, for you will never say you have a friend more loyal to you than Oceanus."

"What?" asked Prometheus. "You have come all this way to gaze at my suffering? You were brave enough to leave Tritio to journey to this battlefield? You, a friend of Wor, who helped him become leader."

"Prometheus, although you possess a subtle mind, I would like to offer you some good advice. Understand your character and adopt new habits. For the Athenians have a new ruler now. If you keep hurling out offensive words, with such insulting and abusive language, Wor may well hear you, even though he is far away, high in space, and then this present heap of anguished pain will seem mere childish play. Set aside this angry mood of yours and seek relief from all this misery. You should hear me as your teacher and stop this kicking out against the whip. You know, Wor rules all by himself and has no one he must answer to. I will go and, if I can, attempt to ease your pain."

"I am happy things turned out so well for you," said Prometheus. "You supported my cause, but you escaped all blame. Now let me be and do not make my suffering your concern. You should take care this journey you have made does not get you in trouble."

"I am confident Wor will free you from this suffering."

"You have my thanks, and I will not forget. But spare yourself the trouble. Just keep quiet, and do not interfere. I may be miserable, but my distress does not make me desire to see such pain imposed on everyone. You saw what Atlas had to suffer, and they reduced Typhon to ash. Take care, in case one day that heart of his vents its rage on you. Be on your way."

As they listened, D'Auria, Tori, Nadio and Ay-ttho wondered who Atlas and Typhon were and what they could have done to enrage Wor.

"You want me to leave," said Oceanus. "And I am eager to go. My new ship is quick. You would like it."

They watched as Oceanus returned to his ship and left.

"I don't want to meet this Wor," said Nadio.

"I wonder what the zoxans gave Prometheus in return," said D'Auria.

"There is another ship coming," said Ron.

"What a great place to hide," said Tori. "This moon is busier than the Gaia space station.

"I think it's just passing by. Oh no, wait. It's landing."

"What ship is it?" asked Ay-ttho.

"Zoxan."

They watched on the scanner as the ship landed near Prometheus. Out of the ship stepped a Zoxan in some kind of mechanised space suit, which made it look even more intimidating than usual, even in the imperfect resolution of the holographic projection.

The Zoxan approached Prometheus.

"Where are we?" it asked and then seemed to double up in pain.

"I am Prometheus."

"What behaviour did you come here to accept such punishment?"

"The will of Wor and Hephaestus' hands."

"What crimes are you punished for?"

"I have said enough. I will not tell you any more than that. Why are you in pain?"

"The Athenians kicked me out of my house. And now I'm wandering alone, not knowing what to do next. Wor sent an asteroid to destroy us. Wounded while trying to escape. I don't know where I am. I just keep running from place to place."

"You are on Future's moon. You have many options from here, however, do not take the portal to Lysithea because in that system is the home of the Athenians. Choose any of the others, though I can't guarantee the Athenians are not there already."

"Oh, no. I may as well die here."

"I wish I could, but I am designed to endure until they toppled Wor."

"Don't they deactivate themselves if they are dishonoured?" said Nadio.

"Shhh," said D'Auria.

"You think Wor will be overthrown?" asked the Zoxan.

"That would please you, wouldn't it?"

"Why not? I am only suffering because of him."

"Then it will happen."

"But who will topple him?"

"He will do that himself."

"But, how?"

"He will find a partner. One he will regret."

"His partner will depose him?"

"She will, because she will bear him offspring whose power is greater than his."

"I thought Athenians didn't have offspring," said Nadio.

"Shhh," said D'Auria

"Can Wor avoid this?" asked the zoxan.

"No. Only I can help."

"But who will free you if Wor doesn't?"

"Your offspring's offspring."

"What? Offspring of mine? How do you know all this?"

"Never you mind."

"You claim to know what will happen to me."

"You must take care to avoid Athenians."

"Obviously."

"But in the end, you will bear Wor's offspring."

"What? You are mad."

"Offspring of this offspring will release me."

The Zoxan doubled up in pain again, staggered to her ship, and left.

"What in the worst place was all that about?" asked Ay-ttho.

"We should ask him more about why he is saying these things," said D'Auria.

"I don't think we should," said Nadio.

"What about you, Tori?"

"Why not? I still have most of my suit on."

"Be careful," said Ay-ttho. "We have only just found you again."

D'Auria and Tori climbed the crater wall again.

"Sorry to bother you again," said Tori when they reached Prometheus. "We couldn't help but overhear your conversation with that zoxan just now. We were wondering why you seem to think that Wor will be overthrown by his offspring's offspring?"

"They may be what I want, but they will come to pass," he said.

"But how do you know?"

"Chains more onerous than mine will weigh his neck down."

"Yes, yes. But are you not worried that Wor will discover you are predicting his downfall?

"Why should I fear when I am destined not to die?"

"But how could you possibly know that? Wor could decide to inflict more punishment. "

"Then let him do it. I am quite prepared for anything he may inflict."

"D'Auria, Tori," Ron interrupted. "Another ship is coming."

"Oh no," said D'Auria.

"I can't believe it," said Tori.

They both scrambled down the bank again.

"It is another Athenian ship," said Ron as Tori and D'Auria staggered back onto the bridge.

"You devious, hot-tempered schemer who betrayed the Athenians by giving their secrets to the Zoxans," the Athenian told Prometheus. "Wor wants to know who this partner is that you predict will bear him offspring."

"Wow, word travels fast," said D'Auria.

"Oh, the gods!" Nadio exclaimed. "Do you think he has been monitoring Prometheus? He will know that you two went up there. We need to get out of here as quickly as possible."

"Relax. They probably just intercepted the Zoxan and got it to talk."

"Provide the name of who will bring on Wor's fall from power," the Athenian continued. "And don't give me any of your enigmatic riddles. Set down clearly every fact and do not make me ask a second time."

"What you are doing here, Hermes?" Prometheus asked. "You are proud and arrogant, quite fitting for a servant of Wor. You all are young and so is your power. But I will live to see Wor disgraced. I'm not afraid of you upstarts. You should hurry back the way you came. You will learn nothing from me."

"You brought this on yourself, Prometheus."

"I would not trade being nailed to this rock for the life you lead as Wor's slave."

"It sounds as if you find your present state a source of pleasure."

"I would love to see you enjoying this."

"You think I am to blame?"

"I hate everyone who received my help and then abused me."

"I see your madness is no mild disease."

"If madness means one hates one's enemies."

"You have not learned to show a sense of self-control in how you think. You should consider if this stance of yours will help your cause."

"What I am doing now has been foretold, determined long ago."

"It seems to me I am wasting my words. If these words of mine do not convince you, think about the storm of torment which will fall upon you. You should think hard."

Hermes turned, returned to his ship, and took off.

"Why is Prometheus so stubborn?" Tori asked the others.

"Hermes is coming back," said Ron.

He expanded the holographic image so that they could see Hermes' ship return and begin an attack run towards Prometheus.

Hermes let loose a barrage of fire so ferocious that it destroyed the top half of the crater wall in a ball of fire and Molten rock.

CHAPTER 42: THE NEW PROMETHEUS

The force of the explosion shook the Mastery of the Stars and rock rained down on the freighter.

"Damage report?" asked Ay-ttho, once the inundation of geology had subsided.

"Nothing significant," said Ron. "But it would be wise to go out and do a visual inspection. There is a lot of debris. We might have to move some of it before we take off so as not to risk any more damage."

"When you say 'we' you mean us, don't you?" said Tori.

"Of course. I can deploy some maintenance drones."

"That would be nice, thank you. Right, let's go."

This time, Tori and D'Auria were joined by Ay-ttho and Nadio. When they stepped outside the ship, they realised there was not much of a crater wall left. Rather, a new crater had been created, which had pushed debris down on top of the Master of the Stars. The maintenance drones soon got to work shifting the rubble.

Tori climbed up the now smaller crater wall to see inside the new crater.

"You had better come and see this," he said to the others.

They climbed up to see what was so interesting and were all stunned by what they saw. In the centre, the rocks were still glowing red, but in amongst them, also glowing red, was the skeletal remains of Prometheus.

Tori had already entered some way into the crater to get a closer look.

"Be careful," shouted Ay-ttho. "It looks very hot."

"I can't believe it," said Tori, staring at Prometheus's remains.

"What is it?" asked D'Auria, going after Tori.

As they watched, they could see that between the metal framework of Prometheus's charred remains, tiny tendrils were moving and joining up with each other. It was barely discernible, but after a few moments, both Tori and D'Auria were convinced that there was something inside Prometheus's shell and that, whatever it was, it was alive.

"What do you think it is?" asked Ay-ttho, after she had a closer look.

"I don't know," said Tori. "If I didn't know better, I would say that it looks as though Prometheus is fixing himself."

"Who's Prometheus?" asked Sevan, who had turned up late.

Tori pointed to the crumpled and twisted pile of smoking metal that was slowly being pulled together by ever-growing masses of tendrils that stretched and twisted and intertwined.

The more they watched, the more the wreckage resembled the shape that Prometheus had, until recently, enjoyed.

"What kind of creature is capable of that?" asked Tori.

"A very dangerous one," said Ay-ttho. "We should go. Ron? How long before we are ready to take off?"

"The drones are working as fast as they can, but it will take a while before it is safe to attempt a takeoff."

"We should take him with us?" said D'Auria.

"Are you mad?" said Nadio. "If someone as dangerous as Wor sounds, chained him to a moon and then sent someone to blow him up and he still isn't dead, why would we want him on our ship?"

"What if he's on our side?" said Sevan.

"That's the dumbest thing I've ever heard."

"No, wait," said Tori. "What if Sevan is right? What if Prometheus were on our side? We'd stand a much better chance against both the Zoxans and the Athenians. I would have no worries about going to Lysithea if Prometheus were with us. What do you think, Ay-ttho?"

"Okay, let's lock him in the brig and hope he wakes up in a good mood."

She asked Ron to send some drones to carry the remains of Prometheus to the sick bay.

They returned to the ship and waited while they installed the remains of Prometheus in the brig and they took the rest of the debris from the top of the freighter.

"So, tell me," Ay-ttho asked Tori. "What happened after I left you on Angetenar?"

"Well, I hid. Obviously. The Ao-jun were going house to house, killing everyone they found, so I stayed out of the way until they had lost interest and the majority had left. There were several of us hiding together and, after the worse of the Au-jun occupation had ended, some tried to rebuild their lives. Some decided to try to leave, so the next time a ship arrived, a group of us hitched a ride. The aim was to avoid the Zoxans but you know how the saying goes: all portals lead to Future. It was difficult to find any opportunity that didn't involve passing Future. I travelled via the outer world but no matter where I went, I ended up heading towards Future. When I hitched a ride on a freighter to Rechinia, I risked it. To my surprise, the Zoxan organisation was clearly in collapse. The entire system was completely disorganised and could pass through the Future system easily, just by paying a few bribes."

"It seems the Athenians have taken over now," said Ay-ttho. "So, it might not be so easy."

While they waited, they went to the brig to see Prometheus. His original form was clearly visible, as were the tendrils stringing him back together.

"It looks like he is burning through the floor," said Tori.

"Don't worry," said Ron. "He won't burn all the way through. The brig floor is thicker than most other areas of the ship."

"We are ready for takeoff," Ron interrupted their spectating.

"Okay, let's go," said Ay-ttho, and they all traipsed back to the bridge, leaving Prometheus to repair himself alone.

"The plan is," said Ay-ttho. "To stick to the dark side of the moon for as long as possible and then take as wide a trajectory as possible hoping we are less likely to be spotted by either Zoxan or Athenian if we are not taking a direct route to the portal. It will take longer, but hopefully it will be safer."

Ron did as Ay-ttho had said, and steered the Mastery of the Stars away from the moon so that it remained between the ship and Future, taking a wide trajectory so that they would cross the portal corridors rather than travel along them. At the zenith of this spiral was the portal to Lysithea.

Sevan suddenly felt uncomfortable and realised his fellow crew members were turning to stare at the entrance to the bridge. He turned as well and saw the large, though still very unfinished figure of Prometheus stood in the entrance.

Ay-ttho, Tori and D'Auria reached for their weapons almost simultaneously and pointed them at the Athenian who raised his half finished hands as if to say that violence was unnecessary.

"How did you get out of the brig?" Ay-ttho demanded.

Prometheus raised an unfinished finger to an unfinished mouth and shrugged.

"It appears he burned all the way through the brig floor," said Ron.

"I thought you said it was thicker there?" Ay-ttho complained, noticing the Prometheus was burning dark footprints into the floor of the bridge.

"It is."

"Then what's to stop him from burning through the floor of the bridge?"

Prometheus walked awkwardly to one of the control desks, leaving a trail of charred footprints, and placed half a finger into the end of a terminal. They followed him with their weapons.

"He is communicating with me," said Ron. "He apologises for the floor of the brig but says it was necessary for his regeneration. He stored a large amount of energy from the blast and is using it to create reactions with the elements within the floor to create material for his body. He is essentially made from our floor. But he says that he promises that his material needs are almost at an end and that he hopes he won't damage much more of our ship."

"Ask him if he has any hostile intentions towards us," said Ay-ttho.

"He says he does not mean harm to any of us and that he is grateful for us taking him on our ship. He hopes he does not put us in any more danger than we are already in and asks us where we are going."

"Tell him."

"He is concerned that Lysithea's proximity to Tritio means we are almost certainly going to encounter Athenian ships."

"What does he suggest?"

"He admits he knows of no other route to Lysithea."

"There might be a way," said Nadio. "If we could get a tachyon transmission to Cyrus, then Cyrus could get Effeeko and use the Horizon to bring him to anywhere we want."

"It's worth a try," said Ay-ttho. "Ron?"

"I'm already onto it."

"Do you need anything?" Ay-ttho asked Prometheus.

"He says you are very kind," said Ron. "He is going to go to another part of the ship where the marks he makes on the floor are less obvious."

Prometheus left the bridge.

"Very considerate," said Sevan.

"Considerate?" said Nadio. "Have you seen the mess he has made of the floor. I can't imagine what the brig looks like."

"I'm going to rub oil into the box," said Sevan before leaving.

"Why didn't you think of that before?" asked D'Auria.

"What? Rubbing oil into the box?" asked Nadio.

"No, asking Cyrus to bring Effeeko to us. She could have brought him to Rechinia, or even Tritio."

"We'll, if you're so brilliant, why didn't you think of it?"

"Stop it you two," said Ay-ttho. "We can't change what's already happened."

Ron, reduced the velocity of the ship to give Cyrus a chance to respond and they waited. While they waited, they went to the brig to see what damage Prometheus had done to the floor. A Prometheus shaped hole had been burned all the way through and, as they peered down, they could see that he had almost burned through the maintenance gantry below.

"Where is he now?" asked Ay-ttho.

"He's in one of the cargo holds, trying to spread his footprints around," said Ron.

"He'll ruin the whole ship."

"But at least he won't make any more holes. Wait... I have a message coming in from Cyrus. She says that the Athenians have also invaded Lysithea and do not go there. Her ship is damaged and she cannot fold. She does not know the fate of Effeeko or the other Angetenarians."

"What? But we have to do something."

"Do what?" asked Tori. "Take on the entire Athenian fleet by ourselves?"

"We can't just leave him there," said Nadio.

"But how do you expect to get through the portal and still avoid the Athenians?"

Nadio didn't respond but just sulked.

"Ay-ttho?" said Ron. "Prometheus has an idea for you."

"Okay, where is he?"

"In the hold."

"Right. Does he want us to go down there?"

"No, he can still only communicate via me. But he was saying that, in the same way he can communicate via me, he could also communicate to Athenian vessels."

"Okay," Ay-ttho didn't know what the point was.

"He thinks he could convince the Athenian fleet that we are on their side and that they should give us safe passage to Lysithea."

"Let's do it," said Nadio.

"Hold on a unit," said Tori. "How can we be sure it will work?"

"We can't, but it's the only plan we have."

The others reluctantly agreed and Ron accelerated towards the Lysithea portal.

Even at a distance, they could see there was a reasonable amount of traffic coming and going.

"Here we go," said Ay-ttho. "The moment of truth."

CHAPTER 43: A AUTOMATIC DRAGONFLY

As they approached the portal, they were met by an Athenian patrol ship.

"They want our identification and manifest," said Ron. "Prometheus is communicating with them directly."

There was a long awkward pause while they waited to see whether Prometheus's plan would work.

"What's happening, Ron?" asked Nadio.

"He's talking to them. They are asking lots of questions."

Nadio paced forward and backwards.

"Stop that," said D'Auria. "You're making me nervous."

"That's it," said Ron. "They're letting us go."

"He did it!" said Ay-ttho.

Ron steered the ship towards the portal where they had to queue due to the large volume of traffic.

"Ron? Please ask Prometheus why Wor decided to invade the Zoxans?" asked Ay-ttho.

"He says that Wor has expansionist ambitions. He wants to replace all species with his own which is why Prometheus turned against him."

Once they had passed through the portal, they headed straight towards Lysithea where small skirmishes were happening in the planet's orbit.

"Prometheus says the Athenians are probably picking off the craft of those Saturnians and Tritions trying to escape," said Ron.

He took the ship straight to the forest bio-dome where Effeeko and the other Angetenarians had been. The bio-dome was broken and the forest was in flames. They landed and disembarked to search for Effeeko on foot.

After a mega unit had expired they re-assembled at the ship. No-one of them had encountered any colonists, not even Saturnians.

"They must have taken them somewhere," said Ay-ttho. "If they had just killed them, there would be some evidence. Ask Prometheus if he can find any evidence of prisoner transport."

"He says there is evidence of a large amount of activity on Zanzenburg."

"Let's go and check it out."

Within only a few units into the flight, Ron triggered the silent intruder alarm.

"What is it?" asked Ay-ttho.

"There is something on the ship that wasn't here when we landed on Lysithea."

"What is it?"

"I'm not sure."

"Do you know where it is?"

"It's in the mess."

"Okay, seal it in. We'll go down there."

Ay-ttho and the others looked through the windows of the mess but could not see anything."

"Where is it?" asked Ay-ttho.

"It is on the third table from the door."

Ay-ttho looked.

"I can't see anything. Looks like there's a small insect."

"It is the insect."

"What? You daft uxclod. You brought us down here to tell us we trapped an insect. Just kill it. Spray it with something."

"It's not an ordinary insect. It's an automatic dragonfly."

"What's an automatic dragonfly?"

"Oh yes," said Nadio. "I've heard about those. They belong to the electric bowmen."

"The who?"

"No, the electric bowmen. You've heard of the mechanical bowmen? Elite troops mainly used for assassinations. They famously killed the first President Man and President Chuba."

Ay-ttho nodded.

"We'll, the electric bowmen were like an upgrade created by President Hours."

"Okay, but what is an automatic dragonfly when it's at home?"

"They are like the spies of the electric bowmen. They send them out to find a victim for them."

"So someone on this ship is a victim?" asked Tori.

"Possibly."

"Prometheus is trying to communicate with it," said Ron.

"Wow, Prometheus can do everything, can't he?" said Tori.

Ay-ttho sensed both sarcasm and jealousy in his voice.

"Prometheus says it's called A. He says he can't deactivated it," said Ron. "He says we should try and get it off the ship."

"And how does he propose we do that?" asked Tori.

"He's on his way there to catch it right now."

"Of course he is."

Prometheus entered the mess, caught A, took it to an airlock, threw it inside, locked the door and blew it out into space.

The Mastery of the Stars was soon in orbit around Zanzenburg and, as previously agreed, they surveyed the surface fully before deciding to land anywhere.

Athenian troops carriers were travelling back and forward depositing prisoners they had captured in other systems. In some cases this caused problems such as when rival species found themselves sharing the same space or, even worse a species found itself sharing a space with its predator.

Ron scanned the planet for Angetenarians.

"Lots of Ao-jun," Ron said. "Some Saturnians. Plenty of Indigenous Futurians and Zoxans. Some Herseans. A few Zistreotovians. Plenty of Tritions."

"No Angetenarians?" asked Nadio.

"Not yet. Cheng Huang colony. Genuihines. Thugs."

"Thugs?" Nadio and D'Auria said, almost in unison.

"Yes, quite a few. Here we go. I've found some Angetenarians. Very few. And they are mixed with Saturnians so there's a good chance they are from the Lysithea colony."

"Shall we go down?" asked Ay-ttho.

"Ron? Are you able to identify any obvious danger in the vicinity?" asked Tori.

"The whole situation on the surface is potentially volatile but I am sure there are no risks that Prometheus could not handle."

Tori ground all sets of his teeth.

They descended through the atmosphere and flew low along the green valleys which were now teeming with refugees. They flew over a plateau, on which the Angetenarians had constructed a large camp. Queues of refugees were waiting outside, so they assumed it must be a processing centre of sorts.

"We can't land," said Ay-ttho. "The refugees might hijack the ship."

"What do you propose?" asked Tori.

"Ron? Where exactly are the Angetenarians?"

"They are inside the centre."

"If we return to orbit, can you keep tracking them and tell us when they leave the centre?"

"I'll try."

"There is no try, there is only do or do not."

"Then I'll do."

"Good, let's go."

They waited patiently in orbit. At least, most of them waited patiently. Nadio was distinctly impatient.

"They could be doing anything to them in there. We should go and get Effeeko."

"Nadio, that camp is full off Athenians. We can't take them all on," said Ay-ttho.

"What about Prometheus?"

"He's not invincible. Otherwise, they wouldn't have been able to chain him to a rock. Besides, he hasn't finished regenerating yet."

Eventually, Ron told them they had emerged from the camp and they descended to the planet's surface once more.

At the opposite end of the camp, they saw huge queues waiting to board transporters.

"Where are they, Ron?" asked Ay-ttho.

"They are in one of those queues, waiting to board a transport."

"Send their location to my communicator. And don't let anyone on the ship while we are gone."

"I will come with you."

Ay-ttho turned to see a still unfinished Prometheus stood by the entrance to the bridge, his feet still smoking as they drew elements from the floor to continue his regeneration.

Ron landed only long enough to let Ay-ttho, Prometheus, Nadio, D'Auria and Tori to descend from the ship. Although the refugees at this side of the camp didn't appear to pay much attention to them, they didn't want to risk anything.

Checking her communicator, Ay-ttho led them towards the huge queues waiting patiently for the transports.

"There's something very odd about them," said Tori.

"I know what you mean," said Ay-ttho.

All of the refugees waiting in line were staring forward at the refugee in front of them. It was almost as if they were in some kind of trance.

"What has happened to them?" asked Nadio.

"Some kind of brainwashing?" Tori speculated.

They followed Ay-ttho, picking their way through the queues.

"There he is," said Nadio, rushing over to one of the queues. "Effeeko, it's me, Nadio."

Effeeko just stared straight ahead.

"Effeeko! What's the matter? Effeeko! Look at me."

Nadio tried to pull at his arm but Effeeko just pulled his arm away.

"He's been brainwashed," said Tori.

"Effeeko!" Ay-ttho tried standing in front of him but he stared right through her.

"I don't think it's brainwashing," said Prometheus.

"Oh no?" said Tori. "Then please do tell us what you think it is."

"I think they have replaced their marbles with something else."

"Such as?"

"An Athenian marble."

"What are you talking about?"

"Wor is set on domination of what was the old republic and beyond. But creating new Athenians is very costly and time consuming. I think he's found a way to put the Athenian marbles into the marbles of other species."

"So you are saying that Effeeko is an Athenian now?" asked Nadio.

"Essentially."

"Then what has happened to Effeeko?"

"Good question. He might still be in there somewhere or he might have gone altogether."

"You don't know that for sure. You're just guessing."

"You are right. I am."

"We can't let this happen," said Ay-ttho. "We have to stop them."

"And how do you propose we do that?"

"Whatever is doing this to them is there in that camp. We have to attack the camp."

"We have to get Effeeko to the sick bay first," said Nadio.

"You take Effeeko to the ship," said Prometheus. "I will deal with this."

Prometheus walked off towards the camp.

"Come on Effeeko," said Nadio, trying to drag him out of the queue.

But Effeeko was going nowhere. No matter how much Nadio attempted to pull Effeeko out of the queue, he wouldn't budge.

"Whatever Prometheus is doing," said Nadio. "We can't let him destroy whatever they are using to do this."

"Why not?" asked Tori.

"Because whatever they used to do this to Effeeko, we might need to reverse the process.

Ay-ttho and Tori went running after Prometheus, while Nadio and D'Auria stayed with Effeeko.

"Where is Sevan?" asked D'Auria.

"I don't know. Probably rubbing oil into his box. And I don't care. I just want to get Effeeko out of here."

Tori and Ay-ttho caught up with Prometheus just as he arrived at the exit of the camp where thousands were filing out to join the queues.

"Prometheus? We need to be careful. We might need their equipment to reverse the process," said Ay-ttho.

"Understood," said Prometheus, who approached a senior Athenian officer.

CHAPTER 44: THE DYING RACE

"General Prometheus?" the officer was surprised. "But I thought you were..."

"As you can see, I am not. I wish for you to give me an immediate tour of this facility."

"Of course, Sir. But first I will need to check..."

The officers didn't have a chance to finish his sentence because Prometheus grabbed his neck. Something metallic snapped and then the officer fell to the ground.

"Would you like to give me a tour?" Prometheus asked the next officer.

"Er... yes... of course."

Prometheus, Ay-ttho and Tori followed the officer towards one of the huge tents through which the prisoners were being processed.

"So what exactly is happening here?" Prometheus asked.

"Do you not know, sir?"

"Of course I know. I want to know whether you know."

"Oh, right. Well, this is where we process the prisoners. They go through the process of having their marbles replaced by Athenian marbles."

"And what happens to the victim?"

"The original marbles are suppressed."

"But they are not eradicated?" asked Ay-ttho.

"No, that process takes too long. It would reduce efficiency. "

"And can the process be reversed?"

"In theory, but it would be a lengthy process and there are obviously ethical issues regarding the new Athenian that occupies the marbles."

"Why are you doing this?"

"I have been ordered to do this."

"No, I mean, why are the Athenians doing this?"

"We are a dying race, sir. We cannot find resources quickly enough to make new Athenians. Professor Christie discovered a method to transfer Athenian marbles into those of other species and so, all we have to do now is manufacture Athenian marbles."

"Where are the marbles created?" asked Prometheus.

"Follow me."

The Athenian led them to a huge machine. Prisoners were being forced into one end and then they were emerging, calmly, from the other.

On top of the machine was a huge sphere.

"This is where the marbles are made," said the officer.

Prometheus took the officer's weapon and began firing into the sphere.

Ay-ttho and Tori were as stunned as the Athenian officer but held him back from Prometheus. The other Athenian guards began to fire on Prometheus. Ay-ttho and Tori dragged the officer to cover but Prometheus remained where he was, seemingly unaffected by the small arms fire ricocheting off his, still repairing, body.

"The General has gone mad!" the officer shouted. "We must stop him."

Ay-ttho punched him in the face, knocking him unconscious, freeing her and Tori to return fire on the Athenian guards from their position of cover.

Outside, D'Auria and Nadio could hear the commotion.

"You stay here with Effeeko," said D'Auria. "I'll go and see what's happening."

Despite receiving innumerable shots to his body, Prometheus was still able to fire on the sphere which was beginning to disintegrate.

Meanwhile, Athenian reinforcements had arrived and Prometheus began to falter under the barrage.

"Let's get out of here," said Ay-ttho, seeing that the sphere was about to collapse about them.

They ran along the length of the machine, the way they had came, to where prisoners were still emerging, oblivious of the fighting going on around th.em. Ay-ttho and Tori had to fight their way out of the giant tent where they met D'Auria.

"What's happening?"

"Prometheus is destroying the machine. Let's go."

Nadio was still waiting with Effeeko when they arrived.

"Come on," said Ay-ttho. "We have to go."

"What about Effeeko?"

"Sorry Effeeko," said Ay-ttho, before punching him in the face and knocking him unconscious. "Let's carry him."

Ay-ttho and Tori carried Effeeko away from the processing centre, unnoticed by the Athenian guards who were running towards the fighting.

"What about Prometheus?" asked Nadio.

"He'll have to fend for himself," said Ay-ttho. "Get Ron on the communicator and have him pick us up."

In the sky, they could see a fleet of Athenian fighters arriving with reinforcements.

"What about all the other Angetenarians and Thugs here," asked Nadio.

"We can't rescue everyone," said Ay-ttho. "Let's look after Effeeko first. Then we can think about this place."

Ron met them on a rise some distance from the processing centre. They hurried on board, took Effeeko straight to the sick bay and strapped him down onto one of the beds. Nadio stayed with him, while the others rushed to the bridge.

"Where to?" asked Ron.

"Right now, anywhere," said Ay-ttho.

Ron lifted the freighter high onto the sky and almost immediately, Athenian fighters peeled off from the fleet to intercept.

"What are we going to do, now Prometheus isn't here," said Tori with a hint of sarcasm, but he knew that they could have really done with Prometheus at this point.

"I still have the data he transmitted last time," said Ron. "I will try sending it again."

The Athenian fighters escorted the freighter while they verified the data but, once satisfied, they returned to their fleet and Ron was free to continue their journey.

"Where now?" asked Ron.

"No point going back to Lysithea now," said Ay-ttho. "We'll have to risk passing Future again."

"We could do a lot worse than going back to Rechinia," said Tori.

"I agree," said D'Auria.

"I could get some more books," said Sevan, who had suddenly appeared on the bridge, his face buried in the book he was using to learn how to look after his box.

"Sevan? Did you know that Effeeko is in the sick bay?" asked Ay-ttho.

"Is he? How nice. I'll pop by to say hello."

Sevan wandered off the bridge again, his face still buried in his book.

On the route to the Future portal they passed substantial traffic coming the other way, mainly Athenian military ships.

The Athenians had set up checkpoints on either side of the portal but Ron transmitted the same codes that Prometheus had used and they appeared to work because the Athenians allowed them to proceed.

The Future side of the portal was still littered with disabled ships and the planet itself was still shrouded in clouds of dust. The fighting appeared to have ended suggesting that the Athenians had finished off the last of the Zoxan resistance.

At the Zistreotov portal, they had to join a queue of ships waiting to pass the Athenian checkpoint.

"Maybe they are searching ships," Tori suggested. "What if they find Effeeko?"

"Nadio?" Ay-ttho said over the intercom. "We might be searched. Give Effeeko a sedative."

Nadio did as he was asked. Effeeko had regained consciousness and his Athenian personality was protesting about being restrained. Any searchers would immediately discover they had kidnapped Effeeko if he were allowed to remain conscious. Nadio administered the sedative and Effeeko immediately fell into a slumber.

Tori was correct, they were searching ships and when they reached the front of the queue a patrol of Athenian guards boarded and searched the entire freighter.

They accepted Nadio's explanation that Effeeko was restrained because he had been fitting and paid little attention to Sevan polishing his box; they assumed it was he who was singing.

Satisfied the freighter was not sheltering zoxan fugitives, the Athenians allowed the Mastery of the Stars to continue on its journey.

Ron headed straight for the Leda portal and them onto Rechinia where they landed in the same hangar as before.

Ay-ttho asked the caretaker if there was anywhere good to eat nearby and the caretaker told the of a hostelry called the Sun which was basic but good value. Nadio said he would stay with Effeeko and Ay-ttho promised to bring him something back.

The Sun was small, dark, wooden floored and frequented by an assortment of unsavoury looking creatures. D'Auria found a small table in the corner that could just about accommodate her, Tori, Sevan and Ay-ttho.

"So, you managed to prise yourself away from your box," D'Auria said to Sevan who still had his nose buried in his book.

"I miss him already," he said, suddenly noticing the type of establishment to which Ay-ttho had taken them. "Do you think they have fushy or pish here?"

"I'll find out."

D'Auria got up and walked over to the serving counter. She came back a unit later with four glasses of what looked to Sevan like dishwater.

"What is that?" he asked when D'Auria placed the cloudy liquid in front of him.

"Apparently it's better than fushy or pish," she said.

Sevan looked unconvinced and sipped the liquid cautiously.

"It's very bitter. But it's not bad."

"I've had it before," said Tori. "It has a very calming effect. It's made from Inferno Root."

"I thought that was illegal in the Republic," said Ay-ttho.

"It was but the Republic is long gone."

Ay-ttho felt the strange sensation of being watched again. When she looked at the window it was almost as if something had just moved out of the way before she looked up.

"Do you ever get the feeling we are being followed?" she asked.

"Always," said D'Auria. "Inferno root has that effect."

"I don't think it's the root, we've only just started drinking it. I'm going to take a look outside."

The street outside the Sun was deserted but Ay-ttho had an uncomfortable sensation that a nano-unit earlier someone or something had been there.

"I don't like this place," she said when she returned to the others.

"Relax, sit down," said D'Auria. "Have a another."

"Do you remember that night in Hygiea?" asked Sevan

"Not really."

"Exactly. There were some incredible drinks. What were they called?"

"Whimsical lotus," said Tori.

"That's right. That stuff was as rough as the worst place."

"Do you remember the fantasy hell?"

"Oh yeah, it was like a cooked version of this," Sevan raised his glass. "But much worse."

"It wasn't the whimsical lotus or the fantasy hell that got you that night," said Ay-ttho. "It was the crimson punches."

"We didn't drink crimson punches, did we?" laughed Tori. "That would explain everything."

"No, it wasn't the crimson punches," said Sevan. "It was definitely the fantasy hell. Terrible stuff."

"That's right, you got all paranoid. Did we go to a singing room?"

"I thought we agreed never to speak of it again," said Ay-ttho.

"That's true," said Tori.

"Anyway, let's order some food. I need to take something back to Nadio."

"Do they have a menu?" asked Sevan.

"Do they look like they have a menu?"

Sevan shrugged.

"I'll ask what they have."

Ay-ttho went to the counter. She returned a unit later with the same dissatisfied expression.

"All they have are Gurtions protein cobs, Pasteurized Blorn rinds or Edoato astro-beetle."

"I love blorn rinds," said D'Auria.

"What are they?" asked Sevan.

"Try them. You'll like them."

"Alright," said Ay-ttho. "I'll get blorn rinds for everyone."

"And another round of drinks," said D'Auria, raising her empty glass.

Ay-ttho delivered their rinds and another round of drinks and then left them to take Nadio's rinds back to the Mastery of the Stars.

As soon as she got outside of the Sun, the sensation she was being watched returned. It was a different sensation than when she had been followed by Tori. This felt more like a thing.

She took a roundabout route back to the freighter, looking around all the time to see if I was being followed. She was almost back at the hangar when she saw it, only for a moment, but it was undeniable. The tiny fluttering shape of A, the automatic dragonfly that Prometheus had thrown out of the airlock. Ay-ttho knew immediately what it meant and ran all the rest of the way back to the ship.

CHAPTER 45: FIRST FROM THE SUN

"Ron, tell the others to get back here as soon as they can," said Ay-ttho, as soon as she arrived on the ship.

"Of course. Might I tell them why?"

"I just saw the automatic dragonfly that Prometheus threw out of the airlock. The electric bowmen might not be far behind."

Ay-ttho rushed to the sick bay, gave Nadio his rinds and explained what she had seen.

"They are probably after D'Auria," said Nadio. "We should leave her to them."

"What if they are after the box?"

"The box? No, they are after D'Auria for certain. She has done enough bad things in her life for several electric bowmen."

"She has been exonerated for some of them."

"Whatever."

When the others returned from the Sun. Ay-ttho met them on the bridge.

"What are we going to do?" asked Tori.

"Get out of here as quickly as possible," said Ay-ttho.

"They'll only come after us," said D'Auria. "Do you want to be running for the rest of your lives?"

"That's all we seem to do anyway," said Sevan.

"I say we stay and fight."

"That's fine for you to say, D'Auria. They're probably after you, anyway. Why don't we leave you to stay and fight?"

"Fine by me, because I'm certain they are not after me. They're after you for whatever you did that caused you to be in suspended animation so long."

"How about you? Thugs don't live 85 solar cycles, you must have been in suspended animation too."

"Well, I guess we both have our little secrets then, don't we? But my secret doesn't warrant being hunted by electric bowmen. Does yours?"

Ay-ttho was silent.

"I thought so."

"Look, this doesn't get us any closer to a solution," said Tori. "D'Auria is right."

"I am?"

"If we run, they will only come after us and we will run forever. However, if we stay, we will face some of the most formidable assassins the known universe has ever seen."

"So, we run," said Sevan.

"We run," said Tori.

"You can run," said D'Auria.

"I think we will," said Ay-ttho.

"And where will you run to?"

"We'll go towards Mytilene."

"The same way that Chuba fled."

"Yes, but we'll get beyond Ptolemy."

"We'll see."

"Are you coming with us?"

"I'm tempted to see where and when they catch you but, no thank you, I'll stay here."

"At least then we will find out if they are after you or us."

Nadio entered the bridge and approached Ay-ttho.

"We can't keep running," she said. "We don't have enough credits."

D'Auria reached into her bag, took out a card and handed it to Nadio.

"I've been meaning to give you this," she said.

"What is it?"

"It is the credits that Ay-ttho and Scotmax gave me. Not the original credits, I drank those. But it is the same amount. I was never comfortable about it."

Nadio touched the card to his communicator.

"26,000?"

"Yes, that should keep you going for a while."

"Then why did I pay in the Sun?" Ay-ttho complained.

"Right, then there is no time to waste. We should go. Where will you stay, Auria?"

"I'll find somewhere. I hear the Sun has some rooms."

"May the gods be with you," said Ay-ttho.

"You don't believe in the gods, but thank you. And thank you all. I hope I haven't been too much of a burden for you all."

D'Auria's comment was met with a murmur of polite dissent.

She waved them goodbye, stopped by her cabin to collect what meagre possessions she had, and then descended from the ship into the hangar.

Half way across the hangar floor, she pulled her weapon and shot something in the air. She walked over to where it had fallen and picked it up, it was a tiny automatic dragonfly.

"Better get going," she shouted.

Ron closed the doors and the Mastery of the Stars took off. D'Auria sat at the edge of the hangar and watched the freighter disappear into the sky.

"Mytilene," said Ay-ttho.

"Already programmed in," said Ron.

"Will we need to stop for supplies?"

"Not advisable. Although you would be fascinated by the impressive Mytilenean warships in orbit. Perhaps I can pass close enough for you to get a view."

"That won't be necessary."

"Mytilene was also home to one of the seven sages."

"Sevan sages?" asked Sevan.

"In the rotations before the old republic, the seven sages who made laws and settled disputes ruled this region of the universe. Pittacus of Mytilene held the support of the old religions in the rotations before the modern gods."

"Who were the other sages?"

"There were Thales of Miletus, Bias of Priene, Solon of Tritio and Chilon of Ao-jun, but the other two are unknown."

"That's enough history, thanks Ron," said Ay-ttho. "Let's focus on running away, shall we?"

"You forget I can focus on many tasks simultaneously. It would be wise to avoid Mytilene. I sense a great deal of Athenian activity there. I am heading straight for the Cilician portal."

"Good."

"Sevan? You might be interested to know that Cilicia was the home of the famous hunter, Bellerophon."

"Ron!" Ay-ttho complained.

"Sorry."

Sevan returned to his quarters to rub oil into the box where Ron told him tales of the mythical sea creatures of Cilicia well out of earshot of Ay-ttho. When they crossed the portal to Ptolemy, Ron told him tales of ancient explorers that had fought over the planet, which had once been fertile but had become a barren wasteland.

"It is where the mechanical bowmen assassinated President Chuba," he said. "There is a monument that has become a site of pilgrimage for Chuba's followers."

"He still has followers."

"Oh yes. For every president, there are those who think they were the best president ever. Even supporters of President Xocliw come here to celebrate her victory over Chuba and sometimes the two sides clash."

"Even after all this time?"

"Especially after all this time. Time has a way of modifying facts into opinion and the more time goes by, the stronger those opinions can become and the more estranged they become from reality."

"You can be very wise sometimes, Ron."

"I know."

"What comes after Ptolemy?"

"We'll, there's the thing. This is why Ay-ttho feels this is such a good escape route. There haven't been expeditions beyond Ptolemy that have returned so the area remains uncharted."

"Never?"

"Incredible, isn't it? The region does not appear on any star charts."

"Do you think the electric bowmen will follow us in?"

"Almost certainly."

"But between you and me, I don't think they are the only ones looking for us. I didn't want to worry the others but I have detected our signature in deep space scans."

"You didn't want to worry them but you are happy to worry me."

"Sorry about that."

"So we are being pursued by more than one group?"

"Apparently, let's just hope that only one of them wants to kill us."

"Thank you, Ron. That's very reassuring."

After he had finished rubbing oil into the box, Sevan went to the sick bay to see how Nadio was coping with Effeeko.

"How is he?" Sevan asked.

"The Athenian has been talking to me. He is aware of Effeeko inside his marbles."

"Weird. You haven't been able to speak with Effeeko."

"Not yet, but he is definitely in there somewhere. The problem is that the Athenian doesn't belief any of this is real. He has no recollection of who he is or how he got here so he thinks this is all a dream."

They were interrupted by Ron telling Sevan when the ship would be passing through the portal on the far side of Ptolemy because he had told Ron that he would like to be on the bridge with the others when they passed through the portal.

"Are you sure about this?" asked Tori. "We don't know what is on the other side."

"No, but we know what is on this side," said Ay-ttho.

"But what if there is a black hole on the other side?"

"Then we have to hope that it leads to a white hole somewhere else."

This made Sevan extremely nervous, and he watched with trepidation as the freighter entered the portal.

"There's no star," said Tori, when they emerged from the other side.

"There is," said Ron. "It just appears very dim because a Sinik sphere surrounds it."

"What's a Sinik sphere?" asked Sevan.

"It is a mega-structure that encompasses a star and captures a large percentage of its solarpower output."

Sevan didn't appear to be any the wiser.

"It's a way for a civilisation to meet its energy requirements once those requirements exceed what can be generated from the home planet's resources alone. Because only a tiny fraction of a star's energy emissions reach the surface of any orbiting planet, building structures encircling enable a civilization to harvest far more energy. There weren't any in the old Republic because they shared resources between systems."

"But that doesn't explain why this system isn't on the star charts," said Tori.

"At least it wasn't a black hole," said Sevan.

"Maybe they just want to be left alone," said Ay-ttho.

"The question is, what measures are they willing to take to ensure that happens?" said Tori.

"We are about to find out," said Ron. "I have detected several craft emerging from the Sinik sphere."

"Armed?"

"Very much so."

"Probably a good idea to talk, then."

As the craft drew closer, it became clear that they were large, plentiful, and formidably armed. They formed a cordon around the Mastery of the Stars.

"We will escort you. Please do not attempt to flee, fight, or remain. You will come with us peaceably," Ron relayed the announcement to the bridge.

"They speak good Future Standard," said Tori. "We had better follow them, then."

Ron navigated the freighter within the cordon until they reached the sphere, which turned out to not be a sphere at all but a network of immense rotating cylinders with gaps in between. The escort manoeuvred within one of these gaps and then into an immense air lock which closed behind them.

A vast door ahead opened, and they escorted the freighter into the vast rotating cylinder.

What astonished Sevan was the sheer immensity of the project. The cylinder was huge, the size of a continent. Green forest and countryside stretched away for hundreds of units, probably more, and all around them. It seemed to stretch on forever, but he knew this wasn't the case because he had seen the extent of each cylinder from a distance.

The escort landed on an empty stretch of grassland. A light in the centre, which obscured the terrain immediately above them, illuminated everything.

"Take your belongings and leave the ship. You may take your weapons, they will be useless against our ships," came the next announcement.

"Can you send a voice communication, Ron?" asked Ay-ttho.

"Of course."

"What makes you think we are going to leave our ship?"

"Because if you don't leave voluntarily, we will make you leave."

"Why would we leave?"

"You have entered our system without being invited. In order to preserve our security, you must never leave. You will take your belongings and leave the ship."

"Wait a unit. You are going to dump us with no explanation?"

"We have explained. For the safety of our system, you must never leave. Hostile species surround us, and this is how we defend ourselves. "

"Ron?"

"They have control of the ship, I'm afraid."

"Ron! You really have to stop this from happening."

"Sorry, but there was little I could do, and that was ineffective. They have very sophisticated technology."

"We'll, I'm not just going to stand by and let them chuck us off our own ship."

No sooner had Ay-ttho finished speaking than doors on the escort ships opened and many large walking machines descended from the ships. They were large, but not too large to board the Mastery of the Stars. They had no heads, and each had four arms which concluded in formidable looking weapons.

"I don't think we have a choice," said Tori.

CHAPTER 46: THE ELECTRIC BOWMEN

D'Auria watched the electric bowmen enter the hangar. They looked a lot older than he had expected, but then they had probably been pursuing the Mastery of the Stars for over 85 standard solar cycles, so they could be forgiven for looking a bit rough.

They looked at D'Auria. D'Auria pointed to the sky in the direction that the Mastery of the Stars had left. The electric bowmen looked in the direction D'Auria was pointing, and then one of them reached into a pouch and pulled out a small object.

He lifted the object up to the sky in the palm of his hand. The object unfurled tiny dragonfly wings and flew up into the sky.

"Do you mind telling me what they did?" D'Auria asked.

The electric bowmen looked at D'Auria, turned and left.

*

Sevan, Nadio, Ay-ttho and Tori sat on top of the piles of equipment they had unloaded from the Mastery of the Stars. They had, in fact, emptied the cargo holds as well as stripping the sick bay and most of the crew quarters.

Their captors had been very patient but, once everything had been unloaded, they left with the Mastery of the Stars. They also took the space suits that had been unloaded and put them back on the freighter.

Sevan had been pleased to discover that they still had a consignment of hoverboards but that elation had soon passed with the realisation that they were now stranded.

"So, what now?" asked Ay-ttho.

Nobody answered. Everyone was out of ideas.

"I wonder what D'Auria is doing now," said Sevan.

"Who cares," said Nadio.

Effeeko grunted. He was still strapped to the bed they had wheeled off the ship.

"We need to build a shelter," said Ay-ttho.

Sevan stopped rubbing oil into his box and got up to help.

"How do we get off this place?" asked Tori.

"I don't know," said Ay-ttho. "Ogenus was different. They always dropped prisoners off in the same place. Here, they might never return."

They worked together to construct a shelter, and everyone shared a sense of achievement when they had finished.

"How long can we last on the supplies we have?" asked Nadio.

"Not sure," Ay-ttho admitted. "Tori and I should go into the forest during the next rotation and see what there is to hunt."

Ay-ttho used the word rotation but in reality, the light always remained overhead and it was only because of periodic dimming of the light that the illusion of rotations was maintained. It was into one of these periods of dim light that the group was about to enter.

Sevan slept uneasily; worried about what creatures might live in the cylinder's forests. When the light brightened again, Tori and Ay-ttho went into the forest to see whether there was anything worth hunting.

Nadio stayed with Sevan at the shelter to look after Effeeko, whose Athenian personality had been pleading to be released. Every so often, when it had become too irritating, Nadio would give Effeeko a sedative, but now they were stranded, he knew that he would have to ration the medication.

A few mega units later, Tori and Ay-ttho returned. Ay-ttho had a small mammal slung over her shoulder and Tori was carrying a bundle of wood.

"There's no shortage of food," said Ay-ttho. "We saw lots of cukids and other animals we can hunt. There's also an abundance of fruit trees and edible plants. It's almost as if they designed this place to sustain us."

"That's nice, but how do we escape?" said Nadio.

"If they hadn't taken our suits, I would have suggested tunnelling until we reached the cylinder shell and then break through, but even then, we wouldn't have a ship. To be honest, I don't know. Maybe we shouldn't try to escape. We have everything we need here. We are safe."

"Everything except our freedom."

In the rotations that followed, the group took steps to make their fledgling settlement more comfortable.

Tori and Ay-ttho began felling trees to construct a more permanent shelter. They had identified a sheltered site closer to a water source and built a structure that would allow them to transfer everything they had unloaded from the freighter.

Occasionally, artificial rain fell, and on the first occasion it had taken the group by surprise. Sevan marvelled at the variety of birds, insects and animals that populated the cylinder. He would have considered it a paradise had he chosen to be there.

One rotation, Distant sounds of explosions and fighting interrupted their work on the shelter. They rushed to a clearing from where they could see some kind of battle taking place around the massive doors of the huge air lock and one end of the cylinder.

Someone or something had blown a hole in the inner door and was fighting what appeared to be a losing battle against the same kind of ships that had escorted the Mastery of the Stars.

The ship crash landed on the same grassland that contained their original shelter and they rushed through the forest to safeguard their supplies.

When they reached the end of the forest, they could see the crashed ship some distance from their makeshift settlement. The escort ships were already beginning to land around 'the wreckage.

Ay-ttho was halfway to the shelter when she halted. She signalled for the others to stop as well. She was staring towards the wreckage but, a nano-unit later, she turned and ran back towards them.

"The electric bowmen!!! Go, go!"

The others turned and ran as well, back to the forest, their weapons drawn.

Meanwhile, the electric bowmen had emerged from the wreckage and were exchanging fire with the machines that had descended from the escort ships.

Despite their apparently formidable firepower, the machines were being picked off one by one by the electric bowmen who were slowly, but surely, making their way down the slope towards the forest where Ay-ttho and the others were sheltering, watching with interest the battle unfolding in front of them.

Their interest soon dissolved into concern as the bowmen, despite their worn appearance, were making quick work of the machines and were heading towards the section of the forest where the group was hiding.

The escort ships opened fire of the bowmen with great accuracy, but every time a bowman was grounded by a laser bolt, they struggled back to their feet and continued on their way, returning fire on the ship's and still making their inexorable way towards the forest.

Once they were within range, Ay-ttho and the others opened fire on the bowmen, who were now being assaulted from all sides. However, despite clearly missing chunks of their anatomies, the bowmen continued onwards and began firing into the forest.

Ay-ttho and Tori were both excellent shots but, although every direct hit would floor a bowman, it didn't stop them from getting up again and continuing their journey. They had blown the legs of one bowman off, but he still dragged himself along the ground, firing into the forest.

"Let's pull back," said Ay-ttho, as the bowmen got too close to the mark.

They retreated through the forest, laser bolts pursuing them as they ran. Once the bowmen reached the forest edge, it sheltered them from the pursuing machines and they could hunt their quarry with relative freedom.

Sevan was beginning to feel the situation was hopeless when there was another massive explosion in the distance, followed by a rushing wind.

"They have breached the airlock," said Nadio.

"Why would they do that?" asked Tori.

"To kill us," said Nadio.

"It doesn't make sense," said Ay-ttho. "There are easier ways to kill us and they still have to stop the bowmen from leaving."

Despite the rushing wind, they could still hear sounds of distant fighting followed by the sound of smaller craft getting closer. Shots were being fired into the forest and Sevan wondered what new machines their captors had sent.

When the group reached the clearing where they had been building their new shelter, they could see the small fighters above the canopy, firing into the forest, presumably targeting the bowmen.

One of the fighters landed in the clearing. The door opened and a suited creature the size of a small zoxan emerged.

"The vrequx," said Ay-ttho.

The creature was gesturing for them to get into the fighter.

"We have no choice. The atmosphere is being sucked out of the cylinder. It's our only chance of survival."

Nadio and Tori ran to the shelter to get Effeek'o, who was still strapped to the sick bay bed. They followed Ay-ttho and Sevan into the fighter. The vrequx immediately closed the door behind them and the fighter took off.

The vrequx directed the to strap into seats at the rear of the bridge before strapping itself into a seat behind what Sevan assumed must have been the pilot and co-pilot.

Through the observation window, Sevan could see a considerable amount of fighting between the vrequx fighters and more of the escort ships that had arrived.

"What are the vrequx doing here?" asked Tori

"We did quite a bit of damage to their ship," said Ay-ttho

"So they came Halfway across the universe for revenge?"

"Possibly."

"It doesn't matter why they came," said Nadio. "They won't let us leave."

Sevan thought Nadio had a point. The fighting was furious and large numbers of escort ships had arrived.

The vrequx were now trying to fight their way back out of the holes they had created in the immense air lock doors. The cylinder's atmosphere was still rushing out of the hole, taking all manner of debris with it, some of which was colliding with the escort ships and adding to the damage caused by the vrequx.

The vrequx front line which was engaged in a battle sheltered their own fighter, not just against the escort ships, but also against the rest of the airlock to widen the holes to enable their escape.

Both sides were losing a battle against the escaping atmosphere and, when a vrequx fighter lost control, it caused a knock on effect of collision which initially blocked the hole temporarily with a variety of ships from both sides, before they were all such out into space.

Now they were free of the cylinder, the vrequx tactics changed. The fighters were now heading for the Ptolemy portal, pursued by the escort ships, who were determined to prevent them from leaving the system.

They had ushered their own fighter to the front, and the rest of the fighters were covering their escape. However, one by one, these fighters were being picked off until, when they were very close to the portal, only a couple of vrequx fighters remained against a fleet of the escort ships. By the time they reached the portal, these fighters had also been destroyed and the last they saw on the unknown system was the vast fleet pursuing them.

"We're finished," said Sevan.

"I wouldn't be so sure," said Nadio.

"Why not? You saw the size of the fleet. They'll come through the portal after us and finish us."

"You are forgetting one thing."

"What's that?"

"Their desire for their system to remain a secret."

"I don't follow you."

"No. And neither will they."

"Why not?" Sevan was getting frustrated.

"Sending their vast fleet through the portal would reveal to everyone on the Ptolemy system what lies the other side of the portal. They don't want that. I predict at the most they will send a small long-range fighter to pick us off."

"Oh great, so we are still doomed."

"The odds are much better."

With that, the vrequx fighter emerged from the portal.

"You know we have to go back for the Mastery of the Stars, right?" said Ay-ttho. "The others stared at her in disbelief."

*

Enjoyed this book? You can make a big difference.

Reviews are the most powerful tools in my arsenal for getting attention for my books. Much as I'd like to, I don't have the financial muscle of a large publisher. I can't take out full-page ads in the newspaper or put posters on the subway.

(Not yet anyway)

But I have something much more powerful and effective than that, and it's something those publishers would kill to get their hands on.

A committed and loyal bunch of readers.

Honest reviews of my books help bring them to other readers' attention.

If you've enjoyed this book, I would be very grateful if you could spend just five minutes leaving a review (it can be as short as you like).

Thank you very much.

Get a free and exclusive bonus epilogue to *Surviving the Zoxans*, only available here.

Building a relationship with my readers is the very best thing about writing. I occasionally send newsletters with details on new releases, special offers, and other bits of news relating to my novels.

If you sign up to the mailing list, I'll send you an exclusive epilogue to *Surviving the Zoxans.*

You can get the epilogue, for free, at: https://BookHip.com/ PCBRKMH[1]

---

1.   https://bookhip.com/PCBRKMH

Not ready to leave Sevan and the Team?
Book Five in the Mastery of the Stars Series
Coming soon in 2024

ABOUT THE AUTHOR

M J Dees is the author of eight novels ranging from psychological thrillers to dystopia, to historical, to humorous fiction, and the Mastery of the Stars sci-fi novella series. He makes his online home at mjdees.com[2].You can connect with M J on Twitter at @mjdeeswriter[3], on Facebook at facebook.com/mjdeeswriter[4] and send him an email at mj@mjdees.com if the mood strikes you.

---

2. http://www.mjdees.com/

3. http://www.twitter.com/mjdeeswriter

4. http://www.facebook.com/mjdeeswriter

ALSO BY M J DEES

The Astonishing Anniversaries of James and David: Part One

How do you know if you have achieved success? No matter how successful he becomes, James doesn't feel happy. Meanwhile, his twin brother, David, seems content regardless of the dreadful life-threatening events which afflict him year after year. The Astonishing Anniversaries of James and David is as much a nostalgic romp through the 70s, 80s and 90s England as it is a shocking and occasionally tragic comedy.

Get it now[5]

Fred & Leah

At a time of war, soldiers are not always the only casualties.

On September 3rd, 1939, Fred knew he would have no choice but to go to France and fight. However, when he found himself among the thousands of men stranded after the Dunkirk evacuation, he did not know whether he would see his wife, Leah, and his two children again.

It leaves Leah trying to raise her two children by herself, but even she can't stop the bombs from falling on her street.

M J Dccs' fourth novel and his first historical novel, Fred and Leah, is based on a real-life love story of two people whose lives were irrevocably altered by war.

Get it now[6]

Albert & Marie

What would you do if you were convinced you were going to die?

Swept up in the frenzy of patriotism, Albert volunteers to serve his king and country.

They shipped him off to the trenches of France along with almost every able-bodied man that he knew, leaving his estranged wife and his child behind.

Convinced he will die a horrible death, he seeks comfort in the arms of Marie, a local French woman who gives him hope his last days might become bearable.

Unfortunately, to do so would mean committing bigamy and he is caught between love and the law.

Get it now[7]

---

6.   https://buy.bookfunnel.com/jvqhvcibuu

7.   https://buy.bookfunnel.com/y99ybm832n

DEDICATION

To Margarido, the latest addition to our family.

ACKNOWLEDGEMENTS

I am indebted to my beta reading team, especially Peggy Coppolo and Jim Zimmerman, and, of course, my Advance Review Team.

Milton Keynes UK
Ingram Content Group UK Ltd.
UKHW010749110923
428455UK00014B/783